# Around The Way Girls 8

# Around The Way Girls 8

### Tina Brooks McKinney,
### B.L.U.N.T., Meisha Camm

www.urbanbooks.net

Urban Books, LLC
97 N18th Street
Wyandanch, NY 11798

Got Me Twisted © 2011 Tina Brooks McKinney
Arrested Development © 2011 B.L.U.N.T.
Greed © 2011 Meisha Camm

ISBN 13: 978-1-60162-616-5
ISBN 10: 1-60162-616-9

First Mass Market Printing June 2014
First Trade Paperback Printing June 2011
Printed in the United States of America

10 9 8 7 6 5 4 3 2 1

Distributed by Kensington Publishing Corp.
Submit Wholesale Orders to:
Kensington Publishing Corp.
C/O Penguin Group (USA) Inc.
Attention: Order Processing
405 Murray Hill Parkway
East Rutherford, NJ 07073-2316
Phone: 1-800-526-0275
Fax: 1-800-227-9604

# Around The Way Girls 8

## Tina Brooks McKinney, B.L.U.N.T., Meisha Camm

# Got Me Twisted

by

*Tina Brooks McKinney*

# Chapter One

## *EBONY QUEEN*

*It's strange how one bad decision can have a domino effect on so many lives.* This thought resonated in my mind as I watched them lower my mother's body into the ground. It was not the send-off I would have chosen for her, but beggars couldn't afford to be choosy. Thanks to my mother's error in judgment, I was so broke I couldn't afford to pay attention, let alone bury her in the style she'd become accustomed to. Hell, I was lucky to get this much. New York City, just like other cities, was strapped for cash, and budget cuts were the only things people were talking about. Vital programs were being scratched, so instead of having a three-man crew whose job it was to bury the indigent, I had a man and a shovel who was anxious to get this part of his job finished. I should have felt grateful for the meager service, since it was the best the city was willing to do, but I wasn't. I wanted to believe my mother was dancing on streets made of gold, but it was hard to do when her body was encased in a shitty box.

My mother, Candace, was a true diva. If she wasn't already dead, she would've had a stroke knowing her final resting place would be in a plain pine box. She believed diamonds were another article of clothing and she raised me the same way. It broke my heart just thinking about the simple brown dress she wore, also provided by the city. I never felt so alone and miserable in my entire life. Guilt plagued me but there was nothing I could do about it.

My neighbors gawked, coming out of their fancy apartments, to witness my disgrace as the FEDs came and confiscated everything we owned. I was twenty-one and had never worked a day in my life. But I never had to because my mother had a plan, a vision that ended the day she was killed. I thought I was prepared for every contingency in life, but I was sadly mistaken. All my training was contingent on having money, and I was broke as a joke without a pot to piss in or a window to throw it out of.

My mom's only brother, Leon, sent me a bus ticket to Atlanta and a couple dollars for spending money. He would've come to the burial;

however, he was busy burying his wife Kym, who was killed the same day as my mother. I reminded myself that I should have been feeling grateful to him since he offered my grown-ass a place to stay, but I wasn't. I was angry, bitter, and to be honest, I wanted revenge. I wanted everyone involved in my mother's death to suffer the same way I was suffering.

My mom used to call me her ebony princess. She said I took the best from her: my dark brown skin, straight brown hair, and a big ol' butt. She told me I would grow up to be a queen. Of course I told her I was already a queen, and she quickly countered by saying there was only one queen bitch in our house, and I wasn't it. Now that she was gone, I inherited the title but there was no throne. I didn't feel like the queen as I looked around at the few people who gathered to pay their final respects.

"Are you okay?" someone asked me, gently touching my shoulder. I recoiled from the touch. None of the faces surrounding me looked familiar, and I hated them all, but it didn't matter. "I'm fine," I mumbled, but I really wanted to yell and scream, *Get the fuck away and give me a moment!* I was sick of people asking me the same question over and over again because they didn't want to know how I really felt. They expected me to put some smell-good on it so I lied, told 'em I was fine. What I really wanted to say, *Hell no, I ain't okay. My mother is dead.*

Another thing they said that was getting on my damn nerves was, "Is there anything I can do?" *Hell yeah. Bring my mother back and while you're at it, tell the FEDs I want our shit back.* Those slimy fuckers took everything. My mother's jewelry, furs, clothing—hell, the bastards even took her shoes. They boarded up the front door of our penthouse apartment and sent my black ass packing with only the clothes on my back.

This should not have been happening to me. My mother's boyfriend, Mel, the lyin' piece of shit, was nowhere the fuck to be found. He'd promised my mother he would protect us, but the bastard removed all evidence of his life from our house the moment the news of my mother's death hit the wire. I was gonna find the little-dick motherfucker and make him pay for leaving us. The very least he could have done was make sure his woman had a proper burial.

Though I promised myself I wouldn't cry, it wasn't working. *How could I not cry?* My life, as I knew it, was over, and I was ill prepared to do anything about it. My mother loved money, but she obviously wasn't good at keeping it because there was nothing left. I tried to stand tall, I wanted her to be proud of me, but I couldn't help it. On the outside I looked like a queen. On the inside, however, I was a sick, twisted sister. Everyone I loved and trusted had let me down. This was not the life my mother planned for us.

Mel, my mother's sponsor, was a small-town drug dealer from lower Manhattan. He harbored aspirations of growing his operation into something much bigger, but he hadn't found anything bigger than a corner to sling dope from. Mom pumped him up, gave him the courage to go out on his own and as a result, he provided for us. The FEDs questioned me for hours, and I didn't tell them anything. The truth of the matter was that even though I was my mother's best friend, her ebony princess, I didn't know anything. The only thing I did know was my Aunt Kym was involved, but the FEDs already knew that.

The man with the shovel shouted, "Let us pray." He brought my attention back to the present. However, I didn't know what to pray for. I felt I should be realistic, but my mind wasn't cooperating. I didn't want to move to bumfuck Atlanta, but the answers to all my questions had to be there. Besides, my uncle was the only person who stepped up to help me. All the other wannabes my mother associated with were nowhere around. I wanted my mother and my life back. I wanted the fairy-tale ending my mother predicted I'd have.

The tears fell and it was like a dam breaking. Through my tears, I watched the city employee throw dirt on my mother's box. My heart pounded as I watched in horror. Visions of bugs and shit passed before my eyes, and I felt like fainting. Her grave would be marked by a simple rock. The only thing I had left of my mother was a satin pair of Jimmy Choo shoes I had smuggled out of our home.

"I'll be back, Mom, I swear. I'm gonna get you an elegant marker befitting a queen, I promise."

# Chapter Two

## *RESHUNDA WYLDE*

"Dad, can I drive the car today? I have graduation practice tonight after school and I don't want
to catch the bus in the dark." I knew the answer
to the question before I asked it, but part of me
wanted him to say no because it would mean he
was at least paying attention to me. I didn't care
about graduation practice. In fact, I didn't care
about much since my mother died. I'd graduate
because I knew I needed at least a high school
diploma, but anything after that didn't seem as
important to me. I didn't feel like celebrating, even
though I knew that's what she'd have wanted.

"Yeah, the keys are on the counter."

My dad was grieving as well, but instead of
leaning on me, he avoided all contact. It had
been two months, and he still kept his pain
inside, but it was hurting us both. My best friend
Valencia was trying to keep me on point. She was
the one who talked me into going to graduation
practice. She said that we needed to fake it until

we made it . . . or some shit like that. Although Valencia also lost her mother, her situation was a lot different from mine. Her mother was in jail, so she could still communicate with her if she chose to. My mother, on the other hand, was dead. My dad said he hoped she was rotting in hell for all the pain she caused, but I preferred to think of her in heaven watching over me.

"All right, I'm gone." I didn't expect a response from him. He didn't talk much anymore. He loved me, I was sure of it, but I was bothered that he didn't understand we were both grieving and needed each other now more than ever.

Crying had become second nature, and I was tired. My mother meant the world to me, and I didn't know how I was going to make it through life without her. To make matters worse, I was having trouble adjusting to having my cousin, Ebony, from New York living with us. Her mother was also killed. A double homicide, and to make matters worse, Valencia's mom was the only suspect in custody. Ebony resented Valencia because of it and this presented a problem for me.

Ebony was cool and all, but we only had a two-bedroom apartment, and I was beginning to feel like it was Ebony's room and not mine. She wore all of my clothes and rarely lifted a finger to wash them. Dad said we didn't have enough money to buy her some new things, said we had to make do with what we had. Humph, easy for him to say, he didn't have someone else's nasty ass wearing his drawers.

I suggested family counseling, since my mother was the backbone of the family, but he claimed we'd be fine in time. I was still waiting for that to happen. I swatted away my tears as I drove the few blocks to Valencia's apartment. She lived on the other side of the railroad tracks and it was like stepping into another world. I didn't like getting out of the car so I called her on her cell.

"Come on, hussy, we're going to be late." I pulled down the visor to inspect my face. My eyes were red, but there was nothing I could do about it now.

"I'm coming, I just need to put out the trash."

She was huffing through the phone like a Hebrew slave. *Put out the trash? That's a man's job.* I thought to myself. I saw her coming around the back of the building, wiping her hands on a piece of paper.

"Yucky-poo, don't be putting your nasty hands on the seats," I shouted.

"Bitch please, ain't nothing wrong with my damn hands. Besides, you act like this car is all that." She got in, slamming the door and folding her arms over her ample breasts.

I smiled. Valencia was beautiful. She was tall, slim, and light-skinned, and when she got mad, her whole face turned red. I enjoyed pushing

Valencia's buttons just to see her face change. It was comical to me.

"I'm just sayin', why ain't your daddy putting out the fucking trash?" I pretended not to notice her anger as I pulled away from the curb.

"I put the trash out myself to save the roaches the trouble of carting it out their damn selves. They leave shit all over the place when they try to carry it themselves."

*What the hell? Was she serious?* I shot her a questioning look and she caught me.

"Oh God, don't tell me you thought I was being serious." Valencia was laughing so hard she rolled over on the seat.

My cheeks heated up when I realized she was fucking with me, again. "Shit, how the hell was I supposed to know. We don't have no roaches in our house." I started laughing too 'cause I actually pictured roaches carting shit out under her door.

"Girl, you've got to step up your game or else folks gonna be tellin' you all kinds of shit and your dumb-ass will believe it."

"I don't believe everything I hear . . . I just listen more when it's was coming from you." We were silent for a moment. That was the closest thing to a compliment I was gonna give her so I hoped she recognized it.

"Word." She nodded, accepting the compliment. We pulled up in front of the school and parked.

"What's up for tonight? Got any plans?" I asked.

"Not really, after practice I was just gonna go home. Why? What's up?"

"Ebony wants to hang out at the mall, so I told her I was going to swing by and scoop her up so we could hang."

"All right then," Valencia said with a sad look on her face.

"You can come with us."

"Naw, I'll pass. You know me and your cousin don't get down like that. Besides, I don't have any money, and I don't do window shopping."

I locked the car. I was getting tired of being caught in the middle. I felt like I had to make a choice between hanging out with my best friend or my cousin, and I hated that shit. My cousin didn't have any friends in Atlanta, and she used it against me when there was something going on she wanted to do. We walked to our respective classes in silence. I was excited that we were down to the final weeks of school; however, it made me sad that my mother wouldn't be around to see me graduate. She talked about the importance of having a high school diploma almost every other day. She wanted more for me than she had for herself. When I walked across the stage, I would be doing it for the both of us.

"All right, I'll see you at practice."

"Peace out."

# Chapter Three

## *EBONY QUEEN*

I was waiting for Uncle Leon to leave the house so I could do some snooping. I wanted to see if he still had my Aunt Kym's things in his room since all the other rooms had been checked. I was hoping to find out who her Atlanta connect was. I wasn't satisfied living in the dump my uncle called a home and I was 'bout to make things happen for me to change my situation. With any luck, he might know who killed my mother and provide me with a means to make some quick money.

I knocked on my uncle's door to see if he'd left the house while I was sleeping. Since I'd moved in, Leon rarely left his room except to go to work. If he ate, he took his meals in his room. "Leon, can you run to the store and get me some tampons?"

"Huh?"

Damn. I was disappointed that he answered. "My period, it started and I need some tampons." I was lying my ass off, but it was the first thing that came to mind.

"Shit, don't Reshunda have some?"

"I checked in the bathroom but I didn't see any. I'm bleeding really bad." I snickered.

"Aww damn, that's entirely too much information," Leon groaned. I knew it would get to him. Men hated to hear anything about the complications of being a woman.

"Did Aunt Kym leave anything in the bathroom?" I prodded.

"I threw all her shit away—ain't none of it left in here." He didn't bother to open the door, and I could tell by the tone of his voice he was done with the conversation. I didn't mean to upset my uncle, but I didn't want to waste my time rooting around in his room for something that was not there.

"Don't worry about it. I'll use some toilet paper." I was slightly disappointed but I was not down for the count. I had one other option to make the type of money I needed to make, and that was dancing. I'd been taking dance lessons since I was three years old and those lessons were about to pay off. Though I was sure my mother wouldn't approve of me dancing, I couldn't think of anything else I was able to do short of selling myself on the street.

Finding the club my mother often spoke of was easy. Finding the nerve to go in was an entirely different ballgame. According to the Internet, Cheetah was a private strip club with all white dancers. My mom said drugs flowed freely into the club and because of the clientele they weren't hassled by the police. The ratings weren't great but I intended to turn things around if they would have me. I grabbed the door handle and slid inside the dimly-lit club. At first, I was overwhelmed by the smell of smoke but I quickly adjusted to it. I searched for a bathroom so I could change my clothes.

I'd taken MARTA, Atlanta's subway downtown and had to walk over two blocks to get to the club. I expected a bouncer or someone else to stop me at the door but I assumed that since it was mid-afternoon, it wasn't necessary to have someone sitting at the front counter. I slipped into the bathroom unnoticed. I was literally shaking as I pulled off my clothes and touched up my makeup. I was expecting someone to come in and grab me at any moment, which intensified my nervousness.

*The first thing I'm gonna buy is a car and some decent clothes*, I thought as I removed the shirt and jeans that covered the bathing suit I'd swiped from my cousin. As I rolled my clothing up, I knew there was a good chance I would be thrown out of the club on my ass. So I had one chance to make a good impression, a bold one, one that could not be denied. I wore the stilettos my mom had worn the night before she died. I'd smuggled them from the house before the FEDs forced me out. Leaving my clothing in the stall, I stepped close to the mirror to admire my appearance.

"Not bad." But it wasn't edgy enough. I could not afford to be turned away. I needed money bad and I was sure this was where I needed to be to make it. I untied the string from my neck, freeing the twins. If my double D's didn't grab the attention I needed, I was barking up the wrong tree. I tossed the top into my bag and used my hair to conceal my boobs.

"Perfect." I turned from the mirror and sashayed my sexy-ass out the bathroom. Inside I was shaking, but on the outside where it counted, I was one bad bitch. My alter ego, Queen Deep, took over and sauntered to the center of the stage.

Queen Deep looked down on the men seated at her feet who stopped moving as if frozen, drinks held midair. She smiled. Four white males gaped at her, tongues practically hanging out their mouths, and she hadn't moved a muscle. She scanned the room, looking for the manager of the club. Impressing the men gathered at the bar was important, but without the approval of management it would all be a waste of time.

Queen Deep bent over, eye level with the patrons, and licked her lips. Her hair brushed the stage, the twins saluted. The man directly in front of her dropped his beer. The glass bounced off the bar and landed on the floor.

"What the fuck—" A red-faced man stumbled into the room, adjusting his pants.

"Shut up," the gentleman whose glass hit the floor commanded.

The sound of her butt cheeks clapping overshadowed the country music playing in the background. She knew she had their undivided attention.

She stood up, whipped her hair over her shoulders and turned slightly, allowing the gentlemen a side view. She snapped her fingers and the DJ started playing a sultry beat she didn't recognize.

A fifty-dollar bill floated to the floor. Queen Deep bent over backward, her toned legs held high in the air, her boobs dangerously close—she puckered her ruby red lips—lowering her legs one at a time, she flipped over. Licking her lips, she turned, facing the room and executed a perfect split. She posed with her legs wide open, a tiny strip of material covering her clit as the bills continued to litter the floor. In less than five minutes, Queen Deep became the first black dancer for Club Cheetah.

I counted my money during the cab ride home. Reshunda and I were going to the mall so I needed to get home to change.

"She'd better not bring that bitch Valencia with her."

"Excuse me?" The cabdriver asked. He'd been eyeing me ever since he picked me up from the club. *Dream on, motherfucker.* I chuckled.

"Just talking to myself." I stuffed my money deep in my purse. I didn't like Valencia, and she made it clear the feeling was mutual. Unfortunately, due to circumstances that had nothing to do with us, we were forced to tolerate each other. The cabdriver stopped a block away from the apartment building just as I instructed him to do.

"Can you come back, say around ten o'clock, and pick me up?" I could've asked Reshunda for a ride but I didn't want her to know about the club just yet or about what Queen Deep did there.

"Uh . . ."

I slipped a fifty-dollar bill into the tiny slot that separated us. "Well?" I opened the door, my impatience written all over my face. I could not stand indecisive people. Either you do or you don't, you will or you won't, plain and simple.

"Yeah, I'll be here." I slammed the door, walking away from the cab without looking back. He almost sounded like he was doing me a favor even though I tipped his ass fifty dollars. This confirmed my decision to make purchasing a car my first order of business.

"Asshole," I mumbled. I was already counting the money Queen Deep and I would make.

"You ballin' out of control, ain't you? Where'd you get money?" Reshunda inquired. She'd been acting funny ever since we got to the mall.

"This cheap shit? You should have seen me shop when I had some real money. This is some change I got from one of the corner dudes trying to get up in my stuff."

"You fucked him?" She spit the soda she was drinking out of her mouth. Droplets clung to her chin as she tried to wipe away the mess.

"Hell no. Girl, there are more ways to get money from men than fucking them. Didn't your mother ever teach you that?" I was surprised at how backwoods and naive my cousin appeared.

"No, I guess she never got around to it." From the hurt look on her face, I could tell I'd bruised her little ego. I realized that at times I sounded a lot more harsh than I meant to be, but what could I say, it was the New Yorker in me. I was going to have to work on that, especially when I was dealing with Reshunda. Up north, we don't waste words; we said what we meant and keep it moving.

"Reshunda, I'm sorry. That didn't come out the way I intended."

"Oh, it's okay. You didn't offend me." She turned away as if something had suddenly caught her attention, but I saw the wetness in her eyes. She wasn't a bad kid, just a little slow when it came to ways of the world.

"Hey, do you like this?" I held up a cute yellow halter I'd been eyeing, but I was willing to get it for her as a peace offering.

"It's cute," she sniffed. I grabbed two pairs of shorts and another top and pushed her off into the dressing room.

"Here, go try these on." Her face lit up like a neon sign and her frown completely went away. As she disappeared from view, I realized that I didn't need to teach her shit about how to get money 'cause she worked the hell out of me to the tune of sixty bucks without even trying. I laughed. "Humph, my cuz may have some potential after all."

# Chapter Four

## *VALENCIA ROBERTS*

"Reshunda, wait up." She was practically running down the hallway. If she heard me calling her, she didn't acknowledge it. We hadn't spoken in a while and this was the first time I'd seen her in over two weeks. I had called her several times and left messages, but she never returned my calls.

"What the hell is this heifer's problem?" I walked to class trying to figure out what, if anything, I'd done to warrant the silent treatment from Reshunda. We'd been friends for over seven years but we never stopped speaking to each other even when we were arguing. My mind kept recalling the last time we'd seen each other and it just wasn't making sense to me. The last time I talked to her, she asked me to go shopping with her and her cousin. I said no but that shouldn't have surprised her, since she knew how her cousin felt about me. It wasn't like I didn't want to hang out with her. Why would she wait one week before graduation to pull some shit like this? I knew the answer; it was right in front of my face. Ebony. There was no other explanation.

Reshunda and I had an appointment in the counselor's office to confirm our choices for college. Our plan was to attend the same school and possibly share a dorm room. We should have done this during the first couple months of the school year, but with all that had been going on, neither of us had gotten around to it and now we were running out of time. I waited for Reshunda for a few more minutes before I decided to meet with the counselor alone. Reshunda wasn't as passionate about school as I was. She did okay in school but had to constantly be reminded to do her homework.

For me, going to school was the only means I could think of to escape the life I was living. However, in order to go, I would need financial assistance because Gerry, my stepfather, had made it clear on many drunken occasions that his only obligation to me was to provide a roof over my head until I graduated from high school. After that, I was on my own.

I rapped on the glass pane of the counselor's door.

She was seated at her desk and looked up when I knocked before she waved me in. "Valencia, come on in. It's good to see you."

Bad memories assaulted me as I closed the door. The last time I'd been in Mrs. Wells's office it was to find out that my mother had been arrested. It was all over the news and she wanted to make sure I was going to be okay. I hated that my life was put on front street, and I was looking forward to starting over at a new school in another city, where people didn't know my name or my family history.

"Hi, Mrs. Wells." I took a seat, pulling out the paperwork I had been given in the beginning of the school year.

"Where is your partner in crime? I thought she was coming with you," Mrs. Wells said, laughing, as she came around her desk.

"I don't know, she was supposed to be here." I didn't know what else to say. Even though I didn't understand what was going on with my friend, I wasn't about to say it to Mrs. Wells. That would be like talking behind Reshunda's back, and it was something we swore we would never do to each other.

"Wait right here, I need to get your file." She stepped out, leaving me alone with my thoughts. Reshunda weighed heavily on my mind, but I realized she was going to have to decide for herself if she was going to continue going to school. I could browbeat her into signing up, but if her mind wasn't in it, it would be a big waste of time and money. Leaving her would be hard, but it was time I started putting myself first.

"Well, I'm glad you made it. Let me see what you've brought me." She held out her hands and I passed my paperwork to her. Using my file and the papers I supplied, she started typing on the computer. It made me nervous thinking about what she could possibly be typing as her fingers flew over the keyboard. Her head was bowed so I couldn't read her facial expression, or her computer monitor.

It didn't take long before I had her attention again. I didn't realize I'd started to sweat until a droplet dripped into my eye, startling me. Mrs. Wells handed me a tissue, her face severe, which didn't make me feel any better. I felt like I was in the principal's office instead of my counselor's.

"It is warm in here." She picked up my folder and used it to fan herself while she waited for her printer to stop.

I nodded my head in agreement.

She grabbed the papers from the printer and reviewed them. Apparently satisfied, she pushed them toward me. "Valencia, your grade-point average is great and under normal circumstances, you would've been eligible for several scholarships and grants."

The only words I heard were *normal circumstances*—everything else was grayed out.

"Normal circumstances? What does that mean?"

She cleared her throat and started talking to me as if I rode the short, yellow school bus on the regular.

"Each year, every college is allotted a certain amount of money for scholarships. My job as your counselor is to help you apply for those scholarships and to find any grant money that may be used to supplement those funds. However, those funds are limited. This is why we asked each of you students to fill out your paperwork early. We should have started planning for your future last year. If a plan was in place, it would have been simple to narrow down which paperwork needed to be filed. Now, since it's the end of your senior year, there aren't any scholarships left. There may be a few grants, but most of them are for colleges here in Atlanta and you indicated that you want to attend college out of state."

She didn't need to say anything else. My hopes and dreams were evaporating right in front of my eyes. I used the tissue she'd given me to wipe my eyes so I could see the paperwork. The words were blurred and I couldn't read it.

"I tried to get here sooner, Mrs. Wells—"

"Honey, don't cry, it's not the end of the world. There may be other options."

"Options? What options?" I clung to her words like a life vest thrown from a sinking ship.

"Well, your parents can cosign with you for a student loan."

I used to think Mrs. Wells was very bright, but obviously the bitch spent her spare time smoking crack. Rage the likes of which I hadn't felt in months surged through my body. I wanted to reach across the desk and smack the shit out of her. I took a few seconds to compose myself. I shouldn't have had to remind her of the circumstances that prevented me from coming to see her earlier. I was certain every stinking detail was listed in my file and the bitch hadn't bothered to read it.

I tried to hide my anger when I spoke. "Are you fucking kidding? Don't you remember calling me to your office to inform me my mother had been arrested?"

She started shaking her head with an uncomfortable look on her face.

"No? Seriously, is that what you're trying to say to me?" I stood up placing my hands on her desk, eye level with her. I wanted her to really see the words coming out of my mouth. Her face had turned a brilliant shade of red but I didn't give a fuck.

"Well, I'm sure you remember calling security to remove my stepfather from your office when he showed up to get me, pissy drunk with his dick hanging out his pants? How 'bout when he peed in your trash can. Does that jog your memory?" I was screaming at that point.

"Valencia, please sit down. There's no need to raise your voice!" Her lips were tight, her pupils dilated. I was ready to snatch the bitch and catch a case just like my mother.

"Then do your damn job and help me. I'm sorry I didn't meet your deadline but I had some other shit on my mind." I sat back down, but a visual of the worst day of my life kept replaying in my head. I assumed Mrs. Wells would've called security, but to my surprise she kept shuffling papers around on her desk as if my outburst hadn't happened at all.

"Let me see what I can do. Can you come back tomorrow at the same time? I should have some answers for you then." Closing my file, she stood up.

I continued to stare her down as I walked backward out of her office. She wouldn't forget me again.


"Long time no hear, bitch," I said as Reshunda came out of her English class. She jumped at the sound of my voice. I stepped in front of her and boxed her in. I was still hyped up from my encounter with Mrs. Wells, so it wasn't a good time to mess with me.

"You scared me." She looked around anxiously.

"Are you looking for someone?" I didn't like the vibe she was giving me, and I wasn't in the mood for any more bullshit.

"Yeah, you know Caleb, don't you? Well, he said he would walk me to my next class."

I wanted to believe her but something was not right. She was off somehow and I could not put my finger on it.

"Oh, really . . ." I turned my head and scanned the almost empty hallway. I decided to ditch the rest of my classes and I was hoping to get Reshunda to go with me, but she appeared uncomfortable as hell just standing near me.

"Yeah. Don't you remember I told you he was cute?" I followed her eyes, hoping to see Caleb headed in our direction. I didn't want to catch Reshunda in a lie, especially about some unnecessary dumb shit.

"What happened to you at the counselor's office?" I was angry.

"Huh?" She wouldn't look at me. She glanced at her watch.

"We were supposed to meet Mrs. Wells at eleven."

"Damn, I forgot. Uh . . . I need to get to class."
She started walking around me, suddenly very
interested in school.

"Fuck class. Let's get out of here. I really need
to speak to you."

"What?"

I'd seen the look in her eyes before. She looked
trapped. "All right then, I'm out." I wasn't about
to beg the bitch to go with me. I didn't know
what the fuck her problem was, but I was not
sticking around to find out. I really wanted to
talk to her about what happened in Mrs. Wells's
office, but she hurt my feelings.

"Valencia, wait."

I wanted to keep walking but I didn't know
how to turn my back on my friend.

"What?" I demanded, with my hands on my
hips.

"Fool, stop trippin'. Let's get out of here." She
smiled and grabbed my arm. Her sudden change
in attitude made me suspicious and it did not
mix well with my precariously emotional state.

# Chapter Five

## *RESHUNDA WYLDE*

Valencia and I went to the McDonald's closest to our apartment. I didn't want to talk to her at school just in case our conversation got loud. I'd been meaning to call her over the past few weeks, but something always seemed to get in the way. We weren't talking on the way and that in itself was unusual, but I didn't know what to say and Valencia had this sullen look on her face. I kept trying to think of something to say but my mind remained blank.

"So what's up?" I asked when we got our food and sat down. I tried to front like everything was one hundred between us, but failed miserably.

"You tell me. You're the one acting all shady." She picked at her fries. Valencia was starting to get on my nerves. She acted like we were lovers instead of friends.

"Shady? How am I acting shady?"

"For one, you don't call anymore."

"Damn! I've been busy and shit."

"Busy, doing what?" She stuck another fry into her mouth, her eyes piercing mine with their intensity.

"School shit, what else. Wasn't it you who told me I needed to knuckle down? That's what I've been doing." I stretched the truth but I prayed she wouldn't see through my bullshit.

"Is that so? Then why didn't you meet me at Mrs. Wells's office for our eleven o'clock appointment?"

She had me, I was busted. I remembered we were supposed to meet the counselor but I'd been putting off that visit even before my mother died. The truth of the matter, I didn't feel like going to school. Ebony had told me it was a waste of time and money. She said all I needed was a high school diploma because of the economy and I was inclined to believe her. Every day on the news, they talked about the college graduates who couldn't get jobs because of the economy.

"Damn, I forgot. Why didn't you call and remind me?" I realized my mistake as soon as the words left my mouth.

"Bitch, I've been calling your ass for weeks. You know what! Fuck this shit." She stood up and pushed her fries onto the floor. "I ain't gonna beg your ass for nothing. Peace out." She walked to the door with her head held high.

I felt like a piece of crap. I ran after my friend. "Val, wait. I'm sorry."

"Talk to the hand." She kept on walking, taking a piece of my heart with her.

We'd been through so much together, I couldn't believe I'd taken her friendship for granted. "Bitch, I said I'm sorry, damn it."

"Reshunda, I ain't up to no games. It's been a fucked-up day—so I don't need any of your bullshit." She continued to walk.

I had a hard time keeping up with her because Valencia was at least two feet taller than me. Plus, she was damn near running trying to get away. I reached out and grabbed her arm but she snatched it back.

"Damn." I stopped in my tracks. I'd never seen Valencia act this way, and suddenly I knew exactly how she felt.

"What?" she spat. Her hands were balled into fists, which was also a first for me.

I'd seen Valencia jump on someone else but she never took this stance with me. I wasn't really worried about her hitting me, but it bothered me nevertheless. A small group of people who'd been standing around on the corner watched us.

"Would you calm your angry-ass down so I can talk to you?" The last thing I wanted was to create a scene because it could make the situation a lot worse than it already was.

"It's hot as a hell out here. I'm going home."

"Fine, I'll call you later."

"Whatever." My mind told me to run after her and try to make things right but my stupid pride would not allow it. I was caught in the middle. My best friend and my cousin hated each other and each of them were vying for my attention. I was left feeling guilty for spending time with either of them.

"Shit." I started walking home, but with each step I became more and more determined to either squash whatever the problem was with Ebony and Valencia or tell them both to leave me the fuck out of it. Ebony never came right out and said she didn't want me to be friends with Valencia, but she'd get this funky look on her face every time I mentioned her name.

"School over already?" Ebony startled me when she pulled up to the corner in a black Honda Civic.

"Where the hell did you get this car?" I asked as I took a step off the curb. It wasn't a new car but it was certainly newer than my father's car and it was sporty.

"A friend. Get in."

I was nervous about getting into the car. I was pretty certain she hadn't stolen it but who's to say her friend didn't steal it. I didn't want to get caught up in some bullshit, especially if she hadn't bothered to question the owner about the validity of its title. I slowly walked around to the passenger side and got in. Hell, I didn't even know if Ebony had a license, but my stupid-ass still got in the car with her.

As soon as my ass hit the seat, she took off, barely giving me time to close the door and put on my seat belt. "Damn, can you slow the fuck down? You ain't in New York." I immediately regretted my decision to get in the car.

"What?" Ebony asked as she eased her foot off the gas and gave me a sheepish grin. "Hey, isn't that your little friend?" I followed her finger as she pointed to Valencia. She blew the horn and had the nerve to wave as she sped by. I wanted to crawl under the seat when I saw the look on Valencia's face.

"Why the fuck would you do that?" I demanded. If I had any doubt about Ebony trying to break up my friendship with Valencia, it was cleared up then.

"What are you talking about? You told me to be friendly to her." She had this silly look on her face as if she didn't understand why I was so upset, but I wasn't fooled by her little act.

"If you were going to fucking wave, why didn't you stop and give her a ride?" I was furious.

"Oh, do you think she wanted a ride?" Ebony asked, trying to play dumb.

"It's a hundred fucking degrees outside. You know what, stop the fucking car. I'm not playing these games with you."

"Are you serious?" Ebony's foot never left the gas as she sped up the street.

"Yes, I am."

Her lips curved into a pout as she pulled the car over. Ebony was a spoiled bitch, used to getting her way, but it was not going to happen this time.

"I'm getting my nails done, if you go with me, I'll treat."

She was trying to buy me off again, but this time it was not going to work, even though my nails were a hot mess.

"Ebony, you need to understand and respect that Valencia is my friend. What you do to her, you do to me. If you don't like her, that's your problem, but you're going to have to find another way to deal with it. I won't be stuck in the middle."

I slammed the door behind me and took off at a slow trot to fix things with my friend.

"What do you want?" Her voice was devoid of emotion when she opened her door.

"Valencia, stop it. Can I come in?"

She stepped out of the apartment, closing the door behind her. I could tell she'd been crying.

"I thought you said you were going back to class."

She wasn't going to make this easy for me, but if the shoe were on the other foot, I wouldn't have either.

"I stopped by to apologize for acting like an ass for the last few weeks."

"That's an understatement."

Her verbal barbs were beginning to annoy me. She folded her arms across her body, but to me it felt like she was pushing me away.

"But you have to recognize the part you played in it," I pleaded, trying to get the focus off me.

"Me? What did I do? I didn't change, you did."

She looked astonished that I would even go there with her.

"I didn't change." I wanted to say so much more but didn't know where to begin.

"Yes, you did."

She started counting off my infractions on her fingers.

"You stopped taking my calls and you damn sure didn't bother to call me. Hell, we don't even walk to classes anymore. What's up with that?"

She was flinging things at me so fast I didn't know which one to address first.

"Damn, it sounds like we are dating and shit." I started laughing, but Valencia was still holding onto her anger and failed to see the humor I was trying to interject.

"Who put that dumb shit into your head? Wait, let me guess. I'll bet money it was your cousin."

"What does my cousin have to do with this?" Now I was mad too.

"She has everything to do with it and you know it. We have never been at odds with each other until she came along."

I couldn't take it anymore. The two closest people in my life were pulling me in different directions and it was tearing me apart.

"I said I was sorry, dammit and I'm done begging. Y'all got me twisted."

# Chapter Six

## EBONY QUEEN

"Damn, there ain't nowhere to park!" Part of me was agitated because all of the spaces were taken, but the other part of me was elated because that meant the newsletter the club sent brought out some new patrons. New patrons equated to mo' money for me. Things had changed since my first night at the club—I became a headliner with a whole new set of perks. They told me they were going to do a feature article, but I had no idea it would become a full-blown campaign. The other girls in the club hated me, but I was used to that. I was about to leave the parking lot when one of the club's bouncers came out to meet me.

"Ebony, leave your car with me, I'll take care of it."

"Another perk?" I asked, grinning from ear to ear. I liked the star treatment the club was giving me.

"Something like that. The boss doesn't want anything to happen to you."

"I like the way he thinks. Thanks, Rick." I blew him a kiss as I stepped out of the car. I knew the names of all the guys working the club but it was part of my strategy. If I treated them right, they would look out for me if shit ever got ugly in the club.

"Not a problem," he said, winking at me. He wasn't a bad-looking guy, but I wasn't looking for a love, I was there to make money and he couldn't afford me.

"This baby is new, so make sure you take good care of her."

"I got you, ma." He winked again as he got behind the wheel. I watched him safely maneuver my car into a tiny space before I went inside. They say membership has its privileges, and I was going to take advantage of each and every one offered to me. I entered the club through the side door heading to the back rooms to get dressed. I was eager to get out on the floor; the sound of dollars hitting the floor called my name.

I was making a lot more money than I originally anticipated, for a few hours a night. However, the real money wasn't made on the floor, the real money was in the back rooms, exclusively available to the men that could afford to be there.

Access to these rooms wasn't granted to everyone and it wasn't only about the money. Money was paramount but you also had to be someone to enter those doors. These were the rooms the celebrities visited where their privacy was guaranteed. I hadn't made it inside those sacred rooms yet, but I knew it was only a matter of time. I did, however, luck up on a man who sponsored my car.

Cheetah's didn't approve of us meeting the gentlemen outside of the club, but as far as I was concerned, what they didn't know wouldn't hurt them. I did a F&B with the credit manager of Honda in Covington: He fed me and I bled him dry. I sucked the cum out his balls and the money out his wallet. Not bad for a few hours' work and the best part about it, I didn't have to share that shit with anyone.

Cheetah's made all the dancers parade down the stairs into the main showroom but I wasn't feeling that shit. It was a nightly cattle call with each girl trying to outshine the other. I stood at the top of the stairs and watched the other girls move. It was ridiculous to me and if there wasn't money involved, I wouldn't have done it, but I was about making mine.

I waited until the last dancer took her spot on the floor before I descended the stairs. We were required to dance two full songs before we worked the room for private dances. Unlike the other girls, I didn't compete for attention, it was given to me. I waited until the first record had played before I strutted onto the stage. I struck a pose in the middle of the stage as the other dancers slithered around in various stages of undress.

Their bodies begged for money and to me, made them look pathetic. I waited. As the second song ended, the girls left the runway to dance in their designated areas. Little, if any money had been tossed on the floor and what was there wasn't enough to pick up. They had wiggled their asses for two songs straight and hadn't made a dime. This equated to a freebie and Queen Deep didn't do shit for free.

The DJ played an oldie called "Gold Digger" by Jamie Foxx. I used the drumbeat as an intro, following it with my hips. I'd borrowed a white shirt from my uncle's closet. It fell to my knees and touched the tops of my thigh-high fishnet stockings. The first three buttons of the shirt were undone. A red tie, loosely knotted, was around my neck. The tie was so wide, it could almost be used as a sash. I had on black spiked heels, which made my legs appear even longer. I also had on a hat that I'd purchased from some thrift store. I knew I looked hot and when I was sure all eyes were on me, I tipped the hat and threw it on the floor.

Queen Deep took over my body and I watched as she worked the runway like a hooker on the stroll. Everyone in the room appeared to move in slow motion, giving her their undivided attention. It was like taking candy from a baby. As she began my striptease, money rained inside and around her hat. I was having what could only be described as an out-of-body experience because Queen Deep was doing things I never would have done and I was granted a bird's-eye view. She unbuttoned the rest of her shirt and allowed it to drop to the floor . . . more money hit the floor. More money rained . . . the harder she rocked her hips. Soon there was a thundershower in the joint when Queen Deep went deep; hips dipping on the way to that first bounce of ass flesh, what she called the uptown bounce because it pulled money out of men's pockets. The bounce started with the firm, full roundness of her ass and jiggled, working its magic up into her titties. She cupped them in both of her hands as they shook like jelly. When she bent over, spread her legs and touched her toes, the first twenty-dollar bill hit her in the crack of her ass . . . and stuck there. She didn't realize how turned on she had become until the floor became covered with bills, and then a sudden rush of blood to her clit pushed her pussy into overdrive.

She got down on her knees and began seducing the women who were brave enough to enter the club. I was a little surprised to see them but it didn't make Queen Deep stop her seductive dance. She turned me on, so I can only imagine how they felt. She parted her legs and waited, finger crooked, singing, *She gives me money!* Her voice was hetero-sexy! She paused, waiting for them to give her enough motivation to continue.

"Do it," the blonde lady said as she slid a fifty-dollar bill into the moist strip of cloth that barely covered Queen Deep's swollen lips.

"Thank you baby." She blew the woman a kiss and the crowd went wild; even the dancers stopped shaking their money-makers. She made a clap with her ass cheeks to the music and then she fondled my twins. My nipples were taut, standing tall and firm as she blew on them. She pulled my hat toward her, fondling the money. She pulled the bills from her stocking tops and G-string and stuffed that into the hat too. The men were begging her to take off the rest of her clothes, but I wouldn't let her. By the time the song ended, I didn't need Queen Deep to do my dirty work anymore. I could handle it from here on out because I had the confidence to dance alone. I collected my money and left the stage.

I was elated and floating on a currency high. I couldn't wait to get to my dressing room to count my money.

Some redheaded bitch snatched my arm and twirled me around, causing money to spill out of my hat. Behind her were several other dancers. The ballsy bitch looked like she wanted to bust a cap in my ass and was the obvious spokesperson for the group.

"Who the hell are you and what da fuck was that about?" She spoke with an Italian accent. Her tiny breasts bounced against her thin chemise cover.

"I beg your pardon?" Homegirl was lucky I didn't punch her in her fucking face. I didn't take too kindly to people putting their hands on me. I snatched my arm back, daring her to try to touch me again.

"That stunt you pulled out on the stage. You're not supposed to be grandstanding and shit."

"Yeah," the other ladies cosigned. They moved closer to the redhead in what could be construed as a show of solidarity. There was not a black face among them and it didn't matter. I was glad to be back in charge because Queen Deep was a lover, not a fighter, and I was about to whip some ass if any one of them heifers stepped to me again.

"Then I suggest you take it up with the manager 'cause I'm not the one." I tried my best not to laugh at the hatred on their faces.

"Hey, what's going on here! Break it up," Trent, the manager, announced as he walked into the center of the congregation. He was a no-nonsense type of guy and most of the ladies were afraid of him. I walked past the ladies with their mouths wide open into my private dressing room and slammed the door.

"Get back on the floor. You aren't getting paid to just stand around, damn it."

I had my ear pressed against the door, listening.

"Who is that bitch and how did she get her own dressing room?" one of them demanded.

"That ain't none of your business and if you want to continue working here I suggest you move your ass," he replied. I laughed this time because he put those bitches in their place. I was in the process of changing my clothes when I heard an urgent knock on the door.

Thinking I was going to have to handle one or more of the ladies, I snatched open the door. "I know you bitter bitches don't want no parts of me." I held a straight-edged razor in the palm of my hand and I was prepared to use it.

"Oh, my bad." I stepped back from the door and allowed Trent into my room. I placed the knife on the vanity just in case I needed it. His eyes roamed my body but I didn't attempt to cover myself from his lustful looks.

"Damn, you know how to use that, ma?" Trent asked, eyeing the weapon.

"You damn right and I'm not afraid." Actually, I was a little afraid, but I wasn't about to let him or anyone else know it.

Trent's face broke into a smile, as if he wasn't worried about the nasty business in the hallway. "Just be careful you don't wind up cutting yourself."

"No worries, I know how to handle mines." If he noticed the double entendre he didn't acknowledge it.

"You were fantastic tonight. I've gotten so many requests for you, I can't keep up."

"This is what you wanted, isn't it?" I thought he came in my dressing room to complain, but obviously that wasn't the case. I wanted him to get to the point so I could continue making money.

"Yes, of course." Trent was a man after my own heart. He loved money just as much as I did. I walked away from him to finish getting dressed. I was confident he would look at my

fat ass, so I made sure I jiggled it extra hard. It
didn't bother me to give him a free show. He was
going to be my fast ticket to the top. I pulled a
gold lamé two-piece outfit out of my bag that I'd
picked up from the Rave.

"Do you mind if I get dressed?" I smiled at him.
I could tell he was thrown off his game when I
stepped out of my thong. He didn't answer, but I
could tell by the swelling of his dick that he didn't
have a problem with it. I discarded the stockings
for the next set. I wasn't going to wear anything
but the gold thong and bikini top, which barely
covered my large titties.

"Damn ma, thank God I have enough sense
not to shit where I eat because I'd be tearing
that ass up right now." He grabbed his dick for
emphasis.

I wanted to laugh at his arrogance. Although
Trent was a handsome older man, he couldn't
afford me. I wasn't about to give up my goodies
for a manager.

"Perhaps another time, another place," I said
suggestively, even though that shit would never
happen. Not unless the motherfucker hit the
lottery for millions. I looked over to Trent and
he appeared to be deep in thought. His brows
were knitted together as he combed his goatee
with his fingers. Something about his pensive

look made me nervous so I edged closer to my knife. I wanted to be ready just in case he lost his fucking mind and tried to take something that didn't belong to him. My money was laid out on the vanity next to the razor and I wasn't about to play with my money or my sex.

"You remind me of someone I used to know," he said. His dark brown eyes, normally clear, appeared to be cloudy.

"I hope that's not a bad thing," I flippantly replied.

"No, it's cool. Look, on the real, I can't let you back in the main room tonight. The girls are ready to kick both our asses."

I started laughing. I wished a bitch would try to step at me. I'd slit her throat with my razor and keep it moving.

"What are you saying? You want me to go home?" My heart sank because it was still early and I knew I could triple the money I'd made in just one song.

"Hell no, but I do need things to calm down a little before you go back out there. I want you to do some photos for our newsletter and Web site. We did the special e-mail blast but I think we need to turn up the heat. Maybe even your own personal video greeting. Starting tomorrow, you will be working the executive room."

I was speechless. I thought I was going to have to fuck my way to the executive rooms but this nigga was giving me the key. My hands trembled as I put the finishing touches on my outfit.

"All this sounds nice, but I came here to make money."

"How much do you think you'd make if you were out on the floor right now?"

I could only speculate, but I wasn't going to lowball it.

"Two thousand easily," I bluffed.

We stood in the middle of the room staring at each other and I could tell he knew I was bluffing. He looked over at the pile of money I had stacked on the vanity and it scared me.

"Okay, I got you. Take the pictures, do the video and I'll have your money ready for you when you're done."

"That's what I'm talking about." My clit twitched. Trent didn't realize just how close he came to getting broken off, but I quickly dismissed the feeling. Screwing Trent could fuck up my money and I was not about to do that.

# Chapter Seven

## *VALENCIA ROBERTS*

Reshunda and I started walking. I wasn't sure we'd ever get back to normal, but I wanted to try.

"We never really talked about what happened to our mothers." She stumbled and I could tell she was shocked by my statement.

"What is there to talk about?" Reshunda's whole demeanor changed.

"There's no need to get mad about it. It's done and there's nothing we can do about it."

"Why do you even want to talk about it then?" Reshunda demanded.

We were getting close to our school so we went around back to the outdoor tables we used for the cafeteria eating area. We sat on the benches.

"Because I have so many questions. Don't you?" I thought she was going to ignore me, because she didn't answer right away.

"Yeah, I have questions, but who am I going to ask? My mother?" She stared at me with a defiant look in her eyes. She tried not to cry but it was a losing battle. Her shoulders shook as she let it go. We'd been here before. I put my hand around her shoulders as we both cried.

"Did your mom say anything, or was she acting differently?" I asked.

Reshunda's shoulders shook even more. "No, I wasn't speaking to her that day, I was in my room with the door locked when she left the house. I'm so mad, she died before I could say I was sorry."

My heart hurt for my friend. "I think she knows."

She pulled away and wiped away her tears. "How do you know?"

She was angry again, but I couldn't blame her. I went through periods of irrational anger myself. There were times I just wanted to hit someone and it took everything in me not to do it.

"Moms know. It's like they have this maternal instinct that lets them know everything about their kid. You know what I mean, like when you're in the other room doing something you shouldn't be doing and they bust you. I think they're born with that shit, or maybe they even develop it once they have a child. Hell, I don't know, but I know it's something like that."

She looked at me like I were crazy, but it got her laughing and it was good.

"Yeah, she was good at it. Heifer made me sick, I couldn't get away with shit," she agreed.

"Tell me about it." I had been busted on a number of occasions so I knew from firsthand experience.

"Val, did your mom say or do anything that was out of the ordinary?" Reshunda's voice was so low, I could barely hear it.

"Not really. Your mother called, I answered the phone. She sounded upset, but I assumed she was pissed off at your dad or something. My mom asked her about some dude named Trent and the next thing I knew she was running out the door."

"Trent, who the fuck is Trent?" Reshunda demanded.

"I ain't got a friggin' clue. I was hoping you knew."

"You know what you gotta do, right?"

"Yeah, I know. It's getting dark. Let's go home."

I had put off going to visit my mother for as long as I could. My conversation with Reshunda convinced me to put aside my fears and swallow the bitter pill I'd been holding in my mouth, that my mother was behind bars. Guilt tormented me because I felt bad about not visiting her sooner, but part of me was ashamed of her. She spent so much time telling me to do the right thing, and there she was knee deep in shit and facing life in prison.

"I'm going to see my mom today." I announced to Gerry, my stepfather. He grunted. We didn't have too much to say to each other, but it wasn't a new thing. He never talked to me. If he wanted to tell me something, he always told my mother, which made her the bad guy. I understood this and kind of respected it, since he wasn't my father. However, ever since my mom was gone, he didn't have anyone to speak for him so we just coexisted in silence.

When he didn't answer, it made me mad. "Have you seen her?"

He looked at me like I sprouted another head. "For what?" he barked at me and it caught me off guard.

"For starters, she's your wife." I could've listed a lot of other reasons, like 'til death do us part, in sickness and in health, blah, blah, blah, but it shouldn't have been necessary.

"She didn't act like my wife."

I didn't know what to say. Something was obviously wrong between them, but as far as I was concerned he should've at least visited her.

He got up from the table, letting me know the conversation was over.

"What about an attorney? Did you get one for her?" I didn't give a shit about what was going on before she went to jail, all I was concerned about was the here and now.

"With what? I don't have that kind of money to throw around. Your mother should've thought about it before she got involved with the bullshit she was in." Instead of going into his room, he went out the front door. He didn't even have a shirt on, only a wife beater with a hole over his right tit. He was livid, but so was I.

# Chapter Eight

## *RESHUNDA WYLDE*

Valencia got me thinking again. She also made me realize that it was okay to feel the loss, but I had to push past it to get better. I'd been keeping a lot of emotions and resentment inside and it was hindering my growth. I needed more out of life and the only way I was going to get it was to improve my situation. I looked around my room and immediately felt disgusted. Ebony was a pig, and it was clear she must have had a maid or someone else cleaning up behind her.

I pulled the laundry basket out of the closet and picked up my clothes Ebony had either worn or tried on and discarded. It didn't make any sense. She changed clothes more than me and she didn't even go to school.

"I wonder what she does all day? It damn sure ain't cleaning up after herself," I said out loud. She was asleep when I left for school and most days was gone when I got back. On the weekdays, she shopped and it was another thing that troubled me. I wondered where she got all the money she flashed.

"Where the hell have you been?" I asked Ebony when she stumbled into my room. She startled me because I'd been sleeping when I heard her come in. I glanced at the clock—it was well after three in the morning.

"Girl, you scared the shit out of me." I turned on the light so I could see her. Her words were slurred and her makeup smeared. She dropped her heels in the middle of the floor and pulled a short dress I'd never seen before over her head and deposited it on the floor as well. She didn't have on any underwear either and didn't seem to mind standing in front of me naked as a fucking jaybird. I couldn't help but to notice how nice her body looked.

"You didn't answer the question." I folded my arms across my chest, annoyed she'd already started junking up the room I'd just cleaned. I drew the line with washing her clothes but I did lump her clothes into a pile in the closet.

"Where's all my stuff?" Ebony complained as she flopped down on the bed.

My eyes were drawn to her large breasts. I wondered how she managed to get them in my small tops without ripping the seams.

"In the closet. You had so much shit on the floor I couldn't even walk in here."

She laid back on the bed, closed her eyes and basically ignored me.

"Turn off the damn light."

Oh no, she didn't come in and start barking off orders like she was the boss of me.

"You need to pick your stankin'-ass clothes up off the floor. The maid quit."

She chuckled like I was joking but I was dead serious. I was done playing nice with my cousin.

"What the hell you got stuck up your ass?" She attempted to rise up on her elbows but failed miserably. She fell back across the bed, turning her face away from the light.

"The only thing up my ass is you. You've worn all my clothes—without asking, I might add—and then you tossed them on the floor. You come in here at all hours of the night and don't say shit to nobody, and you walk around here like your shit don't stink." I had worked myself up to a good mad, but even though I touched on a lot of things, I hadn't said half the things that were really on my mind.

I'd been walking around on eggshells with Ebony because she had lost her mother, but the bitch didn't give a rat's ass about me and my feelings. Never once did she acknowledge that I'd lost my mother as well. Everything was about Ebony, and something in my gut told me this wasn't new behavior for her. She probably treated my aunt the same way, but it was going to stop tonight as far as I was concerned.

"You are not my mother!" she hissed at me and rolled over, placing a pillow over her head.

"Thank God for small favors."

Drunk or not, she lunged from the bed.

If she meant to scare me she had picked the wrong bitch this morning. "What? I'm supposed to be scared?" Her eyes narrowed to tiny slits but I didn't know if that was from anger or if it were due to her inebriation. My bet was on inebriation, since she was rocking on her feet.

"You might want to sit your drunk-ass down before you fall down."

She weaved back and forth.

I wanted to fuck with her so badly and dance around the room but I was too upset to play games. Ebony needed to get her shit together.

"Why the hell are you fucking with me? I ain't do nothing." She stumbled back to her bed.

I shook my head in disgust. Although Ebony and I needed to talk, it would be fruitless to try and do it tonight. I wanted her to remember what the fuck we talked about. I turned out the light and tried to go back to sleep.

"I thought so," she said with false bravado before the telltale sounds of snoring filled the room.

This only aggravated me more. I wanted to get up and go someplace else but there wasn't anywhere else to sleep in our tiny apartment. "Shit," I mumbled as I turned over.

"What time is it?" Ebony asked when she finally woke up.

I ignored her. I normally slept late on Saturday but I'd been up since Ebony's early-morning arrival.

"Did you hear what I said?"

"I heard you." I continued to sip the coffee I had brewed. My father and I shared a cup before he went to work. It was the first time we'd done something together in a long time, and I decided to make it a weekly ritual for us.

"What the hell is wrong with you?" She went over to the teapot but it was empty. She slammed the pot down but picked it up again, irritated.

My smile was hidden behind my cup. "Ain't nothing wrong with me. There is a big-ass clock on the wall, why can't you look for yourself, or must I do that for you too?" I hoped she didn't miss the sarcasm dripping from my voice.

"Reshunda, I don't feel like no shit this morning." She walked over to the kitchen sink and ran some water into the pot.

"In case you haven't noticed, the sun doesn't rise and set around Ebony."

"What's that supposed to mean? You've been ragging on my ass since last night."

"Oh, you remember that?" I was surprised, especially since she fell asleep so quickly.

"Yeah, ain't nothing wrong with my memory."

"Good, then remember this: Do not wear my clothes again without asking and keep your shit off the floor. If you want to sleep in filth, that's on you, but the next time I come into my room, and I stress the *my room* part, and find shit on the floor, it's going in the trash."

"I wish you would throw my motherfucking clothes away."

I felt like we just went full circle. She obviously didn't get anything I was trying to tell her.

"Whatever—throw something else on the floor." I got up and went back in the bedroom and slammed the door behind me. Her dress from the night before was still on the floor and I promptly tossed it in the trash can. Once I finished the laundry, I hung all my things in the closet. I pushed all of her things to the far right side, away from mine. Most, if not all of her things still had price tags on them, which annoyed me even more.

"Why the hell is she wearing my shit when she has all this new shit!"

Ebony came in the bedroom waving a paper towel like a flag, but I was still heated. I tried to ignore her as she removed her dress from the trash and hung it in the closet. If she was pissed, she didn't let on, but I think she got my point.

"You got plans for the day?"

"No." I turned up the volume on the television. I knew where this was going. Ebony would talk me into going to the mall, she'd buy me some trinket and we'd put off talking until the next time I got sick of her shit.

"I waved the white flag, damn it."

It was hard to stay mad at Ebony because we looked so much alike. I gave her my undivided attention. "Where were you last night and all those other nights?" If she wanted to talk, I was ready to listen. She remained silent so I returned my attention to the television.

"I didn't want to tell you because I knew you weren't going to approve."

"Tell me what?" I was all ears, especially if it meant I could be ballin' out of control like she was.

"You promise you won't tell Uncle Leon?"

I needed to think about that for a minute. I wasn't a snitch, or anything like that, but I'd be damned if I was going to sit back and be quiet if Ebony was into some stupid shit.

"Are you fucking around with drugs?" In our neighborhood, slinging dope was nothing new. If Ebony chose that path to fortune, she was on her own.

"Hell no, I ain't stupid."

The jury was still out on that one as far as I was concerned. I waited for her to continue.

"I'm not telling you unless you promise to keep my secret a little longer."

"Okay, I promise, heifer, but if you're lying to me and it's drugs, I'm singing like Beyoncé."

# Chapter Nine

## *VALENCIA ROBERTS*

DeKalb County's jail wasn't far from our apartment complex, but it felt like it was light-years away as I walked through those doors. Guilt for taking so long to visit my mother seemed to weigh down all my limbs. I almost gave in and went home but I needed to see her; I had too many unanswered questions. I loved my mother, but I couldn't shake the feeling that she'd abandoned me at a time when I needed her most. I was so ashamed of myself for forsaking her regardless of the reason, because I knew she would never have done that to me.

Even though I had seen many reality shows about the lives of inmates, nothing I'd seen prepared me to witness it firsthand. The lines were ridiculous. Mothers with their young children stood in the hot sun for hours waiting for a thirty-minute visit; cranky children, crying because they weren't being allowed to play. But that wasn't the worst part of it. The worst part was seeing my mother shackled behind a plate of glass.

Visitation was on the fifth floor. They called us back in groups of four. We were told to walk single file down the hall, hugging the wall. When we were told to ignore the inmates if they called out to us, I felt like I was in elementary school all over again. Walking past the inmates was unnerving so I couldn't imagine having to sleep in the same room with half of the women that we'd passed.

An officer took us to a larger room, which was divided into four rows. At the end of the row was a glass door. I didn't notice the steel gate in front of the door right away.

"Your inmate will enter through the glass door," the officer informed us.

I was relieved we'd get some form of privacy, but I was still nervous. I waited for over thirty minutes before I saw my mother, which is when I noticed the gate. I thought my heart was going to break when I saw her. Her hands were shackled behind her back as she shuffled along on shackled feet. I struggled to hold back the tears, but I was fighting a losing battle. As the officer bent down to unchain her feet, I lost it. I felt like I was watching an episode of *CSI*, but this was life, in prime time and living color. Unlike television, I couldn't change the channel just because I didn't like what was showing.

My mother's eyes reached mine beyond the glass. She smiled in recognition but it quickly died as reality set in. I could feel her pain and I knew she felt mine. No child should witness their parent behind bars. She shuffled toward me as if her feet were still shackled. I raised my hand and touched the partition, which separated us, and lifted the phone.

For a minute she didn't move. I felt like she was drinking me in like a cold glass of water on a hot summer day. After a few more seconds, she sat down and raised the phone to her ear.

"Hi," I whispered. I wanted to hate her for leaving me alone but it was a selfish thought.

"You shouldn't have come."

It hurt that she didn't want me to visit her. If she only knew how difficult it was for me to come, she might not have said it. I was so concerned about me, how I felt, I hadn't really given her feelings much consideration. Tears flowed freely from both our eyes.

"Of course I was going to come. I'm not going to lie to you. I was scared, but you should've known eventually I would come."

She nodded her head as she wiped her nose. Snot dripped freely from both of our noses. The only difference was I was able to use a tissue out of my purse to wipe mine away.

"You doing okay?" I asked, but after I said it, I realized how dumb of a question it was. How the hell could anybody be okay in jail?

"Yeah, how about you?" She reached up and touched her eye.

I hadn't even noticed it was black until she did that. It wasn't a fresh bruise but it was apparent she didn't want to talk about it, so I didn't press the issue.

"I'm making it." I didn't know what else to say to her. Everything that was going on in my life seemed so trivial compared to what she was going through. "What are they saying about your case?" We only had thirty minutes so we didn't have time for all the niceties.

She shrugged her shoulders and it pissed me off. When she was on the outside, she would have slapped the shit out of me for doing it. Now, I understood how she felt.

"I haven't been told anything yet."

"What is your lawyer saying?" She'd been locked up for almost two months, so I assumed she'd been appointed a lawyer and would know something. She looked up with a hopeful expression on her face.

"Gerry hired a lawyer . . ."

Damn. I didn't even see it coming. More tears leaked from my eyes, as I realized I was going to have to be the bearer of bad news. As hard as I tried, I couldn't get the words out of my mouth, so I just shook my head.

Her smile turned upside down as she slumped back against her chair.

I wanted to offer her some encouragement, but what the hell could I say? "Aren't you entitled to a public defender?"

"Yeah, so they say. I guess I'll see one eventually." She didn't sound bitter but I would have been raising hell if it were me.

"There is one lady in here who has been waiting for a year to see a public defender."

"Damn." I shook my head. This wasn't acceptable.

"I'm sorry I missed your graduation."

I didn't even want to talk about the ceremony because it would only remind me of the pain I'd been carrying since her arrest. At the graduation, I didn't have any family to stand for me when I walked across the stage. If it wasn't for Reshunda yelling and screaming like she'd lost her mind, the auditorium would've been silent. "We can talk about it later, we don't have much time left." Both of our eyes gazed at the clock on the wall. The second hand practically galloped around its face.

In spite of the circumstances, I was happy to see my mother. I hadn't realized how much I missed her until she walked through the door.

"I'm innocent," she whispered.

Relief washed over me because I needed to hear her say it. In my heart, I knew she wasn't capable of murder. This is what I wanted her to say and I prayed it was true.

"What happened?"

"I don't know all the details, but I've had plenty of time to speculate on what went down. Kym called me and said she had to make a run. We were supposed to go to the mall but she had to cancel at the last minute. However, she didn't go into any great detail about the run." Her eyes glazed over as she got lost somewhere in her mind.

"Mom." I snapped my fingers. "We don't have a lot of time." I hated to keep reminding her to stay on point but I needed to make sure I had a full understanding of what went down before I had to leave.

"Sorry, in hindsight, taking the ride with her was the stupidest thing I've ever done in my life."

I didn't say anything because I agreed with her, even though I didn't know all the details. That trip landed her here, in jail, so there had to be quite a bit of ignorance involved.

"Anyway, she told me her sister-in-law, Candace, was making some major moves in New York in the drug game. I asked her what she had to do with it because to my knowledge she didn't do drugs. Kym said she introduced Candace's man to a guy named Trent and business in Atlanta was going good. Kym said the only thing she did was introduce them and I believed her."

"So how the hell did you get into this?"

"Kym was my friend, but I swear, I didn't know anything about what she was doing until she called me. It's very important to me that you believe me."

"I do, Mom, but what happened? How did you get here?"

"Shit hit the fan, that's what happened. When we got to the meeting, everybody was all pissed off. Kym said Candace usually made the exchanges, but she'd never actually touched the drugs before. Kym would meet Trent after the drop and he'd break her off. This time, Candace said she couldn't come and Kenny insisted that Kym go with him to make the exchange."

"Mom, that was dumb on so many levels." If things were different, there was no way my mother would have tolerated me calling her dumb.

"Tell me about it. When the cops questioned me, I didn't know anything, but when they brought me here, I found out the real deal. The guy Candace was dealing with in New York was DEA gone bad. According to the rumors I've heard, Candace was killed because she was stealing like a motherfucker from him. He wanted to meet Kym to find out if she was involved in the shit."

My mother was throwing a lot of information and names at me. I didn't bring a pen so I tried my best to remember everything she said. "So what's the name of the guy Candace dealt with?"

"I don't know, we didn't get around to introductions. He shot both of them and hauled ass. He left me standing, so the cops are throwing the book at me because one of their own was taken down."

"His name has to be in the police report. Can't you tell the police he was crooked and dealing for himself?"

My mother shook her head. "It don't matter. They need someone to pin this on and I just happened to be the last person standing." She appeared nervous.

I could tell she wasn't telling me everything she knew about this man. "Why didn't you run, Mom?"

"I couldn't. My friend was lying on the ground bleeding. I couldn't just leave her—"

"What about this Trent guy?" She never really explained where he fit into the entire equation. I was grasping at straws. I understood where my mother was coming from when she spoke about leaving her friend. I'd probably do the same thing for Reshunda, if the situation was reversed.

"I don't know where Trent is. Most of what I'm telling you I heard here and you can't trust everything you hear up in this bitch."

"Well, you have to tell everything you know to the public defender so he can start looking for him."

"The public defender's office is the biggest joke in here. The woman I shared a cell with when I first got here didn't get to see her PD until the day of her trial. She's on trial for murder too, so they had to postpone her case so they could prepare. The fucked-up part is that she's been in here since 2008 and still hasn't had a trial."

"Three years? Are you serious?" I could not fathom my mother being behind bars that long.

"Yeah, and if that wasn't bad enough, this bitch tried to rape her and my celly killed her. Now, even if she gets off on the original charge she'll probably get at least ten to twenty years for the lady she killed. But I don't blame her. I'll do the same thing if some bitch rolls up on me like that."

"Time," the guard called out and stood behind my mother, waiting for her to stand.

Big tears rolled down my mother's face as she stood. She put down the phone and probably didn't hear what I said.

"I'm gonna get you out, Mom! I promise, I'm gonna get you out. . . ."

# Chapter Ten

## *VALENCIA ROBERTS*

I didn't take the bus home from the jail; I needed to walk. I needed to feel the wind against my face. There were so many things I took for granted, and freedom was one of them. Seeing my mother behind bars made me more appreciative and my priorities shifted. My mother used to warn me about being in the wrong place at the wrong time and I finally understood what it meant. She put herself in the wrong place at the wrong time.

I needed to make some fast money. If I was going to keep my promise to her, I needed to hire a lawyer. I couldn't rely on the criminal justice system to help. I would have to do it myself. However, I was at a loss as to how I could make the amount of money I needed in the short period of time I had before I left for college. My counselor was able to get me a full scholarship to a pharmacy school in Boston and I couldn't wait to leave. I would have to do two years of undergrad work before I could shift over to my major, but I was cool with that. Mrs. Wells surprised me with the news the day before graduation and I hadn't had the opportunity to share it with anyone. Leaving would be bittersweet, but I didn't get it twisted; I was going no matter what happened.

I stopped by Reshunda's house, hoping she'd be home. I had so much on my mind, I just needed to talk. I knocked on her door but Ebony answered. I wanted to be nice to the bitch but something about her appeared fake and I couldn't stand fake-ass bitches.

"Hey Valencia, how've you been?"

Stunned by her reception, I stood in the doorway. I felt like I'd knocked on the wrong door and stepped into another dimension.

"Why are you being nice to me?" I wasn't even gonna fake the shit with her.

She laughed and turned away from the door, waving me in.

"I understand what you mean, but I've decided to turn over a new leaf."

*Whoa, what the fuck was going on?*

Reshunda came out of the bedroom. "Who was at the door? Oh, hey Val, what's up."

Both of them were wearing these shit-eating grins that made the hairs on the back of my neck stand up.

"Okay, what's up?" I had this nagging feeling in the pit of my stomach and something told me to turn around and take my black ass home.

"Nothing, we were about to get something to eat. Do you want to come?"

I expected Ebony to come up with an excuse not to hang with me, but she shocked me again.

"Yeah, come on, it's going to be fun." She slung her bag over her shoulder and opened the door.

I was hungry and I probably had enough money in my purse to order something off the dollar menu at McDonald's, but sharing that information with Ebony didn't appeal to me one bit. My eyes shifted to Reshunda, praying she'd give me an out. However, she was still grinning as she linked arms with me, practically dragging me out the door.

"Girl, come on, Ebony's treating."

They didn't give me a chance to say no. We walked out of the apartment and stopped at the same late-model Honda Civic I'd seen her driving a few days before.

"Whose car is this?" It was one thing to borrow someone's car and take it back, but this one was parked in front of their house and I was reluctant to get in.

"It's mine," Ebony proudly announced as she used the key to open the door. Reshunda looked a little stunned, but it did not stop her from jumping into the front seat. Still trying to figure things out, I got in the backseat.

Instead of going to McDonald's we went to Olive Garden. I loved Olive Garden, but it was definitely not in my budget. As a special treat, my mother used to bring me there when I did well in school. I started to tear up as I remembered those special moments we spent there. I needed to speak to Reshunda about what was going on with me, but it would have to wait until we were alone.

"Get whatever you want," Ebony announced as she ordered herself a glass of white wine.

"I want lobster tails," Reshunda announced.

"I'll have the soup and salad." Even though Ebony said she was treating, I wasn't trying to break the bitch.

Laughing, Reshunda slapped me on the arm. "Girl, stop lying. You know you want some lobster too."

I didn't appreciate Reshunda calling me out and I waited for things to get ugly. "Shit, did it ever occur to your ignorant ass that Ebony might not be rolling like that. Hell, she just brought a fucking car." I sat back and shot Reshunda an evil eye.

"Valencia, if you want lobster, get it. It's cool. Let's make a toast." She raised her half-empty glass. Reshunda raised her glass of water and I did too.

"What do we toast to?" Reshunda inquired.

"To the future. I mean, who knew that the three of us could stand to be in the same room together," Ebony said, chuckling.

We clicked glasses, but I was not amused. Part of me agreed with her toast because were it not for the sins of our mothers, I'd never choose Ebony as a friend. But I still had questions. I couldn't understand how we went from happy meals without cheese to lobster tails and wine. I was bugging when Ebony ordered an entire bottle of wine after finishing the first glass. Since Reshunda and I were underage, she would have to drink the whole bottle or leave it behind.

I waited until our food arrived before I started asking questions. "Can one of you tell me who hit the fucking lottery?" Reshunda shot a look at Ebony. I felt like I was standing on the outside looking in and it made me feel uncomfortable.

"Shit, will one of you say something?"

"Go 'head, Ebony, tell this nosy bitch what's going on."

I didn't take offense to Reshunda calling me a bitch, but it would've been a whole different conversation if Ebony had said it.

When we finished eating, Ebony raised her glass again and emptied it. "I've been working at a club downtown and believe me when I say the money is good."

I damn near choked because this was the last thing I expected her to say. "Is she for real?" I asked Reshunda.

She nodded her head yes. It seemed like everyone in the room had stopped what they were doing and all eyes were on our table, but it was just my imagination. I didn't give a rat's ass about Ebony's decision to degrade herself. However, I was concerned about how her decision would affect Reshunda.

"Okay." They continued to stare at me as if they were expecting a different reaction.

"That's it? What do you think about it?" Ebony had a bored look on her face.

I had an opinion, but I didn't think she wanted to hear. "What does it matter what I think? Hell, I ain't nobody."

"That's what I'm saying," Ebony slurred. She'd consumed the entire bottle and was back to ordering by the glass. She was clearly drunk at that point.

"Ebony, you said you were going to be nice," Reshunda said, pouting.

"I am being nice. I bought the bitch dinner, didn't I?"

Reshunda gulped air, her eyes wild and uncertain because I'm sure she expected me to go off, but Ebony didn't offend me. She said exactly what I'd been feeling but had enough tact to keep to myself. But that didn't mean I wasn't gonna let her fly-ass remark sit on the table alone.

"Right, right. Dinner was lovely but why should I care if Ebony shows her ass like some stank ho? It ain't like I give a fuck about her anyway." There was no animosity in my heart. I just kept it real, but maybe a little too real for Ebony's taste.

"Ah shit, here we go." Reshunda started to get up from the table but I wasn't trying to show my ass in public and she should have known that about me. However, Ebony was operating off of liquid courage and started loud talking both of us.

"See Reshunda, I told you this high-yellow-stuck up-boogie-bitch thought she was better than us. Well, I'm about to break my foot off in her bright-yellow narrow ass."

Reshunda went around the table to block Ebony from getting out of her seat. For a second I thought she was about to side with her cousin against me.

"Just pay the damn check, Ebony, and let's get out of here."

"I ain't going anywhere until I show this bitch who the fuck I am."

I remained seated, watching their interaction, cause the shit was funny to me.

"Pay the fucking check and keep your voice down," Reshunda hissed. When Ebony didn't bother to reach for the check, Reshunda grabbed her purse off the table. She whipped a hundred-dollar bill off a fat roll and tossed it on the table.

I wanted to stay and make change but I decided to follow them just in case Ebony decided to drive and I had to knock a bitch out.

As we walked out, Ebony continued to make an ass of herself, shouting obscenities at the other patrons who gawked at her like she had escaped from the circus. Ebony continued her rant when we got outside. "Didn't I tell you that bitch was going to turn her nose up?"

Reshunda glared at me like I'd done something wrong. "Yeah, but you didn't make it better." Reshunda opened her door and got in, slamming it behind her.

Ebony went around to the driver's side and attempted to get in.

"Oh hell to the no! Reshunda, are you seriously going to let Ebony drive?"

Reshunda looked like she'd just woken up. "What?"

As much as I disliked Ebony, I didn't want to see her body wrapped around a pole. "She can't drive, she's been drinking." It took everything in me not to call Reshunda a dumb bitch when she jumped in the front like it was all gravy. I marched around to the front of the car and took the keys from Ebony, who was having a hard time sticking them in the lock. I was prepared to punch her out if she attempted to fight with me, but she obviously had enough sense not to argue about it.

We didn't speak until after I'd parked her car in front of their apartment.

I thought Ebony was sleeping but I was wrong. "So when you gonna tell ol' girl you stripping too?"

I thought it was more drunken chatter but one look at Reshunda's face let me know it was true.

# Chapter Eleven

## *RESHUNDA WYLDE*

Ebony was off the chain tonight and all I wanted to do was get her silly-ass in the house and shut it down for the evening. What should have been a pleasant evening spiraled out of control, turning downright ugly. I didn't want to believe Valencia would be judgmental about me dancing. It was written all over her face that she didn't approve. I probably could've made Valencia understand what led me to dance, but thanks to Ebony, I almost certainly wouldn't get the chance. I slipped my key in the door and shoved Ebony inside.

"Can I speak with you for a moment?" Valencia asked.

I didn't realize she'd followed us to the door. She wasn't loud or ugly so I decided to hear her out. "Yeah."

"Why you got an attitude with me? If anyone should be mad, it should be me."

"Mad about what, Valencia? You always talking about why you should be mad. What the fuck did I do to bruise your little ego this time? It's always about you, isn't it? Do you ever think about anyone else but yourself?" I was tired and did not want to have this discussion.

"First of all, heifer, I thought we were friends, but more importantly—cause I feel like you set me up—if you wanted to tell me something you should have told me instead of having your stupid-ass cousin deliver the message. And since you want to know what really bruised my ego, as you so eloquently stated, I'm pissed because if I hadn't shown up on your doorstep today, I still wouldn't have known what was going on with you. Friends don't do friends that way, but it's obvious you don't know a damn thing about being friends." She turned around and started to walk away.

"Fuck you, Valencia," I shouted to her retreating back.

"Naw, bitch, fuck you. My mother may be in a fucked-up situation right now, but at least she knew how to treat a friend." She continued to walk away. I was not about to let her say something so fucked up and get away with it.

"What's that supposed to mean?" I was ready to punch her dead in the face. In all the years that we'd been friends, we'd never come to blows.

She stood in front of me heaving and blowing out her nose like she really wanted to hit me,

and it frightened me to see how bad things were
between us.

"I saw my mother today. She told me what
happened the night your mother was killed but I
don't feel like talking about it now." She backed
away from me.

I ran toward her but my heels were slowing
me down so I took them off. "If I cut my feet I'm
gonna kick your ass," I yelled.

"Then turn your black-ass around and go
home."

"I want to hear more about what happened
with your mom." I knew how hard it was for
Valencia to go to the jail and I felt like I failed her
when she needed me most.

"I said I didn't want to talk about it," she said
over her shoulder. She was speed-walking and I
was catching hell trying to keep up with her.

"Come on, Val, you got my attention now."

"Should have had your attention the moment
I knocked on your door."

She was really being a bitch. But if I allowed
myself time to step back and think about it, I
couldn't blame her.

"You want me to get down on my knees and
beg?" I was joking, hoping to get her to laugh
with me.

"Yeah."

I didn't realize we'd walked so far until she
climbed the stairs to her apartment. When she

got to the door she didn't even look at me. She opened it and went inside without saying good-bye, kiss my ass or anything else of that nature. I knew I had hurt her deeply but she'd hurt me too when she said I wouldn't know anything about being a friend. Of all the things we'd said, this would be the most difficult thing to forget.

I stood there looking at the closed door as memories fast-forwarded through my mind. I was tired of thinking and more than anything else, I was tired of feeling bad. These were supposed to be the good years, but lately all I felt was pain. I knocked hard on Valencia's door. We needed to squash whatever was going on and get back to the business of being friends.

"Valencia, open the damn door . . . don't have me standing out here looking like a goddamn fool," I shouted. Things on the other side of the door were quiet but I knew Valencia hadn't gone far. She wasn't above making me sweat. I waited for a few more seconds and I hammered on the door again.

"Shit girl, you might as well open the door because you know my stubborn ass will stand out here all night." I wasn't kidding either, especially since going home meant dealing with Ebony's drunken-ass.

After a few seconds more, Valencia cracked open the door with a scowl etched on her face. "What now?"

I could feel the attitude seeping through the door but I couldn't trip. I had to keep reminding myself that I would act the same way if the situation was reversed.

"Girl, I'm sorry. I fucked up." She didn't respond but at least she didn't shut the door in my face. "I was going to tell you about my dancing. I was waiting for the right time."

"Right time for what?" Valencia folded her arms in front of her chest.

"Can I at least come in the house? My feet hurt."

She looked behind her and I didn't like the expression on her face. She looked afraid. Even though we'd been friends for years, Valencia kept her home life private and not open to much discussion. My life wasn't perfect but at least it was better than hers.

"Do you want to come back to my house so we can talk?"

"What about your cousin?"

"She'll be asleep. She tries to act all hard-core and shit but she can't handle her booze."

"That's okay, I'll take my chances on my own turf just in case you nut up on my ass." She opened the door wide enough for me to come in. I don't know what I was expecting to see. Her life behind the door was such a mystery to me, I expected to see abnormal shit. Instead I saw a normal, dark living room. She held her fingers to her lips and motioned for me to follow her. Once inside, she closed and locked the door.

Her face visibly relaxed once the bedroom door was closed.

"Where's your stepdad?" I whispered.

"He's, uh . . ." The uncomfortable look returned to her face and I was sorry I even mentioned him.

"Don't worry about it," I said as I sat down on her bed. Her room was so neat, it made me feel like a slob. Nothing was out of place. I shook my head because this completely contradicted what I'd imagined her room to look like. My room was hardly ever clean, especially since Ebony moved in. I wasn't a slob, but I tended to leave my dresser drawers open and some dishes on the dresser.

"Why are you shaking your head?" Valencia had started to relax once we were in her room, but I felt her tense up again.

"I was just looking at your room. You've seen my shit, I can't keep it clean to save my soul. I'm embarrassed."

She laughed and I joined her. It felt good to laugh with her again.

"You ain't even lyin'."

"Hey, you didn't have to agree with me."

"It is what it is." She sat down on the bed next to me. She didn't have much by way of furniture but she didn't need much since she was alone.

"So you went to see your mother. How'd that go?" For a minute, I thought she wasn't going

to answer me. Tears welled up in her eyes. I'd
expected that. She sniffed and wiped away the
moisture. I got up from the bed and grabbed
a roll of toilet paper, which was sitting on the
dresser, and handed it to her.

"Thanks," she mumbled.

I gave her a moment to get herself together. I
completely understood her pain. I kept a roll of
tissue under my bed for the nights I cried myself
to sleep. She didn't say anything else but that
was okay too. For a brief moment, I even wished
I could trade places with her because I would've
traded the world just to see my own mom again.

"She's standing tall."

At first, I thought it was a strange thing to say
until I thought about all the shows on television
that talked about life in jail.

"How did she look?" I was trying to be slick to
see if the women had fucked with her.

"She looked tired."

Vivid images danced before my eyes and none
of them were good for her mother. "That's under-
standable." I didn't know what else to say.

"She was surprised to see me. Said she thought
I'd forgot all about her."

My heart went out to my friend and I wanted
to give her a hug, but Valencia wasn't the most
demonstrative person in the world. If she wanted
or needed a hug, she would let me know. "Why
did she say that?"

She shook her head but didn't answer the question. "Can you believe she hasn't even seen a lawyer yet?" Her eyes blazed with anger.

"What! She's been locked down for three months and she hasn't even spoken to a lawyer? That doesn't seem right."

"She's in a holding pattern. They haven't even charged her yet." I felt myself getting angry as well.

"That's crazy. How can they hold her if she hasn't been charged with a crime?"

"I don't know. That's why she needs a lawyer." Tears started flowing freely down her face.

"What about your stepdad? What does he say?"

Her face twisted up momentarily, stopping her tears. "That motherfucker don't give a shit," Valencia shouted. "She could rot in jail for all he cares. All he wants to do is sip on that fucking bottle all day. That's the only thing he cares about."

If she was worried about her stepdad hearing her, I couldn't tell. In fact, I think she wanted him to come in the room and face her. I wished that there was something I could do but I couldn't think of anything that would help.

"She said she didn't kill anyone."

If she expected a response from me, she wasn't going to get it. Even though I sympathized with my friend, nearly everyone in jail claimed they didn't do it. She was upset because her mom was in jail—mine was six feet under. Big difference.

"I need to make some money to hire a lawyer. Waiting for a public defender isn't going to cut it."

A light went on in my head. I had the perfect solution to Valencia's money problems. "Why don't you come work at the club with us? Ebony's been dancing at this club downtown. She's making mad money and she just put me on." I closed my eyes and waited for the explosion I knew would be coming. Instead, silence filled the room.

"How much you making?"

My eyes popped open in shock. This was not the response I expected. "Come again?"

"You heard me. How much money are we talking?"

"You're not mad?"

She didn't answer me, but at least she didn't start yelling at me and shit. "Why should I be mad? If you're making money, I want to shake my ass too."

I'd been avoiding her because I didn't want her to know about the club, when all along it was me that had the problem with it.

"Damn, I was afraid you were going to judge me."

"When Ebony first said something, I was judgmental, but not for the reasons you think. I honestly don't believe there is anything wrong with dancing. My fear is that it could lead to other things. Don't get me wrong. A couple of weeks ago, I might have been judgmental, but now, humph, it is what it is."

Valencia gave me something else to think about. She wasn't to blame in all of this. Now I was going to have to convince Ebony to put Valencia on at the club. I started laughing.

"What's so funny?"

"Ebony said you were going to lose your stuck-up mind when I told you."

"You know, I'm sick of your cousin calling me stuck-up. She doesn't even know me." Valencia's eyes narrowed.

I knew it meant she was pissed so I had to cut her off before she took it out on me.

"Don't get your panties twisted in a knot with me. I'm just the messenger."

She backed down a notch. "I know, but I'm tired of her fucking with me." She eased back down to a comfortable position on her bed.

"I told her to leave you alone but when she starts drinking, she starts talking out the side of her neck. She does the same damn thing to me."

"Humph, still don't make it right." We sat in silence, each of us lost in thought.

"So how did all this happen? How long has this been going on?"

"I've only been doing it for a few weeks but Ebony's been doing it for a minute. Probably since she moved here."

"Figures, bitch just got here and already she's making money."

We both laughed.

"She said she found the club on the Internet. She bought the car the first week she started!"

"Damn, it's like that? You sure that's all she's doing?"

"That's all she did last night. If she's doing something else, I didn't see her do it."

"Humph," Valencia grunted.

I wasn't even going to ask her what she meant because I didn't want to get into an argument with her. I wasn't exactly proud of dancing for money and if Ebony hadn't opened her fat mouth, I doubt I would've ever told Valencia.

"How long were you planning on keeping this a secret from me?"

Valencia read my fucking mind like I had tarot cards painted on my fucking forehead. "Damn, I don't know. I haven't even been able to wrap my arms around it my damn self. I didn't go to the club thinking I was going to dance. I only went to watch Ebony, mainly because I thought she was lying about it. I damn near shit a brick when we walked into this gentlemen's club and folks started greeting her like they were family and shit."

"Oh yeah?" Valencia had this strange look on her face that I couldn't put my finger on.

"Yeah, first she took me to the main area and showed me how the girls got down. She asked me if I thought I could do it and I was like, hell yeah. She laughed at me and you know how I get when I think folks be laughing at me and shit."

"I know that's right. You start wilding out and losing your damn mind."

She started laughing, but I didn't really appreciate it because I didn't like anybody laughing at my expense.

"Girl, will you stop taking yourself so seriously? I wasn't laughing at you, I was laughing with you. If the shoe were on the other foot, I'd be trying to show that fake bitch I had what it took too."

I cringed when she called Ebony fake. It was so hard being in the middle. I didn't want Ebony clowning my best friend, but by the same token, I didn't want my best friend clowning my cousin. "Valencia, I had a talk with Ebony today and I told her she was going to have to lay up off of you. I let her know that I wasn't about to sit around and listen to her dog you out."

"Wow, I'm glad you finally told the bitch what time it was."

I cringed again but I wasn't going to back down. I cleared my throat. "You are gonna have to follow the same rules. You are my friend, don't get me wrong, but that's my blood and you're gonna have to respect it and her. I'm not saying you got to like her, just don't be disrespectful in front of her face or mine. Feel me?" If Valencia was offended by my comments she didn't let on.

"So finish telling me what happened. Damn, I wish I could've been there."

"Oh, I almost forgot what we were talking about." It took a minute to get my thoughts in order. Now that the secret was out of the bag, I had so much to tell her I didn't even know where to pick up.

"Okay, so we watching and shit and I noticed all the girls were white so I asked Ebony what was up with that."

"Don't keep a bitch hanging, what did she say?"

She was beginning to annoy me. It was my story and she was trying to rush how I told it.

"Hold your horses, heifer. Every time you interrupt me you make me forget where I was." She looked sheepishly at me and I immediately regretted snapping at her.

"Ebony said she looked on the Internet and found out that the club only had white dancers, so she hightailed it down there and stole the show. All them white girls hate her ass and I guess they be hating on my ass now too." I waited for Valencia to say something, but she didn't say a mumbling word.

"Well, aren't you going to say something?" I demanded.

"I was waiting until you told me it was all right to speak. The last time I said something you damn near chewed my head off."

"I didn't chew your head off. I just wanted you to let me finish what I had to say before I forgot."

"So, what happened next?"

She sounded excited to hear about my five minutes of fame and I was eager to share it with her. When I tried to talk to Ebony about it, she just blew me off, so I was happy I was finally able to share it with someone.

"She took me back to her dressing room and let me put on one of her outfits. She's got some skeezy shit."

"I'll bet."

I shot Valencia a warning look, letting her know that I heard her underhanded dig. "Anyway, we changed clothes and somebody knocked on the door letting her know she had five minutes before her set began. She actually worked the stage and she called me up at the end of her set. We did a dance together and when it was over we walked the floors, taking requests."

"Requests? What the fuck were they requesting?"

I couldn't help but to giggle at the serious expression on Valencia's face. "If a guy wants you to dance for him, he calls you over. When you dance on the stage the men throw money at you if they like what you're doing. For a table dance, they pay for calling you over and then you get tips from that person if they like you. Ebony said you got to make the guy paying for the dance seem special, that way he tips extra. She said if the guy really liked you, he'd buy you a drink and ask you to sit with him. She said I shouldn't sit with anybody that didn't pay me and to never sit with one person too long."

"Ebony says this, Ebony says that. Damn, can you tell me the story without the Ebony infomercial?"

"If it wasn't for Ebony, I wouldn't have been in the club in the first place," I said. I got up and slipped my shoes back on. I was tired of going back and forth with Valencia and decided it wasn't such a good idea to tell her about my dancing after all. Especially if she was going to keep throwing negative energy at me every time I mentioned Ebony's name.

She followed me as I walked down the dark hallway to the front door. She reached around me and pushed her palms against the door to stop me from opening it.

"I'll talk to you later," I whispered as I waited for her to remove her hands. I didn't want to wake up her stepdad, so I didn't dare raise my voice.

"Reshunda, it's dark and it's late. Why don't you spend the night and we can speak with Ebony in the morning?"

"You promise to chill out on my cousin?" I nodded my head. "What about your stepdad?" In all the years that Valencia and I had been friends, I'd never spent the night there.

"It will be all right. He's passed out and won't even know you're here."

She was still whispering, so I got the impression she wasn't as sure of his sobriety as she pretended to be.

"All right." I took a step back from the door, anxious to get back to the safety of her room. I wasn't really feeling like walking home alone anyway, but she didn't need to know it.

# Chapter Twelve

## *EBONY QUEEN*

I woke up at 4:30 in the morning. My head felt like a little man was inside beating on a drum and I had to go to the bathroom something fierce. I lay in bed for as long as I could before I finally mustered up the energy to go. I dangled my feet for a few seconds on the side of the bed, trying to get my head right. My clothes were piled up next to my bed and I made a mental note to pick them up before Reshunda got in my ass about them. I stood up and started walking to the bathroom. I was being extra careful because I didn't want to wake Reshunda. The bathroom was in the hallway and I had to pass her bed to get to the door. I'd almost made it when I tripped over my shoes and fell to my knee.

"Shit," I yelled. My right knee started throbbing so I quickly got off of it, sitting in the middle of the floor. Mumbling obscenities, I massaged my knee, trying to ease away the pain.

"I hope I'll be able to dance tonight," I whimpered. After a few seconds, the pain started to subside. I looked around the room, surprised I hadn't woken Reshunda up. She was normally a light sleeper. As I glanced over to her bed, I noticed it hadn't been slept in.

"I wonder where that heifer is?" I vaguely remembered her running after Valencia but wasn't sure it really happened. I got up off the floor and limped to the bathroom to pee. I was going to have a long talk with Reshunda when she got home. I was going to tell her to stop running after Valencia like she had a dick. They were starting to worry me. I didn't know much about friendships, since I'd never had a closer friend other than my mother, but their friendship appeared lopsided to me. If this was what it was like to have a friend, I'd say fuck it because friendships required too much work. Thinking about my mother made me want to cry. I was done crying, though. I went back to bed, pulled the covers up over my head and promptly fell asleep.

The sun had lit up the room by the time Reshunda brought her ass home. I wasn't in the mood for talking so I pretended not to hear her open the door. She totally disregarded the fact that I was still sleeping. She snatched my clothes up from off the floor and threw them in the trash.

"Damn," I mumbled. I forgot to pick them up and I knew I was about to hear about it. I sighed deeply. She slammed the closet door, which was a true indicator she was mad.

"Shit, must you make all that noise?" I allowed one of my eyes to open so I could make sure she wasn't about to go upside my head or something like that.

"Must you be such a fucking slob?"

"Damn, it was just a dress," I exclaimed as I opened the other eye. She was standing in front of my bed, holding my shoes.

"What about these? If it was dark in here, I would have broken my fucking neck."

Shit, I forgot about those too. I shook my head. It was going to be a long morning if I wasn't able to get her to shut the fuck up. "I'm sorry. I tripped over them myself and I said I was going to get them but I guess I forgot."

She had the weirdest expression on her face.

"What's wrong?" I wiped my lips, thinking I had drool hanging out the side of my mouth or something, but they felt dry to me.

"You apologized. I've never heard you do that before. Damn, I didn't think you were capable."

"Oh, you got jokes this morning." Reshunda was on some shit today and I didn't feel like dealing with it. When I sat up, I noticed she wasn't alone. A loud groan escaped my lips; the morning was going to be longer than I'd originally thought.

"Morning," Valencia said.

She was so chipper, I wanted to put my foot in her ass. I nodded my head in her direction. I had the feeling I was about to be tag-teamed. It was one thing for me and Reshunda to have our little fights, but it was something totally different when there were witnesses. Reshunda sat down on the bed next to Valencia. Both of them were staring at me.

"What the fuck are you two staring at?" I was getting pissed. I still had a slight headache and this unexpected intrusion wasn't helping one single bit.

"Sorry," they both said at the same time. Reshunda grabbed the remote off the dresser and turned on the television. Since they were making themselves comfortable, I decided to get up and take my shower.

"What time is it?"

"Ten o'clock," Reshunda answered. She continued flipping through the channels.

Before I got up, I checked under the sheets to make sure I had on some clothes. I didn't remember putting on anything the night before and I didn't want to put on a show for Reshunda's little friend. I was counting down the days until I'd be able to move into my own apartment. I had my eye on a pretty little condo downtown, where the action was. I had also looked at a few apartments near the job but I wanted to make sure my money was right before I made that move. As I was leaving the room, Reshunda stopped me.

"Valencia wants to work at the club too."

Her words stunned me. "And do what?" I knew exactly what she was talking about, but I decided to play stupid.

"Stop playin', you know what I'm talking about."

Valencia, who had been lounging on the bed, sat up. "Girl, you just started working there your own self, so how you going to start inviting other folks to come dance and shit. Who said the manager even wants another girl?"

"You got the manager eating off your right tit. You could hook her up if you wanted to," Reshunda shot back.

"What's in it for me? Besides, you haven't really danced yet."

"What do you mean, I haven't danced yet? I danced last night, don't you remember?" Reshunda might have felt the barb I threw at her but chose to ignore it.

"Humph, you've got to be able to work the whole room. You ain't ready for that," I snidely answered, belittling her ability. In actuality, she did a good job, and with a little work, had a lot of potential, but I hadn't counted on Valencia wanting to dance too. If she started working at the club then she'd be around us all the time and I wouldn't be able to put my plans into motion. I didn't like Valencia's attitude but I tolerated her for Reshunda's sake. Plus, I was looking for a sponsor and I didn't need the extra competition if Valencia could work a pole better than I could.

"You said we were the baddest chicks the club ever saw," Reshunda said eagerly.

She didn't appear to notice my reluctance about accepting this new idea and it pissed me off that I was going to have to spell it out for them. "We were, but damn, you took that shit and ran with it. If she wants to dance at the club, she's going to have to go down there and get the job just like I did."

"Reshunda, stop begging this bitch. It's obvious she doesn't want to help us," Valencia said as she threw me the evil eye.

I started counting in my head, trying to cool down. It didn't bother me that she called me a bitch because I was a bitch and a good one at that. She did get my goat when she said I didn't want to help my cousin. She was way out of line with that one.

"Heifer, please, you got me twisted. I never said I didn't want to help Reshunda. I said I didn't want to help you." I watched the different emotions run across her face but once again she surprised me. I expected her to leap off the bed and take a jab at me, but she didn't.

"Seriously, is this supposed to shock me or something? 'Cause you've made it clear from day one how you felt about me, but it's all good, bitch, I feel the same way about you." She stood up and walked to the door. Reshunda, give me a call later." She shut the door behind her, ending our brief discussion.

I was glad when Valencia left. She was a fake-ass bitch and I couldn't stand her. She walked around like she was better than everybody else and I was tired of pretending to like her stuck-up ass.

"Why are you so fucking mean to her? She ain't never did anything to you." Reshunda was pissed.

"Why do I have to be nice to her? She's your friend, not mine." Reshunda and I had a great relationship outside of her bitchy friend and I was tired of fighting about it.

"I didn't ask you to kiss her ass or anything, just be civil. Is that too much to ask, damn?"

"Why did you have to ask her to dance at the club, knowing I don't like her?" My neck was rocking and my hands were on my hips, but it didn't intimidate Reshunda because she was working her neck too and waving her arms as well.

"I didn't ask her to dance and I wouldn't even have told her about the club if you didn't open up your big-ass mouth in the first place."

Damn, she was right, I was the one who let the cat out the bag. Deflated, I sank back down on the bed.

"Fuck it, if she gets in, she gets in. The bitch can't touch me 'cause I know how to work my ass."

Reshunda didn't even respond. She walked out of the room and a few seconds later I heard the front door slam.

"Damn."

# Chapter Thirteen

## *VALENCIA ROBERTS*

I wasn't mad when I left Reshunda's house because things turned out exactly how I thought they would, but even better. I didn't expect any help from Ebony, but at least Reshunda knew I wasn't the problem. If I didn't need the money so badly I would've said fuck it and let them have the stinky club. But I needed some fast money, and short of robbing a bank, I didn't know any other way to get it. I went back home to find something impressive and seductive to wear to the club. I wasn't sure what I was going to do to entertain a pack of horny men, but desperate times called for desperate measures.

I'd tossed every stitch of clothing I owned on the floor and still hadn't found anything that was sexy enough for an audition. I considered going naked, but that would definitely give the wrong impression. I wasn't going there for anything other than dancing. I needed money but I wasn't no ho.

***

I pulled open the door to the Cheetah Club. I was so nervous, I felt like I was going to pass out. I paused in the darkness to allow my eyes to adjust. My hands were shaking but I managed to pull it together and walk inside. The foyer of the club was empty but I could hear music. Without any signs to direct me, I followed the sounds and put my game face on. I was wearing some booty shorts under my jeans and a simple tank top, which emphasized my breasts. In the empty hallway, I removed my jeans and tied the legs around my neck. It wasn't a fashion statement; I didn't have anywhere else to put them.

Taking another deep breath, I strutted into the room and waited for a reaction. Several girls stood in the corner of the room, talking. They looked me over but didn't otherwise acknowledge me. There were a few men sprinkled throughout the bar, but it definitely wasn't busy. It was still early, however. Every nerve ending in my body told me to turn around and leave but I couldn't. I promised myself that I would help my mother and if dancing was the only way I could raise some money, I was going to make it do what it do.

The club wasn't officially open and the few men seated at the bar seemed more interested in getting their drink on than anything else. "I'm looking for the manager," I said, trying to sound more confident than I felt. The men at the bar eyed me from the top of my head to the toe ring on my foot.

"Manager ain't available, you're gonna have to deal with me." A black guy, possibly thirty-five to forty years old, actually quite attractive if I were looking for an older man, waved me over.

I strutted over to him, making certain to maintain eye contact with him while working the lust in his eyes to my advantage. I hadn't met a man yet who could resist my charm when I turned on the switch. I could damn near see the blood rushing from his forehead to his dick as his eyes tried to take in all of this. And I mean *all of this*! I watched his eyes light up as he observed my wide hips and narrow waist. When I straddled the seat next to him, his fingers twitched and his Adam's apple bobbed. I rocked forward, allowing the roundness of my breasts to entice him, holding them a breath away from his touch. I was there for a pussy show and if he didn't know, he'd better ask somebody. Judging from the bulge in his pants, he knew what time it was.

"My name is Vee and I hear you're looking for dancers."

"Is that so? Well, someone told you wrong. We don't need any more dancers." He turned around on his stool as if I didn't even exist.

This was a first. My heart pounded in my chest. I was not about to let this arrogant prick stop me from doing what I came there to do. If they hired that tramp Ebony, they damn sure were going to hire me.

"Now, you need to look at me. Teasing is a form of art that I've perfected. It takes precision and I'm willing to bet you money there ain't a limp dick in this bitch because of it." I followed his eyes as he looked around the room. I gave him a moment to assess my goodies and the stiff dicks that I'd inspired. I allowed him time to gauge the money my body would generate. "Now tell me," I let my voice caress his earhole. "Tell me that I don't have your blood rushing. Tell me that you ain't harder than you've been in years." I stood up, feeling my titties doing a Bankhead bounce and my ass cascading like chocolate lava. "And tell me you won't be back tomorrow for more and more and more."

He cleared his throat and coughed.

I smiled as I continued my verbal assault. I plucked a cherry from a glass on the bar and popped the red fruit into my mouth while gazing deeply into his eyes. His expression remained stoic as I swallowed and licked my lips seductively. I took the stem and twirled it in my mouth, tying it in a knot. I wanted to throw up. I hated this pussy-power seduction, but it was necessary to get what I needed and homeboy bought my routine, hook, line and sinker. I had the man speechless.

"Obviously you don't have the juice," I said. "I need to speak to someone who does." I blew the words into his ear and his body jerked. I'd seen that shit on TV and it looked sexy so I tried it.

He turned around again. He looked me up and down, licking his lips.

"Little girls shouldn't play grown-up games."

Was he threatening me? I tried to get a sense of what he was feeling but he had a serious poker face and it made me nervous.

"I stopped playing games when I was ten." I edged closer to him.

"I told you we didn't need any dancers." He was saying no but his body was saying yes.

"What's your name, Mr. Man," I spoke very slowly and softly.

He had to move his head closer to hear me. His chest was a whisper away from my boobs and I pretended this game of sexual teasing was exciting. I looked deep into his eyes and I knew I had him.

"Spears." He pulled back, shaking his head as if he were breaking from a trance. "What are they feeding kids these days?" he said to the men in the room who laughed with him, but they were enjoying the show too.

"Spears! If you don't let that fine-ass woman dance, I'm gonna test your blood for sugar! If he don't want you, you can dance for me. baby!

"In fact, fuck him. Come over here and get this money right now," another man shouted, gripping a fistful of money.

"Let her dance, man. Ain't shit else going on in here," one of the guys yelled.

The girls that were still in the room acted like they were about to act a fool, so I kept talking.

"That's too bad. I saw some of the ladies on your Web site and I wasn't impressed." I took my time getting up. I spread my legs wide, giving the other two men at the bar a sneak peek. My eyes were glued to the dicks of both men closest to me. Not surprisingly, they were fighting the hardness that was poking against the fabric of their dress slacks. I smiled.

"She's here, man, why don't you let her dance?"

"Yeah, let her dance. We could use some entertainment," seconded the other man at the bar. I wanted to kiss both of them; they boosted my self-esteem. I didn't move a muscle. I didn't want to appear as anxious as I felt. Spears shrugged his shoulders, as if he couldn't care less what I did, but I refused to let his lackadaisical attitude bother me.

"If you let this go," I said, "your boys are going to wonder what kind of man you are. Like Prince said, 'I think I wanna dance'." I sauntered over to the nearest table and stood in front of the mirrored walls. Sucking up all the courage I had inside, I seductively pulled my top over my head.

Spears nodded his head toward the DJ's booth and the lights dimmed in the club.

My hair was tousled, giving me a fresh out-of-bed look that men dream about. I smiled at my reflection and winked. When I turned around, my breasts sprang free and I was encouraged by the collective gasp from the men at the bar. My nipples puckered, reacting to the cool breeze from the air-conditioning and they stood like erotic soldiers, popped tall and ready for battle.

The lights came up and I immediately started moving my hips seductively. Everyone else in the room disappeared as I danced. This was my time. My space. My sexy that all of these swinging dicks was gonna pay money to look at. I turned my hips to the side and gave them my T&A profile. I knew it was a banging sight and their lustful shouts only confirmed it.

"Oh yeah!"

"Shake that money-maker! Shake that money-maker!"

"Ah, shit! Shake what your mama gave you! Get-er-done!"

*Now it's on! Time for these fellas to take a ride.*

I bent over to the front and touched my toes. I mashed my titties together and licked at both of my nipples. I slapped my ass while I looked them in the eye, changing their heartbeats with the sound of my hands whipping my full ass. I did the butterfly dance, from the front and the back, one man screaming for me to stop. I let them see my tits jiggle. I fired their imagination; hit the spot where carnality resided. I teased them with a promise of tomorrow. My sex is hotness, and in my world, that is all that matters. In school I took dance and gymnastics and I used every move I was taught.

I pulled a small bottle of baby oil from the back of my bikini. I unscrewed the top with my lips and poured the oil over my head. As the oil dripped from my hair, I worked it into my skin, making my body shimmer. The music wasn't the best but I made it work for me. I made love to the mirror and if anyone was watching, they felt what it would be like to make love to me. As the song came to an end, I dropped down low, resting my arms on my thighs and waited for a response. My heart was pounding and I was sure it could be heard by everyone in the room.

Someone came out of what I later found out was the DJ booth clapping. He tossed two hundred dollars on the table. "Fuck me again." He shook his head and walked off. The front of his pants was wet.

I struggled to hide my smile. If he was any indication of how I performed, it was all good. He must have been the person who lowered the lights.

"Stop fucking around, Spears, and hire her."

Spears just looked at me with a scowl on his face. I didn't like him. There was something about his eyes that made me feel off-kilter. My hair was in my face so I pushed it away as I waited. It was only a few seconds but it felt like a lifetime. I tried to act like I was comfortable with the intensity of his stare and it took everything in me to stand there, near naked, before his watchful gaze.

"Young girls bring drama and I don't need no drama."

"I say let her dance. I like the way she moves," said the first guy at the bar.

"Man, she made my dick hard and my shit stopped working so long ago I forgot what it felt like. Let the bitch dance."

The second man openly stroked his dick and I wanted to reach between his legs and snatch his nuts right out the sack. I wanted to turn my head from his blatant expression of self-gratification, but if I was going to get this money, I had to get used to this type of knee-jerk reaction.

"Let me see something else," Spears asked.

I thought about it for a brief moment but decided not to do it. If he liked my dancing, one was enough. "No, the first one was a freebie. The next time I take off my clothes I expect to get paid." I slid on my jeans and put my money in my back pocket. Even though I needed this job I wasn't about to let him or anybody else exploit me. If my boldness resulted in my not getting the job, I was just going to be like Willie Lump Lump and keep it moving.

"You a bad bitch, ain't you?" Spears chuckled but it wasn't intended as a compliment.

"Yes, I am." My voice was low but I think he got my message. He had one more time to call me a bitch. Sometimes I used the word with Reshunda, but in general, the only time I let someone call me a bitch was right before I kicked their ass. It was not a term of endearment as far as I was concerned and this asshole betta recognize.

"Spears, I asked you to stop fucking around and hire the girl." The white man who I thought was the DJ spoke sternly.

Spears dropped his head and mumbled to himself. "I already told her she got the job, man, back off," Spears stated. He waited 'til the white guy went back to the booth before he spoke to me again. "You got the boss's eye. However, I run this. Don't bring all that drama up in this camp. I'm gonna be watching you. Be here at eight."

He got up off his stool and left the room, leaving a bitter taste in my mouth.

"Hey, don't worry about him," one guy said, pointing at Spears's back.

"Yeah, every now and then he gets his head stuck up his ass and today's one of them days. You got my dick hard, so you're all right with me." He peeled several bills off his stack and slid them to me.

I took the extra money before I slid my top back over my head and adjusted my hair.

"See you tonight." I walked out, barely able to contain myself. I felt one step closer to getting my mother out of jail, and for the first time in a long time, I felt good.

# Chapter Fourteen

## *RESHUNDA WYLDE*

"Girl, when did you start working here?" I screamed when I caught up with Valencia coming out of the main room. She was looking good and I was excited to see her.

"For starters, I haven't seen you and since you don't pick up the phone and call nobody . . ." She was about to steal my joy and I wasn't about to let it happen.

"When did you get the job?"

"I got started working the same day Ebony gave me her ass to kiss."

Valencia was all smiles so I didn't trip. "You go, girl, you're here now and that's all that matters. Look at you all fixed up and shit." She turned around so I could admire her outfit and I felt a slight twinge of jealousy. Valencia looked good in everything. She had an effortless beauty and it'd been a long time since I'd seen her take time to apply makeup. Her hair was curled and it looked like a lion's mane.

"Thank you, boo, I've been doing a little extra since I had to audition to get the job."

She caught me off guard. "Are you serious, you had to audition?" I was stunned. If Valencia, with all her beauty, had to audition, I wondered what Ebony had to do in order to get top billing at the club. My stupid behind thought all she had to do was fill out an application.

"What? You thought I was going to walk up in here and they be like 'we need you' or some shit like that? Everybody can't have a hookup."

I could tell she wasn't being spiteful when she said it. She was just stating the facts.

"This ain't a fucking social club," snarled a man I'd never seen before. The bass in his voice scared the shit out of me.

"I gotta change. This thong is riding me like a bicycle without the seat, all up in my ass," Valencia snapped back with the same amount of vigor.

I watched their exchange with growing curiosity.

"Then hurry the fuck up and get back on the floor." He disappeared out the door into the main room.

"Who the hell was that?" I demanded. I had half a mind to go after him and let him know he couldn't be talking to my friend like that.

"That's Spears. Come go with me to the dressing room. That motherfucker is getting on my damn nerves."

I followed Val into the dressing room. Several women were in various stages of undress and I felt uncomfortable being around them. Thus far, I hadn't spent any time with the other dancers and, by the looks of things in the community dressing room, I thanked my lucky stars that I didn't have to. I changed in Ebony's dressing room so I wasn't exposed to the backbiting and petty arguments going on in the tiny room. I could tell from the evil stares that I wasn't welcome into their space, so I kept my eyes low and waited for Valencia to change so we could get the fuck up out of there. She grabbed a few things from her locker and we left.

"What did you have to do for your audition?" I asked, when we were alone in the bathroom.

"I just danced, but the owner was in the club and he made Spears hire me, and he's been pissy to me ever since."

"I'm scared of you! I haven't met any of them yet and from the way Spears was handling you, I don't want to."

"I'm not scared of him. I just want to do my thing so I can get what I need."

Valencia was always bold and confident but something about her had changed. "You were awesome. And did you see Ebony's face when you walked down the stairs?" I was still excited just having my girl with me and getting paid was an extra bonus.

"Yeah, she looked like she wanted to shit a brick!" Valencia made a face mimicking Ebony and it was hysterical. I laughed so hard I started crying.

"Oh God, you look just like her." I should have felt ashamed of myself for laughing at my own cousin, but funny was funny.

"We'd better get back out there. What time are you leaving?"

"Probably around twelve. Do you want a ride? I've got my dad's car."

"Yeah, that would be cool. I hate catching the bus dressed like this." She smiled and winked at me.

"All right, then. I'll meet you at the front door at twelve," I said, as we exited the bathroom.

"She's going to be mad at you when you get home."

She was right, but I would deal with Ebony when I saw her. For now, I was enjoying being with my friend again, almost like we used to be.

"Hey, since we both got money, how about we go get something to eat."

A smile lit up Valencia's face but it was quickly wiped away. "I can't spend this money. I've got to save everything I make so I can hire my mother a decent lawyer."

I couldn't believe how quickly I'd forgotten the reason she was there in the first place and I wanted to kick myself for even making the suggestion that she go out and blow her money.

"Sorry, boo, I wasn't thinking, but don't worry. I'm gonna help you get that lawyer. You can have half of what I make until you get enough to hire someone." I could tell by the look on her face that she was shocked.

"Are you serious?"

"Of course, you're my best friend." I felt better being able to help for a change. She rushed toward me and gave me the tightest hug as we cried.

"Thank you so much. You don't know how much this means to me and my mother."

"And I'm still treating you to dinner with the money I have left." We both laughed.

We took our time getting dressed since Ebony had kicked us out of her dressing room. Things were so different now that Valencia was there. Ebony made me feel inadequate when it was just the two of us, but with Val, I felt like we were playing on an even field.

"Wait, isn't that Ebony at the bar?" Valencia asked.

I looked back over my shoulder and, sure enough, Ebony was at the bar with two older white men. She had a drink in both hands and didn't seem to mind that the men had their hands all over her body.

"Oh shit, she's drunk. Look at her." Ebony was taking shots and the men at the bar were cheering her on. I was conflicted. Ebony was a grown-ass woman but I was afraid she was in over her head. "Should we do something?" I was really talking to myself because I knew Valencia had no love for Ebony, but she was still my cousin.

"I think we should stay and make sure she gets home all right. I didn't want to tell you this, but word in the dressing room says your cousin's is into some other type of shit."

"What do you mean?" A cold chill went up my spine and I shivered.

"Drugs were mentioned, but since I don't deal with those silly bitches, you know they weren't going to say anything to me about it. Let's just stick around and see what happens."

"Thanks, I was hoping you would say that, but since we're still underage we can't go in the bar."

Valencia shook her head. "That's some bullshit. We're old enough to shake our ass but they're protecting us by not letting us drink. How the hell does that make sense?"

"I know, but what can we do?" I felt the same way as Valencia but I wasn't ready to test the rules that were drilled into our heads when hired. The club would lose its license if we were caught drinking in the main bar. The rules were a little different in the private lounge, but since Ebony wasn't in that lounge, we were forced to stand by and watch her make a fool of herself.

"Why don't we wait in the car? These heels are killing me. We can catch her when she leaves and make sure she's okay before she does something stupid, like get behind the wheel of her car."

"Good idea." Valencia followed me outside to my car. My father had officially given it to me because there was no telling when he would be sober enough to ever get his license back. He said he'd buy himself another one when he was ready.

"I hope you don't take this the wrong way because I'm not trying to pick a fight with you—"

"Say what's on your mind." I immediately tensed up because we had just gotten to a familiar place and I thought she was about to ruin it.

"Uh, maybe I should keep my big mouth shut."

"No, go ahead," I urged her.

"Your cousin, she seems like she's changing and I don't mean for the better." I could tell her comment wasn't coming from a bad place so I couldn't take offense, especially since I agreed with her.

"Yeah, I know what you mean. She's getting phone calls at all hours of the night, slipping out the house and when she does come back, she's fucked up."

"Don't you think you should say something to her? I mean, I don't want her to get hurt or something like that."

My heart began to beat faster because it was almost like she was reading my mind. I was worried about Ebony's behavior and it had been on my mind for a few weeks, and I felt like there was no one I could talk to about it. Before I knew it, I was crying.

"Hey, are you crying?" There was alarm in Valencia's voice.

I tried to wipe away the tears but they kept coming faster. "I'm so scared for her but she ain't gonna listen to me. She thinks she knows every damn thing." I had tried to tell Ebony to slow her roll but she was quick to remind me that she was older and to stay in my lane.

"What about your dad, do you think he could talk some sense into her?"

I could tell that Valencia was really worried and this surprised me. I wiped away the last tear as I spoke. "She won't listen to my dad. Hell, how can he give her advice when he spends most of his time fucked up?" I pulled my car around to the side of the club and turned off the engine. I was tired and a little annoyed that I couldn't eat and get in bed because of Ebony's wild ass.

"One day, my mom was real upset. She'd been on the phone with my Aunt Candace. She was yelling and screaming at her. When I came into the room, I could tell she'd been crying, but when I went to hug her she pushed me away and told me to go to my room. I pretended to leave but I stayed in the hallway and listened."

"When was this?" Valencia asked.

I had to think about it because I'd tried to pretty much block all those negative thoughts from my mind. "It was probably a week or two before she died. I don't know for sure, but it sounded like my auntie was fucking around with the guy my mother introduced her to. My mother was trying to tell her he wasn't the one to fuck with but my auntie wasn't trying to hear it."

"Damn girl, why didn't you tell me this sooner?"

"Why, what does it mean?" I had no idea where Valencia was going with this.

"I got to go see my mom."

"Why, what's going on?" I was nervous. If Valencia had figured out what really happened that night, I needed her to share it with me. I reached in my purse and grabbed my money and handed it to her.

"I'll tell you what I think once I talk to my mother. Don't worry, I'll go see her tomorrow."

"Here, it's twenty-five hundred, put it toward the lawyer fund." She didn't get a chance to respond.

"Shit, there's Ebony."

# Chapter Fifteen

## *VALENCIA ROBERTS*

Ebony came out of the club with one of the men who'd been buying her drinks. I recognized the look on his face but Reshunda and I were not about to let it go down the way he planned it. It was a good thing we hung around because nothing good would have come out of this situation. Reshunda and I leaped out of the car and rushed toward Ebony.

"Hey cuz, I was looking for you. I need a ride home," Reshunda said.

I was a little slow on the uptake but I caught on quickly. She passed her keys to me as I stepped back so I wasn't directly in Ebony's limited line of vision. She was so busy trying to stand up straight while looking through her purse she almost fell over. The man holding onto her licked his lips every time she faltered, but we were about to ruin his fantasy.

"Huh?" Ebony looked startled. Her eyes were red and unfocused. She was going to have a hell of a hangover in the morning. Even though I disliked her, I didn't like seeing her like this. She was a beautiful woman, but I didn't see it at that moment.

"I need a ride home. The guy I was kicking it with turned out to be a jerk," Reshunda said.

I backed up. She apparently didn't want Ebony to know I was waiting with her and I was cool with that. She might've shown her ass if she knew I was hanging around.

"Where's your friend?" she asked as her eyes rolled around in her head like marbles.

I smiled. She was wasted but not enough to forget about me.

"Uh, I think she left a while ago," Reshunda lied.

Ebony was so drunk, I doubted if she would've seen me even if I was standing right in front of her. Her eyes were locked on Reshunda and she appeared to have forgotten the man who was still holding her upright.

"I don't mean no harm, lady, but I told Miss— umm—" He pointed at Ebony, "I told her I would see her home," the perv interjected as Reshunda tried to pry Ebony's arm from his fingers.

He acted like he was about to pitch a fit, so I decided to stick around to make sure I wasn't going to have to run his stupid ass over.

"It's okay. Thanks for your help. I'll make sure she gets home." Reshunda continued to pry his fingers away, and she damn near fell in the middle of the sidewalk.

"But she's supposed to come with me!" He poked himself in the chest, upsetting his own precarious equilibrium.

"You should go somewhere and sleep it off," she admonished in a scolding tone.

"Is everything all right out here?" One of the bouncers stepped forward and helped Reshunda push Ebony in the car.

She slumped over in the backseat and slid out of view.

"Thanks," Reshunda mumbled to the bouncer, as the drunk guy took the hint and stumbled away. She got in the car and locked the doors. Once she was safe, I followed them home. When we got there, she waved me on. I rolled down the window.

"I'm sorry we didn't get a chance to eat but I'm glad we stuck around at the club." She glanced over her shoulder at the car.

"Yeah, me too. Give me a second to park and I'll help you get her in the house."

"Child, please. Go on home, I'll get the car in the morning."

"What about Ebony? You gonna leave her in the car?" I asked as she started walking to her apartment.

"I'm not about to carry that bitch, she'll be all right."

I tried not to laugh but it was funny. Together, we might've been able to get Ebony's dead weight up a flight of stairs, but it would have been a struggle.

If she wasn't going to sweat it, neither was I. "All right then. Call me later, but don't forget I'm going to visit my mother and see if I can get a lawyer. Thanks."

"You're welcome. Stop by when you get back. I ain't going anywhere."

I shook my head as I drove. Even though Reshunda and I were technically grown, we still needed guidance. We were raising ourselves and it made me feel sad.

"You shouldn't have come back so soon. I don't want you to keep seeing me this way." My mother had another black eye.

I hired a lawyer and couldn't wait to tell her, so I rushed over to the jail but the news would have to wait. "What happened to your eye?" I demanded through the phone. Blood rushed to my head and the room began to sway before my eyes. I grabbed the counter and forced myself to sit down.

"It was a slight disagreement. Don't worry about it," my mother said, shrugging it off.

"Disagreement? Are you fucking kidding me? Disagreements do not result in black eyes!" If I wasn't motivated to get my mother out of jail before, I was now. This was totally unacceptable and if she thought for one minute that I was going to sit around and let this continue she was out her rabbit-ass mind.

"Hey—don't forget who you're talking to." Her look held a more intensified meaning. In other words, it meant, *I may be locked up now, but I will tear that ass up the second I get out of here—so, shut it down.*

"Did you have the doctor look at it?"

She laughed at me. "No, sweetheart, it doesn't work like that in here. As long as I'm not bleeding or infecting others, they don't give a shit. I believe they like it when we fight, gives them some entertainment."

"That's fucked up." The words slipped out my mouth. I wanted her out of there so badly, I could taste it.

"I'm not going to tell you again to watch your mouth, young lady."

I wasn't trying to disrespect my mother, I was just mad. "I'm sorry."

"Sweetie, you can't keep coming here. It tears me up inside and it's not fair to you."

"Mom, it's tearing me up too, but I can't just not come." I pleaded with my eyes. I didn't know what I would've done if she forbid me to come back.

"Okay, but not so often. I just need a few dollars on my books and I'll be okay."

"You have money on your books. You should get it by Tuesday and I hired an attorney." I could tell she was stunned by the look on her face but her eyes quickly narrowed.

"How did you . . ." If she wanted to know more, she didn't finish asking.

I swallowed a huge lump in my throat because I didn't know what I would say if she pressed the issue. We'd always had an open relationship so it would've been difficult to keep the truth from her.

"Thanks," she mumbled, lowering her eyes but not before I saw her pain.

"I talked to Reshunda last night. She remembered overhearing a conversation her mother had with her aunt. She said her mother was arguing with her about some man she was messing around with. Do you know who she might have been talking about?" I watched my mother's facial expressions as they changed from sadness, anger, and finally fear.

"Why? Has anybody been around the house? I'll kill that motherfucker if he comes anywhere near you."

The hairs on my arm stood up and I leaned forward in my chair. "No. Who is 'he' and why would 'he' come around me?"

Her face relaxed when the guard came over near her chair. I sat back and tried to act calmer than I felt. The guard walked away.

"He's a local hustler, turned out to be a real piece of shit. His name is Trent." She looked around again and this time she lowered her voice to almost a whisper. "The night he shot Candace and Kym he said if he didn't get his shit back he would kill their families. I think he would have shot me too if he knew I was hiding in back of the room. Honey, I promise to tell my lawyer everything when I get to see one."

I nodded my head. "But I don't understand why Ms. Kym would get involved with a buster in the first place if he were such a scumbag?"

"Because I introduced them. She said she wanted to make some extra money and so did I. Since you and Reshunda were graduating from high school, we both wanted to do something nice for y'all." She started crying and it nearly broke my heart to find out all this trouble was because of us.

"Mom, why would you do such a thing? You know me, I'm not high maintenance. I would've been happy with a card and a slice of cake."

"I know, sweetie, but a woman's daughter only graduates from high school once. I wanted to make it special for you. Besides, it was a one time thing for me. Once I collected my money, I was done, but Candace and Kym, well . . ." She shook her head without saying any more.

"Please stop crying, Mom, there's nothing you can do about it now." Although I wanted her to quit crying, I needed to hear the rest of the story. I was curious as to where my mother met such an unsavory character, but I wasn't going to press her on it just yet.

"Candace was screwing this guy in New York. Kym said he was paying the bills but Kym, I found out, was messing around with Trent." She paused, peering at me through lowered lashes.

I impatiently waved her on.

"She told me it was Candace's idea to skim a little off the top before they delivered the product to Trent. Candace would bring the drugs in and they would take a little and cut what was left with baking soda and some other shit. I forget what else they used."

"Somebody has been watching too much TV," I mumbled. My mind was racing one hundred miles a minute. I was trying to figure out how my mother was connected in all this because it wasn't making any sense. A vital part was missing from her story.

"What did you say?" my mother asked, jolting me back into the conversation.

"Uh, nothing," I replied. I gave her an innocent smile that only a mother would believe.

She smiled back at me, but only for a moment. "I'm guessing that Trent and Candace's friend got to talking and grew suspicious of them." She hunched her shoulders.

"But how did you know where to find them?"

"Kym's phone must have dialed mine by accident. She normally met with Trent on the third Wednesday of each month. When I heard her voice, she sounded scared and when she said something about a gun, I got in the car and took a chance they'd met in their regular place."

"Where was that?"

"The Cheetah Club in midtown," I could feel the color drain from my face.

"Mom, they weren't killed there."

"I know, but that's where they met each month."

"The strip club?" I had to be sure she wasn't mistaken, but somehow I knew she wasn't. This was too much of a coincidence to ignore.

"Don't go getting all excited and shit, they didn't go there to dance. Candace and Kym never saw anyone other than Trent when they went to the club."

I got this eerie feeling in the pit of my stomach. Instead of answering the questions, my mother only confused me more.

"How did you know Trent?"

Her eyes darted around the room and she had this pained expression on her face. She didn't answer right away, which confirmed my fears that I wouldn't like what she would say. I held my breath, anticipating the worst.

"Honey . . ."

"Oh shit." Bad news almost always was predicated with a sweet nothing in front of it.

"I didn't want you to find out. . . ."

A tiny voice in the back of my mind said put the phone down and walk away, but my stupid ass hung on. I felt like I was hyperventilating but I didn't relinquish my death grip I had on the phone.

"We used to date before I married your stepfather," she said.

I let loose some of air I had held captive in my lungs. *This news wasn't so bad—it was almost a decade ago*.

She began to cry again but I was so relieved it wasn't any bad news I hardly noticed.

*If she didn't utter another word, I would be good. I envisioned her saying some dumb shit that would change the way I felt about her.*

"He's your real father . . ."

Her words didn't immediately infiltrate my brain, but when they did I was filled with murderous rage. For at least a minute, I couldn't say anything. Everything and nothing made sense. I felt like I was reading a bad book, only this book wasn't fiction, it was my life. My mother told me my father was dead and I never questioned it so, I didn't spend my life wishing for something I couldn't have. I never wondered what it would've been like to have a dad.

"Are you fucking kidding me? You've been lying to me my entire life?"

"Time, Roberts."

I looked helplessly from my mother to the guard who had stepped into the room to take my mother back to her cell.

"No, please, I need more time."

My mother leaped from her chair and placed her hands behind her back. The guard slapped the handcuffs on her wrists and led her out of the room. I waited for her to say something to me, but instead she kept her eyes averted and head down, refusing to look at me. If I could've gone through the plate of glass separating us,

I would've punched her in her other eye. I sat in the chair, stunned and confused. There was more to the story, but she was the only one left standing to tell the tale. Part of me didn't want to know, but the other part knew I had to in order to move on.

# Chapter Sixteen

## *EBONY QUEEN*

Scared, I woke up cold and alone in the back-seat of a car. I had no idea where I was and how I got there. I'd heard about blackouts before but had never experienced one.

"Oh shit," I whispered. My imagination got the best of me as I looked around the strange car, trying to find a weapon.

"Fuck!" I couldn't see anything on the dark floor. My hands were free and I intended to use them if anyone even thought about touching me. I finally got up the nerve to peek out the window after a few seconds to see where I was. I couldn't believe it when I saw my own house.

"Asshole." This shit would have been hysterical if I hadn't been so afraid moments before. I almost crapped in my pants and the whole time all I needed to do was go in the damn house. Feeling stupid, I chuckled, but it was short-lived because I didn't remember driving home. That was not good, but at least I'd made it safely. *You made it, but what the fuck are you doing in the backseat? Why the hell didn't you carry your dumb ass into the house?* I shivered. The temperature had dropped since I had left home and I couldn't wait to get inside to get warm.

I felt like shit when I got out of the car. My neck was stiff, my head felt like a tiny man was stomping around, and I had to pee. I found my purse on the front seat and started looking for my keys. I had to go to the bathroom really bad and my hands were shaking from the cold. I was at the front door when I stopped dead in my tracks. I remembered what started my out-of-control drinking.

"Oh hell no!" I shook my head side to side, trying to rid my mind of the image of Valencia's face as she walked around the main room of the club. Bile rose in my mouth and I made a feeble attempt to stop it from spilling out, but was only partially successful. It tasted bad coming up but it was worse going back down. I stumbled back to my car to sit down. Valencia's face flashed before my eyes, filling me with rage. Cheetah's was an exclusive club, so how the hell had she managed to get her stank-ass up in there? This had to be some kind of mistake. I had to be dreaming, or on some other shit, but I couldn't even think about going to bed until I had some answers. I forgot all about going to the bathroom.

"Where the fuck are my keys?" I emptied the contents of my purse on the front seat of the car, but my keys were not there. I searched the floor but they were not there either. "Bitch, you had to have them to get home!" After a few more fruitless seconds, I gave up the search and took the extra key from my glove compartment.

"I knew this bitch would come in handy." I smiled and started the car. With any luck, Trent would still be at the club because he had some explaining to do. I was still tipsy, but considering the circumstances, I thought I drove pretty good. Trying to restore missing pieces of memory took up most of my concentration but I managed to get to the club without hitting anything. It was a short drive and by the time I got there I had almost convinced myself I'd been having a nightmare. "Get a grip, bitch. There is no way in hell the club would hire Valencia to dance. There's no fucking way. Why the fuck am I tripping?" I stumbled out of the car, fairly certain that I'd made the whole thing up.

Inside the club, the crowd had thinned to a more lewd and cruel type of atmosphere than I'd become accustomed to. Money spent, these

patrons were looking for a freebie or someone
to keep them warm, but I didn't care because
I wasn't there to make money. I was looking
for Trent. Although my mind was relatively
sober, my body didn't get the memo. I staggered
through the club searching for the back door. If
Trent was still around, I knew he'd be in the back
room playing cards with his buddies. He used
the guise of the club to run a high-stakes poker
game. I let out a sigh of relief when I opened the
heavy oak door and saw him immersed in heavy
plumes of cigar smoke. He looked up, obviously
annoyed by the intrusion, but his friends seemed
to be amused.

"You treating us to entertainment tonight,
Trent?" they jeered.

"Negroes please, I can't even afford her ass,
so I know you can't." Trent joked but I didn't
think his remark was funny. I would've cussed
his monkey-ass out if he wasn't my employer. I
might have been drunk but I wasn't stupid.

"Ebony, this room is off limits to the help." If
he were trying to be demeaning, it didn't work.
Although his voice was stern, I thought he was
frontin' for his boys. I wasn't trying to piss him
off, I was just trying to get some answers.

"I'm so sorry, Trent, but I really needed to
speak with you. The girls outside told me I would

find you in here." I immediately switched my temperament from a mad bitch to a subservient temptress, honey dripping from my words and then I burped like the corna' drunk. *Shit.* My face burned with embarrassment. However, my shame quickly turned to laughter. Part of me was humiliated, but the other part of me, thought that shit was the funniest thing I'd ever done. "Wow, did you hear that shit?" I giggled uncontrollably.

"You're drunk, Ebony." Trent pushed back his chair and rushed toward me.

He surprised me with his swiftness. I stepped back quickly and lost my footing. My arms wind-milled as I tried to keep from falling. Laughing did not help but I couldn't help it.

Trent roughly grabbed me, his boys cater-wauling behind him. He dragged me out of the room, shutting the door behind him. He swept me up in his arms and he pushed open another door that I'd never noticed before. He carried me down to the basement.

His cologne hypnotized me and I greedily inhaled his scent. "You smell good, baby." I wanted to lick his neck; he smelled delicious.

He dropped me on the sofa and walked away. "You messing with my money, Ebony. You'd better not be fucking with my product," he replied curtly. A large vein pulsed in his neck.

I could tell I'd pushed Trent's buttons. I tried to pull myself together. "I'm sorry. I may be a little drunk but I ain't touched your stuff," I burped. I wasn't used to Trent's rough treatment. I stood up abruptly but the room started to spin, so I sat back down.

"Shit." Trent walked over to the bar and poured himself a drink. He was an extremely handsome man and if he weren't my employer, I would have done some freaky shit with him just to change his funky attitude.

"Can I have a drink?" I asked, batting my eyes and poking out my chest.

He didn't appear to be amused. "You've had enough. Now tell me what you wanted to speak to me about so I can get back to my game." Irritated, he slammed his empty glass on the bar.

Suddenly sober, I got right to the point. "I don't like the new girl you hired."

He shot me a strange look. "And? The rest of the girls don't like you. What the fuck do you expect me to do? Fire everybody?"

"I don't give a flying fuck about the other girls, but I don't think this last girl can be trusted." Trent was a shrewd businessman and if I wanted him to change his mind about giving Valencia a job, I would have to convince him that she was also a threat to him.

He studied me as if he were sizing me up. "Trusted? Cut the shit, Ebony, you don't even know the girl."

"I know the bitch and I'm telling you she can't be trusted." I really didn't want to get into how I knew Valencia so I prayed he wouldn't ask me any more questions.

"What's up with that? I think you are afraid to have a little competition."

I felt insulted. If things were different, I might have taken a swing at him. I had to convince him that keeping me and Valencia wasn't going to work.

"That bitch can't lick the bottom of my shoes. I'm your money-maker and you know it."

"I hear you, but I still think you feel threatened by her," Trent taunted me.

"Fuck you and her. Coming to see you was a bad idea. Perhaps, I should start looking for another club, one that will appreciate me." I was no longer dizzy when I got up from the chair. I needed some fresh air because I felt like I was going to suffocate in the small cellar. I looked around for my purse but it wasn't there. Shit. I sat back down, trying in my head to retrace my steps. I stood to leave. I must have left my purse in the car again.

"Calm your pretty-ass down. I'm just fucking with you." Trent had a wide smile on his face.

Elated, I tried to contain my happiness. This pretty motherfucker was going to make me fuck him right there on the sofa. I was suddenly horny as hell.

"So, you'll fire her?" I started fiddling with the back of my dress, trying to take it off.

"I can't. I didn't hire her." Trent went back to the bar and poured himself another drink, but this time he poured one for me.

I tossed it back like an old pro, the brown liquor burning its way to my stomach. "Then who did?" I was pissed. I'd been at the club for several months and I never saw anyone else in the club usurp Trent's authority. I felt like I'd been blindsided with this new information.

"The owner. She caught his eye, so he hired her."

My blood boiled. I'd been barking up the wrong tree the entire time I worked at the club. I wanted to go to Valencia's house and rip every strand of hair out of her head. I was livid. Out of all the titty clubs in Atlanta, she brought her slutty-ass to the one I worked in. *Un-fucking believable.*

"Fuck." I was ready to go. The owner obviously operated under the radar so I was going to have to find out who he was and convince him to change his mind about Valencia. The club wasn't big enough for both of us.

"You still want me to drop off that package?" I asked over my shoulder, as I walked toward the stairs. Trent paid extra when I delivered packages for him. I was pretty sure he was pushing dope but I didn't care, as long as I got paid.

"Bitch, please. Do you really think I'm gonna give your drunk-ass a package? You must've bumped your head. Get out of here and sleep it off. In fact, carry your ass out the back." His eyes narrowed and his posture was defiant. Trent had never shown me this side of him before.

I liked dominant men, but there was a time and place for everything and this wasn't it. If I didn't need the extra money I would have told him to kiss my ass. The fucker didn't even walk me to my car. Five seconds ago, I wanted the nigga licking my pussy but now he wouldn't get the chance to smell my funky drawers. I thanked God I found out he wasn't the man I thought he was. If I had allowed him to hit it I would've had to cut him.

My keys were in the ignition, just as I left them. I was fucking tripping. I should've kept my black-ass at the house instead of going to the club and making an ass of myself. It was almost four in the morning and I still had to go to the bathroom.

"Damn, I lost the entire night and I can't remember shit." I fumbled with the keys in the ignition. Trent pissed me off, especially when he said Valencia was bringing competition to the game. He didn't get it at all; Valencia didn't threaten me, I just didn't like the bitch. She had a bond with my cousin that I felt was unnatural and I was determined to break that shit up. I just needed to figure out how to do it. Blue flashing lights painted my car. "What the fuck?" Panicking, I mashed the gas instead of the brakes and smashed into a parked car. "Oh shit . . ." My head thumped against the plastic steering wheel and everything went dark.

"Miss? Miss? Are you okay?" A man was outside my car, trying to get in and knocking on the window.

I shook my head, trying to clear it. My head hurt.

"Miss. Unlock the door."

I didn't know what to do, so I did nothing. My first instinct was to try to run but I would have to back up to do so and my car was blocked by the officer's vehicle. Thoughts of having my face blasted all over through the media brought reality back in focus. I had to open the door. I couldn't continue to sit in the car. The officer shined his light into the car as I reached for my purse.

He butted the window with his flashlight. "Freeze! Put your hands in the air where I can see them," he demanded.

*Damn, what the fuck was I thinking?*

"I was getting my purse," I yelled.

"You should've been opening the door like I told you to."

*Smart-ass. What did he want me to do now?* I kept my hands held high. I was back, in the Deep South, and wrong as hell for drinking and driving. "Sorry," I mumbled.

"Use your left hand and unlock the damn door."

*You have to cuss at me, dude? Really, does that make you feel better?* I hit the switch to open the door and immediately put my hand back up. I could feel the officer's testosterone in the cocky way he was swangin' his tool. He wasn't going to make an example out of me. I was going to follow his instructions to the letter. I wasn't taking any chances.

He pulled open the door and shined the light in the front and backseat.

"Step out of the car, keep your hands where I can see them."

I stepped out, unsure what was going to happen next. In the movies, cops threw folks on the ground and frisked them. I prayed he wouldn't do it to me as he called for backup.

"Sit on the curb."

I wanted to object but thought better of it. The curb was cold and uncomfortable but it was better than being facedown in the street while my car was being searched.

"Have you been drinking?"

*Shit.* "Officer, I had one drink but I'm not drunk. Really, I'm not." Technically I wasn't lying, I only stretched the truth. The drinks I had before my nap couldn't possibly count, especially since I had a nap. However, I couldn't remember how long I'd been sleeping.

"I need your license and registration."

*Was this motherfucker crazy? Where the fuck did he think I was hiding the shit. I was sitting on a fucking curb with my hands raised to God and he wanted my damn license.* "It's in the car. My license is in my purse but my registration is in the glove compartment." *Duh, what an idiot.*

"Do you have any weapons or drugs in the car?"

He sure was asking me a lot of questions. I wanted him to write me a damn ticket and send me on my happy way. I hesitated, thinking about the knife in my purse. I had no clue what the laws were in Georgia for carrying a razor.

"No."

"You sure about that? It sure took you a little while to answer." He rested his hand against his holster. If he did it to frighten me, it worked.

I stood up and walked to the car. "I'm sure."

He kept his weapon on me as I handed him my license and registration. This motherfucker had scared me shitless. I started to cry, I couldn't help it. It finally hit me how much trouble I was in; I was about to be carted off to jail. I dropped my purse and the knife rolled under the tire.

"Put your hands on the trunk and spread your legs." He searched me.

I felt like a common criminal. I'd never been so humiliated in my life.

He slapped cuffs on my hands and placed me in the backseat of my vehicle. He tossed my purse in my lap, minus the knife. "It's not nice to lie to the police."

"I'm sorry, Officer, I forgot it was in there. I'm coming from work and I always take it."

"You're not helping. If you always take something, then how could you forget you had it?"

*Fuck!* His left eyebrow rose as he shook his head. I wanted to tell him to kiss my natural black ass.

"This is a New York license," he said.

"What, it ain't good here?" He had to be the most stupid police officer I'd ever seen in my life.

"How long have you lived here?"

"A year or so." To me, a year sounded a whole lot better than six or seven months. I didn't realize I'd stuck another fork in my ass.

"Georgia law requires you to apply for a license within six months of relocating. I'll be right back, so please don't do anything else stupid."

My heart sank. I grabbed my cell phone as best I could with shackled hands to call Reshunda. She was gonna have to get me a bondsman just in case I needed one. I scrolled through the phone but I didn't recognize any of the names or numbers until I came upon Valencia's name.

"Arrgh! This ain't my phone." I wanted to pitch the bitch out the window but the way my luck was going I would get a ticket for littering. Reshunda must have picked up my phone by mistake. I continued scrolling through the names, hoping to find someone else who I could call, but she was the only name I recognized. Damn. "Fuck!" She was the last bitch on the planet that I wanted to speak to but I didn't have a choice. I pressed the speed dial button and put the phone on speaker and prayed she would answer. I didn't want the officer to know I was on the phone and thankfully Valencia answered on the second ring.

"Bitch, do you know what time it is?" Valencia screamed through the speakers.

"It's Ebony, Valencia. I need a favor." Just hearing her voice made me want to gag. She didn't say anything and I thought she'd hung up.

"What the fuck do you want and how the hell did you get my number?"

Attitude, attitude. If I didn't need her ass, I would have checked her.

"Shit, did something happen to Reshunda?" Her whole demeanor changed.

"No, Reshunda's fine, I guess. She must have my phone. Listen, I don't have a lot of time. I'm being arrested and I need—"

"Wait. What did you say? How the fuck—? Where the hell are you?" She was rapid-firing questions without giving me a chance to answer.

I needed her to shut the fuck up so I could tell her what I needed. "I'm around the corner from the house and I got pulled over. Call her—" The bitch interrupted me again.

"We left your ass in the damn car. Where the fuck did you go?"

I could only play nice for so long. "Are you going to call my cousin or not?" Either she was going to help me or she wasn't. I was sure it was Valencia's idea to leave my ass in the car but I'd deal with that later.

"Bitch, you got it twisted. You called my ass for help, not the other way around."

If I could have gone through the phone at that moment, I would have. I looked over my shoulder to see if the cop was coming. As much as I hated to do it, I had to apologize.

"I'm sorry. I'm sneaking this call so I'm trying to get off before the officer comes back and catches me," I whispered.

"What did you do?" She whispered too.

"Ran a red light, hit a parked car." I wasn't even gonna tell her about the knife.

"And DUI too? For real, for real, you're going to need a lawyer."

"Shit, here he comes. Are you gonna tell her?"

"Yeah, I'll tell her and you know she's going to have a duck-plucking fit."

"Ah shit. A tow truck just pulled up."

"Where are you? I'll come get the car."

I snapped the phone shut when the officer started reading me my rights.

"Ebony Queen, you have the right to remain silent—"

# Chapter Seventeen

## *VALENCIA ROBERTS*

"Where are you? Are you there? Hello," I yelled into the phone, but Ebony was no longer there. Even though I couldn't stand her, I heard the fear in her voice and it scared me. My mother was caught up in the system and I hated that she too was heading down that path. I didn't wish that shit on anyone, even a bitch like Ebony. I got up and put some clothes on. The more I thought about it, the more certain I was that she needed a lawyer. Reshunda would be ready to run out of the house like Captain-Save-A-Ho and we'd wind up spending the remainder of the weekend sitting around the jail. I waited until the sun came up and placed the call to my lawyer before I let Reshunda know what was going on.

"This is Ricardo Mosby." He sounded like he'd been up for hours even though it was only eight in the morning.

"Ricardo, I'm sorry to bother you so early in the morning but I need your help."

"You didn't disturb me, so don't worry about it. May I ask who's calling?"

I had to chuckle at myself. "I'm sorry, I haven't had my coffee yet so I'm a little ditzy. It's Valencia Roberts."

"Hey, Valencia, I haven't been to see your mother yet because I needed to have my ducks in a row before I saw her. I plan to go this morning and see if I can get her before a judge. She's been in there too long without being charged."

"Thanks, that's great news, but I wasn't calling about her. I have a friend who probably got locked up last night and may be in need of a lawyer." I was truly stretching it when I referred to Ebony as a friend.

"Probably? Either they did or they didn't."

"You're right. Let me start again. A friend called and said she had just gotten pulled over by the police. She ran a red light and hit a parked car."

"Yep, you're right. She probably did get arrested. Do you know whether or not your friend had been drinking?"

"Put it this way, the last time I saw her, around two this morning, she was passed out, but hopefully she had sobered up by the time she was pulled over."

"Unfortunately for her, I doubt it. If she was drunk at two, by law she's drunk. Where did she get pulled over?"

"She was in DeKalb County."

"And this just happened?"

"Yes, she asked me to call a bondsman but I called to see if you could help her out. I'm sure she can pay you."

"That's always a good thing, but if she went to DeKalb County, she won't even be processed until around four o'clock this afternoon and then she'll have to see the judge. I hate to tell you this, but that probably won't happen until midnight at best. You probably won't hear from your friend 'til Sunday or Monday at the earliest."

"Are you serious?"

"Yeah, since it's the weekend, my best guess is Monday."

"Damn, my girlfriend is going to show her ass."

"She'd better not or she is going to be there a whole lot longer than that. What's her name?"

"Ebony Queen. She's not really a friend. She's my best friend's cousin. I don't really care for her, but since she called me I'm trying to help."

"Best friend? Is this the same friend you told me about whose mother was killed?"

"Yeah, and the girl that I want you to go see lost her mother too. She's the one who moved here from New York."

"And the plot thickens. Well, I'll check in on her when I go see your mother at noon. Chances are they won't let me see her until she's booked, but I'll try."

"Thanks, Ricardo, I really do appreciate it." A lump formed in my throat but I refused to cry. I was still upset with my mother, but not enough to see her rot in jail for a crime she didn't commit.

"No problem. Tell your friend she should try to come up with some bail money. If this is her first offense it will probably be between thirteen to fifteen hundred dollars. That's just for bail. I'll discuss my fee with Ebony if she decides to hire me."

"Thanks again. I'll wait for your call."

"No problem."

I was putting on my shoes as I finished up the conversation with Ricardo. I grabbed my keys so I could take Reshunda's car back and tell her what was going on with her cousin. I debated about whether or not I should call first, but the news I had to deliver was better served in person. If I told it to her over the phone, I wouldn't be able to stop her from rushing down to the jail to wait. This way, I could try to talk some sense into her before she went down there and acted a fool.

"Heifer, do you know what time it is?" Reshunda asked as she yanked open the door. She still wore her clothing from the night before.

"Going somewhere?"

She ignored me and walked back to her room. She picked up her digital clock and shoved it into my face.

"I'ma ask you again, do you know what time it is?" She slammed the clock back on the dresser and plopped down on her bed. I took a seat on Ebony's bed, especially since I knew she wouldn't be using it for a couple of days.

"Heifer, please. You should know me well enough to realize I wouldn't come over here this time of the morning unless it was important."

"Dag, I'm sorry. I lost my damn phone and I couldn't sleep worrying about it. I just bought that bitch, and what makes it so bad is I had to sign a two-year contract!"

"You're phone isn't lost, Ebony has it."

Relief transformed her face. "Thank you Jesus! I was about to be mad as a motherfucker if I had to pay for a phone I no longer had for two years. How'd you know Ebony had it? That heifer is still asleep in the car," she said, smiling.

"She might be asleep but she damn sure ain't in the car." Damn, I hadn't meant for it to come out like that.

"What are you talking about?" She got up from the bed and peeked out the window. "Where's Ebony's car?"

"Sit down for a minute, I need to tell you something. It's bad but it ain't the end of the world."

Flinging the blinds back against the window, she rushed over to me, grabbing me by the shoulders. "What the hell is going on?"

I tried to pry her fingernails from my shoulders but her grip was firm.

"Ebony's been arrested. She must have woke up and decided she needed to be somewhere. The cops pulled her over and arrested her, and before you go off the deep end and shit, I've already called a lawyer."

"She's what—" She raced back over to the window as if she didn't believe what she saw the first time.

"She called me because she didn't know anybody else on your phone."

"Where the hell was she going?"

"Beats the shit out of me. She may have woke up and thought she needed to go home. Hell if

I know what the bitch was thinking." The last statement slipped out. It was on my mind but I hadn't planned on saying it.

Reshunda turned on me, her eyes blazing.

"You think this shit is funny, don't you!"

If I hadn't seen it for my own eyes, I would have never believed she could flip the script on me so quickly. "Bitch, please. Didn't you hear me say I called a lawyer for her!" She had pissed me off. I reached in my purse and pulled out Ricardo's card and tossed it on the bed. "I thought you knew me better than that. I may not like your cousin but she means something to you so I have to care what happens to her. Real talk, that's what friends do." I turned and stomped out of the room. I was sick of this back-and-forth bullshit surrounding Reshunda and her cousin. I was done.

"Val, wait, I'm sorry. I'm sleepy and I took it out on you."

"Seriously? Is that your excuse?" I was so mad I couldn't even think of anything else to say.

"Uh . . ."

"Forget it, Reshunda. I'll tell the lawyer to call you if he gets to see her." I walked out the door. I was through with her and her silly-ass cousin.

Going away to school was looking better, and I was finally ready to cut the strings with my longtime friend.

# Chapter Eighteen

## *RESHUNDA WYLDE*

Valencia was giving me the silent treatment. She didn't answer the door when I went over to her house and she wasn't returning my calls. I thought she was being childish but I was sure I could get her to forgive me when I saw her at work. After Val left, I tried to get some sleep but I couldn't. I was worried about Ebony, but I was also afraid that I'd finally crossed the point of no return with Valencia.

We'd had our fair share of spats over the years but this last year had been the roughest. A lot of things had been said and some of them would leave permanent scars. The lawyer Val had contacted told me that Ebony wouldn't get to see a judge before Sunday, so I was going to have to go to work without her, which was easier said than done. I didn't realize how much I depended on Ebony until I started getting ready. Nothing I tried on fit the way I wanted it to and I couldn't get my hair right. I was a complete mess. I sat before my mirror but didn't like the person staring back at me.

*Fine friend I turned out to be. How could I let her leave like that?* I asked myself for the hundredth time. *Shit don't matter. We'll be friends again before midnight. She's just trying to teach me a lesson.* I tried shrugging my shoulders, acting like it didn't matter, but I was lying to myself. I slammed down my brush. "Fuck it, it is what it is." I wasn't used to having my room to myself and the pure silence was driving me crazy. I was also worried about how I was going to work the room at the club alone. I had a few good dance moves but my moves weren't inspirational. When I danced with Ebony, I studied her moves and imitated them, but I wasn't sure how things would go without her being there to inspire me. I didn't have enough confidence to make it drizzle, let alone rain!

Ebony once told me dancing for her was like an out-of-body experience and her alter ego took over. I didn't think I had one of those but if I did, I was going have to meet the bitch tonight because I was going to need her.


I called Valencia to let her know I was on the way but she didn't answer.

"I know she didn't catch the bus," I mumbled out loud. However, on a deeper level I knew that she had. I drove over to her house anyway, praying that she'd changed her mind and was going to forgive me.

She didn't answer the door but when I rounded the corner heading to the club I saw her standing at the bus stop. I pulled up next to her; my heart was beating so loudly I just knew she could hear it from where she stood.

"Val, I know you're pissed at me, but get in the car. You can still be mad but there is no need for you to catch the bus."

She took a few steps away from the car.

"Fool, stop trippin' and get in the car."

"The only fool out here is you!" Her long, brown hair whipped into her face as her neck swung wildly.

"Okay, I'm a fool, now get in the car."

She looked both ways several times before she got in.

I was relieved, because as much as I hated to admit it, I didn't want to go to the club without her.

"'Bout time, heifer," Valencia said, as she closed the door and put on her seat belt.

As soon as she sat down, a riot started in my stomach. Butterflies seemed like they were eating a hole in my stomach and felt like I was going to be sick.

"What's wrong?"

I was so sure she could see the discomfort I was having and laugh at me, so I shrugged it off.

"I'm good."

She grunted, which was cool because I really wasn't up for a whole lot of conversation. I turned up the radio. I pressed my foot harder on the gas. My stomach was trying to make a mockery of the burger and fries I ate earlier. I'd been shitting all afternoon and it was starting to get on my nerves.

"What's the matter with you?" Valencia inquired.

"My stomach is all fucked up." I grimaced in discomfort.

"Nerves?"

I wasn't surprised by her intuitiveness. That's the way we were. I nodded. What did surprise me was the fact that she wasn't nervous and she appeared to have forgotten our earlier disagreement.

"You don't have to do this if you don't want to."

"Huh?"

"You don't have to do this. Ebony's not here to impress. If I didn't need the money, I wouldn't be doing it either."

I thought about what she was saying. It was true that I started dancing because Ebony dared me, but since she wasn't there, I couldn't use her as an excuse. If I took to the stage tonight, it would be because I wanted to.

"I like the money," I admitted.

"Then, dance. When this mess is over with my mom, I'm done. I'm not going to allow the allure of money make me settle in. I'm going to school."

My foot hovered over the brake. Valencia's declaration was like a punch to the stomach.

"You got in?" I didn't mean to sound like she was incapable of getting accepted into college, but her decision seemed to come from left field, catching me in the center of my chest.

"Yeah, full scholarship and all."

She had every reason to be proud of herself but I didn't understand why she chose this moment to tell me about it. I wanted to be happy for her but I wasn't. In fact, I hated her.

"Oh yeah, where at?" The words tried to choke me as I tried to pretend I really gave a damn. I had forgotten about my upset stomach and began plotting on different things I could do to make Valencia feel as bad as I did.

"I'm moving to Boston."

My stomach recoiled as we reached the club. Throwing the car in park, I bolted and raced to the bathroom. I could hear Valencia behind me, yelling my name but I couldn't stop. I couldn't explain why I felt inadequate because she was going off to school. Perhaps it was because she was leaving me behind, but there was no time to analyze my reactions as I hovered over the toilet. When I was finally able to raise my head, I was embarrassed.

"Ee-wo, that's nasty." Valencia chuckled as she turned up her nose.

I failed to see the humor. "Nigga, you can save the jokes." I walked over to the mirror and washed my mouth out as best I could. As I stood up, Valencia handed me a miniature bottle of mouthwash. I stared at her for a few seconds before I took it.

"You always walk around with mouthwash? Is there something you want to share with me?"

She shrugged her shoulders. "I'm always prepared."

As much as I hated to admit it, she was. I gave the bottle back to her and she handed me my purse. I surveyed my face in the mirror and attempted to fix my makeup.

"Thanks." I was battling tears. We'd come to the end of the road and I honestly didn't know what I would do with the rest of my life.

"We're going to get through this."

I looked deep into her eyes. Even though I tried to hide my feelings, she knew.

"Since Ebony isn't here, why don't you dance with me in the main room? That's where all the big money is and it would put you that much closer to your goal." The more I thought about the idea the better it sounded to me. If she danced with me, I wouldn't feel so alone. It was a win-win situation.

"I don't know about that. That Spears guy ain't feeling me."

"Spears? How did you get on his bad side? You haven't been here long enough."

"Beats me, he looks at me like I'm the shit on the bottom of his shoe."

"Child, don't worry about him. I got you." I sounded more confident than I felt because I didn't know Spears either. Since I didn't do the same type of audition Valencia had done, I relied on Ebony's status in the club to shelter me. I wasn't sure how that would work, especially since she wasn't there, which was another reason why I wanted Valencia close to me so we could watch out for each other.

"Are you done, yet?" Valencia was tapping her foot, but I knew she was messing with me.

"Yeah, heifer, let's get out there and do the shit."

We had on our game faces.

# Chapter Nineteen

## EBONY QUEEN

"It stinks in here," I shouted through the bars. If anyone other than my cellmates were listening, I couldn't tell. I'd been shouting the same thing for the last half hour with no noticeable results. I was tired but too scared to sleep. Dejected, I finally gave up and went back to my bunk and sat down.

"'Bout time," a voice cried out from across the room.

I looked around, trying to see if they were talking to me. Most of the people who were in the holding cell when I arrived had already been processed.

"What? It does stink."

"And? Do you think somebody gonna come down here with a can of Lysol and spray some shit because your nose is offended?"

"I wasn't talking to you," I mumbled to myself. I wasn't about to start no shit I couldn't finish, so I shut the hell up.

"What you say?" As hard as it was to do, I refrained from responding. If the situation were different and we weren't locked down, I would've jumped but since there was nowhere to run, I decided to keep my big mouth shut. I could talk a good game but couldn't fight a lick. I used words to keep folks off of me. It worked in the past but I always had a way out if it didn't.

"Leave her alone. She ain't no different than we were when we first got here."

This older woman got up from her bunk and came to stand beside me. I wanted to push her away but something about her piqued my interest. "Do I know you?" She looked vaguely familiar but I wasn't about to trust anyone up in this bitch.

"No, but I knew your mother, Candace. You look just like her."

I was stunned. "Are you from New York?" I was thinking this was some kind of bad joke, since my mother didn't know many people in Atlanta.

"No, I'm from Atlanta, but your mother came here a lot."

Suddenly I knew exactly who she was. The resemblance to Valencia was uncanny and if I weren't so self-absorbed I would have seen it the moment I laid eyes on her.

"You must be Valencia's mom." She nodded her head proudly. *Can you say small fucking world? Wow, of all the fucking people that I could meet in jail, I meet the mother of a bitch I couldn't stand.*

"You look so much like your mother, but I wasn't sure it was you until you started talking. You even sound like she did."

I nodded. I used to hear that often when I answered the phone. She brought back pleasant memories that I couldn't afford to think about, at least until I got out of this place. Jail was not the place to appear weak. "I'm sorry, I forgot your name." I didn't know if she could be counted on as a friend or a foe. There's no telling what lies Valencia may have already told her, so I was going to handle her with care.

"I'm sorry, my name is Astoria."

She laughed and my veneer started to crumble. Without thought as to how she would react, I threw myself into her arms. At that moment, I didn't care what anyone thought of me. I was seeking the comfort only a mother could give and it didn't matter to me whose mother it came from.

"It's okay, sweetie, let it out." She continued to pat my back as I cried.

My tears felt like acid on my cheeks as I frantically swatted them away. They were the first real tears I'd shed since my mother passed and with them came the loneliness that I'd been trying to either ignore, or fill with other things.

"I miss her so much," I wailed but I wasn't being entirely truthful. I was angry with my mother for leaving me.

"I know, honey, I know."

I finally felt like I'd met someone who truly understood me, but those feelings conflicted with my desire to hate her. She was here and my mother was not. She was being charged with my mother's murder. I pushed away from her comforting arms.

"You don't know shit," I snarled with venom dripping from my tongue. I was mad at myself for showing any form of weakness, least of all to her.

Her smile disappeared and her eyes narrowed. "You might want to take that down a decibel. I can understand your being upset but I ain't the one you should be mad at." She yanked me forward, causing our chests to collide as she lowered her voice.

"What do you think you're doing?" I demanded.

"Keeping your stupid-ass from making a big mistake. You don't know these people. You start running your mouth and spreading your business around this bitch and the next thing you know, we'd both be dead up in here." She pushed me away as if I stunk but she had a valid point.

I was about to blast her ass and put her on front street. I looked around and noticed all eyes were on me.

"I understand you want someone to hate but I'm not the one and if you're acting this way with me, I can only imagine how you've been treating my daughter." I was busted on all counts; it was written all over my face.

"So?" I puffed up like a damn blowfish and the best that I could come back with was, *so?* If I wasn't so mad, it would've been funny. For months, I told myself what I would do if I ever met the woman who killed my mother and all I said was a lame-ass *so?*

She started laughing, which only fueled my anger. I pushed her, but she quickly shut me down.

"Are you out your fucking mind?" she hissed. "Do you want to wind up in even more trouble than you're already in?" She roughly grabbed my arms, forcing me to sit still next to her. "I know you don't like me and I can honestly understand how you feel, but the only reason I was at the place where your mother was killed was to help your Aunt Kym. I didn't even know your mother was there. Now whether or not you believe me is entirely on you, but the next time you come running at me like a damn banshee I'm going to knock the shit out of you. Do we understand each other?" she demanded.

I wanted to get up and get as far away from Astoria as the bars would allow, but what good would it do? The situation would still be the same no matter where I went. At least now, I had an opportunity to find out what really happened.

I nodded, but she went on as if she hadn't expected a response. "Did you get picked up for DUI?"

Embarrassed, I nodded yes. The alcohol was assaulting my own nose so I knew she got a whiff of it as well.

"Was my daughter with you?"

I was still upset so I didn't hesitate to speak my mind. "I don't roll with that bitch like that," I replied.

"Thank God for small favors."

"What's that supposed to mean? Last time I saw her she was shaking her ass at the club." If my mind wasn't entrenched in such a fog, I might've been quicker to my feet, but Astoria caught me before I could get away. Her nails dug into my arms as she forced me to remain seated next to her. She leaned in closer, allowing her hot breath to heat my already flushed face.

"Careful," she warned, but I was too stupid to heed the warning in her voice.

"I didn't know your little girl could get down like that," I taunted, gaining satisfaction when I saw the pain reflected in Astoria's eyes.

She released my arms but my relief was short-lived. She grabbed my chin with one hand while holding a small knife in her other hand. She held it dangerously close to my neck.

"Are you fucking crazy?" I demanded, which I immediately regretted. I knew this was not the best thing to say to a bitch holding a knife.

"Astoria, what are you doing?" warned another inmate, who was watching our exchange with great interest.

"I'm about to take out the garbage."

*Was she calling me trash?* The inmate edged closer to us and I silently prayed she could talk some sense into Valencia's mother.

"Astoria, look at me."

She did not release her grip on my chin nor did she look away from my face.

"Look at me, damn it," the inmate demanded.

"Yeah, look at her," I said.

"You might want to shut the fuck up before she cuts you," the inmate said.

Astoria turned her head, but she still didn't let me go.

"You're about to start some shit that won't only affect you, it will hurt us all. I love you, girl, like a sista from another mother, but I'm not getting stuck up in no bullshit. You feel me?" the inmate demanded.

Astoria relaxed her grip and I was able to pull my face away. She put the makeshift knife away.

Relieved, I made a mental note not to fuck with her again.

"Thank you." The inmate rolled back over on her bunk, dismissing us.

"Look, I'm sorry. I shouldn't have said what I did, but your daughter and I haven't exactly seen eye to eye." Her posture relaxed and I felt a little more comfortable in the most uncomfortable place I've ever been in my life.

She relaxed a little. "I guess that's how she made the money to hire a lawyer for me."

It was more of a statement than a question, but I answered it anyway. "Yeah, she told my cousin that she wanted to make sure you were okay."

Her eyes began to water and I felt torn between offering her comfort instead of inflicting further pain.

"I didn't kill your mother, a guy named Trent did," Astoria said as her shoulders heaved.

She cried silently, but I could feel her pain. Instead of returning to my bunk, I sat on hers and held her hand. It was the most that I could do for her at the moment.

"When did you start dancing?"

"Shortly after I moved here. What can I say? I can't stay with my uncle forever." Even though I

didn't know this woman from a can of paint, her
opinion of me counted. I searched her face for
clues as to how she felt about my dancing but I
could not read her stoic features.

"What about Valencia?" Her voice was different this time, harder, if that was possible.

"Last night was the first time I saw her," I said,
shrugging my shoulders. I didn't give a fuck about
her child and I wasn't about to pretend I did.

"So you think she's been dancing longer?" She
had started pulling at threads from her orange
jumpsuit.

"I don't really know. I asked Spears but he
told me he didn't hire her. Like I said before, she
don't say much to me." She didn't need to know
that Valencia asked me to get her the job, but I
refused. Especially since I didn't know how long
I was going to have to stay in this hellhole.

"Roberts, you have a visitor."

I could tell she was surprised to hear she had
a visitor by the look on her face, but she also
appeared scared.

"We'll finish this conversation when I get
back." It felt more like a threat than a promise.

# Chapter Twenty

## *VALENCIA ROBERTS*

"Hello?" My phone ringing ended the best dream I'd had in years.

"Valencia, this is Ricardo. Did I wake you?" I sat up straight, wiping the crud out of my eyes.

"Uh . . ." I flung back the covers, searching for my clock to find out what time it was.

He started laughing. "Don't even bother to lie, I can hear it in your voice." He laughed again. He didn't even know me well and already he had me pegged.

"Okay, you got me. What time is it?"

"Almost two. I'm about to go see your mother and I wanted to know if you wanted to take a ride with me."

"Can you do that? I thought it was supposed to be an attorney-client visit." I started pulling on my clothes even though I was still upset with her.

"Since you're the one paying me, you are technically the client. Besides, if you come with me, you can have a little more privacy with your mother."

"I'll be ready in ten minutes but I need twenty-five minutes or so to get to your office." I had my tennis shoes on and was looking for a brush to pull back my hair.

"Give me the address and I'll pick you up." I stopped. I didn't want Ricardo to see where I lived and I definitely didn't want him to come inside. It was silly of me to be so vain, especially since he already knew the address.

"How long before you get here?"

"I'll be there in about fifteen minutes," he replied.

"Okay, I'll be ready." I ran around the room looking for earrings and a matching top to the jeans that I'd slipped on. I raced out to the front room to grab my hat and ran smack-dab into my stepfather.

"Where the fuck are you running off too? Shit, you just brought your raggedy-ass in here." He reeled toward me as I propelled backward. He was stinking to the high heavens. From the smell of him, he probably hadn't had a bath in at least three or four days. Although my stepdad let me come and go as I pleased, it would be just my luck he'd act an ass today, so I decided to tell him the truth.

"I'm going back to see Momma." I held my head down, expecting for him to go off but he surprised me and backed away.

The snarl that normally adorned his face disappeared and for a brief moment he smiled. But just as abruptly as it appeared, it was gone and so was he. He turned around and stumbled back to his room, slamming the door behind him.

I was grateful he didn't tell me to tell my mother to kiss his nasty ass. I shook my head as I eased the front door closed behind me. I silently thanked God for answering my prayers. Soon, I would be leaving this place and the memories it contained. I couldn't wait to say good-bye to the drama.


Visiting my mother with Ricardo was an entirely different process. Although we still had to go through the metal detector, we didn't have to wait long to see her. Ricardo placed his briefcase on the desk as we waited for her to be brought in.

"Relax. You look like a mouse in a roomful of traps," Ricardo said.

"I know, I just hate coming here."

"Good, then I don't have to worry about coming here to visit you." He sat back and put his arms behind his head.

"You got that right. As soon as I get Mom squared away, I'm leaving to go to school in Boston."

"That's what I like to hear. There is nothing like a good education. What do you plan to study?"

Before I could answer, my mother entered the room. She eyed Ricardo first, but her gaze locked on me as her handcuffs were removed. Once again, I could tell that she'd been crying. Ricardo stood and I followed his lead. I wasn't sure if I could to touch my mother.

"Mom." I stepped forward but she pushed me back.

"Since when did you start shaking your ass for money?"

I was stunned into silence. My mother never asked me how I got the money to pay Ricardo and since she didn't ask, I hadn't bothered to tell her.

"I—uh—um—"

"*I—um* hell. Either you're dancing or you're not. Which one is it?"

Ricardo appeared to study our exchange.

I was so embarrassed, I didn't know what to say. I never wanted them to know about the dancing.

"Wait, hold on a minute, Mrs. Roberts, or may I call you Astoria?"

My mother acted as if she was seeing Ricardo for the first time. I was relieved that he was taking control of the situation, giving me time to think.

"Sorry, I wasn't being rude but I just found out my daughter's been shaking her ass at a fucking strip club."

I felt like I was two years old, because my mother made no attempt to hide her irritation with me. I was so ashamed, I wanted the floor to open up and swallow me. I stood up, desperately wanting to flee the room.

"I wish the fuck you would try to leave. Sit your ass down." My mother's hands were balled into fists.

I knew she meant business. I turned on her. "What other choice did I have, Mom? Did you expect me to let you sit in this jail and rot?" My eyes begged for understanding as tears flowed from them.

"Damn that." My mother jumped to her feet as I cowered in my seat.

Ricardo rushed forward and firmly persuaded my mother back into her chair. "Mrs. Roberts, physical violence never solved anything. Now, I can understand how angry you are but I can also understand why your daughter did it. Now, let's all take a deep breath so we can deal with this situation."

My mother shot dirty looks at both of us but she did as she was told.

"Valencia, are you dancing to pay for my services?"

*Was this a rhetorical question? How the hell else did either of them expect me to get money?*

"Don't you dare judge me. I did what I had to do." I wanted to leave so badly but my mother's threat was still hanging in the room.

"Mrs. Roberts, had I known what you daughter was doing, I would have refused."

My heart felt like it was going to leap out of my chest.

"What do you mean?" The words seemed to get stuck in my mouth.

"Just what I said. I'm very upset with you, Valencia, you should have told me."

"I couldn't. Do you know how hard this has been? I can't believe this shit." I jumped up and paced the room. "My mother is in jail—my stepfather is a drunk and couldn't give a shit—I just graduated from high school, what the fuck did y'all expect me to do? Sell pussy? Would that have made you happy?" I screamed.

The officer who escorted my mother in barged into the room, headed straight for her. She was also on her feet.

"Wait, Officer. Things got out of hand, but we're good now," Ricardo said.

He shot warning looks to my mother and me. "I got this," he reiterated. He lowered his outstretched hands, effectively putting us in check. The officer halted, but didn't immediately leave us alone.

"It's okay, Officer, I got this," Ricardo firmly repeated.

The officer gave each of us another hard look and left the room. We sat in silence for a few minutes.

"Okay, now that everybody is on the same page, let's start again. As I said a minute ago, if I had known your daughter was 'working' to pay for my services, I would have offered to take your case pro bono. I have a little girl too, so there is no way I would condone a child working in a club, regardless of the circumstances."

"So you're going to quit?"

My heart was beating so loudly I thought I'd misunderstood what he said.

"I'll stay if you quit working."

I sat back in my chair. As much as I hated dancing in the club, I needed the money for school. The tuition was covered but I needed books and other school supplies.

"Do we have a deal?" His hand was on his briefcase as he waited for my decision.

"She's done," my mother answered for me with a decisive nod of her head.

"What about school? I need money for books and stuff," I whispered. School was very important to me; it was my only way out.

"You will have everything you need. Promise me you'll quit the club, and I'll testify against Trent Spears. I wanted to protect him since he's Valencia's father, but since he allowed his child to dance at the club, I'm done," my mother announced.

"Wait, are you telling us the guy at the club is my father?" I wanted to believe her but she'd let me down before, so it was difficult. How could I be sure she wasn't lying to me again?

"I agree with your mother. You can use the money you gave me for a retainer for your supplies. I'll write you a check when we get back to my office."

What should have been a tremendous weight lifted off my shoulders felt like a trade-off of unreasonable proportions.

"Good. Desperation and degradation lead to terrible decisions, especially when fast money is involved, so I'm glad you are getting out." Ricardo turned his attention to my mother.

I could tell she was still upset with me but was relieved when I said I would quit. She stood up and held out her arms and I rushed into them, in spite of my pain. I hadn't realized how much I'd missed the feeling until I was in her arms again. The mood in the room began to change as we sat down and started discussing how Ricardo was going to handle my mother's case. I still needed to work on how I was going to deal with all this information. I also wanted to know how she knew about my dancing at the club, but I'd deal with that later.

"I'm meeting with the clerk of the court this afternoon and I'm going to request that your case be put in on the docket. I'm also going to ask that you be allowed to post bond. Is there anything in your past that will prevent you from getting a bond?"

"No."

"Good. I'm not going to make any promises but I'll do everything in my power to speed things along." Ricardo stood up and started gathering his things.

I followed his lead even though I wanted to spend more time with my mother. We had a lot to talk about.

"Thank you so much for not only helping me, but my daughter too."

"Don't worry about it. I got a mom and a daughter, so I'm sensitive like that. Just don't tell anyone."

"We won't," we answered at the same time, laughing.

"Just kidding. But you could do me a favor? Have you met another inmate by the name of Ebony Queen?" Ricardo asked.

"Yeah, she's in the same cell with me."

"Perfect. Would you tell her that I'll be in the courtroom as her attorney? She doesn't know me, but tell her Valencia told me to come see about her."

"Okay, I'll tell her," my mother said. The jangle of her jailhouse bracelets drowned out her sobs as she was led from the room.

"It's not fair," I cried into Ricardo's shoulder.

"Things will move faster, Valencia, you'll see." He held me until I was able to stop crying.

"Are you going to wait for me while I go see about Ebony or do you want to hook up later?"

"I'll get with you later. I need to go do a few things."

"I hope you meant what you said about leaving the dancing alone."

"Without a doubt. I never wanted to do it in the first place but I didn't have much of a choice."

"I understand. I just don't want to see you caught up in some stuff you can't get out of."

# Chapter Twenty-one

## *VALENCIA ROBERTS*

*Two Months Later. . . .*

"Shit, how come every time we go out some-where this bitch starts wilding out and gets pissy drunk. Then we wind up in the fuckin' bathroom holding her hair out the toilet?"

"Bitch, shut up and just hold the fucking door." Reshunda glared at me from over her shoulder. She was bent over, braced against the wall, trying to keep Ebony's face from actually touching the basin. It was not a pretty sight, but one that I'd grown used to.

"I ain't gonna be too many more of your bitches." I stepped away from the door, allow-ing it to close. This was a familiar scene and I was glad it was the last time I'd be part of it. I was leaving for school in the morning and this was to be my going-away celebration.

"Valencia, open the fucking door, it stinks in here," Reshunda shouted.

I could tell she was mad but I was mad too. I was sick of doing the same fucking thing every time we got together. If I wasn't leaving, I wouldn't have come, but Reshunda and Ebony begged me to come. Ever since Ebony got out of jail, her attitude toward me was different and while I wouldn't call us friends, we weren't enemies.

I forgave Ebony because she provided the missing piece of the puzzle that resulted in the charges against my mother being dropped.

"Then bring your stank-ass out of there. I don't see why we've got to take turns holding that bitch up because her stupid-ass wanna drink up the entire bar." I was beyond pissed. Although I tolerated Ebony when she was sober, she was a mean drunk and I couldn't stand being around her when she was like that. My mother said that a drunk mind speaks a sober heart or some shit like that. I couldn't really remember exactly how the saying went, but I was close enough to it.

"Bitch, I ain't playin' witchu'. Open the fucking door." Reshunda was kicking at the bathroom door.

"I told you to leave that lush at the house," I spat, as I angrily pushed against the door.

"Fuck you," Ebony sputtered as she threw up again. She completely missed the toilet even though Reshunda was propping her up. If the shit wasn't so disgusting, it might have been funny.

"No, fuck you and your trifling-ass." I stepped into the stall, ready to dunk her head under the water but the stench coming up out of the stall made me back up.

"Ugh, how can you stay in there?" I backed away from the stall again, allowing the door to close. I loved Reshunda to death but there was no way I was going to stand there and breathe in those toxic fumes. I pulled my travel-sized bottle of perfume from my tiny clutch and sprayed some on my clothes and into the air.

"Y'all got me wasting my perfume up in here ."

There was a loud thud and the stall shook.

"What's going on in there?" I started to push open the door again but my nose wouldn't let me.

"None of your fucking business," Ebony snarled.

She was getting on my last nerve. I wanted to bust through the door and choke her, that's how mad she made me.

Reshunda stumbled out of the stall, dragging Ebony behind her. She had a ugly yellowish stain on her once white dress. She grunted as she propped Ebony up against the sink.

"Eww, what's that on your shoulder."

Reshunda gasped as she spun around to see what I was pointing at. Meanwhile, Ebony slithered to the floor, her face slapping the ceramic tile. The sad part about the whole thing was the bitch was so drunk she didn't even blink from the impact.

A barrage of expressions played across Reshunda's face and for a nanosecond, my heart went out to her. Our eyes locked in the mirror and I wanted to cry because Reshunda was wearing the dress her mother brought for her graduation.

"Goddammit," she yelled as her eyes filled with tears.

I started to step over Ebony and give Reshunda a hug but she stopped me mid-step.

"If you would've helped me, this wouldn't have happened." Once again, Reshunda blamed me.

"Come again? How the fuck is it my fault that this bitch got drunk and threw up, again? Did I say *again*? 'Cause if I neglected to mention it the first time, let me say it again. I'm not her fucking babysitter and neither are you." I was so fucking mad I just wanted to hit something or someone. I was about to walk the fuck out of the bathroom until I realized I would be cutting my nose off to spite my face.

"I heard you the first time," she spat back at me. She grabbed several paper towels from the dispenser hanging on the wall and began picking off the particles of food clinging to her shoulder.

I couldn't bear to watch so I averted my eyes, looking at the floor, my eyes bucking in horror.

"You got some shit on your shoes too," I whispered. She wore her mother's four-inch white satin Jimmy Choos I'd secretly coveted.

Reshunda doubled over. "Oh my God." The tears fell this time. Her shoes, ruined, just like her dress. Now the only thing Reshunda had left of her own mother was another bad memory. "Ebony must be on some different shit 'cause her ass is out cold." I poked her leg with the tip of my stiletto. I didn't poke her hard enough to leave a bruise but it was enough to rouse her if alcohol were the only thing she'd been into that night.

Reshunda didn't even look at her. She was in her own little world, dealing with her own demons.

I stepped to her, trying to break her out of her trance. I was still mad at her, but I felt sorry for her at the same time. "Reshunda, we've got to get out of this bathroom. What if someone comes in?" Thus far, we'd been lucky that no one else had come into the room. I shook her to gain her attention.

"Huh?" She was still staring down at her shoes.

My heart went out to her. "Come on girl, get your shit together and let's move this bitch out of here."

She finally came back to the land of the living. "Oh God." She bent down on the floor, near her cousin's mouth.

"I wouldn't stick my face too close to her mouth. She might still be volatile."

Reshunda gave me a sharp look as if I were trying to be funny.

"What? Am I lying?"

She looked back at Ebony and shook her head. "I don't think she's breathing." She stood up and started looking around the room.

"Get the fuck outta here. She has to be breathing, stop trippin'."

"I'm not trippin'. Look at her back, do you see it moving?" She had a point. Ebony hadn't moved since her face hit the floor.

I started to panic, even though I hadn't done anything wrong.

"We've got to call for help." She pulled her iPhone from her purse but I grabbed it from her hand before she could start dialing.

"Bitch, are you crazy? We ain't even supposed to be in this club. They might even arrest us for having fake IDs." I knew I was going over the top but I was so close to leaving Atlanta that I wasn't about to let anything get in my way.

"What? We can't just leave her lying on the floor, that's my cousin," she screamed at me, as if I didn't know their relationship.

"I wouldn't give a fuck if it were Jesus Christ himself, I ain't goin' to jail on some bullshit."

"Give me my damn phone, heifer."

She lunged at me but I held the phone over her head. Things were happening too fast and I needed some time to think about the possible consequences. I looked down at Ebony to see if she was showing any signs of life, but she looked like a corpse to me. I didn't really hate her; she just got on my motherfucking nerves.

Reshunda took off one of her shoes, and held it high over her head. Thankfully it was the shoe without the vomit on it. "Bitch, if you don't give me that fuckin' phone, I'ma beat your ass like I caught you fucking my man."

"What the fuck are you going to say to the police? Think, Reshunda, they arrested my mother for being in the same room with two dead bodies and she stayed in jail for a year just for being in the wrong place at the wrong time. Do you want to sit in jail for a fucking year?"

She lowered her hand but her eyes were still wild and crazy. "I don't know. We can't leave her here!" She looked around the bathroom as if she were seeing it for the first time.

As bathrooms go, this one was a piece of shit, so it wasn't surprising that folks weren't busting down the doors to get in here. Shit, I would rather piss myself before I'd put my ass anywhere near the toilet. "That's what I'm talkin' 'bout. We got to get our stories straight just in case she's dead."

"Dead? Who said anything about her being dead?" Reshunda started walking around in circles, waving her hands in the air.

"Bitch, she ain't breathing. What that mean?" I was getting irritated, especially since time really wasn't on our side.

She stared at me like she wasn't understanding a word I said. "So what do you think we should do?" She appeared to snap. With her hands on her hips she started patting her foot like she was growing impatient with me instead of the other way around.

At no point did either of us consider giving Ebony CPR. I, for one, was not about to press my lips anywhere near her mouth and it was obvious Reshunda felt the same way or she would've been on the floor pounding the hell out of her chest and forcing air into her airways.

"I say we get the fuck out of here and call for an ambulance from a pay phone. This way we can get her some help without getting all jammed up with the fucking cops." I honestly didn't know if the cops would do anything to us at all but I wasn't about to take any chances.

"A pay phone? When was the last time you saw a fucking pay phone?"

Damn, she had a point. Since everybody and their momma had a cell phone, pay phones were few and far between.

"Then we tell them guys at the door, as we leave, that someone in the bathroom needs a little help getting home." I was already heading out the door when Reshunda stopped me.

"Bitch, give me my motherfucking phone. I don't know what type of bitch shit you've been smoking but I'm not about to leave my cousin lying in the middle of the fucking floor." She had a crazed look in her eyes and it was about to be on like popcorn.

"Oh, is that how we about to roll? I started taking off my earrings just in case she wanted to jump up in my shit. "Why you taking this shit out on me? I ain't the one that allowed my cousin to hit the fucking floor in the first place." I was beyond irritated now. I was mad as hell and I was ready to whip her ass. This was not how this night should have ended. We were supposed to be celebrating, not fighting in some stinky-ass bathroom over some bullshit.

"Do you think she's dead?" Reshunda whispered in defeat.

"I don't know, but the only way we're going to find out is to get somebody in here to check on her."

Reshunda nodded and this time she followed me out the door.

"Follow me." Relieved, I grabbed her hand to make sure we didn't get separated. I pushed my way through the crowded dance floor toward the exit. I stopped when I got to the door, Reshunda pulled my hand in the other direction. I snatched right back, pulling her up beside me. My fingernails dug deep into her wrist and I dared her to say anything about it.

"There is a lady in the bathroom throwing up," I yelled into the bouncer's ear.

"And? Happens all the time." He looked over my head, dismissing me. I wasn't going away that easy.

"She's been in there a long time," I yelled a little louder.

"So what, you counting and shit." He started laughing as if he made a joke.

"Naw, motherfucker, I ain't counting, but the bitch is laid out on the fucking floor. I just thought I should tell somebody 'bout the shit."

The beefy bastard finally looked at me. He spoke into his earpiece and nodded.

I had no idea what he said but it was enough for me to get the fuck out of there.

"Thanks, we'll check it out."

"Sorry-ass fucker," I said, dragging Reshunda out the door. Her feet were moving but she wasn't moving fast enough for me. Luckily, we didn't have far to go. We got to the car and Reshunda just stood there.

"Are we going to get in this bitch?" I knew that Reshunda was upset—she should be. Hell, I was upset too. Even though I didn't like Ebony, I didn't want her ass dead. Reshunda continued to stand next to the driver-side door. Frustrated, I marched around to the other side of the car and snatched her clutch from her. She didn't object to my snatching her purse. She just kept staring at the door of the club. There was now a long line of people waiting to go in.

I found the keys and unlocked both doors. Reshunda was in no shape to drive so I led her around to the passenger side and eased her into the car. She was crying softly. I wanted to cry too but probably not for the same reasons. We didn't talk as we sat in the car. I wanted to say something that would break the ice but for the first time in my life, I couldn't think of anything.

We were there when the ambulance arrived and we sat until it left. Neither of us bothered to get out of the car to identify Ebony's body.

"Reshunda, you can't tell anybody about this shit."

She didn't say anything. She kept staring straight ahead.

"Did you hear me?" I was running out of patience. Even though we didn't do anything wrong, I wasn't willing to rely on the police to come to the same conclusion. Our innocence died the same night Ebony did.


I adjusted the seat in her car. I didn't know where to go but I knew we had to go somewhere so we could think. Reshunda was obviously in shock. She was scaring me and I didn't know what to do about it.

"I sure am glad I ain't got to clean that bathroom," Reshunda giggled.

Her comment was so callous I almost lost control of the car. I swung the wheel wide to the left, damn near hitting the car in the oncoming lane of traffic. "Bitch, you scared the shit out of me."

"Don't you fuck up my daddy's car." She continued to laugh.

"Are you okay?" The last thing I expected from Reshunda was jokes and it made me question her sanity.

"I'm straight but I could use a drink."

I looked at her again just to make sure she wasn't about to flip out and do some stupid shit while I was driving. "Fat chance. I don't know anybody that is going to give our young asses any liquor." I didn't really want anything to drink but I was glad that Reshunda was back to her old self.

"Why don't we go to your house? You know your stepfather has so much booze at the house he won't even miss it." She giggled again. Reshunda wasn't lying about the booze so I couldn't get mad. Our closets were packed. My stepfather claimed it to be a perk for working for one of the largest liquor distributors in the state. My stepfather was the classic functioning alcoholic. He went to work every day and did his job, but the moment work was over, he was a straight-up lush who drank until he passed out. He had so many DUIs, he wasn't even allowed to own a car.

I wasn't ready to go to my house but it was actually the best place for us because we needed to have a serious talk and my stepfather wouldn't pose a problem for us. Nine times out of ten he would be in his room, passed out. The only potential problem to going to my house was my mother. If she were up, she'd know right away something was wrong.

"Fine. Do you need to call your father?"

"For what?"

This was the Reshunda that I knew, but she was bouncing back entirely too quickly for me. Not that I wanted to see her crying and shit but I expected something more from her. I stole one more look before I turned the car around and headed to my house. I had a feeling that it was going to be a very long night.

We arrived at my house with no further mishap and for that I was grateful. I undid my seat belt and slid out of the car. I expected Reshunda to be close on my heels but I had to go around to her side and practically pull her out. She was sending me mixed messages. One minute she was pumped up as if nothing had happened and the next she was shell-shocked and catatonic.

"You all right to walk?" I was mindful of the four-inch heels she had on. While my heels were high, they weren't quite that high.

"I'm good," she mumbled.

If I had to pick from the two personalities that she was showing me, I wanted the one that was able to communicate because we had a lot to talk about. I handed her the keys and groped around in my purse until I found my house keys.

Even though Reshunda and I were good friends, I didn't bring her around my house often, especially after my mother got arrested. Even though my mother was back, my stepfather was still drinking it up. Some nights, he would stay up all night drinking his ass off, and other times he sat in the dark and cried. It broke my heart when he cried. I wasn't used to that and neither was my mother. She refused to sleep with him and they were just going through the motions until she could leave him.

I breathed a sigh of relief when I opened the door to a dark apartment. I turned on the lights and watched the roaches scurry. I gave them a moment to get situated as I tried to hide my embarrassment.

"Bitch, stop trippin'. You ain't the only one who has unwanted critters living up in your shit. Stop trying to act all brand new and shit." She pushed past me and went straight to the kitchen and started fixing a drink.

I looked around the room to make sure all the furniture was in order before I went to my room to take off my shoes. "Be quiet. I don't want to wake up my mother."

If the furniture was tossed, it would mean that Dad had another of his crying spells, but today everything was intact, so I breathed another sigh of relief. I rushed into my room and threw the clothes that littered my floor into the closet and quickly shut the door. I pulled up my stained sheets and fluffed the pillows. I stuffed my Snoopy dog under the bed. I didn't need to hear Reshunda's mouth if she were to find out that I still slept with some of my childhood toys. I normally kept my room clean but since I'd been packing, everything was a mess.

"You finished? You act like this is the first time that I stopped by this bitch." Reshunda was standing in the doorway, holding a glass.

"Shit, can't a girl clean up a bit? I had to make room for you to flop your ass down, didn't I?"

"Whatever." She flopped down on the bed and kicked off her shoes. She wasn't sipping her drink, she was gulping it and she had a full bottle of Hennessy sitting next to her. She was about to get fucked up.

"Damn, you didn't fix me a drink?" I asked with attitude.

"Shit, this your house, you should have fixed me a drink since I'm company all of a sudden."

"Your ass didn't give me a chance to fix you a drink." Stuffing my feet into my pink fuzzy slippers, I marched out of the room. I had to keep reminding myself that Reshunda was in shock because I was about two seconds away from giving her head a sunroof. I inhaled deeply, trying to regain composure. I reached up in the cabinet and pulled down a large bowl, checking to make sure no resident evils lurked inside. I opened the cabinet in search of some chips or something. If she was going to do some heavy drinking we would need something on our stomachs. I grabbed the chips and dumped them in the bowl and put some ice in my glass. I could have gotten another bottle but I wanted to drink out of the one Reshunda had to control how much she drank. I wasn't trying to mother her. I just didn't want her puking and shit in my bedroom.

When I went back to the bedroom, Reshunda was sitting on the floor with the bottle between her legs. I put the chips on the floor and changed my clothes so I would be comfortable. "You gonna share that bottle or do I have to get my own?"

She flipped me off and I reached over and grabbed the bottle. She had already drunk one-third of it.

"Girl, you'd better slow your roll, or you'll be praying to the porcelain God just like your cousin." I instantly regretted saying anything about her cousin, especially since she hadn't mentioned her. "I—um—damn—I'm sorry."

"What?"

"I didn't mean to bring up your cousin." I wanted to open my mouth and stick my entire leg in it.

"I can't believe she fucked up my shoe." She went back to gulping her drink like she didn't have a care in the world.

I didn't know what to say and that was unusual for me. "You might be able to get them cleaned or dyed." I was lying through my teeth. If she got them dyed, the stain would still be there, just a different color.

"Bitch, why you lyin'? You know I might as well toss these shoes in the trash right now." She pulled her feet up close to her face. "It's a shame because they really make my feet look little."

"What?" My mind had wandered.

"My feet look small in these shoes. Have you noticed that the average foot size has changed from a five or six to nines and tens? I think it's something they are putting in the food. Like chicken wings."

"Girl, what the fuck are you talking about?"

She gulped from her glass and reached up and took the bottle back from me.

I was so busy trying to keep up with her conversation, I hadn't even had a chance to pour myself a drink.

"Church's is a perfect example. Have you seen the size of their wings? It's not natural and I think the same thing is happening to our bodies."

I reached over and took the glass from her.

"What the hell are you doing? Give that shit back."

"You're talking crazy and you're scaring me." I gave her a hard look, hoping to cut through the wall she had apparently constructed around herself.

"Fine, if you don't want to drink with me, I'll go home." She attempted to get up but was very unsteady on her legs.

"Heifer, sit down. You just need to slow down a little." I gave her back the glass but reclaimed the bottle and poured some for myself. I decided I was going to need something if I was going to get through the night. I didn't care what else happened because first thing in the morning, I would be on a plane.

Reshunda fell back once I'd returned her glass. I was pretty sure she was just talking smack when she said she was leaving, but I didn't want to have to fight her ass if she really did want to go. I went over to my dresser and pulled out something for her to sleep in.

"You might want to get out of that dress. You still have vomit on the shoulder."

She looked at the dress as if she was seeing it for the first time. This time when she attempted to stand, she had no problem. She began fighting with the zipper, trying to get the dress off.

She looked so funny, I couldn't hold in my laughter.

"Shit, don't just stand there grinning like an idiot, help me get this shit off." She had kicked her shoes across the room and was twisting in circles in an attempt to reach the zipper on the dress.

I went to help her but I took my time doing it. I didn't appreciate her calling me an idiot. She continued to wiggle until her clothing fell to the floor. I waited for her to get dressed.

"You know we have to talk about this." I took it slow just in case Reshunda tried to flip out on my ass. She was still drinking pretty heavily, but at this point, so was I.

"I know. I thought if I kept on drinking, we'd wake up and Ebony would come through the door."

"Well, baby girl, I don't think that's going to happen. Do you know what she was on? It had to be more than drinking."

"I don't really know what she took. She's been doing a lot of pills lately, but when I asked her about it, she told me to mind my business."

"The police are going to want to know."

"I know, Valencia, that's what I'm afraid of. When dad finds out she was taking drugs, he's going to be all up in my ass." Reshunda was really acting weird. She professed all this love for her cousin but yet she hadn't said one word about her death. She appeared to be more interested in her shoes than her own cousin.

"Well, what are you going to tell him?"

"Hell if I know. I'm thinking about not saying anything at all and acting surprised and shit when they come and tell us."

"Seriously?" I felt like a muthafucking bomb had just exploded in my room. *Who was this hard bitch sitting in front of me?* For the second time tonight, I was speechless. My feelings were sliced in half. Part of me didn't give a flying fuck what we said about the whole incident. Ebony was okay but I could take her or leave her. I only hung around her because of her relationship to Reshunda. The other side of me wondered how Reshunda would've reacted if it were me lying on the bathroom floor. I asked myself again, *Who was this bitch and was she worth the trouble?*

"Yeah, no matter what we say, it ain't gonna bring her back so why not act like we weren't even there? We can say she got us into the club but she left."

"We shouldn't say a damn thing about the club."

"Good thinking. I'm down with it. Hand me some of those chips," Reshunda said.

I was playing different scenarios in my head as I passed the bowl of chips. Reshunda crunched loudly, smacking her lips. I was going through a mental checklist of the things I needed to do before my flight.

"You do know Trent was your daddy," Reshunda said between smacks.

I felt like all the air in the room had been sucked out, as my body turned cold. I finally had what I needed to make a change that was good for me.

"What did you say?" My hands trembled as I waited for her to answer me.

"Huh?" Reshunda's head had rolled onto her chest and drool dripped from the corner of her mouth.

"What did you say about Trent?" I demanded, getting onto my feet.

She rolled over onto her stomach and began to snore. She'd turned up the bottle, its neck in her Jimmy Choo shoe.

I wasn't upset Reshunda knew who my father was. What hurt me the most was the fact that my so-called friend knew and didn't say a damn thing about it. I was officially done with Atlanta. I'd said it many times before but this time I meant it. In time, I was going to try to forgive Reshunda and my mother but for now, I was going to do me!

I stepped over her, much the same way she stepped over her cousin, and grabbed my suitcase from the closet. Changing clothes, I did a final check of my room before leaving it. I sat at my kitchen table and composed a short note. I finally understood why my stepfather was drinking himself to death. He knew my mother sat in jail, protecting her ex-lover. He knew she chose him over both of us, so, in his own way, he checked out too. The same way I was about to do.

*Reshunda, your car is at the airport, good luck finding it. I wished you loved me enough to be honest with me. Mom, I really don't know what to say to you right now. Both you and Reshunda got me twisted, but I won't live my life with hatred in my heart. I'm sure, in time, I will forgive both of you. But I doubt I will ever forget. I sincerely hope you both find what you're looking for and when you do, be honest with yourself and those around you. Ain't nothing worse than a liar. When you both think back on this, and you will, don't think of my leaving y'all, think of it as me leaving me. I've got to do it this way or never do it at all. I'll holla.*

I walked out the door and never looked back. Despite the pain, I felt good. Never again would I allow anyone to have as much control over me as they did. I loved so hard, I refused to see their faults. No more. I was done with that. I left my rose-colored lens at the house.

I allowed a final tear to fall as the plane taxied down the runway. I was not running from my past, I was leaping to my future.

# Arrested Development

by

*B.L.U.N.T.*

# Chapter 1

*Good In The Hood*

Kelly stared up at the ceiling, chilling, lying on her bed, in a pair of tight, light blue jean booty shorts and a close-fitting black T-shirt that read *Flirt* in white rhinestones. There were a juicy set of lips in ruby red rhinestones that also embellished the T-shirt. The red lips matched the color of Kelly's fiery red hair, which was pulled into a sleek ponytail. She inhaled and exhaled slowly as she enjoyed smoking a blunt of purple cush in the privacy of her bedroom. The scarlet-red walls that surrounded her high-yellow body had black hand-painted Chinese writings on them. The symbols were striking and bold. They stood for love, peace, loyalty, and faith; all of the creeds that Kelly took to heart.

The powerful weed infiltrated her mind as she began reminiscing on the current events of her life. So far, at the age of twenty-six, she was still figuring out who she was and what it was that she really wanted to do. Kelly Morgan was just an around-the-way girl with around-the-way aspirations, but she did know that she had not yet accomplished as much as she had hoped she would. She was going to be turning thirty in a few years and her mother had always told her, before she passed away, that thirty was the age she needed to know what she wanted out of life and have a plan on how to get it.

To date, she had a job working as the main lookout for Buddah, the neighborhood coke and crack king. Her previous employer, her younger brother, Kevin, had turned her on to the opportunity when he got locked up. It wasn't the career path she had in mind, but Kelly was financially straight. She was making more than enough to keep her bills paid, her refrigerator stocked with food, her clothes game sick, her hair, nails, and feet done weekly, and her shoe game on one thousand. She was a long-haired, thick redbone who could probably convince any man she wanted to trick on her, but she was an independent chick and she wanted to get it for herself.

Kelly raised herself up off of her queen-sized bed and waltzed her nice round, plump behind over to her open closet. She thumbed her manicured nails through a plethora of hangers, contemplating what she wanted to adorn her fine ass with on this day. Whatever her choice was to be, ultimately it was going to be a fly one. Kelly loved to look good. The shape of her eyes were those of a temptress, her eyelashes were naturally long and she didn't mind batting them. She was a thick little thing at five foot four, with all of her one hundred and fifty pounds perfectly proportioned.

Working for Buddah on the block was a cool gig. That's where she got her shine on; the block was the shit. She had to know everything and see everything and tell Buddah everything that didn't smell right, which was pretty much what she used to do for her brother, just in a different location. Kevin did his thing in Brooklyn. After being on the streets and doing her thing for so long, she had developed a keen sense for sniffing out undercover cops, and her talent was invaluable.

It was becoming more and more difficult to know who "Jake" was. Most of the undercover police that worked the hood these days were hard to detect. They were getting younger and there were a higher number of African American undercover police officers working the inner-city neighborhoods, which was very good for the employment rate, but not so good for the drug game. They blended in so well with the dudes on the street that niggas was getting knocked off left and right by fucking with what niggas in Colonial Heights labeled on the streets as "ducks." Everyone in Colonial Heights was about getting money by any means necessary. Police were simply in the way.

Kelly hated the police. She had had numerous experiences with them; none of them were pleasant. There was the obstruction of justice and falsifying a police report, which stemmed from a vehicle accident. Both charges were considered felonies. There was the possession of marijuana. She had been caught with a half ounce. They tried to turn a half ounce into a half pound. There was the sodomy charge she had received for giving one of her ex-dudes head in his Escalade. She had been arrested a total of three times. Each time, they tried to hit her with felonies and trump up bogus charges on her. And each time, she came with a lawyer and ate their bitch-asses up and walked out of the courtroom with her head held high.

Back then, she didn't have that much to lose, but now she did. If they ever busted her boss and shut down his operation, that would shut her shit down completely and stop her from being able to ball out. They were a direct threat to her financial prosperity. She knew all the uniformed cops of the neighborhood knew who she was, but they didn't really have a reason to fuck with her; she really wasn't doing anything illegal. All she was doing was informing her boss of the people whom she didn't trust, telling him who she thought was suspect. Kelly didn't feel she had anything to hide or to worry about in regard to her freedom. The worst they could do was label her as a snitch, but it was the cops she was snitching on. She didn't see anything foul about it.

After combing through hangers filled with jeans, slacks, leggings, blouses, sweaters, and belts for what seemed like hours, Kelly had finally decided on what to wear. She grabbed a pair of Rocawear blue acid-washed skinny jeans, and then slid her hands over to a red satin long-sleeve Deréon button-down blouse. She was about to hit her shoe room when her cell phone began to vibrate on her nightstand. She ran over to it and checked the display. It was Buddah.

"Hey, boss," Kelly said, with a smile in her voice.

"Kells, baby, what you lookin' like?" Buddah asked.

"I'm lookin' like new money, playa, what you lookin' like?" Kelly shot back.

"Yo, I need you to be on the block early. They raided Spank's house. They tryin'a come at a nigga and catch me up on some bullshit. I need to be extra careful who we serve today. I need you to be on point," Buddah said. His tone expressed his urgency.

"Cool, I'm on it," Kelly told him, nonchalantly.

"Kells, I'm serious, I need your eyes and your ears to be wide open," Buddah stressed.

"I got you, baby, I told you, I'm on it," she said with assurance.

"Oh, so you got me, you sure you got me?" Buddah asked. His tone had suddenly changed up. He was doing what he had always done with Kelly: play games with his words in a flirtatious manner.

"Yeah, Buddah, of course, baby, you know I got you one hundred and ten percent," Kelly said in a sexy tone.

"Thas whassup. Yeah it's real real good to know that you got me like that," Buddah replied slowly.

"No doubt," Kelly slurred.

"So when you gon' let a nigga get *you?*" Buddah asked her in a low tone.

Buddah had been trying to get with Kelly ever since Kevin had put the two of them in business together, but Kelly wasn't feeling him like that. Nor did she want to mix business with pleasure. And she damn sure didn't want to start something with Buddah that she had absolutely no desire to finish. That would make their working relationship very uncomfortable. In her eyes, he was her boss and that was as far as she was going to take it. She did fuck with his head now and then, but it was strictly for her very own amusement.

"I'm good, Buddah, but thanks as usual for the offer," she told him.

"Oh, I know you good, but like my man Ne-Yo said, 'Baby, I can make you better'!"

Kelly laughed.

"Yeah, okay, Buddah, I promise to keep that in mind. Yo, I'll hit you back. I'm about to get dressed right now."

"Aw shit, Kells, you mean to tell me you ain't even dressed yet? That shit's gon' take another five hours. I need you out on the block now!" Buddah stated in a pressing tone. He was back to business and he needed her.

"You wanna come and watch me get dressed?" Kelly asked, teasing him, as she chuckled lightly, trying to lighten his mood.

"Hell yeah I wanna watch, shit, a nigga want a front-row seat too!" Buddah said with excitement. Kelly's voice was making his nature rise.

"Nah, I'm just fuckin wit' you. I'm good, Buddah," Kelly said, softly.

"See now that's what I'm talking about, just fuckin' *with you*," he emphasized.

"Buddah, stop playin'. I'll be out on the block in a few," Kelly told him, as she pressed her end button on her cell phone.

Kelly hoped that even though she played with him like that, he understood that she had no need for him in that way. She wasn't mad at Buddah for trying to get at her; he wasn't the first nigga trying to get at her and he certainly wasn't going to be the last. As a matter of fact, she enjoyed it when he flirted with her; it was fun. The more shit he talked, the more shit she talked.

Buddah was stressing, but she wasn't going to let him stress her out. He needed to put that shit on freeze. Kelly went back to doing something she loved to do so that she could take her mind off of Buddah and his mood swings. She entered her shoe room. Kelly's shoe room was not by any means the average shoe room. She owned at least two hundred pairs of pumps; over one hundred pairs of boots; another hundred pairs of sandals, and over two hundred pairs of sneakers. Thus, she needed an entire room equipped with a ladder to house them all.

Kelly selected a pair of red Nike sneakers with a navy blue swish. It wasn't the look that she was originally going for, but it matched her outfit, and if Buddah was as much a target as he suspected he was, she really did need to be on point. Kelly had wanted to put on a pair of black pumps, but she didn't want to have to dip off and jet in a pair of stilettos. She had done it before and it was no joke. Her feet stayed swelled up for a week. The thought alone was too painful to relive. Kelly took her sneakers back into her bedroom and tossed them on the floor. She then ran into her bathroom, placed a shower cap on her head, and jumped in the shower for all of five minutes, making sure to wash her "spots."

Once out of the shower, she doused her skin
with baby oil and then slid baby lotion all over
her creamy soft skin. She then dried her smooth
body off with a thick, maroon bath towel and tied
it around her body. Light makeup was applied to
her radiant skin. She really didn't need any at all,
but she placed a little bit of mascara on her lashes
and red shimmery gloss on her pouty lips. She
smoothed her brown eyebrows with the tips of her
fingers and smiled to herself in her bathroom mirror. Kelly smoothed her silky red mane with her
yellow hands from the edges of her temple all the
way up to the rubber band that held it all together.
She wrapped her fingers around her shoulder-
length ponytail and twirled her tresses around and
around. Kelly was feeling the color of her hair. She
had just dyed it two weeks before and the bright-
ness of the red was becoming of her complexion.

"Bitches gon' be hatin' today," she said to
herself out loud.

Kelly got dressed, went into her top dresser
drawer, scooped up her .380 and headed toward the front door. She slid her keys off of her
kitchen table, snatched up her dark-blue denim
Dooney & Bourke bag, put her .380 inside of it,
and left her apartment. Kelly had been living
in the Colonial Heights in the Bronx for four
years. The chicks of the hood who liked her,
really liked her, but the ones who hated on her,

really went out of their way to let her know that they weren't fucking with her. She had a flock of neighborhood niggas from the block hanging on her every word on a daily basis and a lot of their girls had a problem with their men being all up in Kelly's face.

"Well, well, well, if it ain't Miss Thang," Kelly's next-door neighbor, Dora, hollered. She had walked up on Kelly before she could lock her apartment door, yelling as if she was putting out an all-points bulletin.

Dora was a middle-aged woman in her fifties who still dressed like a teenager. Her philosophy was you stay young by looking young. Dora was also a high-yellow female and she saw a lot of her old self in Kelly, before she became a drug addict. She used to be beautiful like Kelly, and she used to rip and run the streets with all of the hustlers that was making noise back in the day, but after years of running the streets, along with the overuse of drugs and alcohol, now she just looked used and abused. She still had somewhat of a shape, but she had some extra bulges in a few places she didn't desire to. Dora still had some pretty-ass hair though; black, short, and straight. She actually had the look of a mulatto.

Kelly locked her apartment door, turned around, and rolled her eyes.

"I knew bitches was gon' be hatin today, but, damn!"

"You better watch who you callin' a bitch, okay? I ain't one of ya' li'l friends, I'm old enough to be yo' mama. You need to respect me," Dora told her in a chastising manner.

"Bitch, please, you could never be my mama, and you need to give respect to get respect," Kelly said sternly, letting Dora know that she would be as many bitches as she wanted her to be.

With Dora's battered dark-gray eyes nearly shut, she spoke angrily. "Don't get too big for your britches, Kelly. Don't let Buddah swell your little big head into thinking you can't be taken down."

"Taken down? Who gon' take me down, boo? It ain't gonna be ya' cokehead-ass," Kelly said, verbally blasting her. Kelly was feeling a mix of surprise and anger. She didn't know where Dora was coming from, but she did know that when someone came at her like that, it was to be taken as a threat.

"You ain't no different from the rest of them li'l bitches he get to work for him. He fuck 'em, give 'em a li'l money, take 'em shoppin', buy 'em a li'l bit of shit, when he get tired of the pussy, he get rid of 'em. And he gon' get rid of you too."

"You sound like a bitch who been hurt. What you fuckin' Buddah, Dora?"

"Yeah, I *was* fuckin' him, until yo' li'l skank ass came into the picture. Now all I hear about is I ain't got time to get wit' you. I gotta check on Kelly, Kelly this, and Kells that."

"Eew, wit' ya' old ass, now that's nasty," Kelly said with a comical-like scowl.

"What, you think this ol' pussy don't work no more? Shit, she still workin'," Dora told her, with the smell of liquor on her breath as she rolled her hips around.

"Dora, man, go head wit' all that nonsense. You high as a muthafucka an' you talkin' shit, and in a minute, I ain't gon' be so nice about it," Kelly said, warning her.

"Like I said, you ain't no different from the rest of them young-ass ho bitches, you just a li'l older, but you ain't gon' last," Dora told her.

"The difference between me and them other bitches is I'm Kelly Morgan and they're not. I don't have to fuck Buddah to keep my position. Do me a favor, Dora, mind your business 'cause you don't know nothin' about mine. Take your drunk-ass on in ya' house and take a fuckin' nap." Kelly walked away from Dora and headed toward the elevators. She couldn't help but to trip off of the thought of Buddah and Dora fucking. She had noticed him coming out of her apartment quite a few times, but Dora was a cokehead and he sold coke, hard and soft, so she thought it was about the business. Kelly had also given Buddah more credit than to want to slide his dick up into someone as unsanitary as Dora.

Kelly Morgan stepped out of the elevator, leaving all of the bullshit that had transpired between her and Dora behind. She was about to hit the block and she had to be on point. Kelly felt like she was the shit when she was on her turf. She felt safe and secure 'cause niggas knew damn well not to fuck with her. Everybody knew who she was and if they didn't know her, they had heard about her. Niggas on the block also knew her brother, Kevin, or "Crazy-ass Kev," the nickname by which he was better known. He had a major reputation in Colonial Heights.

Before she stepped outside of her building, Kelly said, "What's up" and gave dap to a few of the heads posted up in the lobby. They were all huddled together as if they were trying to seek refuge from the fall afternoon air. A few of her neighborhood associates were already outside kickin' it, so she just slid right on in.

"Whas good wit' you, Quisha?" Kelly asked Laquisha, one of her peeps standing in front of the building.

"Everything is everything," Laquisha said, while snapping and popping on her bubble gum. She looked Kelly up and down and down and up to check out what she had put on for the day. She rolled her eyes when she saw that Kelly was rockin' out in her skinny jeans. Laquisha had wanted to wear her skinny jeans, but they were hanging up in her bathroom still damp from her washing them. She had worn hers the day before and so far, she only had one pair.

Laquisha and Kelly were not that tight, but they were all right enough to say that they were cool. Kelly never let Laquisha get too close because Laquisha was the type of chick that you had to watch around your man. Not that Kelly had a steady one, but still, she didn't play that shit. Laquisha was a hot tottie. She was hot in the ass. Deep, dark chocolate in color, Laquisha had extensions with honey-brown waist-length twists in her hair. She had slanted, dark brown eyes, thick lips, thick hips, and bowlegs that niggas loved to watch every time she walked. She was always high and horny most of the time. And she stayed fuckin' somebody's man. More than a few of the chicks in the hood had beef with Laquisha over giving her pussy up willingly to niggas that she knew for sure had chicks at home. Laquisha didn't give a fuck, though. She was ready to go round for round with them at any time. She didn't feel the women were correct in beefing with her, she felt they should be beefing with their men.

Other than her being a trifling ho, Kelly fucked with Laquisha all day.

Everyone else who was standing in front of the building just nodded or waved. There was a different vibe in the air. Kelly could sense it without even talking to anyone. Niggas was standing around looking lost. She took a look around to get a feel of the day and what was in store. She scanned the rooftops of buildings with her keen eyesight, but she didn't notice anything out of the ordinary. Kelly then broke off from the stupefied pack that was in front of her building and checked all of the immediate corners to see if she saw any new faces. There were no new faces; just the same neighborhood crackheads and dopefiends.

Kelly called Buddah to give a report. "The coast looks to be crystal-clear for right now," she said in a preoccupied manner. She was still looking around to see what was what.

"Good, that's real good, Kells. Don't sleep on these niggas, though, Kells. Keep doin' what you do, and get back to me," Buddah told her.

"No doubt, I got you, baby. I'll be in touch," Kelly told him, as she let the call go.

She was going to tell Buddah about her conversation with Dora, but decided not to. That shit wasn't that important. She had matters that held much more weight. She had returned to her building and was standing in front with Laquisha and a few other known heads. Just as she was about to launch her private investigation on what was really good in the hood, a man approached who looked to be a dopefiend. Kelly looked him over real good. She had never seen his face around the way before. He wasn't old at all. He looked to be in his mid-twenties. Kelly knew for certain he wasn't anybody that she knew.

"Yo, anybody over here good?" the unknown man asked, as he slowly scratched the side of his face.

"Good? Nigga nah, ain't nobody over here good on shit. You need to step off with that shit, B," Kelly said.

The man immediately took notice of the red-headed, hotheaded female that stood in the way of him and his score. He knew her type. He had run into her kind too many times before; big mouth, big ass, and too much sense. *But damn, she's fine*, he thought. He had seen plenty of attractive females in his time, but she was nothing short of a delectable delight. Not allowing the beauty of her face or the harshness of her tone to deter him from his mission, he took a deep breath and tried his hand again.

"Look here, sweetheart, I ain't no police. I need some shit real real bad, or I'm gonna end up real sick. Now they told me that diesel pumps over here strong, all day and all night, and I gotsta' get me some of that . . ."

Kelly continued to look at the disheveled man real hard. He looked as if he had been to hell and back again. He held tightly onto his stomach and he was crouched over as if it would literally kill him to stand up straight. Sweat ran down his caramel-colored skin. He wore one of the old red and black lumberjack jackets that Biggie used to rap about, but Money was missing the hat to match. Kelly thought the man *would* make a great dopefiend, but her gut told her that he was definitely an undercover cop. Either way, it wasn't a day for bullshit, so she kept to her story of him coming to the wrong place.

"Well, I guess you about to be real sick, homie, cause ain't no diesel pumpin' over here. Fuck what you heard," Kelly said sarcastically. She turned her back on the man and returned to kickin' it with her peeps that were in front of her building.

The man walked away, disappointed.

*Well, what do you know,* she said to herself. *Buddah wasn't being paranoid after all. That nigga is definitely a duck.*

Kelly stepped away from the crowd and immediately called Buddah. She would have bet all of her money that an undercover cop had just left her sight. It was time to be extra careful. Kevin was already locked up for some shit behind a funky-ass cop. The last thing Kelly needed was for both her and brother to be incarcerated at the same time. One of them had to remain free in order to take care of the other.

"What the nigga look like?" Buddah asked. He knew he was right.

"He a young dude, I mean, for real the nigga look like our nigga, Chop, except his clothes was all fucked up and he *looked* like he was fucked up, but I could tell, Buddah, he wasn't no fiend, for real," Kelly said. Chop was one of Buddah's workers.

"Thas wassup, that's exactly what I got you for. Where dat nigga go?" Buddah asked.

"He got the fuck outta my face talkin' that bullshit. I don't think he's stupid enough to come back. If anything, they gon' send a different duck, you know how they do it," she said, confidently.

"A'ight, thas what it do. Yo, go and hit Broadway. I got a few heads that I need you to check wit' and collect from. Get up wit Chop and Spank, them niggas should have some paper for me, get that, take your cut and bring the rest to me. Keep doin' what you do and get at me by four o'clock. I'm shuttin' the shop down at four, whoever don't have they shit is just shit out of fuckin' luck, cause Buddah ain't goin down for no mufucka," he told her.

"Thas wassup, I feel you, I ain't either," Kelly replied.

She meant exactly what she said, too, she wasn't going down either. Kelly knew the drug game wasn't stable; she wasn't planning on staying in it forever, but the money was too good and had pretty much spoiled her. But she was also aware of quite a few hood horror stories of kingpins who were supposed to be harder than hard being hemmed up, and before you knew it, their bitch-asses were wearing skirts and blaming their lookout and even their mama for their drug stash. She wasn't the one.

# Chapter 2

## Mission Possible

Kelly was glad that she had to go to Broadway to collect for Buddah. Undercover police were sure enough lurking, so she was more than ready to dip out of the hood for a few. All of this talk about going down and being taken down was starting to leave a bad taste in her mouth. She was freshly dressed and looking fly. She had until four o'clock to get up with Buddah to get him straight. It was only twelve in the afternoon. That was plenty of time to play. She was ready to get into some shit; she felt a little mischievous.

"Come on, chick, let's get away from here for a while," Kelly suggested.

"I'm down, you got a ride or we cabbin' it?"

"I'm a' take Buddah's joint."

"That nigga let you drive his whip?" Laquisha asked in disbelief. Laquisha had known Buddah for some shit of years and she knew that Buddah didn't let any females drive his car ever since one of his ex-girls had the next nigga pushing his whip.

"Yeah, I know right, that shit tripped me out too, but yeah, last week he told me I could push it," Kelly bragged.

"You'sa a lucky bitch," Laquisha stated enviously.

Kelly smiled at Laquisha and laughed. She knew that Laquisha thought that she was fucking Buddah. Shit, the whole hood thought that she was fucking Buddah. She knew the real deal though, so it didn't bother her one bit. The ladies stepped away from the crowd at the building and headed toward the Avenue.

"You got a babysitter?"

"Nah, but shit, Mokesha's home, she can watch 'em."

Mokesha was Laquisha's twelve-year-old daughter. She might as well have been the remaining four children's mother because Laquisha hardly gave a fuck. None of Laquisha's children had the same father. Two of them didn't even know who their daddies were because Laquisha herself had no idea. Mokesha was constantly left in the house to care for her younger brothers and sisters while their mother either went out to fuck her dudes, or sometimes she brought the dudes to her apartment. Laquisha's children's ears would be glued to the door as their mother got the shit fucked out of her on the regular. She was in no way being a role model for her children, especially her three girls. But Laquisha was only twenty-five years old. She had been raised that way, so she didn't see anything wrong with the way her children were coming up.

Laquisha was more than willing to go. She had hung out with Kelly a bunch of times and she knew without a doubt that it was not going to be a dull afternoon. Kelly had all the niggas hollering at her, so Laquisha was banking on finding her some new dick for the day. She had already had a fat blunt before she had left her apartment and her pussy was twitching. Laquisha may not have had on her skinny jeans but the Apple Bottoms jeans that she had on hugged her shapely ass like a child gripping a teddy bear. With her bowlegs swaying, niggas was bound to respond.

"Where we goin'?" Laquisha asked. Not that she really cared; she just thought she would ask.

"I gotta go to Broadway to handle some business, but I ain't in no rush to get there, if you know what I'm sayin'," Kelly told her with a sly smirk on her face.

"Yeah, uh-huh, I know what you sayin'," Laquisha said, with a smirk of her own.

"A, yo, you seen that nigga that came up to us in front of the building, right? Did he look like a fiend to you?" Kelly asked Laquisha. She knew what she thought, but she just wanted a second opinion.

"I mean, to me, he did, but shit they all look like they on some shit, that's your bag. I don't know . . ."

After hearing what Laquisha had to say, Kelly thought, yet again, about the fiend that appeared out of nowhere. Yeah, there was no doubt that he looked the part, but there was something about him. He wasn't from around there, so if he was so sick, how did he get there? She didn't see him drive off in a car. Kelly shook off the thought of her being wrong. She always trusted her gut and her gut told her that Money wasn't a dopefiend; he was a duck.

"Yo, you know who got some decent puff?" Kelly asked her girl.

"Nah, it's been real dry lately. Niggas hollering about it's a drought," Laquisha said.

"It ain't never no muthafuckin' drought, they be front'n n' shit," Kelly stated with an attitude.

"You right, you right," Laquisha agreed.

"It's all good, though. Shit, I still got a half ounce of purple cush, but I know this shit gon' be finished with the quickness," Kelly said as she rode through the city in Buddah's navy-blue Acura 3.2. TL, puffing on a blunt of that sweet-ass purple cush.

The ladies jetted down the avenue looking for some shit to get into. Besides fucking everybody's man in the hood, Laquisha was the best booster Bronx had ever seen. She could put an entire rack of clothes under her coat and walk out of the store without a hint of detection. There were times Laquisha had gone down to Macy's on Thirty-fourth Street and come back with enough clothes to clothe the entire Colonial Heights and Polo Grounds put together.

"What you trying to get into, yo?" Kelly asked with a mouthful of smoke, as she inhaled the strong weed.

"I don't really care, it's whatever wit' me," Laquisha said. She had just finished taking a hit of her own and she too was feeling the rush of the purple cush. Shit, she felt like she could lift anything that she wanted to.

They rode along listening to Drake rap about how he wanted to marry Nikki Miraj. Laquisha felt her arm vibrating. *Damn that's some good-ass weed, I'm fucking really buzzin' n' shit,* Laquisha thought, until she realized that it was Kelly's cell phone on the vehicle's console that her arm had been leaning on that was actually buzzing.

"Yo, Kells, your phone is buzzin'," Laquisha told her loudly, over the even louder music.

"I can't fuck with that shit right now. I don't have my earpiece with me," Kelly said.

"You want me to answer it?" Laquisha asked her.

"Nah, fuck it, just see who it is," Kelly replied.

"It's an eight-hundred number." Laquisha told her.

"Oh shit, that might be Kevin," Kelly said.

Kelly loved her younger brother to death. And she missed him very much. Kevin being locked up was not something that Kelly liked to talk about. Her brother was four years her junior, but he looked out for her and protected her at all costs when he was on the streets. And the day he was taken off of the streets, Kelly felt vulnerable in a way that she never thought she would. Kevin was another reason why Kelly hated cops. The cop that had arrested her brother had also testified against him. He was the reason Kevin was not out on the streets, but serving a five-year prison sentence for possession of crack cocaine, possession and use of a firearm, and assault of a police officer. Kelly wasn't present for any of her brother's trial; she was too wrapped up in herself at the time and for that she felt guilty beyond measure. According to Kevin, all cops were devils and needed to be eliminated. He felt they were an abomination in his world and whenever he spoke about the subject, he made his feelings known.

Kelly pulled over so that she could catch her brother's call. She had missed his first attempt, but she knew that he would call straight back. And she was right: Her phone buzzed again and this time she was ready.

"You have a collect call from (Kevin) an inmate of Rikers Island Correctional Facility."

Kelly knew the greeting by heart so she by-passed the rest of the recorded message by pressing 3.

"Whas good, sis?" Kevin asked. He was so glad that she had picked up this time. It was so disappointing to Kevin when he couldn't get his sister on the phone.

"I'm good, Kev," Kelly said, smiling.

"What's going on in the streets?" Kevin asked. He asked this question every time he called her. She wasn't only Buddah's eyes and ears on the streets; she was his eyes and ears also.

Kelly knew that Kevin depended on her to keep him in the know, but she also knew that his calls were most likely being recorded, so most of what she told him was in code.

"Buddah's seeing ducks," she told him.

"Word," Kevin replied.

"Yeah, I saw one too, today, at least I think I did," Kelly said.

"Ain't no time to be thinkin', sis. You need to be knowin'. These fucking devils ain't playin' wit' you, so don't be playin' wit' 'em," Kevin told her. "You see they got my ass caged up like a fuckin' bird."

"I feel you, but I'm on my game, Kev. I don't want you worrying about me. I got this out here. You need to be concentrating on bringing ya' ass home and gettin' ya' shit back on point. So stay yo' ass out of trouble!" Kelly told him.

"Oh, I'm ready for that shit. And they ain't got no choice. They gotsta let a nigga out this muthafucka when my day come, you feel what I'm sayin'," Kevin told his sister.

Kevin had been locked up for four of the five years he had been sentenced to and had been on his best behavior the whole time. He was aching to get back on the streets to pick up where he left off.

"Oh, no doubt, I feel you baby bruh."

"Yo, I just got finished reading the whole entire *Webster's Dictionary*," Kevin said, proudly.

"Get the fuck out, yo, that shit is crazy, Kev."

"Yeah, I know right. What the fuck else a nigga got to do in here? I be bussin' these niggas asses in Scrabble, so that shit is gon' help my game, you feel me?"

"No doubt, I know damn well you be bussin' them niggas' asses, nigga, you betta, nigga."

"You have one minute," the recorded voice echoed.

"I ain't gon' call you back and hold you up 'cause I know you got shit to do out there, but be easy, sis. You make sure you take your time out on them streets. These devils are out to destroy us," Kevin said, as his minute ended and his call was automatically disconnected.

Kelly was glad she had gotten the opportunity to talk to her baby brother. Now that she had heard his voice, she knew her day was going to get better. Talking to Kevin always lifted her spirits. The fact that he was on the down stretch of his bid was a real good look for her brother. And she was hoping that he wouldn't do anything to jeopardize his homecoming. Her mind began to wonder. She started thinking of how good it was going to be to have him home again. All of the new strip clubs she planned on taking him to as soon as his feet hit the concrete. She then thought of all of the clothes she wanted to get him. She had to hook him up with some Coogi and Sean John, Rocawear, and Ralph Lauren. She wanted to have at least ten pairs of sneakers and five pairs of Tims for him to step his feet into. And she was in the process of saving

up twenty stacks for him to have when he came
home. Kelly wanted her brother to be as fresh
and caked up when he came out as the day he
went in. She knew that it would take some time
to get him to the level where he was before he
went in, but she had his back.

"Now, where were we?" Kelly happily asked,
smiling from ear to ear.

"Damn, you would think that was your man
the way you smilin' n' shit."

"My brother's love is better than any love that
I can get from these niggas on these streets, and
he is my man. Shit, while you bullshittin', that
nigga is my main man. Okay, now, again, where
were we?"

"We were going to find some fly shit to wear,"
Laquisha reminded her.

"Oh yeah," Kelly said, smiling. "Let's get it."

Kelly pulled up in front of Rainbow Shops on
Broadway. It was far from the fly shit she had in
mind, but after she thought about it, they didn't
have time to deal with the heavy traffic and
go downtown to Madison Avenue to the Gucci
store. She was good with getting some clothes
from Rainbow Shops; they did have some cute
outfits that she could stunt around the way. Kelly
relit the blunt of purple cush and took a few
more hits off of it. She handed the blunt over to

Laquisha, who also took her last few pulls off of the blunt, which was now smaller than the butt of a cigarette.

Laquisha smashed the butt into the ashtray. "I ain't wear the right shit to pack a lot, so just pick a few light things, a'ight?" Laquisha said, blowing smoke from her nostrils.

"A'ight, thas' wassup," Kelly agreed.

They exited the car and walked into Rainbow Shops. Kelly and Laquisha immediately started dancing and singing to the remix of "Hold Me Down" with Jasmine Sullivan and Mary J. Blige as they began to work the store and look through various racks of jeans and tops, dresses and sweaters. There were a few people in the store shopping, but everyone seemed to be so caught up in the songs that were playing on the radio that no one was really paying attention to what was going on in the store.

Laquisha had stuffed three pairs of leggings in the back of her jeans, making her fat ass look fatter. Kelly had inconspicuously pointed to a few tops she that was feeling. Laquisha was on it as she slid the tops off of their hangers and stuffed them down into the front of her jeans. She continued to look around the store to see what goodies she could lift.

Kelly had more than enough money in her
pocket. She didn't have to steal anything. But
it was what Laquisha did to get money, so Kelly
figured why not spend her money with Laquisha.
She thought maybe it would help her with all of
the mouths she had to feed. As far as Kelly was
concerned, she could never have enough fly gear
to wear and she was getting the clothes for next
to nothing. Plus, it was a thrill to get away with it.
This was the type of behavior that gave Kelly her
adrenaline rush.

After perusing the store and lifting all that she
possibly could lift. Laquisha looked around for
Kelly, who had since separated from her, to let
her know their time was up. Laquisha turned to
her left and peeped a white lady staring in her
direction. She was one of the sales clerks and
she had been watching her. Laquisha was a vet;
she didn't panic. She began to walk the store
until she had finally spotted Kelly in the shoes
and boots section. She walked over to Kelly and
gave her the eye. It was time to go. She couldn't
take the clothes off of her now; if so, she would
definitely be busted. So she played it off and
walked over to the selection of shoes, grabbed a
brown suede knee-high boot that was on display
and asked the shoe clerk to get them in her size.
She then sat down and pretended like she was
going to try on the boots.

Laquisha saw the sales clerk, who had been watching her, walk over to the cash-register area where there were two cashiers and several people in line. The two young black cashiers laughed and joked and carried on a conversation as they popped the security strips off the clothes and rang up the customers, who appeared to be annoyed at their unprofessional behavior. They had no idea what their coworker was up to as she dialed 911 for the police.

It was the perfect opportunity for them to try to get out of the store. Once the sales clerk picked up the phone to call the police, there was going to be a problem. Kelly zigzagged her way through the clothes racks like a mouse in a maze as she headed toward the door to get out of the store. As soon as she pushed the door, Laquisha came running past her.

"Let's get the fuck out of here," Laquisha hastily told Kelly, while running out of the door toward Buddah's car.

Kelly followed suit and ran out of the store with the car keys in her hand. She opened the doors with the keyless remote, ran around the back of the car, opened the door and plopped her ass into the driver's seat. Kelly didn't realize that you had to press the remote twice in order for all of the doors of the Acura to open. This caused

Laquisha's door to remain locked. Laquisha had reached the passenger-side door and began fumbling with the door handle and discovered that her door was locked. She began banging on the window and yelling for Kelly to open the door. Kelly was doing her best, but every time she unlocked the door, Laquisha would do something to the handle and the door automatically locked itself back.

"Stop fuckin' with the door. You lockin' it, not unlockin' it!" Kelly yelled.

Back inside the store, the sales clerk had been waiting forever for someone to take her report and she couldn't wait any longer. She couldn't believe that she was actually trying to report a crime and had been asked by the 911 operator to hold. She slammed the phone down in absolute disgust and she instinctively ran after Laquisha and Kelly in an attempt to stop them.

"Will you two stop talking about a whole bunch of nothing and call the goddamned police, for Christ's sake—those two black girls just stole some clothes from the store!" she screamed angrily.

The sales clerk came up behind Laquisha, catching her before she could figure out how to open the door and get into the car.

"Uh, excuse me, miss," she called out loud.

"Yeah?" Laquisha asked, as she snapped her neck briskly around with pure attitude to face the sales clerk.

"Uh, I'm sorry, but I believe you have some merchandise that belongs to my establishment, and I'm going to need you to come on back into the store," the sales clerk said nervously. Her skin was a pale pink, but it was getting rosier. Her stringy brown hair wavered in the wind as she stood outside in the cool air with no jacket on. She was trembling from the weather, but she was mostly trembling from fear as she confronted Laquisha. After seeing the hateful look that Laquisha's face displayed, she now wished she would have stayed inside.

"Yeah, bitch, you need to be sorry, 'cause I don't have nothin' that belongs to you, so just take your cracker-ass back on inside your fuckin' wack-ass store," Laquisha angrily told her.

Kelly slid the automatic window down and flashed her .380 at the sales clerk.

"Hey, miss, do me a favor, go on back in the store. I don't want to hurt you," Kelly politely told her.

The terrified sales clerk was about to back away from the Acura, but she wasn't moving fast enough for Laquisha so she punched her in the face so hard that she fell and hit the ground. She screamed out for help as she gripped her face and began to whimper and cry. With the window down, Laquisha was able to reach in and open the car door, but the injured sales clerk was in her way. Laquisha used her foot and kicked her out of the way. She jumped into the car and slammed the door shut. She stared at the side profile of Kelly's face and gave her the evil eye. If Laquisha didn't know any better, she would have thought that Kelly was trying to lock her out on purpose to take the rap.

Kelly felt the glare of Laquisha's eyes on her as she pummeled the gas pedal to the floor. Kelly didn't give a fuck what Laquisha was thinking. Her freedom was vital. She didn't have time for Laquisha's slow and confused ass. Kelly's only objective was to be the fuck out of there, and thanks to her, they were out. The screeching wheels of the Ac disturbed the peace as the car lunged forward and Kelly slung the vehicle around the corner of Broadway.

# Chapter 3

*Time for Some Action*

Dante Evans sat behind the wheel of his un-marked police car parked on the corner of 181st and Broadway with his head laid back on the headrest and his eyes closed. He took his pointer fingers and massaged his eyelids. He was tired. It had been a real long day. He was in the middle of training to go undercover and had been assigned to Colonial for the first half of the day. Now back in his NYPD uniform, Dante was thankful that he was nearing the end of his day. The next shift started at four o'clock and it was already a little after two. He was looking forward to a cold beer and reclining in his favorite chair with his feet up. The Giants were playing Chicago and he was betting some of his fellow police officers on his Giants, even though they were not favored to win; he had been a die-hard Giants fan all of his life. And when Dante was on your team, he was on your team for life. Dante's stomach began to growl. It prompted him to contemplate what he wanted to eat for dinner. A few tasty options dashed through his weary mind. There was some leftover take-out Chinese food, or he had some cold cuts and some soup. Just as he was about to make a decision, a call came over his radio.

"Unit 7710, we have a report of a shoplifting incident at Rainbow Shops on Broadway. Suspects are two black females, one extremely dark with braids, the other extremely light in complexion with red hair. Suspects look to be in their mid-to-late twenties and driving a four-door Acura, either black or dark blue in color—first three characters of the license plate X-ray, Umbrella, Victor–the remaining characters are unknown. Suspects are armed and are assumed to be dangerous. Do you copy?"

"Damn," Dante exclaimed in frustration.

He loved what he did for a living, but a tiny part of him was hoping the criminals and derelicts of the city would have taken a break until his shift change, but he was to have no such luck. Dante briefly thought not to respond to the call, but he knew that would not sit well with him. He responded to the call.

"This is unit 7710, copy."

"Roger that, unit 7710. I'm putting a call out for backup."

"Roger that."

Now it was Dante's adrenaline that was beginning to rush. Even when he was exhausted, it didn't take much for him to get that natural high from the dispatcher's voice calling his unit number. Dante's tired eyes transformed into those of an eagle as he drove down Broadway, attempting to locate the car that the suspects were driving. Out of nowhere a navy blue Acura flew past him. It was difficult, due to the fleet of traffic on the street, but he was able to make a U-turn as he headed in the opposite direction. Dante sounded the sirens and turned the flashing red and blue lights on. He was having a hard time seeing the Acura. It seemed to have blended in with all of the cars on the avenue. Dante tried all he could, but his actions were limited. It was hard to impel the vehicle and maneuver due to the squeeze of other cars on the street. The black '09 Dodge Charger with its full body dodged slowly in and out of cars that were blocking Dante's path and his access to the Acura.

"Damn, Laquisha, why the fuck you had to hit that bitch? Now, these fuckin' devils is chasin' us. I gotta meet Buddah at fuckin' four o'clock, man, shit, man!" Kelly yelled, in an agitated tone.

"Man, fuck that, what was I supposed to do, just stand there and let the bitch catch me for boosting some shit for yo' fuckin' ass?" Laquisha asked, with an attitude of her own.

"Oh, so now it was all for me?" Kelly asked. She could have sworn Laquisha had some shit stuffed in her ass for her own self as well. But it was all good; she was used to bitches flip-flopping like a fish when the heat was on and it came down to the come down.

"Then you wanna play fuckin' big and bad and show her your fuckin' gun. That was real fuckin' smart," Laquisha yelled.

"It scared her bitch-ass, didn't it?" Kelly asked, daringly.

Kelly was approaching a red light. She had to make a decision. Was she going to stop the car and risk the possibility of the police catching up to them or was she going to run the red light and risk the possibility of running into who knew how many oncoming cars that were driving through the green light at the busy intersection?

Kelly decided to play it safe. She stopped and allowed the traffic to continue to flow as it should. She thought about calling Buddah, but she didn't want to panic him. Plus, she was a little caught up at the moment. Kelly's heart was pounding just as fast as her mind was racing as she tried to think of what to do next. She should have just gone and taken care of business and collected the money from Chop and Spank, smoked her purple cush, and chilled the fuck out. But, nah, her fast-ass wanted to find some shit to get into. Now she was involved in a high-speed chase with the NYPD.

Kelly's decision to stop at the red light turned out to be a bad one. Officer Dante Evans tapped on her window with the tip of his .45 and motioned for her to roll the car window down. Kelly could have driven off, but something told her if she did, shit would get a lot worse than it already was.

"Man, Kelly, drive the fuckin' car," Laquisha said, anxiously.

"Drive it where, Laquisha?" Kelly asked in exasperation.

"You gon' just fuckin' give up and get us arrested?" Laquisha asked in disappointment and disbelief. All she could think of was the fact that she had her five kids at home waiting on her to walk through the door and fix them dinner. She didn't have time to be getting locked up.

"I need you to shut the fuck up and let me handle this, okay? I got this," Kelly told her.

She rolled down the window.

"Do you realize that you fled the scene of a crime?" Dante asked Kelly, immediately noticing her red hair. That made two redheaded problems for him in one day.

"Crime—uh, no, Officer, I didn't commit no crime," Kelly said nervously.

"Miss, I could arrest you simply for the way you were recklessly driving. That in itself is a crime," Dante told her.

"I'm sorry, Officer," Kelly said, sincerely,

"Can I see your license, registration, and proof of insurance?" Dante asked.

"Uh, I don't have all'lat, Officer, this—this isn't my car," Kelly said slowly.

"I'm going to need both of you to step out of the car," Dante said, as he pointed his gun at the side of Kelly's face.

Kelly froze. *Where the fuck did he come from anyway?* she thought. Kelly had a visual on the Charger the whole time, or so she thought. And she did, but what she didn't know is that there were two Dodge Chargers in pursuit of the vehicle that contained her and Laquisha.

Kelly played it calm, and she urged Laquisha to do the same. Laquisha didn't know, but Kelly didn't have a license.

"Be easy, yo, I told you, I got this," Kelly told her in a light whisper.

Kelly and Laquisha both stepped out of the car. Dante motioned with his gun for Laquisha to get up on the curb. He escorted Kelly by her arm around the front of the car and onto the sidewalk where Laquisha was standing. There were quite a few onlookers as people walked up and down the street, trying to be nosy.

"Uh, I'm sorry Officer, but there must be some sort of mix-up," Kelly said, with her voice half sexy and half sad.

Dante turned her around to face him. He did a double take and looked at his suspect. *It can't be. This is the same girl that just cursed me out and sent me away. Damn, she is fine as hell! She even looks better than she did two hours ago. Now, how is that possible?* he thought. Dante had to quickly put the current situation into perspective. For a split second, he had forgotten that he was an officer of the law on a criminal radio call, with suspects in his presence. He had to remind himself that just because they were females, that didn't make them any less dangerous. He looked at Kelly one more time and all that he had just told himself went straight out the window.

"No, uh, I'm sorry, miss, but there was a report of a theft and the description fits your vehicle. And you and your girlfriend here fit the description of the perps."

The radio dispatcher had said that they were armed and dangerous. The freak in him hoped it was Kelly who had the gun. Damn, he knew

he was wrong, but he was so turned on by the
thought. Like Bobby V, Dante wanted her phone
number right then and there, but he knew that
to just come out and ask her would in no way be
appropriate. Dante didn't want to be on the end
of a sexual-harassment charge. He was a police
officer and she was a suspect in a crime. But he
had to think of something, because there was no
way he was going to be able to arrest her.

The other police officers that had been called
for backup had arrived on the scene. They saw
that Dante had the two females up against the
wall with his gun drawn and that he appeared
to be questioning them. He looked to have the
situation under control, but they checked with
him anyway.

"You all right over there, Evans?" one of them
inquired.

"Yeah, I got it covered," he told them.

Noticing the growing crowd of spectators,
the two additional police officers took it upon
themselves to try to clear the streets. In their ef-
forts to get the mass of people who had suddenly
gathered to go on about their business, they
were met with boos, a host of other unwelcomed
words, and a few pieces of trash that had been
spewed at them. It took them a little while, but
they managed to clear the crowd.

"All right, Evans, we removed your audience. You need us to help you with anything else?" one of the officers humorously yelled out. He saw the pretty young things that their fellow officer had up against the wall. His guess was that the ladies wouldn't see the inside of a jail cell. At least, not this time.

Dante looked behind him and saw that most of the people who had front-row seats to the excitement had gone. He looked at Kelly again. He felt her eyes plead with his for him to say no, he didn't need them. He felt her eyes telling him that it was him that she needed at that very moment, in more ways than one.

"No, but thanks for the offer, I don't need y'all. I told you, I got it covered," Dante turned around and told them.

"Yeah, we know you do," the officer said with laughter as he got back into his Charger.

Laquisha peeped the eye contact between Dante and Kelly. She then peeped out Dante. He was a good-looking dude minus the police uniform. Laquisha didn't give a fuck how she got out of the trouble that they had managed to get themselves into; she just wanted to get out of it, so that she could get home to her kids. Shit, if he wanted pussy in order for him to let them go, she was more than down. Her pussy was still twitching and waiting to be fed.

"I don't usually do this, honestly, I never do this, but something is telling me to let you go," Dante said, apprehensively. His eyes were back on Kelly and he couldn't seem to take them off of her.

"Word," was all Kelly could say, as she looked up at the police officer who she had just previously called a devil. She stared at his police badge and read it aloud, "D. Evans."

"Yeah, the D is for Dante, and yeah, uh, my last name is Evans," he told her, while underlining his name with his finger, his eyes still glued to hers.

Dante Evans was a tall, dark caramel, fine-ass brother and had captured 100 percent of Kelly's attention. She could tell he was nervous. She thought that was cute. He wasn't sucker nervous, though. Kelly was a great reader of people. She knew that this could have turned out completely different and Dante would not have appeared to be so nervously cute. What the hell was she thinking? Was she actually thinking good things about a police officer? She couldn't be. Kelly mentally forced herself to remember exactly who Dante really was. He was a devil, he was a pig, he was who she hated and despised.

"Well, I want to thank you, Dante Evans, for doing something you've never done before,"

Kelly said, flirting with the officer, playing the role so that he would let them go.

Dante smiled at Kelly, causing her to feel a really warm sensation flow through her. She instantly smiled back.

"So does that mean we're free to go?" Kelly asked, still smiling. She was ready to be out. This man was making her feel too strange in a good way. She didn't know where it was coming from and she didn't understand it.

Dante didn't want Kelly to leave. This was his second time within hours of coming in contact with her. That had to mean something. He also recognized that she wasn't the type of woman that he was normally attracted to, but there was something electrifying that transpired every time he looked in her eyes and he never, ever wanted her to leave his presence. He had to think of something to make her see him again.

"You can't go, not yet," Dante told her.

"What? Why? I thought you were going to let us go?" Kelly asked in a slight panic. She thought briefly that he might turn on them as the devils and pigs were famously known for doing, and go back on his word.

"Come on, Officer, you playin' wit' our heads," Laquisha told him. She also began to get nervous again. She had never in her life seen a cop just let someone go after a high-speed chase. She knew the shit was too good to be true. If he was going to arrest them, Laquisha wished that he would just do it and get it over with. The sooner she got locked up, the sooner she could call someone to bail her out.

"I'm not playin' with your heads. I'm doing what I do, I'm doing my job, which is to protect and serve," he said slowly as he studied Kelly's facial features. His eyes landed on her hair as he imagined taking her rubber band out, freeing her beautiful hair, and running his fingers and his face all through it.

"So you protect and serve, huh? Who is it that you protect and what exactly is it that you're serving?" Kelly asked in a sultry tone. She couldn't help it. He kept throwing it at her, and she kept throwing it back.

"Yes, I do, and I would love to protect and serve someone as fine as you," Dante said. *Yes! You said it,* he thought to himself.

Kelly was about to say no when he told her, "Come on now, I did something that I've never done before, for you. The least you can do is the same for me."

"Man, let me find out, Mr. Police Officer, you tryin'a holla at my girl?" Laquisha said.

"Oh, I'm sorry, is this your girl?" Dante asked, waving his hand between the two of them. He knew a lot of pretty chicks were hooking up with other women, but damn.

"Oh hell no, you need to correct that right now, it ain't even like that," Kelly said.

"Okay, well, then why don't you show me exactly what it *is* like," Dante said, smiling, as they verbally challenged one another.

Kelly couldn't help but to smile. He was dead-on about what he wanted and he wasn't going to take no for an answer. Dante blushed as his spirits lightened. He knew that he had accomplished his goal. He was going to get her cell phone number. Dante pulled his phone out and got ready to enter Kelly's information. Kelly couldn't hide the smirk on her face. Did he really think she was going to give him her real number? She smiled at him as she prepared to blurt out a false number.

"Oh, no you don't. I'm not falling for that fake number crap. Call me," he told her.

"What?" she asked him, acting like she was confused.

"Call me from your phone right now," he demanded.

Dante recited his cell phone number to Kelly and she reluctantly entered his number into her cell phone and placed a call to him. He answered his phone with a Kool-Aid smile on his face.

\*\*\*

"Hello, this is Officer Dante Evans. Who's this?" he asked, smiling.

"This is Kelly."

"Kelly, huh? Well, Kelly, you know my last name, how about telling me yours?" he asked, staring at her.

"Morgan," she said.

"Kelly Morgan, great, I'll be in touch. Kelly Morgan, you stay beautiful," Dante said as he ended their call.

Kelly laughed at his sense of humor. Fuck it, if all she had to do to get out of another felony charge was talk shit to this fine-ass, corny-ass cop, then so be it. It could have been a lot worse. Kelly let out a huge sigh of relief. She felt lucky as hell to be walking away from the crazy shit they had just done, but now that she had breezed through it, it just seemed like another one of her crazy adventures that she had gotten away with. Kelly just knew she had angels assigned specifically for her. Her mother used to constantly tell her that God took care of fools and babies. Not that she was calling herself stupid, but she had to admit to herself that a lot of the things she did were the result of her making foolish decisions.

"Yo, that shit was sick, yo," Laquisha said, as she joined Kelly and got into Buddah's Ac.

"Yeah, tell me about it," Kelly agreed.

"Peep how I didn't have trouble getting in the car just now, though," Laquisha said as she slammed the door shut, looking suspiciously at her.

"Word, that shit is crazy, yo," Kelly said.

"For a minute, I thought you was trying to get a bitch caught up," Laquisha admitted.

"Why the fuck would I do that? I don't get down like that," Kelly told her.

"Shit, you never know these days," Laquisha said, shaking her head back and forth.

"No, you never do," Kelly agreed, again.

"Shit, after that crazy shit, a bitch need to blow. You got some more choke?" Laquisha asked.

Kelly agreed with Laquisha: A good blunt would hit the spot after their crazy ordeal. She checked her phone to see what time it was. It was almost four o'clock. She needed to handle Buddah's business. Kelly reached inside of her Dooney & Bourke denim bag and pulled out a grape-flavored Dutch and a bag of purple cush. She held the bag up to her nose and reveled in the aroma before she dropped the items into Laquisha's lap.

"Roll up," Kelly said, as she handled the wheel of the Ac and pulled off.

"You gon' call that nigga?" Laquisha asked.

"Call what nigga?" Kelly asked in return, playing dumb, as if she had no idea at all who Laquisha was talking about.

"You know who, don't front, that cop."

"Hell fuckin' no, I'm not callin' that nigga. You know I can't stand them muthafuckas. Those bitches make my skin crawl."

"Shit, whatever, bitch. Give me that nigga's number, I'll call him."

"Oh, believe me, ho, I know you would," Kelly teased, as if she didn't know what time it was.

# Chapter 4

*Lockdown*

"1817024," the correction officer yelled.

"Right here," Kevin answered.

Long, thick, reddish-brown dreads hung on Kevin's broad shoulders in a large mass. They were identical in color with the freckles that covered his entire face. A few darker freckles were fixed permanently on his rose-colored thin lips. His light brown eyes squinted a lot, and he always held a serious demeanor. Kevin was tall in stature, at six foot three inches. At a solid 285 pounds, his presence was a bit overbearing to some. He stood still in his orange jumpsuit, waiting to be allowed to go into his pod. The fact that he had to be "allowed" to go anywhere had yet to set well with him, but he dealt with it the very best he could.

Kevin Morgan was so tired of being referred to and identified as a number, but he knew there wasn't a damn thing he could do about it. He only had one more year to do in the rat hole that he was in. Then after that, the whole world would be his once more; he would be free. That day was going to be one of the happiest days of Kevin's life, but for now he still had time to serve. He was the property of the prison system and they had a way of breaking a man's spirit if he wasn't mentally, physically, and emotionally strong enough to withstand the pressures that brewed and erupted within those walls.

The stories he had heard about prison from niggas on the streets who had done bids weren't shit compared to what was really going on when he arrived to do his. Kevin had just turned eighteen and he really wasn't ready to spend five years of his life behind bars. But who was ever really ready for some shit like that? Shit was crazy. Niggas was already wilin' out and trying to kill each other on the bus on the way up there. Right then he knew that he had better put his game face on because it was on. He knew quickly that he was going to have to become a man before a nigga tried to make him his bitch.

When he had first arrived it was in the dead of summer back in '05. Niggas was damn near sleeping on top of other niggas due to over-crowding. There were just too many inmates and not enough space. The prison didn't have any air-conditioning units that were functioning properly and the inmates were made to endure the unbearable conditions. There were also many more violations. And sure, they could complain, but that shit wouldn't have done any good because the people they had to complain to were the cause of the problem.

One day, it was so hot Kevin had to take three showers just to stay cool. He would sweat so bad that he would be awakened out of his sleep. Sometimes, he would grab his top sheet and pillow and put them on the floor by the door and sleep there, just to catch a li'l breeze. Three inmates died that summer due to excessive heat.

Niggas didn't know how to act in the heat. Muthafuckas was fighting way more than usual. And muthafuckas' dicks were roaming places they had no business trying to roam. They were raping the fresh inmates and Kevin wasn't immune. His manhood had been put to the test when he first came in. He had just finished his shower and was on his way out when two big niggas pushed him back.

"I always wanted to know what it was like with a dread," one of them said.

Kevin didn't give them time to say any more than that. He began swinging his fists wildly at his antagonists. He managed to catch one of the dudes in the eye and buffed his shit up. He had studied kickboxing when he was a young teen and was able to kick the shit out of the dude who clearly was a "fem." The way Kevin kicked him in his dick he may not have needed "the operation." During the scuffle, Kevin had caught a few to the dome, but he was willing to take that and then some to keep them niggas out of his ass. After niggas had heard about what went down in the shower, Kevin had earned his respect. He had a few light fights here and there, but nothing major. Now that he was close to seeing the outside of the dingy place he called home for the past four years, he was just trying to finish his time.

They were just coming from the mess hall and were counting everyone before they went back into their pods. Kevin was feeling pretty good. He had half-ass enjoyed his meal, which was a dry-ass chicken patty on a stale-ass bun, but still, he liked it. And he had gotten to talk to big sis and she sounded good. It killed Kevin that he had to leave his sister Kelly on the streets to fend for herself. He had always held her down. No matter what the situation, he was always on her side, fighting for her.

Kevin knew all of the game that niggas was spittin' to broads on the street. Although he was younger than his sister by several years, he still was able to hip her to a lot of game. He showed her how to tell if a nigga was really fucking with her or if he was just playing with her feelings. He taught her how to take a man down if he tried to attack her. He taught her how to shoot her first pistol. He had shown her how to survive on the streets without having to have a man to depend on. Kevin was confident that Kelly was out there handling her business. He had schooled her too well for her not to be handling her business the right way.

Once in their pod, a dark-skinned dude by the name of Siggah was trying to get at Kevin to holla at him before they got locked down for the night. Kevin had only been down for four years, but Kev took no shorts and niggas respected that. The whole prison knew what time it was with Kev. He was the leader of his pod. Actually, Kevin was always the leader anywhere he went. That was the type of personality he had—very strong and dominant.

"Ay, yo, Kev," Siggah called.

"Ay, what up, son," Kevin replied.

Kevin knew Siggah, but he didn't really fuck with him. Siggah had a lot of flaky shit with him. He left the streets owing a lot of people a lot of money. He was famous for getting niggas to invest in some pyramid-scheme-type shit and then when it came time for a nigga to get paid Siggah's ass was nowhere to be found. Well, one of his investors did manage to find him and kicked his ass so bad that Siggah was forced to murder the dude, so he was going to be locked down for quite a while. Right now, he was looking at completing seventeen more of his twenty-five-year sentence.

"Yo, I got this nigga that could get us caked up in this muthafucka, I just spoke to the nigga today," Siggah said, with the corners of his black lips twisted. His permanent two front gold teeth had lost a bit of their shine. He had to stretch his neck to look at Kevin. Siggah was only five foot.

"Get us caked up how, dawg?" Kevin asked, looking down at the short dude. He already knew he wasn't fucking with Siggah. His time was too short to do anything to risk fucking up his release date, but just to keep it one hun'ed, he decided that he could at least hear the man out.

"Yo, my man, Bing, he got a crazy train connect, Kev, I mean crazy," Siggah told him.

"Nigga, I ain't got time for that shit, I'm about to be outta here. Tell that nigga to holla at me once I'm out on the streets," Kevin said, smiling inside and out at the thought of him having four years down and only one more to go.

"Shit, Kev, he ain't gon' wait that long to connect. That nigga might be in here by the time you get out," Siggah said, laughing, but he was dead serious.

"Take that shit to another nigga, dawg. I ain't wit' it," Kevin said, as his face straightened up. He was no longer smiling.

"He ain't tryin'a deal wit' no other nigga but you," Siggah said.

"And why is that?" Kevin asked, inquisitively.

"That's jus' what the nigga told me, Kev."

"Who the hell is this nigga?" Kevin asked. He was dying to know who it was that needed to deal exclusively with him or they wouldn't deal at all. That sounded like the same type of duck shit his sister was talking to him about earlier on the phone.

"Yo, this my man, he straight up, no bullshit, Kev," Siggah pleaded.

"I don't give a fuck how straight up this nigga is, if he a real man, he'll understand my situation, and parlay, make sure you relay my message," Kevin told him.

"So, you telling me to tell this nigga that he gotta wait a whole fuckin' year to get at you, dawg?"

Kevin didn't say a word. He knew that Siggah had heard what he said the first time. He wasn't going to repeat himself. He was through talking to Siggah. Kevin went over to his bunk and stretched out his long body and folded his hands behind his head. He just wanted to go to sleep so that a new day would come in. He had to plan for his future and make sure his present stayed mellow. He knew that when your time was short that hatin'-ass niggas would do all they could to fuck your shot up at freedom and he wasn't going to allow himself to become weak enough to fall victim to all of the traps and temptations.

So far, he had gotten through his bid with no major setbacks. He did his time on his hands, busting out over one thousand push-ups a day. Kevin also taught a few of the classes for the inmates. They looked to him for leadership and guidance. Kevin thought it was ironic that everywhere he went people looked to him for answers. It made him proud, especially since he himself had never finished high school. His father once told him that most of the richest people in the world had no college education. He told his young son that the way for a man to have true wealth is through owning his own empire, and ever since the age of thirteen, Kevin had been planning on how he was going to own his very own empire.

Although there was a lot of noise around him, silently he laid still and thought back to the night of his arrest back in '04.

*It was bitterly cold, which was odd for the month of May. It was early evening, yet, the sky was pitch-black. The sun was no longer present in the sky. Still, the moon could not yet be seen. The stars had even decided not to show on this nebulous night. For this being one of the busiest cities in the world, the streets were unusually dark for a Friday night. If Kevin didn't know any better he would have sworn New York City was experiencing another blackout.*

*"Yo, I'm tellin' you, man, it was them mutha-fuckas from Prospect Ave. They on some pay-back shit. They know we hit 'em up before and they know we gettin' crazy money," Kevin said, as they stood in front of the corner store on Amsterdam Avenue.*

*Kevin was the leader and president of the Cypress Crew. He had started the organization in 2002. In Kevin's eyes, they were nowhere near a gang. They had official positions with detailed responsibilities. They had a president, vice president, secretary, and a treasurer who kept accurate records of all of their financial transactions. Now what gang do you know of with that type of structural foundation?*

"Yeah, well 'em niggas is gon' be dead by tomorrow, dawg. You can put that shit on my muthafuckin' son," Rayvon replied.

Rayvon was the vice president of the Cypress Crew, as well as Kevin's right-hand man. He was down for the cause to the fullest. He was a big, brown-skinned dude with little to no words to say, so when he spoke, niggas listened. Some niggas had just robbed Rich, the treasurer of the crew, and Rayvon wasn't havin' it. Niggas knew their status and they were nobody's vic. It was official: Somebody was about to get bodied.

"Fuck tomorrow, nigga, we need to handle this shit tonight!" Leek said, with this face twisted in a scowl. He was more than ready to rumble.

Leek was also a member of the Cypress Crew; he was the secretary. He hated his title because the guys would clown him about him being a man and having the job of a secretary, which they all totally felt was a woman's position. But anyone who came up against Leek knew damn well there was nothing feminine about him. At six foot four, weighing in at 285—when Leek was aggy about a situation a nigga had a problem.

"I'm wit' Leek, fuck waitin' on tomorrow. Niggas gone think we weak. Let's get this shit *in right muthafuckin' now!" Rich said, both angry and excited. He had been the one to have a gun pointed at his temple and he wanted some payback of his own. Niggas made him feel vulnerable and he didn't like it at all. He knew the saying "what goes around, comes around," all too well, but it was his turn to give it, and some unfortunate soul was going to have to take it.*

*Kevin watched as Dante pulled up across the street from the grocery store. He also saw another black car pull up along the curb of the grocery store. The vehicles were too close to Kevin and his crew for his comfort. He placed his hand on his 9 mm Glock as they continued to talk loudly among one another in front of the grocery store.*

*Kevin continued to peep the scene as he noticed Dante place a pair of small binoculars up to his face. He then took note of the black sedan DeVille that had pulled up adjacent to the grocery store. He also took note that no one seemed to be getting out of the vehicles. His instincts told him something was about to go down. Whoever was in the black sedan DeVille apparently was not getting out any time soon and they were there to do wrong. Kevin watched as Dante exited his vehicle and made his way across the narrow street. His presence incited the situation. As soon as his foot stepped on the curb, a hail of bullets flared from the black sedan DeVille, soaring past them.*

*Members of the Cypress Crew immediately drew their guns and started shooting at the black sedan DeVille and anything in its path. The vehicle was able to slide off.*

*"Police, everyone stop shooting and drop your weapons," Dante forcefully yelled.*

*Members of the Cypress Crew began to scatter as they fled the scene. Rayvon was the first to blow the scene by putting his feet in motion as he ran toward some buildings that he planned to get lost in. As Kevin attempted to run, his gun slipped from his hand and dropped to the ground and he went to pick it up.*

*"Freeze!" Dante yelled with this weapon drawn.*

*"Fuck it, man, just shoot me!" Kevin shouted, as he stood up slowly with the Glock in his hand.*

*"Put down the gun! I'm not going to shoot you. I'm not trying to hurt you," Dante said as he slowly approached.*

*Kevin held on to his gun. He wasn't scared to shoot a cop. Shit, he would be considered a neighborhood hero if he did.*

*"Don't do it," Officer Evans told him nervously. "You don't want to face the music on that one, trust me."*

*Two additional police squad cars came with
their sirens blaring. The officers jumped out and
came to Dante's aide.*

*"Man, fuck you, fuck all a' y'all. Y'all don't
understand us. Y'all take advantage of us all
day, every day!" Kevin yelled at the officers.*

*Dante now had the gun at Kevin's head and
was removing the Glock from his hand. Another officer came and roughly brought Kevin
down to his knees with his baton. Dante then
brought Kevin's arms together behind his back
as his knee held him down and slapped the
handcuffs on his wrists. Dante turned him over
and searched his pockets, finding a bagful of
crack-filled vials. Kevin knew at that moment,
that he was basically fucked.*

There were so many things he would have
done differently that night if he had the chance
to do it all over again, but that shit was dead and
in the past. The day was approaching when he
would once again reign supreme on the streets
of Bronx, mainly Colonial Heights. Kevin pretty
much ran the projects.

Thoughts of the punk-ass cop that brought
him down also filled his mind. He was the main
reason Kevin had to serve the time. If it wasn't
for the police officer's testimony, he was about
to get off with probation and some community

service. It was only his first offense and he had proof of employment. But the bitch-ass police officer showed up at the very last court appearance to give his testimony and painted Kevin as a menace to society and deemed him unfit for society.

He thought back and remembered having to sit and watch the pain in his mother's eyes as she cried for them to let her baby go, but instead he was found guilty. Kevin didn't know that at the time his mother had just been diagnosed with breast cancer and was fighting one of the toughest fights she had ever fought in her life. He admired her for being so brave through it all. He knew now that she was trying her best to be strong for him and Kelly. If it wasn't for the bitch-ass police officer who arrested and testified against him he would have been there for his mother's last few years. He could have done special things with her and for her. Kevin felt as if the police officer that arrested him took away more than just years of his freedom. He took away years with his mother that he would and could never, ever get back.

# Chapter 5

*Sleeping With the Enemy*

Kelly stood in the mirror, primping. She was looking rather lovely in her little black dress. She couldn't believe that she was actually going to go out with a cop. She had thought about changing her mind and calling off the date more than once. Paranoia was a big part of the reason. Dante had called Kelly the very same night of their crazy chase and they had been talking every day since. During every one of their conversations, he practically begged her to let him take her out. Although Kelly had continued to turn him down, he kept trying. Every single time he asked her, she would say no and he would go on to tell her about his day and that he couldn't wait to see her again.

She wasn't sure what made her have a change of heart, but she did. In all of the days of talking to Dante over the phone, she began to care for him. Yes, he was a cop, but he was also a man, a fine and muscularly built one at that. She enjoyed listening to his phone voice; it was deep and sexy, and the more she heard from him, the more she wanted to get to know him. As she slipped on her boots, she realized how much she was looking forward to seeing him again.

A call came in on her cell phone. It was Dante. He had just caught an arrest and was going to be late. Kelly told him to call when he was done and she would meet him somewhere. She wouldn't allow him to come to her apartment. There was no way Kelly could be seen with a cop. Just as she had ended her call with Dante another call came through on her cell. Kelly thought that it may have been Dante calling her back, but it was a collect call from Kevin.

Kelly suddenly realized the chaos she would be creating by going out with Dante. It was a police officer who had put her brother behind bars. She knew the hatred that her brother, and that she herself felt toward police officers, and she was about to go out with one. Hell, she had been talking to one every day, listening to his innermost thoughts. And as much as she hated to admit it, she craved to hear his voice again and she desired very much to be near him. Kelly breathed a deep breath and accepted the collect call from her brother.

"Wha's good, sis?" Kevin asked, as usual.

"Uh, what up, bruh, everything is cool, yeah, yeah, and you, you good?" Kelly asked, all in one breath.

Kevin knew his sister. Something was wrong. She was way too quick with her response. It almost sounded as if she had a gun to her head. Kevin became tight, instantly. The thought of any harm coming to his sister and him not being there to help was a constant thorn in his side.

"Yo, you sure you a'ight?" Kevin probed, with anger and frustration building in his voice.

"Yeah, baby bruh, I'm good. I, um, was just getting ready to go out," she said nervously.

Kelly knew that she was straight buggin' but for some reason she thought her brother could see through the phone and that somehow he knew that she was getting ready for a date with the devil. Kelly then thought of what her brother's reaction would be had he known that she was having some unexplainable feelings for a police officer she barely knew. She pictured Kevin yelling at the top of his lungs as he cursed her out, and although he didn't hit women, she pictured him beating the living shit out of her.

"Oh a'ight, you had me shook for a second, you was speedin' an' shit, where you headed to?" Kevin asked in a lighter tone as he calmed himself down.

"Uh, well, I—I'm, uh—I'm about to get up wit' uh—uh, Laquisha—yeah Laquisha, and, uh, we gonna—uhm, hit the club," Kelly stuttered. She had never lied to her brother and she was finding it very difficult to do so.

"Kelly, what's going on? Is somebody there with you? Is a mufucka tryin'a hurt you?" Kevin flipped again and yelled into the receiver of the prison phone.

"No, no, nah, Kev, everything is fine over here. Please, no, don't get upset. I didn't mean for you to take it like that, yo, for real, I was just somewhere else with my thoughts, that's all, I'm still getting dressed, you know how I am wit' that shit," Kelly truthfully explained.

Kelly pleaded with Kevin to relax. She wanted and needed him to calm down. She didn't want him overreacting to her lies. Kelly knew her brother better than anyone. If she were to tell him the truth, he would flip out for real and take his madness out on someone around him, which would result in him catching a bunch of bullshit charges that would no doubt prolong his release. That was the last thing she wanted on her conscience. Kelly truly missed her brother and she couldn't wait to have him back home.

"Yo, you know being in here drives me crazy. I can't take care of you like I promised Mommy I would," Kevin said, regretfully.

Kelly and Kevin's mother had lost her bout and died from breast cancer two years before. It was a wonder seeing her baby boy go to jail didn't kill her first. Kelly was sure that it would. Mrs. Morgan cried her eyes out at every court appearance she ever attended and at every visit with her son. Kevin hated that he had to be escorted to his mother's funeral by prison guards, but even more, he hated that they paraded him in front of his mother's casket and in front of his loved ones with handcuffs on his hands and shackles on his feet. He felt like an animal. Kevin was grateful, however, that they did allow him to go. He knew that they could have been complete dicks about the situation.

"I don't want you worrying about me, I'm fine. Just be on your best behavior, so you can come home as scheduled, please," Kelly told him.

"Yeah, that's the plan, sis. That's most definitely the plan," he told her, with a host of background noise behind him. Niggas was getting rowdy. Kevin felt they were getting a little too rowdy and they were also disrespecting his phone time.

"Ay, yo, y'all mufuckas is dissin' a nigga? I'm on the fuckin' phone," Kevin yelled.

Just as he said that, Kelly could hear a lot of loud voices mixed with loud, thunderous noises.

"Aw shit, sis. They rioting, I gotta go."

Kelly's thoughts were everywhere. She was worried about her brother and what he was facing in prison. She had seen prison riots in movies and on television and they were no joke. Prison was a dangerous environment and it was a place that she was oh-so grateful to have been spared from.

Her brother's time away had been long, but now his time was short and she didn't want anything to stand in the way of his chances of coming home on time. But she knew her brother's temper, so all she could really do was pray over the matter and hope for the best. Kevin was never officially diagnosed, but Kelly had always thought that her brother was bipolar. At times he was real mellow and real laid back, but if he heard some shit he wasn't feeling, in an instant he would flip and act like a ticking time bomb. Kelly didn't like lying to her baby brother, but she knew his deep-seated hatred for police officers. Kevin always had a dislike for police officers, but after the Sean Bell murder and his own downfall, they were considered enemy number one and he hated the very ground they walked on. There was no way she was going to fix her lips to tell Kevin about Dante.

Kelly's thoughts reverted to Dante. She never planned on having to tell her brother that she was thinking about dating a police officer. Shit, she had never in her life thought that she would even consider seeing one. Kelly still had a lot of internal issues about seeing Dante. After all, she was a street chick. He was against everybody she was for. She planned to go out with Dante once, okay, maybe twice, and that would be it. Did she see herself giving him some pussy? Well, maybe, if he played his hand right. Yeah, right—who was she kidding? Kelly knew the nigga was going to get the pussy, but that was going to be about it. After talking to her brother, she realized that she had to snap out of it. There was just too much about her seeing Dante that she had to keep on the low. *Yo, this shit is wack. I'm gon' have to sneak everywhere to even see this nigga,* she thought.

She couldn't tell Buddah about him. He was already under the assumption that he was on the radar and the police's next target. If he found out that she was going to check for a cop, he would accuse her of being a snitch and he would never trust her again. Knowing Buddah the way she did, Kelly was certain that he wouldn't hesitate to slander her name and reputation on the streets by labeling her a snitch. Her mind quickly went to Dora and all the shit she had been popping about Kelly being just like the rest of the chicks that had come and gone working for Buddah. It wasn't going to be her; she was smarter than that.

Laquisha was her only problem. She had peeped Kelly give the police her cell phone number with her very own eyes. She also saw Kelly flirting hard with the cop. Laquisha knew that Kelly took his number because she had to, but Laquisha also peeped the chemistry between her and Dante and she kept fucking with Kelly about it and asking her a bunch of questions, like had Kelly been talking to the cop and if she was going to really see him, but Kelly dismissed her every time. Kelly kept telling Laquisha that she just played the role to get them out of a charge, and that there was no way she would ever fuck with a cop. Laquisha was the last person Kelly could confide in. She had one of the biggest mouths in Colonial and she would most definitely tell the whole hood and with her ho-hoppin' ass probably try to fuck Dante in the interim; so in essence, since Kelly really didn't fuck with anyone like that, she had to keep it all bottled up inside. It was her secret.

Kelly's cell phone rang again. She answered it without checking to see who it was and inadvertently blurted out, "Yeah, Buddah."

"No, uh, this is Dante."

*Wow, Dante, speaking of the devil,* Kelly thought.

"Oh, I'm sorry, Dante, I thought you were my—you know what, never mind. You ready to get up?" she asked him hastily.

"Yeah, I was on my way to pick you up," Dante said.

"Oh hell nah, I mean, nah that's a'ight, I can meet you somewhere, anywhere you like," Kelly said, trying to clean up her blunder.

"Well, I live in Queens. I don't want you traveling all the way out here this late all alone," Dante told her.

"Aw, come on now, I'm a big girl, Dante. Just tell me your address and I'll put it in my phone and I'll be there before you know it," Kelly told him.

Dante was enraptured. He loved her fearless attitude; it matched his own. That was a trait of a good police officer. He had dreamed about holding Kelly ever since the first day he laid his eyes on her, and it seemed as though his dream was about to come true. He pictured her face as he thought about the incandescence of her beautiful skin, the slight roundness of her eyes, her sweet and succulent red, shimmery lips. Dante told Kelly his address and they agreed that she would call should she run into any problems in finding his home.

For a split second, Dante had second thoughts about Kelly coming to his home. His home was his private sanctuary. Was he losing his mind? He had just given his address to a young woman who he had to chase through the streets of New York. A young woman, who along with her girlfriend, had just committed a class-A felony, yet, he was caught up in what his dick was telling him to do. How did he know she wasn't coming there just to case out his joint and have some sort of trouble come to him? He had arrested females like her too many times. Not as pretty as her, but still. Dante silently reasoned with himself. Why was he so drawn to her? He didn't know where his feelings were coming

from. The negative feelings that had arisen about
Kelly left Dante's mind just as fast as they came. It
wasn't just his dick that was talking to him; it was his
head and his heart too. There was something about
Kelly. She was different; someone special. Why, he
didn't know, he couldn't pinpoint the reasons quite
yet, but he would stick it out until he found out. He
promised himself that much.

   Kelly had some second and third thoughts of
her own as she drove toward her destination.
She looked into the rearview mirror of the Ac
and checked herself. What in the world was she
doing? Why was she driving to another borough
to see this man? What was she really getting
herself into by taking this forbidden relationship
further? Along with her brother Kevin, she too
had a pure dislike for police officers, and anyone
who represented an authority figure for that
matter, yet she was on her way to chill with one.
What would they talk about? What could they
possibly have in common? *Probably nothing,*
she thought. Kelly pulled Buddah's car up to the
address Dante had given her. Her mouth fell
open at the sight of his home. He had a beautiful two-story beige cobblestone home with a
circular driveway. Kelly had pulled Buddah's car
behind Dante's Charger. There was also a black
Jaguar parked in front of the Dodge Charger,

and a black Cadillac Escalade parked in front of
the Jag. Dante was waiting for her at the front
door. She got out of the car and walked in his
direction.

"Hey there, look at you, I can't believe you're
finally here," Dante said happily as he greeted her.

He couldn't get over her outfit. She was in a
short black dress with black thigh-high boots
and a bolero-cut black leather jacket. In his
opinion, Kelly was armed and extremely dangerous without a weapon, *or maybe she did have a
weapon,* Dante thought, as he looked at the size
of her purse. He held his hand out for her. Kelly
placed her hand into his. Dante pulled her close
and stole a hug as well as a kiss on her soft cheek.

"Oh, you not shy at all, you gettin' right down
to ya' business, huh," Kelly said softly, laughing.

It was obvious that Dante couldn't keep his
hands off of Kelly; she liked that. Kelly found
Dante to be incredibly sexy out of uniform. She
didn't quite know what to expect when they
talked on the phone, or what type of style he
had or what type of gear he liked, but now that
she was in front of him, she wasn't mad at him.
He was rocking a dark blue Sean John velour
suit with no shirt, just bare brown skin, with his
white-on-white low Nikes. Kelly was all the way
turned up.

Once inside his home, he invited Kelly to have a seat anywhere she liked. Kelly looked around his spacious home and saw that his kitchen had an inviting and open atmosphere. She was also a little hungry. Since their original plan was to have dinner, she suggested the kitchen. Dante thought it was a bit odd that she chose the kitchen, but he did tell her she could sit anywhere she liked, so he went with it. They sat on a pair of stools located under the island that rested in the middle of the kitchen.

"This is crazy. I had so much to say to you on the phone, but now that you're right here in from of me. I'm at a loss for words," he told her.

"Yeah, that's crazy, right," she said, smiling.

"You look good as hell," Dante said.

"Thanks," Kelly replied.

Her smiled ceased, as she silently and seriously admired the African artwork that hung on the walls in Dante's kitchen. She had never seen artwork in a kitchen before, but she thought that it was a fly idea. As Kelly observed the art, Dante keenly observed Kelly. He could tell the way in which she studied his artwork that she had untapped desires and hidden tastes. He wasn't sure, but he had suspected that Kelly had not yet had the opportunity to travel outside of New York City to see all of what the world held. But he was someone who could change all of that for her. In Dante's mind, Kelly was still young, and if she had the right man behind her, she could be molded and chiseled into the jewel he saw through his eyes.

"So tell me, because I have been dying to ask you, face-to-face, did you and your girlfriend really steal that stuff?" Dante asked. He had to. It was simply the police in him.

"Do you think we stole it?" Kelly asked in return.

"Well, really, I want to believe that you were innocent and give you the benefit of the doubt, but my gut tells me that you did what you were accused of doing," Dante told her.

"Now, now Officer Evans, such negative presumptions, isn't everyone supposed to be innocent until proven guilty in a court of law?" Kelly asked.

"Trust me, I'm not here to judge you, Kelly."

"Really? Wow, you coulda fooled me," Kelly said with an attitude.

Dante saw that she was getting tight, but he wanted to see just how far he could go, so he continued to question her.

"Which one of you had the gun?" he asked her.

Kelly wasn't about to tell him the truth. For all she knew, he could have been setting her up for a bigger fall. Kelly didn't like his sudden line of questioning. Was that all that he called her out there for, to interrogate her about the incident at the store? She had hoped Dante didn't get her all the way out there for some sort of crazy sting operation.

"Do you always commit crimes with someone who can later be a witness against you and rat you out?" Dante asked her.

"Yo, are you serious?" Kelly asked him, agitated.

Dante noticed the disgusted look on her face. He realized how much he was really upsetting her and stopped firing his questions.

"I'm sorry, Kelly. I didn't bring you out here to upset you or to make you uncomfortable. You must think I'm some sort of asshole. I was just curious, that's all. I'm a cop and they were just questions that I wanted the answers to, and my mother always told me, 'Boy, if you wanna know something, just ask.' So I just asked you," he said in a humorous tone, trying to lighten the room that his badgering questions had darkened.

Kelly didn't know why, but she wasn't mad at him anymore. Maybe because her mother used to tell her the same thing or maybe it was because he was standing all up in her face with his innocent puppy-dog eyes. She did, however, make note that she would be on her guard with Dante. He looked like he could handle the truth, but who was he really? Kelly thought long and hard. There really was no way of getting around it. At the end of the day, Dante was a police officer, the enemy, and he may have been able to be fucked, but he was in no way able to be trusted.

"Dante, I didn't steal anything from that store. I don't have to steal, okay, I work for mine," she said matter-of-factly.

"Good, I'm glad to hear that. That makes me feel a lot better. So what do you do?" he asked her.

"I do hair," Kelly lied.

"Ah, okay. I hear that doing hair can be a very lucrative profession," he said, knowing that she was lying to him.

"Yeah, I mean, it's okay. It pays the bills," she told him.

"Do you work in a beauty shop?" he asked.

"No, right now I'm working out of my apartment," she said.

"Oh, okay, well, that cuts out all of the overhead," he joked. He wanted to see just how far she was going to take the hairdresser thing.

He saw that Kelly was in no laughing mood and she was becoming quite distant. He had done it again, alienated a female with a million and one questions. Dante didn't know why he had to interrogate every woman he met, but he did.

"Do you enjoy it?" he asked.

"Enjoy what?" Kelly hesitantly asked. He was asking her so many questions she had forgotten what it was he was asking.

"Doing hair, do you enjoy it?" he asked again.

"Yeah, I guess," she said, nonchalantly.

Kelly's mind was completely somewhere else. The more she thought about it, the more she felt comfortable painting Dante the picture that she wanted him to see. She really knew nothing about this man, except that he was a police officer, and with that alone, she needed to watch what she did and said around him.

"Would you like something to drink or even better, something to eat?" Dante asked. He thought that his fine cooking would make a great peace offering.

"What you got?" Kelly asked.

"I've got everything you could possibly think of, and hopefully, I've got you," he said as he stepped off of the stool and eased his body up on Kelly as she remained seated.

No, this man didn't have the balls to piss her off and come on to her in the very same breath. A part of her wanted to rip Dante a new asshole by cursing him out and leaving him standing alone in his kitchen as she slammed out of his house. Another part of her wanted to grab his jacket off of his buff-ass body, kiss his neck, and suck his nipples as she ran her hands across his solid, muscular chest. Yes, he had truly gotten on her last nerve, but as much as she wanted to, she couldn't resist him.

She giggled, and said, "Nah, man, is you crazy? You don't have me. You just had me all on the witness stand 'n shit."

"Aw come on, Kelly. Bottom line is I'm a cop. I had to chase you down Broadway. And if I would have searched you and your girlfriend, I probably would have had to arrest both of you. You had to know that eventually I was going to ask you about it."

Dante stared at her. If he could, he would make his living by simply staring at her. She was that fine to him. "Kelly, please don't think that just because I'm a police officer, I didn't ever do anything wrong. I was born and raised in Brooklyn, not too far from Marcy Projects. I came up in the hood and I was a regular kid who did regular things. I got in trouble all the time as a kid. Then I went to Boys and Girls High School and let's just say I stayed in detention."

"Word," Kelly said. He didn't look like the Boys and Girls type. He looked more like a Brooklyn Tech type of guy.

"Word, my moms was on public assistance and we ate no-frills items brought with food stamps. I remember I would wait all of my friends out in the supermarket so they wouldn't see me using the rainbow dollars, as I used to call 'em. I didn't have what I wanted under the Christmas tree on Christmas, but I had whatever my mother could afford to buy. Shit, a brother had a Voltron, so you know I thought I was doing it big."

Kelly laughed. Kevin had begged their mother for a Voltron too.

"We weren't special or any different. When I turned sixteen I started getting in trouble all the time. I started running with a gang, the Bloods—that is, until I came to my senses," he told her.

"The Bloods? Get the fuck outta here," Kelly said in amazement. She would've never guessed that in a million years.

"Yeah, the Bloods, so you can see that I have quite a past too. We all do. Now, are you gon' hold that against me all night?" he asked in a deep, low tone as his lips got closer and closer to her neck.

Dante paused for the cause and brought her chin up in his hands and looked deeper into her brown eyes.

"Kelly, like I told you, I'm not here to judge you. And I would appreciate it if you wouldn't judge me. People think they know cops and how and what makes us tick, like we're some sort of mechanical robots. But you really don't have a clue. We're human, we feel, we hurt, and we love just like the rest of the people in this fucked-up and crazy world."

"That was deep. I'm feelin' that, what you just said," Kelly said, as her eyes stared into his eyes.

"Thas' wassup, I'm glad you feelin' that," Dante said, as he winked at her.

Kelly liked Dante. She liked him a lot. Yes, he was a cop, but he was cool and very down-to-earth. And she liked having him all up in her face. His skin was dark and smooth; a big contrast to her own. He smelled real good and he looked even better. Their eyes met as he wiggled his nose gently against hers. Kelly then allowed Dante to place his tongue in her mouth and kiss her softly. He held her head gently as their tongues met and they got sensually familiarized with one another.

"So, you gon' let a brother cook for you, or what?" Dante asked her. He was a very good cook.

"It's gon' take a lot more than that to get me," Kelly slurred.

"I don't want you to think I'm cheap. I was going to take you out to eat," Dante whispered in her ear when he finished his kiss, as he ever so lightly nibbled on her lobe.

"It's all good. I can eat something you got here. I'm not hard to please," she told him, as she stuck her tongue out once again for him to grab hold of.

Dante was hard as a brick. The little black dress that Kelly had selected was tempting him to touch her in places in which he knew he would have to ask permission. And the pair of black suede thigh-high boots she had on was driving him absolutely nuts. *Sexy* wasn't the word for her; he was ready to grab his thesaurus in order to find a better word to describe her alluring appearance. He did notice Kelly liked to wear her hair in a ponytail. At least, that's how it appeared to him. He grabbed her by her ponytail, pulled her head back, and shoved his tongue in her mouth.

Before they both knew it, they were naked, with the exception of Kelly's thigh-high boots. They looked as if they were grappling with each other as their bodies scrambled on the ceramic-tiled kitchen floor. Dante's tongue was all over Kelly. He sucked her titties skillfully as he ran his hands all up in her hair. He had relinquished her hair of its rubber band and now had thick strands of red hair all in between his fingers.

"Damn, I love sucking your titties, they're so pretty," Dante panted.

"Thank you," Kelly panted back.

Dante licked and kissed her all over. Kelly noticed that he licked, sucked, and kissed every-where except her pussy. He purposely avoided licking and sucking her pussy. She knew it. She knew there was going to be something about

Dante that turned her off. Apparently the nigga was either turned off by eating pussy or scared of eating pussy. This wasn't going to work for her. She loved being fucked, but foreplay was important to her. Her pussy wasn't as wet as it should have been all the time. And she liked the extra lubricant to get it right. *Maybe it was too soon.* Some guys wanted to wait to get to know the female before they ate her pussy. *Maybe that was it,* she thought.

"So, uh, what is it, you don't go down on the first date?" Kelly asked. She figured why be in the dark about the shit when he could shed some immediate light on the situation. After all, this was a very important matter.

Dante smiled at her. Oh, he went down, he just wasn't sure that Kelly was ready to receive the gift of a lifetime. Without saying another word, he kissed and licked his way down to Kelly's clean-shaven goodies. He slowly licked her clit, and then began to lightly nibble on it. Kelly liked what she was experiencing so far, so she slipped her fingers down to her pussy to pull it open for him. She wanted Dante to show her pussy extra-special oral attention. He took the hint well as he began to lick the insides of her walls, moistening her entire pussy. He grabbed back on to her clit and began to go to work. Dante did tricks with his tongue like a muthafuckin' genie. He tricked the clit back and

forth and forth and back and slipped his finger to
the tip of the opening of her fat pussy and began to
tap it lightly. He then jolted his finger lightly in and
out of its wetness. Soon after Kelly was writhing
uncontrollably, her body was jerking itself and in a
complete frenzy. She tasted so sweet to him.

"Tell me how you want it," he asked her, with
his tongue slowly jetting in and out of her pussy.

"I like it just like that," she assured him.

He continued to tongue and finger her fat
pussy. Kelly loved the sensational feeling of
his labor. Her head was spinning. She wasn't
planning on fucking Dante this fast, but he was
soaking that pussy up real good with his tongue
and when the pussy was soaking wet she knew
that she wasn't going to be able to hold out much
longer. It was getting too good to her. She was
going to need his dick inside of her very shortly.

Dante rubbed on his thick dick as he sucked the
juices that flowed from Kelly's juicy pink pussy. He
then picked Kelly up off of the floor and placed her
back onto the bar stool. He stood in front of her
rubbing his big, black shiny dick. He kissed Kelly
deeply in her mouth, and then pulled her head
back and pushed her head down toward his dick.
He didn't place it in her mouth. That was to be her
decision. Kelly waited a few seconds. She looked
back up at Dante, who was standing with a sincere
look in his eyes. She then placed her hands around

the shaft of his dick, then slowly slipped the head of his big dick into her waiting mouth.

"Yeah, Kelly, stroke that dick, baby, yeah, lick the hole wit' ya pretty-ass, yeah work that tongue, baby, I like the way you working that tongue, suck my dick," Dante told her.

Kelly didn't know how she did it, but she was able to get her mouth around Dante's massive dick. She marveled at the size of his goodness as she licked his dick all over its head and used her hands to jerk the sides as she popped his dick in and out of her mouth. She loved the way he talked to her while she was sucking his dick.

"Ah, yeah, you suckin' me right, ah, ooh, ah, yeah, rub my balls, aw shit, we can do this everyday," Dante told her. She was getting him off.

Her eyes fluttered as she looked up at him with his big dick stuck in her mouth.

"Yeah, look at me, ah yeah open your mouth," he said.

Kelly opened her mouth wide as Dante pounded his heavy pole of flesh on her luscious tongue. He pulled out of her mouth—he didn't want to cum just yet. He wanted to enjoy all of her. Kelly sexily bit her bottom lip. Dante began to tap his dick into her cheeks and her nose and then the tip of juicy lips before shoving his dick back into her wet mouth.

"I wanna get you in my bed. I need to lay your pretty-ass out and give you the royal treatment. Something tells me, you deserve it," Dante told her as he shoved his dick in and out of her oral moistness.

Kelly managed a smile, even with a big dick in her mouth. *That's right, nigga, I damn sure do deserve the royal treatment, that's what the fuck is up,* Kelly thought. In her mind she was indeed hood royalty.

Dante carried Kelly all the way upstairs to his bedroom.

Kelly never had a man carry her anywhere; she thought that shit only happened in the movies.

Before laying her down on the bed, he thought he would give her a treat. Dante stood in the middle of his bedroom. "Put your legs around me," he said. He held her by her ass cheeks and spread them apart as he planted her on his pipe. Dante slid her up and down on his dick while he stood up. His hands slid up and gripped her shapely yellow hips as he bounced her thick ass up and down on his fat dick.

"Ah, yes, I love it all in my pussy like that," Kelly admitted.

"Yeah?"

"Yeah, you like that tight-ass pussy?" Kelly asked. She knew it was tight because she hadn't fucked in a while.

"Yeah, you know I like it." Dante began to sweat.

"Yeah, fuck that tight pussy," Kelly demanded. She loved his strength. He was extremely muscular and it seemed effortless for him to straddle her around his waist and glide her up and down.

Dante loved the way Kelly talked dirty to him. Most of the women he fucked were like mutes. Or they were too shy to say what they liked or what they wanted, but not Kelly. She was right up his alley.

After what seemed like an hour, Dante's legs were getting a bit weak, so he laid Kelly out on his king-sized bed.

"This bed was made for you and me, you're my queen," Dante said as he climbed on top of her.

Dante placed his dick back into Kelly's haven of what was becoming his little piece of heaven. He sank into her softness as they became one. He slid his dick in and out of her like a drill press.

"Damn, you got some sweet pussy, girl. Oh yeah, you got some real sweet, sweet, pussy. Daddy's gon' lick it again for you, okay? You down for that?"

"Yes," she feverishly panted.

All Kelly could do was smile. She just couldn't understand how this man, who she couldn't stand, was now rocking her world while mentally seducing her. She loved a man who knew what to say to a woman. And he was most definitely oiling her rusty joints with pure sensual liquid.

Dante pulled his hot dick from out of her pleasure portal. He slid his caramel brown body down and stretched his long arms and ran his hands up the back of her thighs down to her calves as he buried his face in her love. He licked her pussy walls up and down and then found his way back to that magic button as he suckled her clit once more. Cum dripped from the head of his dick, signifying the enjoyment of his actions.

Kelly's eyes rolled in the back of her head as he ate her pussy. He was no doubt the best lover she had ever had. She was cumming. "Aah, sssh, yes, aah, my pussy's cummin'."

"Yeah, cum all in my mouth."

For the first time in her rebellious adult life, Kelly did as she was told by this officer of the law as a stream of liquid traveled from her pussy down Dante's throat. He sucked her pussy dry and kissed the tip of her clit when he was done.

"Now it's my turn. Turn over."

Dante loved to do it doggie style. He rubbed his dick all over Kelly's creamy soft ass cheeks before he entered her gently. He found his rhythm and he began to dig her pussy out. He grabbed her hair like a rein on a horse and rode her on home.

"Give me that," he told her as he pulled her to him and poked his tongue in and out of her ear, while poking his dick all up in her. "Ah, yeah, Kelly, give me all a' that," he said as he pulled out and shot cum all over her ass cheeks.

"Mmm, I like that, that was real nice," Kelly said, smiling as she climbed down from his bed. "You got a washcloth I can use?"

"Sure."

Dante went to fill her request for a washcloth.

While he did so, Kelly looked around his bedroom. She noticed he was very neat for a man. She was used to niggas' cribs having dirty clothes, half-eaten food, and all kinds of crazy shit thrown all around. She wondered if all police officers were this neat. Kelly walked over to his dresser. She always had a thing for dressers. As a young girl, every time she entered her mother's bedroom, she would always check to see what she had on her dresser. She would play with her jewelry and spray her perfume on and pocket whatever loose change her mother left. Kelly's eyes landed on a picture of Dante with a female. They both had on police uniforms. *Hmm, I wonder who that is?* she thought.

"A penny for your thoughts," Dante said as he walked back in his bedroom with a washcloth and a towel.

"Oh, nah, I was just looking at your pictures."
Kelly walked back to the bed. She didn't want
Dante to think she had been snooping around in
his shit. A lot of people kept personal items on
their dressers, Kelly concluded.

"Ah, I see. So you're wondering who that girl is
in the picture with me?"

"No, I'm not. It ain't none of my business who
she is!"

"Then why are you reacting like that?"

"Like what?"

"Like that," Dante teased her. He could tell
that Kelly wanted to know who the female was
in the picture, but if she said she didn't want to
know, then he wasn't going to tell her.

"So," Kelly said, waiting.

"So what?" Dante asked, playing dumb, knowing exactly what she was waiting for.

"Who is she?" Kelly asked. She didn't know
why she wanted to know. After all, all she had
planned to do with Dante was fuck him once or
twice and be out. But after the treatment he had
just given her, she didn't know what she wanted
out of him.

"That's my partner, Deborah."

"Cool. Y'all fuckin'?" Kelly asked dryly. She
just wanted to know.

"No, Kelly, we're not fuckin'"

"Oh, okay, cool."

"Come here, you."

Dante grabbed her and playfully threw her on his bed. He then hopped up on it as well.

"You're so perfect for me," he said to her, looking deeply into her eyes.

"Why do you say that?" Kelly asked.

Kelly couldn't imagine how a street chick could be perfect for a police officer. The two really didn't go together in her book. Now, if he meant that her pussy was perfect for him, then he was talking some good shit.

"I love everything about you. I mean, look at you—you're fuckin' beautiful. You try to act all tough on the outside, but I can tell that on the inside your heart is good. You only do what you're doing because you think it's cool. I mean, I'm sure you do it for financial means too, but you need to look inside yourself. I think you're destined for great things, Kelly Morgan."

*Wow*, Kelly thought. His words were a lot to take in. She wasn't expecting Dante to get all emotional and philosophical with her. He had just served her up some bomb dick and all she wanted to do was chill. She really wanted to smoke a blunt, but she didn't think that he would approve. Kelly wondered if this was one of the differences with police officers, because gauging by his conversation, they were definitely different intellectually than the guys she was used to dating. Not that she had dated many, but the ones that she had dated were street dudes and totally thugged all the way out.

Kelly never thought of herself being destined for greatness in anything but the drug game. She was just an around the way girl and wasn't sure who Dante was looking at. And she wasn't trying to get caught up in what he was saying. Yes, he had the best dick she ever had to date, but she didn't want to get too wrapped up in this man. He wasn't someone she could consider having a future with, so there was no need in her taking anything he said too seriously. *Damn, why did he have to be a cop? He's so perfect other than that,* she thought.

"If you had something else that you were interested in, I bet you would pursue it, if you thought you had the opportunity. Am I right?"

"I don't know, Dante. I never really gave it much thought."

"Well, you need to think about it. Take your mind beyond your neighborhood. Step outside of your usual zone."

"Okay, I will."

"Ever thought of becoming a police officer?"

Kelly couldn't help but laugh. *Now I'm sitting right here. I ain't see this nigga bump his head, but this nigga had to have bumped his head on something because he straight trippin'!*

"Nah, for some reason, I don't see that happening," Kelly said softly. What she really wanted to say was, *Muthafucka, you must be crazy! I would eat a pile of dog shit and drink some cat piss before I would become one of you stinkin'-ass pigs!*

# Chapter 6

*Partners in Crime*

Buddah had been laying low. Shit was all good just a week ago, now he had the police breathing fire like a crack torch down his back. He had just spoke to Kelly and told her to get her phat ass over to his place. They had to map out a plan. They had to move their work regardless of police presence. Money still had to be made.

Buddah got his nickname honestly. He somewhat resembled the religious statue. He was dark tan in color, a little pudgy with a bald head, but unlike the statue, Buddah had a handsome face. He was good people. He looked out for Kelly like crazy and would do just about anything for her. When Kelly first came to work for him she was a little rough around the edges. Her coming from Brooklyn and transitioning to the Bronx way of doing things took a minute. She had to be shown that she didn't have to be so hard with everyone. She learned that softness worked better with the customers up there.

After he showed her a few things about how he did things, opposed to how her brother did things, she became the most valuable asset on his team.

Kelly used the code knock so that Buddah would know that she was at the door. He immediately opened the door for her. Kelly stepped into his crib looking and smelling good. She had on an off-white long john, long-sleeve shirt with a pair of painted-on Baby Phat jeans. Her rust leather down vest with matching rust strap up knee high boots. Buddah watched her ass as she walked down the corridor of his apartment. *Damn, I wanna hit that shit so bad!* he thought.

"So what's the deal, Buddah?" Kelly plopped herself down on his couch and removed her vest.

"Shit, we got problems," Buddah said.

"We ain't got no problems. We just have to work smarter and not harder."

Buddah felt better just having her there. He knew that she would make him feel better. Buddah was very attracted to Kelly. She was a go-getter and she was a fine-ass bitch. He had tried to fuck with a couple of the chicks that he had working for him before, but it never worked out. He felt that Kelly would be different.

"Ever since they raided Spank, shit been fucked up," Buddah complained. He had lost a lot of money from that raid. Now he couldn't move like he needed to. His pockets were suffering, which meant Kelly's pockets were about to suffer.

"Yo, shit is drying up. Niggas actin' like they ain't got no work."

"Switch up the connec'," Kelly told him. She grabbed the blunt out of the ashtray that he already had smoked off of and lit it.

"What you mean?"

"What you mean, what I mean? Get another connec'!"

"You know somebody?"

"Damn, Buddah, you don't know nobody else that got coke in this big-ass city?"

"Nah, I've been fuckin' wit' the same niggas for the past few years. Yo, them niggas always stayed good, but now, since that shit wit' Spank, they on some otha' shit, like they ain't got shit. Man, I know them niggas got some shit."

Kelly watched as Buddah tried to put Humpty back together again. She was amazed that he only fucked with one connect. You never depend on one connect to get you what you need. She thought about it: She did have a cocaine connect out in Brooklyn that she could get at to see if they could be straight. Kelly called Rayvon, her brother's VP.

"Hey, Ray. This is Kells . . ."

Great, he was straight and he was going to be able to get them straight. So that solved that.

"All right, it's handled. My nigga said he'd be through in about two hours. I didn't want to say too much over the phone, but he knows what time it is," Kelly assured Buddah.

"Damn, man, I'm tellin' you, you ain't nothing but that shit, ma!"

In Buddah's eyes, Kelly had saved the day. Feeling the euphoria of the moment, he thought that now would be a good a time as any to try his hand. He sat next to Kelly on his couch and tried to kiss her. Kelly stopped him.

"Nah, Buddah."

"Come on Kells, what you mean, nah."

"I'm sayin' nah. I mean, I know we play around a lot, but for real, yo, I don't want you like that. Come on now, don't fuck shit up between us."

Buddah backed off instantly. If she said no, then it was no. He just couldn't be that close to her and not try at all. He hoped that one day her nah would turn into a yes, and until then he would just keep hoping. Kelly knew what would put an end to his attempts.

"Ay, yo, what's this I hear about you fuckin' nasty, dirty-ass Dora!"

"What? Man, get out of here!"

That's what his mouth said, but Kelly could tell by his facial expression that he had been fucking her. Which was all good to her since she just wanted to know.

"Uhm, sure."

"She told you that crazy shit?"

"Nah, nigga, your face just told me everything. Ew, Buddah, you nasty! What would make you want to put your dick in that nasty bitch?" Kelly asked, as she laughed.

Buddah didn't answer her; he couldn't. He was embarrassed.

"Yo, that's on you, Buddah. But for real, my nigga, you know you can do a lot better than that."

"Man, she just a piece of pussy."

"Yeah, well, I know one thing, you'll never, ever have a chance of getting this pussy now that I know you fuckin' and suckin' that stinkin'-ass pussy!"

"Ah, shit, Kells, don't fuckin' play, you wasn't givin' me no pussy."

"True, so true," she said. She was just talking shit because she was high off of the haze that Buddah had in that blunt.

Buddah and Kelly heard the code knock and looked at one another. Spank was still locked up and Kelly was already there so it could only be one other person. Buddah went to his door and opened his apartment door for Chop.

"What's good?" Chop asked.

"Waitin' on Kells's people from Brooklyn," Buddah told him as they walked down the corridor to join Kelly in the living room.

"What's good, Kelly?" Chop asked her, as he gave her dap.

"Chillin'," she replied.

Chop put the money he had from his last run on the living room table. He began counting it out. Kelly watched as the stacks of bills piled up in front of her. Thoughts of Dante started running through her head. He wanted her to think about becoming a police officer. Police officers didn't make the money that she was seeing piled up on that table.

Buddah had returned from getting them some Heinekens. He handed them each a beer.

"We got like seven stacks right here," Chop told him.

Seven thousand was a decent pull, but they were used to at least fifteen a day. The raid and Spank's absence were taking a toll on the payroll.

"Fuck it, when Rayvon come through and get you straight, get me straight, 'cause I'm goin' out there."

"Man, you ain't going nowhere, you better stay doin' what you do and look out," Buddah told her.

"Look Buddah, I gotta stack for my brother's homecoming. I ain't got time for shit to be fuckin' up right now. If it wasn't for me, you wouldn't even be gettin' the work. So, uhm, yeah, like I said, when it get here, give me that. Thank you."

"Your brother ain't comin' at me 'cause all of a sudden you feel like you wanna sell some coke. You know the rules, Kelly. You don't touch the drugs."

That was the rule. And she never had touched the drugs. But now there was a need to touch them, therefore, it was time to break yet another rule.

"You and Chop can't work all that shit off. So, whas' up, let me get my lick."

She wasn't taking no for an answer, and Buddah could very well see that. Fuck it, if that's what she wanted, who was he to stop her? She was her own woman and she was a grown woman, and he knew Kelly well enough to know that when she said she wanted something she wanted it and she was going to get it.

There was an un-coded knock at the door. Kelly went along with Buddah, both of them strapped, to make sure there were no surprises waiting on the other side of the door. Kelly gave the okay for Buddah to open the door once she saw through the peephole that it was Rayvon. Rayvon came inside and immediately picked Kelly up and hugged her for a long time.

"Yo, it's been mad long since I seen you, yo," Rayvon told her.

"I know right."

They all walked toward the living room.

"So what's poppin', yo? What you need?" Rayvon asked her.

"Let him know what you need," Kelly said, looking at Buddah.

Buddah excused the two of them and showed Rayvon into his kitchen so that they could handle their business. Chop stayed behind with Kelly. He was waiting for Buddah to break him off his pay for the day.

"Yo, this undercover cop came up to me the other day. I told Buddah I swear that nigga look just like you," Kelly told Chop.

"What the fuck you mean he look just like me. I ain't no fucking cop!" Chop got mad instantly.

"Yo, calm the fuck down. I never said you was a cop, all I said was—"

"Nah, fuck that, I heard what the fuck you said."

Rayvon and Buddah came running into the living room when they heard the commotion. Rayvon had a 9 mm in his hand, ready to shoot Chop. No nigga was going to be talking to his man's sister like that.

"Ay, ay, what the fuck is goin' on out here?" Buddah asked.

"Yo, this nigga straight bugged out when I told him about that undercover cop that I said look just like him. Nigga actin' like it was really him the way he flippin'."

Buddah looked at Chop. Chop had been working with him for three years, but still, he really didn't know too much about him. Kelly had apparently struck a nerve. Did he have a duck on his team this whole time?

"Yo, Buddah, man, I know you don't believe this bitch. Man she ain't even from around our way for real. She down wit' them thieving-ass niggas from Brooklyn."

Rayvon didn't take Chop's comment well. He was from Brooklyn, and who was this nigga calling a bitch?

"Yo, nigga, you need to watch ya' mouth, before you be watchin' ya' mouth, you understand what I'm sayin'." Rayvon let Chop know that he would shoot his fucking lips off and give him a clear-eye view of them.

"Yo, dawg I don't even know who the fuck you is, son," Chop said.

"You don't need to know who the fuck I am," Rayvon said as he pointed the 9 mm in Chop's face.

"Yo everybody needs to just calm down. There's too much going on," Kelly said.

Kelly looked at Chop. She now saw him in a totally different light. He may have been working for the other side all along and she missed one.

"Yo, Buddah, straight up, I ain't fucking wit' this nigga no more."

Kelly meant what she said. Chop was cut off.

"Ay, yo, Chop let me get at you in the kitchen for a second."

"Nah, nigga, fuck all'at, you need to get at me right here!"

"I'm sayin' man, I don't know," Buddah started.

"What the fuck you don't know? You gon' let this bitch decide who work for you? I been down wit' you before this bitch even came on the scene. Nigga, I just brought seven stacks in this muthafucka."

Buddah walked over to the table and grabbed up half of the money.

"Here." He handed the money to Chop.

"You stupid, man, but it's cool . . . Just remember, you're only as strong as your weakest link," Chop told Buddah as he looked at Kelly.

Kelly stared back at Chop as he walked toward the door to leave Buddah's apartment.

Buddah hoped that Kelly was wrong about Chop. If she wasn't, Chop would be back. Shit if she was, Chop would be back no matter what.

"Ay, Kelly, you gon' be aight, 'cause you can come back to Brooklyn with me right now," Rayvon told her.

"Yeah, I'm good, and as long as you got my man right here straight, I'm straight," Kelly said, referring to Buddah.

"Oh, he straight." Rayvon confirmed.

"Cool, then I'm straight," Kelly told him with a smile.

"A'ight, well, I got some other shit I gotta handle so I'm out." Rayvon left her there with

Buddah, but he planned to come back. He told
that nigga to stop calling Kelly a bitch, but he
wouldn't listen.

"We gotta get all of this shit off now." Buddah
told her. "Chop put in work."

"Fuck Chop. Let me get that." Kelly held out
her hand for her package.

She walked out of Buddah's apartment. She
didn't have time to be playing with these niggas;
she had some money to make.


Three hours had passed and Kelly was halfway
done. One package down and one more to go and
she would have the seven thousand that Chop
had thrown on the table. She was trying to figure
out a way to cut her time in half and make double
the money. Kelly was on the block going hand
to hand. She didn't have a choice, since she had
made Buddah get rid of Chop,

"Kelly!"

Dante jumped out of his patrol car. He couldn't
believe his eyes. He knew she was a lookout, but
he had no idea that she was now selling drugs.
There was no way she was going to be able to
become a police officer if she kept behaving in
such a destructive manner.

Kelly saw Dante and rolled her eyes. *Damn,*
she thought, as she sucked her teeth.

"You know we've got to stop meeting like this," he told her.

"No shit! Dante, what are you doing around here?"

"I'm doing my job. They gave me this area today. What the hell are you doing?"

"What does it look like I'm doing, Dante?"

"Honestly, Kelly, I can't even believe what you're doing. I can arrest you."

"But you won't," she said, almost daring him to.

"Get in the car," he yelled.

Dante grabbed Kelly tightly by her arm, shoved her into the backseat of his patrol car, and slammed the door. He then got in the driver's seat and slammed his door even harder before he drove off. Quite a few people in the hood heard and saw what had transpired between Kelly and Dante. The whole neighborhood was buzzing with rumors. They didn't know if Kelly was getting locked up, but they saw her leave in the clutches of a cop.

"What the hell are you trying to do, Kelly, ruin your life?" Dante asked her angrily as he watched her through his rearview mirror.

"You don't know anything about me or my life."

"I know a lot more than you think I know."

"Really?"

"Yeah, really. Stop all of this, Kelly, before it stops you."

Dante had driven quite a distance away from where he had seen her selling drugs. He pulled over and got into the backseat along with her.

"Kelly, there is no way you will be able to become a police officer if you keep trying to get arrested."

"Why the hell do you keep talking about that shit? Who the hell said I want to be a police officer? That's your wish for me, Dante, not mine. That's the last thing I want to be."

"You haven't allowed your mind to grasp the thought, Kelly. You have the skills. You've got exactly what it takes to make a great police officer. You're just wasting your keen senses and gut instincts on bullshit street deals. You could do good work by using those same skills and help rid the hoods of the people that are killing them."

"People like me, Dante?"

"You're not one of them, Kelly. You just think you are, just like when I was out there wilin'. I thought I was a gangster. I thought I was a Blood."

"I can't be no cop, Dante. Everything I've been taught and everything that I believe in goes against what you stand for," Kelly said sincerely.

"That's only because you won't allow your mindset to change. You have to change your mindset, Kelly. Start believing in yourself, that you can do good."

Kelly thought about what Dante was saying to her. Why did he make sense to her? She wanted to find every reason not to agree with him.

"Y'all don't even make a lot of money."

"That's not true, Kelly. Shit, we make a very decent living. You see how I live. You don't see me hurting for anything."

*Yeah, the nigga did have the Jag and Cadillac truck in his driveway, hmm, shit,* she thought.

He could see her opening up to the idea.

"I have medical coverage. Does your current position give you that? Especially with what they have you out there doing. I mean, you say they care about you, right?"

"Whatever, Dante."

Kelly looked at him and smiled. She couldn't help it. He made her smile.

"What about my weed smoking?"

"Well, that's easy, you're going to have to quit."

"I can't."

"Yes, you can."

Kelly wanted to forget about trying to be a police officer right then and there. There was no way she was going to be able to stop smoking weed. She didn't even want to.

"Kelly, are you addicted to marijuana?"

*Fuck marijuana—this is purple cush; this ain't no regular shit,* Kelly thought.

Kelly knew she was addicted to weed, but she never had to admit it. Now that she had, it didn't sound good.

Kelly didn't like needing anything. She was now determined to get the cush out of her system and try a different way of life. She wanted to at least give herself a chance. She owed it to herself, and she owed it to her mother.

"All right," she reluctantly agreed.

"All right, what?" Dante wanted her to make the decision to change her life. He couldn't make her.

"All right, I'll stop smoking."

"And . . ."

"And, what?" Kelly asked. But she knew what he was waiting to hear.

"And I'll think seriously about being a police officer." *Wow. I can't believe I just said that shit,* she thought.

# Chapter 7

*What's Done In the Dark
Must Come to Light*

The television was so loud Kelly didn't hear the thunderous knock on her apartment door, but after the kicking started she couldn't help but hear the noise. Whoever was at the door was going to get cursed out. Kelly was watching her favorite show, *The Game*, and Tasha Mack was about to try to get Rick Fox back. She turned the volume down on her forty-inch plasma and threw the remote back onto the large pillow of her gray suede sofa.

"Who is it?" she yelled, grabbing her .380.

"It's me, Dora."

"Dora, I don't have time for your bullshit right now," Kelly yelled as she put her .380 back into its hiding place near her front door.

Kelly ran back to her television to see what she had missed when Dora went at her door again.

"This bitch," Kelly said in frustration. She was missing her show and she was pissed off.

Kelly ran back to her door and unlocked it and quickly ran back to her television. She allowed Dora's trifling-ass to come into her apartment, that's how much she wanted to see her favorite television show.

"What the hell do you want, Dora?" Kelly asked her, looking back and forth between Dora and her TV screen.

"I just want you to know that because of your bitchin' snitchin'-ass, Buddah got locked the fuck up," Dora yelled.

"What? What the fuck you mean, Buddah got locked up?" Kelly asked in disbelief.

She had just spoken to Buddah the night before and everything was all good. He told her that he was shutting shit down early again and that he was going to need his car because his truck was in the shop. She dropped his car and his keys off to him at his crib, got another two packages, and dipped. That was the last she had seen or heard from him. Kelly didn't know what the fuck was going on, but she knew if Buddah panicked and experienced a case of loose lips, her ship was going to be sinking soon. She had hoped that Kevin's rep held enough weight with Buddah for him to keep his mouth shut about her involvement in his drug operation.

"What the fuck you gon' do now, bitch?" Dora said, spitting while she spoke.

"Yo, Dora, get the fuck out my crib with that bullshit, yo," Kelly told her.

Dora wouldn't leave Kelly's apartment. She was drunk and she was high and she had apparently been crying. Dora kept ranting and raving about Buddah and Kelly fucking around behind her back. She told Kelly that she knew that she and Buddah were having a sexual relationship.

"Bitch, you was fuckin' him. I know you been fuckin' him now get him outta jail, bitch, or give me the goddamn money so I can go an' get my dick outta jail, you stinkin' ho bitch," Dora cried in a drunken rage.

Kelly walked briskly over to one of her stash spots near the front door and grabbed her .380. She walked back over to where Dora stood and pointed the gun directly at her and cocked it. Kelly didn't care about Buddah being locked up at the moment, this bitch was in her apartment bugging the fuck out and that's exactly where she could die, right there in her apartment. Kelly really didn't give a fuck.

"Ga' head an' shoot me! Shoot me, bitch! I got people that know I was coming right on over here. So ga' head bitch, cause yo' ass'll be locked up too," Dora screamed.

All Kelly could think of was Dante asking her was she stupid enough to do a crime with known witnesses that could rat her out. As Kelly stood with the gun in her hand, she reflected on the craziness of her actions. She knew that her mother would turn over in her grave if she was there to see what it was that Kelly was doing and who she had become. She took the clip out of her gun and put it in the jacket pocket of her red velour jogging suit and calmly sat the gun down on her living room table and sat herself down on her sofa. She needed to think and she needed to think rationally.

"Dora, look, I don't know what the fuck happened to Buddah, but I'ma find the fuck out. Now what I need you to do is get the fuck out of my crib, yo," Kelly said calmly as she looked up at Dora's sweaty face. It was obvious that Dora's intrusion to come and inform Kelly of the current events was a result of one of her many crack-smoking intermissions.

Kelly was so calm that Dora knew that she needed to get her ass out of the apartment, because if the clip went back into that gun for any reason, the outcome was not going to be good. Dora couldn't help herself; she was leaving, but not without having the last word.

"You better find out, and you'd better let me know too, bitch," Dora said angrily, slamming the door as she exited.

Kelly had to get her mind right. Dora had just knocked her off of her own high. She went and got her weed from her bedroom, came back and sat in front of her television, hoping that BET was doing a marathon of *The Game*, but when she saw Bernie Mac's black ass complaining about his nieces and nephew, she realized she was going to have no such luck. Kelly sucked her teeth and let out a huge sigh. That bitch had made her miss *The Game*. Kelly took a Dutch out the five-pack box of vanilla Dutch Masters, removed the plastic wrapping, and inserted the cigar into her mouth and rolled it around in her mouth to lubricate it. She continued to roll her blunt as she contemplated who to contact about what had really happened to Buddah. She had to be careful. Until she knew what went down, she didn't know who she should even be talking to.

*Shit, Dora could have been making the whole thing up with her high ass,* Kelly thought.

As Kelly scrolled through the contact list on her phone, another knock came on her apartment door. She had finished rolling her blunt and was just about to set fire to it. She put the blunt away and she also put the clip back into her .380 and put her .380 back in its secret place.

"Bitch, I done already told you to take yo' junkie-ass home," Kelly yelled. That was it, she was ready to drag Dora's ass back inside of her apartment and beat her ass to a bloody pulp. She didn't care who knew. Kelly opened her apartment door ready to go to work on Dora's drunken-ass, but it wasn't Dora this time.

Laquisha stood in the doorway looking at Kelly's twisted face. She could tell that she was heated and ready to do some damage. Kelly immediately stepped to the side for Laquisha to come inside. She was hoping that she had heard something on the block about what happened to Buddah. Colonial Heights was worse than a Facebook bulletin. If one person knew what happened, the whole hood would soon know what happened. But Kelly needed the uncut version, and if anyone in the hood had the uncut version of what went down with Buddah, it was Laquisha.

"Yo, you heard what happened?" Laquisha asked her.

"Nah, what?" Kelly asked, real curious to hear the answer.

"Yo that same dude you said was a fake-ass fiend bagged Buddah up last night."

"What? Get the fuck outta here! But I told his ass about him! Why the fuck would he sell to him?" Kelly said, confused. She had described the dude to Buddah and didn't understand how he would be stupid enough to sell to the duck-ass cop.

"I don't know exactly how it happened, all I know is he's blaming you for it," Laquisha said.

"Blaming me? Why the fuck is he blaming me?"

Kelly's head was spinning after what Laquisha had just told her. One of her fears had become a reality. She was being labeled as a snitch, by none other than Buddah. She knew she had to talk to him and set his ass straight. She wasn't no fucking snitch. He landed himself behind bars because of his own stupidity and she would be damned if she was going to join his dumb ass.

"I don't know why the nigga blaming you, but the whole hood is talkin' about that shit," Laquisha told her.

Kelly's cell phone rang. She had a collect call coming through; it was Kevin. She accepted the call.

"Yo, sis, where the hell you been? I've been trying to get at you for two fuckin' days," Kevin screamed over the phone.

"I'm sorry, Kev, my phone was off for a split second. I know you must have been thinking all kinds of crazy shit, but I'm good, yo," Kelly told him.

Kelly had turned her phone off whenever she spent time with Dante. She had just come back from a weekend at Dante's house. She had been going out there every weekend since her first visit, which was six months ago. She knew what she had said in the beginning about fucking with police officers, but Dante's dick and brain game was on one thousand. And he had been working on her sexually, mentally, and emotionally and she was now under his spell. She didn't want to have to keep lying to him about her life, so she figured if she didn't have to talk to anyone while she was with him, then she wouldn't get caught in a web of lies.

"Yo, you been actin' real funny lately. Leaving the hood every weekend and not telling nobody shit. You my fuckin' sister, where the fuck you been goin' Kelly?"

"Who you got watchin me, Kevin?" she asked him, angrily. Kelly wasn't a child and she didn't like being watched.

"You already know I got eyes and ears all over, what the fuck you thought?"

"You know I'm not wit' that eye spy shit Kevin, I'm grown," she said, sounding like an afflicted child. There was no way Kelly was going to tell her brother where she had been going.

"I mean, shit, fuck Buddah if that nigga is takin' up too much of yo' time. Let me know and I'll set that nigga straight, but yo, you can't be disappearing on a nigga, yo. You had me mad worried, plus you my main fucking eyes and ears out on them streets. You can't just leave when the fuck you feel like it," her brother told her.

"Kevin, Buddah got locked up. I'm trying to find out what's what now." Kelly realized now that she had fucked up big-time. She chose pleasure over business and now Buddah was caught up in some heavy shit and he was blaming her. And why shouldn't he blame her? She was supposed to be available to him at all times.

"Buddah got locked up? When? Yo, Kelly, man, what the fuck is you doin' out there?"

Kelly wanted to tell her brother that lately she didn't know what the fuck she was doing out there. The street life had always been her way of life, but after having Dante in her ear souping her up, she was ready to put R. Kelly's "I Believe I Can Fly" on her ringtone, put on her cape, and fly the fuck out of the hood.

"Yo, Kev, I've been thinking, about me working for you when you come home," Kelly started to say.

"What Kells? Go 'head and say some stupid shit out ya' mouth like you quittin' the business," Kevin told her.

"I'm sayin', I'm not the only person you can get to do the job," she said.

Dante had been talking to Kelly and getting into her mind more and more every time she came to visit him at his home. He had declared his love for her and in addition to sexing her, cooking for her, and pampering her, he began mentoring her. Disregarding her first reaction to his mention of joining him on the force, he continually talked to her about becoming a member of the New York City Police Department. He explained to her everything it would take for her to become an officer of the law and he thought that she would make a perfect candidate for the Police Academy. They had a class starting in a few months and he wanted Kelly to be in it. Even though she was still skeptical of becoming an officer of the law, she really took his words to heart about her true potential. Kelly knew that everyone she knew would think that she had straight lost her mind, but this was her life and she owed it to herself to be all that she could be. And she owed it to her late mother.

"Yo, I don't know what or who the fuck is gettin' up in that head of yours, but don't get it fucked up. We got a business to run when I come the fuck out of here, you hear me? Our family business, so clear that shit up with Buddah ASAP."

"You have one minute," the recording recited.

This was one time Kelly was glad she didn't have much more time to talk to her brother. He wasn't trying to hear a damn thing about her wanting to do better for herself. He was only concerned with his own agenda.

"I got you, Kev. I'll get shit straight. Everything good, yo, just be easy. I don't want—"

Kelly's call ended with her brother before she could tell him that she didn't want him stressing about unnecessary shit, but she had more important shit to handle and she needed to get back to the matters at hand.

Laquisha had been listening closely, trying to read between the lines of the conversation between Kelly and her brother. Kelly wanted to quit—how interesting that sounded. Right after she meets a cop, her boss gets knocked, now she wants to get out of the game. Kelly could have kept lying to Laquisha all she wanted. Laquisha knew damn well that Kelly had hollered at the police officer that had almost arrested them that day on Broadway. Laquisha didn't know why Kelly thought she was so stupid, but she was about to let her know that she was far from stupid.

"Damn, bitch, let me find out the dick was so good, that nigga got you turnin' in ya peeps."

"I ain't got time for the bullshit, Laquisha. I have to find out what happened to Buddah, so if you got something to say about that, then say it, other than that, you can get the fuck up outta here too."

"What the fuck you mean you have to find out what happened to Buddah? Your lover boy probably had something to do with it. You probably helped him set the nigga up. That nigga straight played yo' ass, and you let him," Laquisha said.

Kelly looked confused at what she was saying. How could Dante have Buddah set up when he didn't even know who Buddah was?

"First, you said it was the dopefiend who arrested him, now you're saying Dante had something to do with it. Which one is it?" Kelly asked her.

"You ain't know? They're the same person. That's what the word is anyway."

Kelly wasn't trying to hear a word Laquisha was saying. It was obvious to her that Laquisha didn't know what the fuck she was talking about. It was also obvious that she wasn't going to get any real information from Laquisha about what had really happened to Buddah.

"Okay, bitch, time for you to go too," Kelly snapped.

"That's cool. I'll leave. Shit, I don't wanna be associated with no fuckin' snitch anyway."

"Bitch, whatever. Ya fuckin ass don't know what you talkin' about, so don't go spreadin' no shit, or you'll find yourself caught up in some shit that you really don't want to be in."

"No, I think it's you who's caught up in some shit that you don't want to be in. Matter a fact you got quite a lot of shit that you caught up in. Buddah's shit and that cop's shit, huh, looks to me like you're full of shit."

"Be careful or instead of shoving clothes up ya ass, I'll shove my .380 up that muthafucka."

Laquisha knew that it was time for her to jet. She didn't trust Kelly. And that's why she had told Buddah not to trust her ass either. Laquisha was dying to be Kelly's replacement and this was her perfect opportunity.

"You always threatening to shoot somebody, but I ain't see you pull that fuckin' trigger yet," Laquisha told her.

"*Yet,* bitch, that's the key word."

"Yeah right, whatever, Kelly," she said as she opened the apartment door and let herself out.

Kelly definitely wasn't feeling her past two visitors. The two of them had put so many things in and on her mind that she didn't know which thought to think about first. She didn't need Dora and Laquisha spreading shit out on the block that they had no clear knowledge about, especially if it was pertaining to her. Kelly still had some business to handle out on the streets and she didn't need the whole hood against her. *Fuck them bitches, I need to find out what happened to Buddah,* she thought as she quickly realized that was her first priority. Her mind shifted; she had more important shit to deal with.

Kelly was trying to put some shit together on her own without talking to anyone. There really wasn't anyone she could talk to anyway. She was supposed to be the eyes and ears in Colonial, but it seemed as though the hood now knew everything and she knew nothing. She played back the events of the past few weeks. So the so-called fiend that came up to her was Dante in disguise and he was the one who busted Buddah. Somehow she felt that there was much more to it. And she was going to find out exactly what that "much more" was.

Her cell phone rang. She didn't recognize the number, but she answered it anyway. It was the telephone company, MCI, prompting her on how to set up her phone to receive calls from Brian Levy, aka Buddah. She feverishly ran to her bedroom and got her debit card out of her wallet and set up the account.

Buddah didn't take long to call her back.

"Yo, Buddah, what the fuck happened?"

"You tell me, Kelly."

"What you mean?"

"You fucking wit'a cop, man?"

"What?"

"You heard me. You fuckin' wit'a cop."

"Yo, who told you that shit?"

"Don't worry about who told me. All you need to know is that I know."

Buddah hung up in her face. Well, that pretty much told her what he was thinking. Kelly wasn't going to fold just because niggas had her fucked up. Yeah, it may have *looked* like she had something to do with Buddah getting caught up, but she knew that she didn't. Not wanting to believe that Dante may have gone behind her back and arrested her boss, Kelly thought about Chop. She wondered if he had anything to do with Buddah getting caught up. He was real sour when he left Buddah's crib and he surely had a beef with her. Kelly was going to make it a point to see what was up with Chop too. Shit, she couldn't trust anyone.

The block was full of people when Kelly came out of her building. Everyone who caught her eye either gave her the evil eye or had something smart to say under their breath. She could hear them and she could also read their lips. They were saying she was a snitch and pig lover. She didn't give a fuck. She was looking for Chop. She had some questions for him.

"Ay, yo, you seen Chop?" she asked a crackhead.

"Chop's over there. He dead," the crackhead told her, looking at Kelly as if was way late.

"Dead?" Kelly said in disbelief.

She ran over to the crowd of people and parted her way through. Sure enough, there was Chop, sprawled out in the middle of the block with a gunshot to his head.

"Yo, what happened?" she asked one of the onlookers.

"They said a nigga drove up, got out his whip and just came up, shot him point-blank 'n shit. Yo that nigga whole shit is gone," the man said, referring to the back of Chop's head.

"Ain't nobody see who did it?" Kelly asked.

"Nah, and even if they did, ain't nobody sayin' shit," he said as he walked away.

Kelly's whole world was crashing down around her. She had no idea who wanted to kill Chop, but shit, Chop sold drugs, it could have been a customer, it could have been another drug dealer, and shit, it could have been anybody. Kelly thought long and hard about all of the events that had occurred in the past several months and all of a sudden the street life that she loved so much didn't seem so glamorous.

# Chapter 8

*Him Or Me*

The thought of Kelly seeing a police officer was fucking with Kevin hard. What was fucking with him even harder was the way he found out. He had to hear it from a nigga he ain't even fuck with. And he had to physically show the nigga that he didn't appreciate the bad news. All he could see was a grimy-ass boy in blue with his hands all over his sister. What the hell did this man, this devil, this cop, have over his sister? Kevin knew that his sister shared his sentiments in regards to the "swine of the earth" as he so often called them. He just couldn't understand what would make his sister even give the nigga the time of day. He knew his sister looked good and could have any one she wanted, so it had to be something about this nigga. And he was going to make sure he found out exactly what it was.

Shit was floating around in the air in the prison about Kevin's sister being sexually involved with a cop and being a snitch. It didn't take any time for the word on the streets to make it behind the walls. Niggas in the pod was asking all kinds of questions and making a bunch of fucked-up comments about shit they really knew nothing about.

Kevin was trying his best to ignore all of the negative words that were flying through the prison about his big sister, but it was becoming one of the hardest things he ever had to do in his entire life. For the first time since his arrival, niggas wasn't respecting who Kev was and they weren't showing no fear for "Crazy-ass Kev" either. The niggas who didn't have anything to lose was fucking with him on the regular now. They kept trying to break him.

"Ay Kev," called one of the Mexican inmates who was in for murder.

Kevin wasn't going to respond, but he decided, fuck it. Niggas wasn't running him, he ran niggas.

"Yeah, Ramon, what's good?"

"You think your sister could ask her pig boyfriend to help me get my green card, homie?"

"Nah, nigga, but tell your mother I can help her out with these nuts."

Ramon charged full force at him. He had no choice but to defend himself, throwing a host of punches to Ramon, catching him in his nose as his knuckles busted his nose open and blood began to flow from Ramon's nose. The two men scuffled as Kevin lifted Ramon up off of his feet and slammed him to the ground.

The other Mexicans that were in Kevin's pod immediately came to the aid of their homeboy as they descended on him and tried to annihilate him. They pounded their fists into him one by one and then all at once. A multitude of red whelps began to appear and formed their place on his light skin. Not one of Kevin's so-called boys stepped in to help him. Siggah stood there watching with his black hand over his open mouth. They all watched as Kevin took the worst beat-down he had ever received in his twenty-two years on this earth. The more they hit him, the madder at his sister he got. He was almost home, but now he was going to have to go to the hole.


Kevin sat on the floor inside of the two-by-four boxed-in cell like a caged animal. He had landed himself in solitary confinement and they hadn't brought him any food in the past seventy-two hours. He was about to start singing a song as he listened to the beat of his stomach growl. He was trying to determine whether it was a rap song or an R&B joint, but the growl in his stomach had a crazy sound to it. It was extremely long and incredibly strong. Kevin wondered how people could fast for days and weeks for their religion. *More power to 'em,* he thought. He couldn't see himself ever fasting.

It had been a minute since he had spoken to Kelly. She wasn't answering his calls. He knew that she was trying to get away from the family business and now he knew why. *Why didn't she tell me she was fuckin' wit' a cop,* he thought. But he already knew the answer to that question. Kevin knew that there was no way his sister would willingly tell him that she was fucking with a police officer. He was more than anxious to hit the streets. His sister had crossed the line. He wanted to know why it happened, when it happened, and how the hell it managed to happen. He was a man and he knew with a proper dick down any female was subject to be a victim. He figured that must have been the case because his sister was acting as if she had been sprinkled with fairy dust. He had a few more days and he would be able to try to call her again. If she didn't take his calls then he planned on writing her a letter. One way or another he needed to get his point across to Kelly. He had to make her see the grave mistake that she was making by mingling with the enemy.

\*\*\*

What seemed like forever was finally over. Kevin was out of the hole. He was transferred to a different pod so that he couldn't associate with the Mexicans that he had the altercation with. He was hoping that the niggas in his new pod wasn't on the same shit his last pod was, but he quickly learned the opposite.

"Aw shit, they sent the fuckin' cop-lover over here with us," one of the black inmates said.

"Look, yo, my time is short. I don't want it wit' y'all niggas and for real, the way I'm feelin' right now, y'all don't really want it wit' me, so I'm asking if a nigga feel froggy, leap and let's get this shit out the way, other than that, a nigga ready to do his time and get the fuck up outta here, so I can go deal wit' some real shit."

"Man, fuck all that peace-offering shit. You already know what it is."

"Well then nigga, stop talkin' and let's get to it," Kevin said as he threw up his hands. He was ready to go again and add some more time to his stay.

Kevin threw the first punch. He needed to work off the frustration and anger he was feeling anyhow. He thought he'd rather take it out on this punk-ass muthafucka than to take it out on his sister, but she was going to hear it from him, that was for damn sure.

The dude didn't even give Kevin a good fight. He didn't know why the nigga ever spoke out of turn, if he couldn't back the shit up. Kev looked down at the dude that he had knocked the fuck out. He looked young. He later found out that the kid had just come in and was trying to establish his rep by stepping to Kevin. Too bad it turned out to be a bad move.

COs got wind of Kevin's second fight, but he had a few of them on his side, so they kept this altercation under wraps and actually took the rookie to the hole to teach his ass a lesson. Kevin was then sent to a totally different unit where, amazingly, niggas didn't have a word to say. They left Kevin alone to deal with the unwelcome information.

The next few days he spent trying to get at his sister. He was tired of her avoiding him and he was getting more and more upset. He thought they were tighter than that. And it seemed to Kevin as though his sister was putting this nigga, this cop nigga's needs in front of his own. And he wasn't feeling that one bit. It was Kevin who took care of her when he was out on the street. He was the one who set her up from jump. How dare she turn her back on him and not even talk to him. What if he needed something, what if something was wrong with him or something bad had happened to him? *Wouldn't she want to know?* he thought to himself.

After several attempts were made and him still not making contact with Kelly, Kevin laid down on his bunk in his new pod. He was furious. His sister had truly betrayed him in his eyes. He was literally fuming out of his nostrils and his mouth at the same time, thinking of his sister laughing it up with this nigga and ignoring his calls. He knew that she had to see his calls come through on her cell phone. For her to straight ignore him was blatant disrespect.

One of the older cats, who went by the name of Joe, saw Kevin going through some changes as he lay on his bunk and he came and hollered at him.

"You got'sta take it easy, man. You not gon' get nowhere with all that anger you got inside of you." Kevin looked at Joe. He was tired. He didn't want to fight any more and he knew that Joe was right. The more he stayed angry, the more he was liable to get into more trouble and his time would get longer and longer and that shit was not the move.

"Yo, thanks, my man, you right. I gotta get shit back in control. I have to control the situation. I can't let the situation control me," he said, slowly coming back to himself.

Kevin now waited patiently to catch up with his sister. He stopped calling her for over a week. He wanted to know what she would do then.

\*\*\*

Kelly had been avoiding her brother's calls for over a month. She had never done anything like that before and she knew that her brother must have been going crazy wondering what was going on, but she just couldn't tell him that she had fallen head over heels in love with a police officer and that she was thinking of becoming one herself. It had been over a week since she had seen the 800 number flash up on her cell phone. At least when she saw the number, she knew that her brother was all right. When she stopped seeing it, she began to wonder and then her wonder turned to worry, so when she heard her cell phone ring and saw the 800 number for her brother's prison come up, she answered immediately.

"You have a collect call from (Kevin) an inmate of Rikers Island Correctional Facility."

It had been so long since Kelly heard the prison recording that she had forgotten which button to press and had to listen to the entire option menu. She finally heard her option and pressed 3. The conversation that she had been dreading for the past thirty days was now about to go down and she was not happy about it, but she needed to make sure that her brother was all right.

"Hey," Kelly said, sullenly.

"Hey. That's all you got for me?" Kevin asked her.

"Well, I know you probably know already. You know everything else," Kelly said nastily.

"Nah, I don't know shit, you got something you wanna tell me?" Kevin played dumb.

Kevin wanted his sister to come clean. She had been playing games and hiding from him long enough and if he was going to be able to fuck with her at all when he came home, he needed her to act like his big sister, the same big sister that had been down for him since his birth. The same big sister he used to take baths with when he was a toddler and they would play barbershop. Kelly would smear the bubbles all over his face and make a mustache and Santa Claus beard out of the bubbles and then she would shave his face.

"I repeat, Kelly, you got something you wanna tell me?" Kevin asked very calmly and very slowly.

"Come on, Kev, don't make me say it." Kelly knew that he knew, she could tell by the way he was handling her.

"Don't make you say what? That you've been fuckin' sleeping with the devil?"

"You don't know him, Kevin, you can't judge him if you don't know him."

"Are you fuckin' kiddin me, yo? Yo, Kelly, I don't know what the fuck is goin' on wit' you out there. You duckin' a nigga, like you can't talk to me. I'm ya fuckin' brother! I'm all you got left out in this world and you gon' duck me for some bitch-ass cop."

"Kevin, you don't understand," she pleaded.

"I don't understand? What the fuck is it that I don't understand, Kelly?" he asked venomously.

Kelly was silent. She was waiting for the recording to come on saying they had a minute left. She didn't want to talk to her brother anymore. She knew she wasn't going to be able to tell him what she was feeling inside. There was no way that he was going to understand.

"What the fuck? This nigga fuckin' put it on you? What, he gave you some dick that got you seeing stars? This nigga done fuckin' brainwashed you?"

"Ain't nobody do shit to me."

"*You have one minute left.*" There went the magic words Kelly had been waiting to hear.

"Kelly I'ma call you back and you better answer the phone."

"Kevin, I gotta lot a shit—"

"You better answer the phone, Kelly."

The call ended. Kelly could tell that her brother was heated and he was just getting started. She wasn't in the mood for it. She had enough shit to deal with. Spank was still locked up. Buddah was accusing her of being a snitch and having him locked up. Chop was dead. The whole hood thought she was a snitch and she had a man who she had feelings for that she had to hide from the world who wanted her to change her life and become something she'd always hated. And to top it all off she had stopped smoking weed. Kelly felt a headache coming on.

Her phone rang again. It was her brother calling her back. Kelly contemplated whether she should answer the phone. She knew that her brother was alive and well and pissed the fuck off. That was pretty much all she needed to know. The phone rang and rang until it finally stopped. She didn't answer it.

Three minutes later her cell phone rang again. It was her brother calling back. Kelly decided to answer. She couldn't keep what was going on in the streets from her brother. Kelly needed to tell him what was going on. She had to admit to her herself that she needed some advice.

She answered her brother's call and quickly went through the preliminaries.

"Yo, Kelly, I don't deserve this," Kevin told her.

"I'm sorry, Kev, and you right, you don't."

Kelly explained to her brother how she got caught up with a police officer even though he wasn't trying to hear it. She also told him about what went down with Buddah and Chop.

"Fuck that nigga Buddah, if he wanna think you ratted his ass out then so be it. It really ain't nothing you can do to change that nigga's mind, a nigga gon' think what he wanna think, especially if he caged up 'n shit."

"I know, you right, and I'm not fuckin' trying anymore. I got other things I'm working on," Kelly said.

"Yeah, like the family business. I'm not taking no for an answer. I don't give a fuck about your little boyfriend either, 'cause you gon' get rid of that nigga."

"Kevin . . ."

"Kevin, my muthafuckin' ass. You know how many niggas I had to fight in here over you fuckin with that devil-ass pig?" he asked angrily.

"But—"

"Yo, you know I have to do two extra months because of you?" he asked as he gritted his teeth.

Kelly didn't say a word. That was the last thing she wanted to do, but she had managed to do it anyway. She caused her brother extra time in prison. She felt like shit for that.

"But you know what? Don't even sweat that shit. Just be ready to get it when I come out. With Buddah off of the streets, Colonial is all ours."

*"You have one minute left."*

"Get rid of that nigga, Kelly, or I will. You get what I'm sayin'? We got money to make."

# Chapter 9

## Mixed Emotions

The entire apartment was quiet. There were no televisions on, no radios playing; no noise at all. Kelly was all alone with her thoughts. She sat back on her sofa in her emerald green Victoria's Secret pajama set with her arms crossed and her bare foot up on her coffee table. What filled her pretty head were thoughts of Dante and how he had gotten all up under skin and in her heart. She also cogitated that he may have had something to do with Buddah's arrest. That would have meant that he was playing her all along. That meant that he knew exactly who she was from the very beginning. *This nigga probably think I'm green as a bitch,* Kelly thought. *But I got some shit for his ass.* Dante may have been playing her in the beginning, but she knew that feelings that Dante had for her now were very real.

Dante had been blowing her cell phone up with calls and texts for the past few weeks, but she wouldn't answer. She had been avoiding him. She had to finish getting off those packages of coke that she had left and she didn't want him all up in her shit and trying to stop her, so she went out to Brooklyn and let Rayvon help her. It was money over niggas at all times. She was able to hustle up all of the money she needed to get her straight and her brother straight for his homecoming. Now she was back in Colonial Heights and it was time for her to deal with Officer Dante Evans. She called him.

"Hey baby," Dante said, excitedly. He was very happy to hear her voice.

"Hey, I need to see you," she told him flatly, getting right to the point.

"Okay, cool, I should be leaving the precinct in a few more minutes. You want me to come to your place?"

"No, I'll come to you."

"Kelly, you don't have to keep driving all the way to Queens."

"If it ain't broke, don't fix it, right?" Kelly asked and then ended the call without saying good-bye.

Dante looked at his phone to see if he had lost his signal or if Kelly had in fact hung up on him. His phone looked to be fine. He could tell that there was something different about her from the brief conversation they just had. He wondered what it was that had her sounding so solemn and serious. He knew that he had not heard from her in a few weeks, but other than that things had been going great between the two of them. He knew that her boss was off of the streets so she shouldn't have had any drugs to sell. He hadn't seen her out on the block, so he figured she was keeping to herself while going through withdrawal from the weed. He kept trying to check on her, but she wouldn't respond. All Dante could think about was Kelly graduating from the Police Academy and joining him on the force. He was so glad that she had called him. Dante realized how much he actually missed her. Lately, Dante Evans was on top of the world on and off the job. The crazy dispatch calls with random reports of violence weren't so crazy anymore now that Kelly Morgan was in his life.

Kelly went into her bedroom and got some things together. It was Friday so she packed an overnight bag just in case she felt like staying over. She didn't know what Dante was going to tell her and she didn't know quite yet what she was going to say to him. For all she knew Laquisha was on some straight hatin' shit and she wasn't the cause of Buddah ending up behind bars. If that was case then she was due for a weekend full of some good dick. She grabbed her leopard-print teddy that came with leopard-print faux-fur-covered handcuffs and a leopard-print blindfold. She added them to her overnight bag. Kelly took a shower and got dressed. She threw on a pair of black leggings with a smoke-gray blouse on top. She went into her shoe room, got up on her ladder and selected a pair of suede smoke-gray flat calf-length boots.

Kelly took a cab out to Dante's house. Once Buddah needed his car back, it made her realize that she needed to get her own car and now that she was gettin' a lot more money she was going to do just that. Luckily she was able to get two more packages out of the secret stash in Buddah's apartment before the cops shut it down. She felt that she deserved the come up after the way Buddah had treated her. *That nigga didn't even wanna hear what I had to say,* she thought.

As she rode through the city streets her mind went to her brother having to do extra time behind her actions and it still bothered her. She knew how much he wanted to come home on time and now he was going to have to stay in prison longer, all because of her. *I know that nigga wanna kick my ass right now,* she thought to herself. *This nigga got my ass gone.* She had been tripping because of Dante and she couldn't deny it. Now her brother was paying the price.

Kelly had not seen her brother face-to-face since their mother's funeral. Her brother wouldn't allow her to visit him in prison. He told her that he didn't want her to see him like that and that the next time he would see her would be as a free man. She thought about everything Kevin had gone through for her and all that he had done for her and she realized that she had betrayed their relationship in a huge way by being with Dante. She was so busy satisfying her flesh that she had blocked her only brother out of her head.

*What if Dante did have something to do with Buddah being locked up?* Kelly thought. She didn't really know if that would have been enough to keep her from seeing Dante. *I mean, shit, he didn't touch me. He would never hurt me.* His dick had her that whipped. But her brother was threatening Dante's life—now, that was another story. Kelly knew exactly what her brother meant when he told her to get rid of Dante or he would: He meant that he would get rid of him permanently and she didn't want any harm to come to him. She had to stop seeing him.

She also wasn't feeling the fact that her brother wanted to come straight home and get money in Colonial Heights. She could see them going out to Brooklyn to do their thing. After all, that's where they were from and she had just made a killing out in BK. After everything that had happened around Colonial, she didn't want to remain there. There was too much bad blood between her and some of the key figures in the hood who had love for Buddah and who believed that she had sold him out. Kelly thought for sure that if she did continue to pump over there that she would end up having to kill someone. Then she would be the next one to be arrested and she doubted that Dante would be able to protect her from a murder charge.

*Damn, I need a blunt,* Kelly thought as the cab pulled up in Dante's driveway. She hadn't had a blunt since she told Dante she was going to quit so that she could pass the drug screen for the academy. But it wasn't about him, and it wasn't about the possible police gig. It was something that she had to prove to herself, and so far she had been weed-free for three weeks. It was driving her a bit crazy. She thought about everything too much, but she did like the fact that her mind was clear from the cush.

She paid the cabdriver and got out of the cab. The driver popped the trunk, hopped out, and got her bags. Kelly used the key that Dante had given her on her third visit to his home. He made it clear to her that he wanted her there with him at all times. She came inside and dropped her overnight bag on the floor. Smelling the goodness coming from the kitchen, she walked right on in.

"Hello."

"Hey baby," Dante said, lovingly.

They shared a long, wet kiss.

Dante had dinner cooking, some Raheem DeVaughn playing, and plenty of scented candles lit. He couldn't wait to get his hands on her. It had been weeks since he felt the moistness of her insides and he craved to touch her. All he could do was think about her selling drugs in her neighborhood. He couldn't wait for her to start training at the academy. He had to get her away from the streets if they were going to be together. He could see her in her uniform now. *She gon' look fine as hell in all that blue,* he thought.

"So, first you disappear on me and I don't hear from you for weeks. You don't return my calls or my texts. Then I get a call and you're over here within the hour. What's so important that you had to rush all the way out here?" Dante asked, as he turned to give his attention back to his brewing pots.

Forget the questions, Kelly wanted some dick first. She knew that things were going to get a little rocky after their Q&A session. She had some harsh things to say and although this was to be her last meeting with Dante, she would have had the best sex she ever had at least one more time. She came up behind Dante while he was still cooking at the stove and reached her hand around to rub his dick through his sweatpants. That was all the answer he needed. His dick responded to her touch as it thumped her on her hand. He turned the stove off, grabbed her by her hand, and pulled her along with him. They ended up in his bedroom, on his bed.

There was no foreplay this time. He pulled her boots off and slid her leggings and panties off and plunged his dick into her wetness, his finger into her ass, and his tongue into her ear all at the same time. She was overwhelmed with a sudden sensation of a climactic eruption. He took her to heights to which she had never gone. And she never wanted the feeling to end. *Oh my God, this nigga got some good dick, it's just too good. I don't wanna give it up. Oh God, oh my God, this is the best I've ever had in my life. Oh Jesus . . .*

"I don't wanna cum yet," she panted as she slowed his movement with persuasion from the touch of her hands on his ass.

She enjoyed the slow strokes of his dick as she came back down from her natural euphoric high. She then pulled away from him. Kelly wanted to use her toys.

"Where you goin'," he asked, as she suddenly jumped out of his bed and went over to her bag.

Kelly pulled out the handcuffs and the blindfold. There was no need to put on the teddy at this point so she left it in the bag.

"What you gonna do with those?" Dante asked with a smile on this face.

"What you think I'm going to do with them, Officer Evans?" Kelly asked with a sly smirk on her face.

Kelly connected Dante's wrists with her furry handcuffs that came equipped with a push-button release. They were much better than the handcuffs with the keys.

"How does it feel to be cuffed, Officer Evans?" Kelly asked him softly in his ear.

"Actually, it doesn't feel so bad," he said.

Dante had the fur protecting his skin from the steel in which real suspects and prisoners feel. Kelly placed the blindfold over his eyes, removed the handcuffs, slid the fur off of them, and placed the handcuffs back onto his wrists. She cranked them as tight as they could possibly go, squeezing the steel into his wrists.

"Now, how does that feel?" she asked him with sarcasm in her voice.

"It feels kind of tight and cold," he reluctantly admitted.

"Now you know how we feel when y'all put them shits on us," Kelly chillingly told him.

She shoved her tongue down his throat before he could answer her and gave him a deep kiss as a single tear ran down her face. This had been a wild ride, and even though she liked wild rides, it was time for her to get off of this one, *but not without one last run,* she thought to herself. She then slid her soft, high yellow body onto Dante's dark skin and straddled him. She held his dick in her hands and spat on the head before she inserted it into her juice box. She rode Dante's dick like a jockey rode a winning racehorse. She removed the blindfold and looked him in his eyes. Her pussy slid on and off of his dick as he began to lose himself in her love. She pumped on his dick like a nigga trying to get that last bit of gas out of the pump as she came to a climax and so did he.

Kelly removed the handcuffs from Dante's wrists. He stretched out his arms for her and she laid in his arms. He snuggled with her and cuddled with her in his massive bed. Kelly was enjoying him. Even with all of the drama surrounding their union, she couldn't think of any place she would rather be than in the comfort of his strong arms. She felt safe, like she used to feel on the block. She didn't feel safe on the block anymore. Now that Spank and Buddah was locked up and Chop was dead, to her, shop was pretty much closed.

"I wrote something for you. I want you to read it," Dante told her, as he reached over and went into the drawer of his nightstand and retrieved a piece of paper and handed it to her. They sat up together as she read the letter to herself.

> *Dear Kelly,*
> *I have told you that I love you and that is certainly true. I just need to explain what love is to me. Love is a decision and I have decided to love you. Decision translates into energy and I have become more energetic in my daily life. When we make passionate love I'm overwhelmed by the love you express to me, not only with your body, but with your heartbeat. When I hold you in my arms I want you to feel secure. If there was an army brigade with guns drawn on you, I would take every bullet for you. I feel the love coming from your pores. When you sleep, I listen to every breath that you take. I have your back as I*

*know you have mine, and therefore, I can lead from behind. I will support you in all that you do. I've never met a woman as courageous, smart, and sexy as you. Your mind fascinates me and your sensuality titillates me. All I ask is that you remain real with me.*

Kelly took in the words that were written with love on the piece of paper she held in her hand. She had never heard anything so beautiful. Dante seemed to be the man of her dreams and she wished that's what this all was, a dream. Just as Dante had made a decision to love Kelly, and she now had to make a decision; a very, very important decision.

She looked into his eyes. She was going to miss looking into his beautiful eyes.

"This is very sweet and very deep," Kelly said, truthfully.

"I mean every word of it," he told her.

"Dante, you say you love me, but you don't know anything about me."

"I know enough to know I want you by my side and I never want you to leave it."

"I'm not who you think I am."

"Well, if you're not Kelly Morgan, the sexy, book-smart, street-smart, caring, loving, generous, wild-spirited lovely gem of a lady that I love, then no, I don't know who you are."

"Dante, please, you're not making this easy for me at all."

"What am I not making easy for you, Kelly?"

"I'm not gon' be able to come out here anymore."

"What? What are you saying to me, Kelly?" he asked her as he desperately held onto her face with his hands.

"I can't see you anymore. I'm not who you think I am."

Dante's mind was racing. What was she talking about? He knew that by seeing someone like her that there would be some risk involved. They were from two different worlds and he was trying to squeeze her into his world. Dante thought that maybe he had gone about it all wrong.

"Kelly, no—see, you're the air I breathe. Baby, I need you."

Seeing Dante pour out his feelings made Kelly love him even more. He was showing her that he could be vulnerable behind that bulletproof vest he wore as a shield over his heart. But she knew the deal: She had to stop seeing him or Kevin was going to kill him.

"What about starting at the Police Academy? Huh, what about our plans, baby?"

"There is no way I can join you on the force, Dante."

"Why can't you join me, Kelly, what's stopping you?"

"I'm a fuckin' criminal. That's what's stopping me, Dante. I am the people who you go out and arrest every day. I can't arrest myself. I can't arrest the people that I have known and grown up with all of my life."

Kelly got out of his bed.

"You're not a criminal, Kelly," he adamantly told her, as he jumped out of his bed and went after her.

Dante had been a police officer for seven years and he had seen the most barbaric criminals there were to see. He had been in the presence of capital murderers and rapists, kidnappers, and notorious bank robbers. He knew Kelly deep down inside and she may have wanted to be a criminal, but she really didn't have what it took to carry it off, in his honest opinion.

"Dante, like I told you, you know nothing about me. You should have just saved yourself the trouble and arrested me when you had the chance."

"Kelly, I know more than you think I know."

"Yeah, well, I'll tell you some shit that you don't know. I feel it's damn near my duty to break each and every one of the laws you muthafuckas set."

"Kelly!"

Dante yelled at her, but at the same time he couldn't help but be turned on by her rebelliousness.

"Dante, what? I'm telling the truth."

He knew who she was and he respected her for it. Kelly had lied to him in the beginning, but he knew the woman who was standing in front of him now was the real Kelly Morgan; the uncut version and he couldn't get enough of her. Her plan was to come and turn him completely off so that he would stay away from her, but little did she know, she had done just the opposite.

"Yes, you've been in trouble before—several times before, to be exact—but you don't have any felonies. I checked you out myself."

"Oh, so now you're fucking checking me out too, Dante. What? Did you plug me into your little criminal computer system and run my rap sheet?"

"Well, yeah, I did," he truthfully admitted.

"So you never trusted me? You mutahfucka. You ain't shit!"

"Kelly, come on, that's not fair. You know who I am."

Kelly knew now that Laquisha was telling the truth, it was Dante who had Buddah arrested. Here he was asking that she remain real with him, yet he had not been one hundred percent real with her.

"So what do you know about me, Dante?"

"Come on, Kelly, please. Stop."

"No, if you know so much about me, why do you still wanna see me? Why haven't you arrested me by now?"

"You know why, because I fell in love with you," Dante said as he looked into her eyes with a silent longing for her to understand exactly what it took for him to be with her.

"So you busted my partner, Buddah, instead. Dante, that's how much you love me?" she asked him with disappointment in her words.

So she knew. He knew that she would find out, he just didn't know how fast. Kelly was good. She had played him the whole time she had been there, yet she still showed love for him, she still made love to him. That told him that he still had a chance to win her heart.

"Kelly, we had been watching Buddah for a very long time, long before you came on the scene."

Kelly looked closely at him. She knew either she had to be slippin' or this nigga threw the dick on her so hard he had affected her eyesight. All of a sudden she could see clearly.

"It was you that day dressed like a dopefiend tryin'a score a hit, but then you had a uniform on when you stopped us, and that was only like a few hours later. What kind of shit is that?"

"I'm in a special program that they're testing out at the precinct. It's for officers who wanna consider going undercover narcotics, sort of like on-the-job training, if you will. It's a great program, Kelly. It's a program I think you would be perfect for."

"Do you know what you've done to my reputation in the hood, Dante? Because of you they think I'm a snitch."

"Who cares what they think, Kelly? You're about to move away from there and come live with me, go to the academy, and become a police officer. We're in love."

"You put my life in jeopardy, Dante."

"I would never let anyone harm a hair on your beautiful head. I love you, Kelly."

Kelly wasn't trying to hear any more about love. Love was the reason why she was standing in front of a man that even though he lied to her and deceived her, she loved in return, with not some, with not most, but with all of her heart. But she had to deny his love for the sake of her safety on the block and his own safety and to keep her brother happy and it was tearing her up inside.

She had to flip the script. She had to find a reason to leave him where he stood. Kelly knew something that would make him upset. She had decided to let Dante in on why she hated police officers.

"Since you know so much, did you know that it was one of y'all punk-ass police officers who were responsible for my brother being behind bars?" Kelly asked with tears in her eyes. Some of her tears represented the loss of Dante's love and what they could have had and some of the tears were a reflection of the story in which she was about to tell.

Dante looked at her, but he didn't utter a word.

"Yeah, some bitch-ass cop ran up on my brother and his friends, and of course he didn't take the fuckin' time to see what was really going down, he was a straight pussy about his, so instead of going up on the situation carefully he fucked it all up. Somebody started shooting at my brother, so my brother had no choice but to shoot back. Then some other cops come and grab my brother while all of his other friends got away. After they searched him they found some crack cocaine and of course they had him for the gun. But he wasn't even doing anything when the cop came up on him. He was just standing there talking," Kelly sorrowfully explained as she got dressed and gathered her things together to put back in her overnight bag. She wasn't going to be staying after all.

"So in honor of my brother, who's coming home in a few months, fuck da police!" Kelly chanted as she walked out of his bedroom.

"Kelly," Dante called in desperation. He had just gone weeks without seeing her and could barely take it. He couldn't fathom the thought of him never seeing her again. His heart was literally hurting him.

Kelly had dried her tears and was already on her cell phone calling for a cab.

"Kelly, please, baby, look, come on now, slow down. I cooked for you. Can we please just sit down and eat and talk about all of this?"

"I'm done talking, Dante, and even after all of that good dick you just gave me, amazingly, I don't have an appetite. Maybe I should go back to smoking weed, huh?"

"No, no, you shouldn't go back to bad habits, Kelly. Let me take you home."

Kelly laughed. "You're kidding, right?" she asked, while she simultaneously made arrangements with the cab service to come and get her.

Dante knew that was a stupid thing to say, but he wasn't thinking straight. Kelly wasn't allowing his mind to function correctly. She was stifling his brain with her sudden rejection. In all of the raids he had been in and all of the compromising positions he had been put in as a police officer; all of the guns he had pointed at him in his lifetime; none of that scared him. What was scaring the very life out of him was the thought of him not seeing Kelly anymore, the thought of him not touching her milky skin, the thought of him not kissing her soft, juicy lips; both sets. She was taking the air out of his lungs. He sat on his sofa just looking at her. He didn't know what else to say. Dante was afraid of upsetting her any more than she already was.

Kelly had to get out of there. It didn't matter what Dante did or said, she loved him and if she stayed around him any longer she would say fuck everything and stay with him, but she knew that there was no way she could do that. Not with Kevin holding Dante's life in his crazy-ass hands.

Her cab arrived. He had to give it just one last try.

"Kelly, please, I'll do whatever it is you want me to do. Please just don't leave."

"Dante, for real, baby, I think you've already done quite enough. I'm out."

# Chapter 10

*Fresh on Arrival*

Kelly was hyped as hell. The day had finally come. Her baby brother was coming home. After five years and two months, he was finally about to join her back out on the streets. The last few months had changed the temperature of their relationship from hot to cold, but Kelly intended to get their old thing back. Kelly couldn't be happier for her brother. He was about to taste freedom again. She waited patiently, standing outside of the prison walls, leaning on her new silver Lexus. She still didn't have a driver's license. She bought her a car from one of the Dominicans in Brooklyn with some of the money she had made from the packages Buddah had left behind. They didn't give a fuck, as long as you had the money, you had a car. It was used but it looked new.

She didn't want to wait in the prisoner release receiving room. There were too many police up in there and she knew that she was reeking of purple cush. After she left Dante, Kelly succumbed to smoking weed again. It was mostly because she missed him and his dick so very much. She was sort of in mourning.

The jail had sent a list of acceptable items that could be sent for Kevin's release. So Kelly sent him a package with his discharge gear ahead of time so that it wouldn't take all day for them to let her brother breathe. In the midst of her waiting, Dante ran across her mind. *I wonder what that nigga is up to? I hope he's okay,* she thought. She hadn't heard from him in a while and she was concerned about him. With him being a police officer and the known danger that he faced every day, she couldn't help but to be concerned. She did still love the man. Shit, now that she thought about it, Dante was right. Their lives were paralleled. She faced the same dangers as he did on a daily basis. She missed him. She had told him that she never wanted to see him or talk to him ever again, but it was all because of her loyalty to Kevin. She really didn't mean it.

"Wha's good, sis?"

"Kevin—oh my God!"

Kelly's bright face lit up even brighter as she smiled in sheer jubilation. She grabbed her baby brother and hugged him tightly. Tears of joy came rolling down her cheeks.

"Aw, come on, man, don't cry. Yo, let me look at you," he told her as he held her arms and just glared and stared at his sister. "Girl, you gon' make me kill all these niggas wit' you out here lookin' like that."

Kelly laughed. She was glad to have her brother's seal of approval.

"You ain't lookin' so bad ya'self, kid," Kelly said.

She had sent him a pair of Rocawear jeans, a brown-and-white striped button-down Sean John shirt, and a pair of chocolate-brown suede Tims. His reddish-brown dreads flooded his head and were getting in his face so he tied them up in a huge knot.

"Here," Kelly said. She reached in the backseat of the Lex and pulled out a butter soft chocolate-brown Rocawear leather stadium jacket and two platinum and diamond chains, one with the pendant of the cross and the other a medallion of the Last Supper.

"Yeah, yeah, now we talkin'. You know a nigga gotta protect his rep."

"You know I know," Kelly told him, still smiling.

Kevin slipped on the leather jacket. It felt real good, but not as good as some pussy was going to feel to him, though. That was going to be his first stop when he hit the block. He had a couple of honeys waiting on his arrival.

"Yo, let's get the fuck out of here. We've been standin' around this muthafucka way too long," Kevin said, as he walked around the car to the passenger side of the Lexus and got in.

Kelly got in and put the key in the ignition. She glanced once more at her brother. It was really good to have him home.

"This you?" Kevin asked, referring to the Lex.

"Yeah, just for right now. You know after all that shit, I had to give Buddah his joint back."

"Man, fuck that nigga, you don't need to be driving that crab-ass nigga's shit anyway. That nigga straight played hisself the way he handled that shit between y'all, but all these muthafuckas is about to catch the fucking vapors."

Kevin had been working on his master plan for a long time—five years and one month, to be exact. Nothing and no one were going to stop him from rising to the top and taking his rightful place back in his organization, the Cypress Crew. He was ready to get back to running the block, but the stakes were much higher this time around.

He wanted his turf back in Brooklyn and he had plans to take over Colonial Heights. He used to be known as the boy from the block with a very large knot. Well, he was back.

"I got you a phone. It's in the glove compartment."

Kevin opened it. He smiled. His phone wasn't the only thing in the glove compartment. His big sis knew what it was. She knew what he was coming back to: the mean streets. He placed his hands on the Kahr K9 semiautomatic pistol and pulled it out of the glove compartment. *This shit is beautiful,* he thought as he marveled at the deadly piece of steel.

"Yo, you crazy for bringing this shit up here, sis."

"Shit, I would have been crazy not to bring it."

Kevin knew she was right and he was more than glad to see that her head seemed to be in the right place. He guessed he had finally convinced her that she needed to stop buggin' out over that wack-ass cop. He reminded her of how close they had always been as siblings and that her loyalty to her family was always to come first. He didn't understand what the hell would make her want to fuck with a cop in the first place. Then she was talking even crazier than that; a street chick wanting to turn police. Who had ever heard of such a thing?

The silver Lex glided down the Cross Bronx Expressway as Kelly bobbed and weaved her Lexus through the crazy New York City traffic, listening to Rick Ross. It was Saturday afternoon and everyone seemed to be out on the road. Kevin took in the scenery of the city. He was so used to the dreariness of the pod and the hole that anything was better. He had almost forgotten what the outside world looked like, and more than that, what it felt like.

"Yo, you aight?" Kelly asked, loudly

She knew this was a big day for her brother. They both had been highly anticipating his release and now it was here. She knew he had to be bursting at the seams, ready to get back into everything and get shit poppin', but she also wanted him to be easy. It had nothing to do with Dante, it was just how shit was going down on the streets, period. There was a lot more larceny and shady shit going on with niggas and niggas was not to be trusted.

"Yeah, I'm great."

"What you over there thinking about?"

Kevin was thinking of all of the contacts he had to line up to get the supply of what he needed. His boys were already waitin' on his call. He was definitely fucking with heroin. That shit was a definite money-maker and money was the only thing that was going to gain him back the power on the streets. That nigga Siggah wasn't shit. But Kevin wasn't going to let one monkey stop no show; he was about to find out what Siggah's man Bing was all about. If he smelled bullshit, he was going to keep it moving, but for right now, this was the only train that was coming into town that he knew of, so he pretty much had to ride it.

"Thinking about all the shit we about to get into. I hope you're ready, 'cause a nigga tryin'a live a champagne life," Kevin told her as he reached for his new Verizon cell phone.

Kelly hoped that she was ready too. She believed in her brother's ability to get it poppin' on the streets again and that was honestly what she was afraid of. Kevin always liked to floss. He brought too much attention to himself. There was nothing wrong with being fly, but Kevin was just too flamboyant with it. He carried around way too much money and he was always flashing it in people's faces. That's what made them niggas rob his crew member Rich back in the day. Kelly silently hoped that in all the time her brother had to sit it down in prison that he had taken the opportunity to review his past actions and that he had realized his past mistakes.

"So this duck you been fuckin' wit', he straight laced or he go to the left?" Kevin asked, wanting to know if Kelly's man took bribes. Yeah, he hated the police, but he had no problem using the pigs for what he needed them for. If they had a cop on the payroll, they would have extra protection and shit would really be all good.

"I ain't fuckin' wit' that nigga no more, and nah, that nigga is as straight as they come."

"Shit, we gettin' ready to see so much paper even a straight pig'll wanna get some," he said with bravado.

They had made it back to Colonial Heights. Kelly had parked the car and they tried to make their way to the building, but Kevin had gotten mobbed at least three times by people who had missed him and who hadn't seen him since he had gotten locked up. He had spent a lot of his time in Colonial before he got locked up. He had pretty much started Buddah out, that's why he felt perfectly comfortable taking his place.

He heard a host of people telling him, "Damn, son, you lookin' good" and "Good to have you home, homeboy."

They had finally made it into the building and into the elevator. They had a few heads in the elevator who knew him also.

"Damn, it stinks in this muthafucka," Kevin said with his face twisted from the sour smell of the piss.

"Well, baby bruh, some things will never change," Kelly told him, smiling.

"You lookin' fresh dressed like a million bucks, my dude," one of the dudes said, while giving Kev dap.

"A'ight, a'ight," he replied.

They stepped off of the elevator and left behind some of Kevin's additional fans. Needless to say, his ego was on swoll. He knew he was home now. He was in his element. He was "the man."

"Hey there." Dora said, flirtatiously while sticking her undone head from behind her apartment door. She never knew Kevin, but she had heard a lot about him and wanted to see what the big deal was. After seeing him, she was immediately on his dick.

"Hey, how you?" Kevin asked.

"Oh, I'm fine, and so are you," she eagerly declared.

"Down Dora, yo' stinkin' ass don't miss a beat, do you? You could probably hear a pin drop with that wack-ass crack you on," Kelly said, fucking with her.

"Yeah, like when I be hearing you in there playin' wit' ya'self."

"I bet you do, you freaky bitch."

Kevin laughed as the two ladies who quickly drew claws. Kelly unlocked her apartment door and they stepped into the dark apartment.

"Surprise!"

The lights suddenly flipped on and captured Kevin's reaction. He was definitely surprised, all right. He had no idea his sister had all of this up her sleeve. All of Kevin's close friends including the members of the Cypress Crew, had gathered for a little surprise get-together to welcome her brother home. She had platters of fried chicken, fried fish, and jerk chicken, and cases of Heineken and Guinness floating around the place—all of Kevin's favorites. He saw a big cake on the table that had a picture of the both of them right before he got locked up. Kevin tried not to show his emotions, but the look on his face said it all. His sister truly went all out for his homecoming.

Trey Songz's "Bottom's Up" came on and the men were graced with yet another surprise, as three thick-ass strippers ran out of Kelly's bedroom and immediately went to work on the men in the crowd. They grinded and slithered their fat asses all over the members of the Cypress Crew. The men were prepared as they flourished the ladies with bills. Kevin wasn't thinking about tricking on no fucking stripper. He had much more important things he had planned to do with his money. He got a condom from one of his boys, grabbed the thickest, cutest one of the three and took her into the room his sister had fixed up for him to stay in until he found a place of his own.

"Yeah, baby, don't stop the show, dance for me," Kevin told her as he took a long swig of his Heineken. The cold liquid tasted so good to him. It had been a long time since he had had an ice-cold beer.

The mocha-complexioned cutie dropped it low and placed her finger in her mouth and slid it into her pussy and then back into her mouth. She then stood up and wiggled her fat ass all in Kevin's face as he sat on the bed.

"Yeah, baby, do that shit, ma, I'ma beat that pussy up. A nigga been gone for a minute," he told her as his eyes rotated with the shake of her ass. He grabbed onto her thunder thighs and pushed his freckled face between the fleshy cheeks of her chocolate ass and inhaled her femininity. He wanted to thank his sister at that very moment for knowing her baby brother so well.

Kevin turned the honey around to face him. He opened his jeans and revealed more of a tree trunk than a penis.

"Oh shit, oh hell no, no wait," the stripper cried out in protest.

"Uh-uh mama, ain't no waitin' now."

Kevin pulled her down on to his bed and held her wrist tightly with one of his strong hands, put on the Magnum his boy Leek had slipped him, and slid his dick into the stripper's hot hole.

"Aw damn, aw shit, ya' shit is a'ight, what's your name?"

"Cheyenne."

"Cheyenne, oohh Cheyenne, you got some goodness, ma, oh yeah, you wanna suck my dick, don't you?"

"Yeah, I can, if you payin'."

Kevin continued to stroke her pussy hard.

"Come on, baby, don't be like that, let me fuck that pretty mouth of yours, a nigga just comin' home. I'll get you straight later, you know who I am."

She didn't know who he was and she didn't care, she was about her paper and niggas understood that if you wanted extra services it would cost extra. He must have been gone for a long time if he thought she was giving him head for free.

"Maybe you can go and borrow the money," she said as he dug her pussy out.

*I know this bitch ain't just tell me to go borrow some money,* Kevin thought.

"Turn over," he told her.

Kevin entered her from the back. His gigantic dick invaded every piece of her hole as he fucked her. He slapped her ass harder and harder.

"Oh yeah, you're pleasing me now, there you go," he told her as he worked toward his nut. He slapped her ass as hard as he could and pushed her facedown into the pillow.

"Ah, ouch, you're hurting me," she said loudly.

"Fuck you, bitch, don't you ever tell me to go borrow money. I don't pay for pussy, bitch. Real niggas fuck for free." He continued to pummel into her. "Give me two days and I'll be able to buy and sell your ass, ah, ahhh, ahhhh, yeah bitch," Kevin said as he came.

He pulled his dick out of her and rolled the rubber off.

"Now get the fuck outta here wit' yo' trick-ass so I can be on to the next muthafuckin' one," Kevin told her as he placed his dick back into his pants and zipped it up.

The female did as she was told as she grabbed her things up and quickly put them on. It didn't take her long. All she had on was a thong and some frilly little top. She burst into Kelly's living room where her girls were still doing their thing and getting their dough. She looked back and saw Kevin coming out of the room. She said fuck the money and her girls and frantically raced past Kelly and out of the apartment.

"What the fuck," Kelly said, as the girl nearly took Kelly's shoulder out of the door with her.

Kelly turned to see her brother bragging to his boys and grabbing his dick. She guessed that the chick was scared by her brother's anaconda. Oh, she knew her brother was hung; she used to change his diapers when he was a baby.

"Yo, y'all niggas hurry up with these ladies. We got some business to discuss," Kevin told his boys.

Kevin and the other members of the Cypress Crew partied with the strippers for another hour before he stressed the importance once again of them getting down to business. Kelly paid the woman who catered the affair and took care of the two hostesses who came to help keep the food trays circulating. The boys had laced the strippers with plenty of bills, plus she had hit them off with a base of 250 dollars each, so they were straight. It had been a long Saturday and night. Kelly was tired and ready to lay it down.

"Yo, baby bruh, you need me?" she asked, wearily. Kelly knew that Kevin needed to kick it with his crew and she felt that they needed to bond as men, without the presence of a female.

"Hell yeah, I need you, you my big sis," he said, feeling no pain. The few beers he had had already soaked into his system.

Kevin commanded everyone's attention as he brought his first meeting of the renewed and renowned Cypress Crew to order.

"I just wanna say it's good to see all y'all niggas again, man. I ain't want nobody to come see me when I was locked up, but it's real good seeing y'all right now," Kevin said.

"You too, man," Rayvon said.

"No doubt," Leek added.

"Yeah, yeah, no doubt, Leek, my man, that's right, ain't no doubt we about to take over these muthafuckin' streets. This city is ours. Colonial is ours and our turf out in Bed-Stuy is ours."

His men agreed while Kelly listened.

"And I'm tellin' y'all niggas right now. I don't want to hear shit about no fuckin' police. Unless they tryin'a be down wit' us, them niggas don't exist to me. We gotsta get money, fuck da police," Kevin chanted.

"What we gotsta do?" Rayvon asked, sauced up.

"We gotsta get money. Fuck da police," Leek confirmed.

"That's right my niggas, and yo, word to my dead muva, if I see that punk-ass bitch-ass police that fuckin' deaded my life for five years, I'm gon' dead that nigga for good."

# Chapter 11

## *Rude Awakening*

It only took three months for Kevin and his crew to fully get back on their game. People had been telling Kevin that there was a recession. Kevin and his crew was seeing about thirty thou' a week; he didn't know what a fucking recession was. Rayvon had his coke connect in Brooklyn and Bing was in the Bronx serving his purpose. His heroin connect was more than on time. They moved the work out just as quickly as the work came in. The Cypress Crew was well on their way to fulfilling his prediction of them taking over.

Interestingly enough, once the drugs started flowing through the veins of all of the fiends in the hood, Kelly being a possible snitch didn't matter. Shit, it was her brother that was hooking up the hood and that's all they cared about. Even the niggas that had mad love for Buddah were on the program. Drugs and money had a way of making everything all right in the hood.

There was a bit more of a police presence in Colonial Heights after Chop's death and Buddah's arrest, but that didn't stop the men from operating. They were just extra careful about it. Kelly was positioned at the very front of the building. She sat on the bench all day and damn near all night and all she did was look out. She saw everyone that came in and out. Leek was positioned in the basement for any surprise visitors. And Rich was the alternate. They had headsets letting each other know who was moving and where.

Kelly watched as squad cars rode back and forth trying to cause a panic, but she wasn't pressed. One word on her headset and everything would be shut down. The main issue was dealing with the undercovers that they still managed to squeeze through. She had sent two away in this day alone and it was only one in the afternoon.

"Ay' Leek," Kelly said, as she positioned the mic of the headset.

"Yeah, what up Kells?"

"I need to take a break," she told him. Kelly had been in front of the building since five a.m.

"A'ight, I'll call Rich and have him come down."

Inside his sister's apartment, Kevin sat in his room, counting money, "Twenty, forty, sixty, eighty, one; twenty, forty, sixty, eighty, two; twenty, forty, sixty, eighty, three."

Rich watched as he counted and counted and counted. Kevin couldn't believe all of the money they were seeing. If he wasn't mistaken, he had just counted nine stacks and the working fiends hadn't even copped yet. Kevin's mouth contoured into a sinister smile as he thought about his current financial position. Rich was smiling also. If Kevin was straight, then his team was straight also.

"Rich," Leek called.

"Yeah, yeah," Rich responded. His headset was in place and he was ready to be instructed.

"Kelly needs you in front."

"A'ight."

"Yo, you good?" Rich asked Kevin before he turned to leave.

"I'm great," Kevin said, contented.

Rich left Kevin alone with his money and with his thoughts. Kevin's mind darted back to his years in prison and how he dreamed of all of what was now in front of him. He was the muthafuckin' man, in his own opinion. Who the fuck could come straight out of prison and do what he did in ninety days? He could see the champagne-colored '10 Mercedes S500 that was on somebody's car lot just waiting for him.

His thoughts were interrupted by the slamming of the apartment's front door. Kevin immediately ran out strapped with his new Kahr K9. Once he saw that it was only his sister, he put the weapon in the waist of his Sean John jeans.

"Ay, sis, what up?"

"What's up is you and all of these muthafuckas all up in my crib fuckin' my shit up," Kelly yelled as she ripped her headset off.

"What you talkin' 'bout yo?"

"I'm talkin' about all of these fuckin' scales and shit, residue, cigar wraps and Black and Milds all over the fuckin' place. Niggas in here eatin', ain't nobody washin' no fuckin' dishes. I'm out all day and night and I come in here and can't even take a fuckin' shower 'cause y'all niggas ain't cleanin' up the tub when y'all done. This shit ain't workin'.'"

"The fuck it ain't workin'! Take yo' ass in my room and look at all that cash and you'll see how much this shit is workin'.'"

"Kevin, this is my crib, yo, not a fuckin' drug house or no trash can."

"Who cares, we gettin' mad fuckin' money. And put your fuckin' headset back on."

"Yeah, Kev, I know we gettin' money, the entire block knows we gettin' money, that's the fuckin' problem. Yo we need to get out of Colonial. This shit is too hot."

"We ain't goin' no fuckin' where, we gon' keep pumpin' right here. Shit, this where the money at. We ain't even seeing it like this in Brooklyn."

"Kevin, you're not going to come in here and disrespect me and my fuckin' crib. It ain't like you don't have money for a place. You got mad cake. You can live anywhere you want."

"I like living here with you."

Kelly could tell that her brother was staying in her way on purpose. He just wanted to cock-block just in case she got weak and tried to see Dante.

"You fuckin' up Kevin, you not thinking with your head because you caught up in this money."

"Shit, the last time I looked around, yo' ass was caught up in it too."

Kelly couldn't deny that she was making more money than she ever had before, but she wasn't as happy as she was when she was with Dante. She had also been peeping the scene and she could tell the police wasn't going to keep their distance for much longer.

"I'm on the frontline, baby bruh, and I see a change coming. I'm telling you, you need to seriously consider calming Colonial down."

"I ain't calming shit down, sis, now I'm sorry about the condition of ya' crib and I got you, but we niggas, and we don't get that type of shit," he told her.

"Y'all keep on fuckin' up my house and a bitch'll fly south for the winter."

Kelly went to her bedroom. That was the only part of the apartment that had yet to be invaded by the filth. She removed her black leather bubble and unzipped her jeans. Her bed was a welcome place as she lay across it. *Fuck this headset. This shit keeps messing up my hair anyway,* she thought. Her brother was out of control. And he hadn't been home six months yet. She was worried that he was going right back to the place he had just come out from and wanted so bad to get out of. And if she wasn't careful, she would be joining him. Kelly was disgusted with her brother and his crew. They were treating her apartment like a drug den. Dante was a man and he ain't got that type of shit. His home was immaculate and she missed it. More than that, she missed Dante. She hadn't been doing so good trying to keep him out of her head. Every time a squad car passed by or an undercover cop came up she was looking, hoping to see his face.

It had been over a month since she had seen Dante's number come across her phone. He used to call every day, but she never answered. He would also text her to let her know that he would always love her and that he would always be thinking of her. She guessed that he finally got tired of not receiving a reply. Kelly wondered if he was seeing someone new. Her heart hoped that he wasn't. She began singing Fantasia's "Bittersweet" in her head.

Her break was almost over, fifteen more minutes and she was going to have to go back to her post. The more she was out on the block, the more she thought about joining the Police Academy. Kelly went over to her hamper that held clean clothes and linens and grabbed a washcloth and towel. She went into the bathroom to wash up quickly so that she could feel fresh for the second half of her shift. She wanted to scream when she saw the toilet seat up, with pounds of piss and a pile of shit in the toilet. The sink and the bathtub were covered with mold and mildew. Kelly flushed the toilet and immediately left the bathroom. She couldn't even use her own shower. She was more than heated. Her cell phone was ringing in her bedroom and she ran to answer it. Buddah was calling. She wasn't going to, but she went ahead and accepted the call.

"Hello," she said.

"Yo, I need you to pay for my lawyer."

"Oh so now you need me, nigga, didn't you hang up in my face?'

"Come on Kells, I mean, shit, what the fuck was I supposed to think?"

"You was supposed to know that I wasn't no fuckin' snitch."

"Look, Kells, I got word that ya' girl Laquisha was sayin' some foul shit about you gettin' a cop's number and you fuckin this nigga and the next thing I know I'm gettin' knocked."

"Fuck that bitch. Her fuckin' word don't hold no muthafuckin' weight."

"I don't give a fuck about the bitch either, but I need to get up out of this piece. They ain't even tryin'a give a nigga no bond. I ain't even do no serious shit, yo, they on some straight bullshit."

"Yeah, no doubt," Kelly agreed, thinking back to how many times they tried to slap whatever charges they wanted on her ass.

"So I can count on you, Kells?"

"Yeah, I got you," Kelly said.

"Thas what it do, yo, Kells . . ."

"Yeah?"

"Yo, my mistake, yo."

"It's all good," Kelly told him.

Kelly figured the least she could do for Buddah was to pay for his lawyer. He had looked out for her for years and everyone was entitled to make mistakes. She knew how Laquisha ran her mouth, so she believed Buddah's story. Kevin happened to be walking by Kelly's room on his way to his own when he had overheard the conversation. Kevin wasn't trying to have Buddah come out and interrupt his monetary flow. Everything was working perfectly, every day was sunny; it only rained money. He joined his sister in her bedroom.

"Ay, what the fuck that nigga squawkin' about now?"

"He asked me if I could pay for his lawyer."

"I hope you told that nigga to kiss your yellow ass."

"No, I told him I would handle it."

"Man, fuck that nigga. After the way he turned on you, we ain't paying for shit for that bitch-ass muthafucka. Tell his ass I fuckin' said so."

"Yo, Kev, that ain't right. He made a mistake and he admitted it."

"I don't want that nigga in Colonial no fuckin' more. That nigga gon' come out and try to get his block back and ain't no haps on that shit. "

Kelly looked at her brother as if he she didn't know who he was because she was beginning to doubt that she did. Prison had changed him immensely. He was selfish and greedy and had no compassion for anyone. Kelly recognized that he was getting a lot of money and that he couldn't be soft, but he was shittin' on niggas that didn't deserve to be shitted on. She was going to find a way to get Buddah's lawyer paid up. To Kelly, it was simply the right thing to do.

"Where the fuck is your headset?" he yelled.

"Right here," she yelled back, as she grabbed it up and put it back on her head.

"Don't do that shit, Kelly, yo. You need to be gettin' back out there," Kevin told her.

"I'm going," she said as she sucked her teeth and grabbed her jacket. *Yeah this nigga done came out and flipped the fuck out,* she thought

"Hold the fuck up," he said to her as he grabbed her arm.

Kevin knew he wasn't looking at who he thought he was looking at.

"What the fuck is wrong wit' you, Kevin?" Kelly knew her brother was truly bugging now that he was putting his hands on her.

Kevin held up a framed picture of Dante that had been on Kelly's dresser. He grimaced.

"I know this ain't the duck you was fuckin' wit?" he asked harshly.

"Yeah, that's him, why?"

Kevin threw the picture against the wall, shattering the glass frame that it was encased in.

"That's the bitch-ass muthafucka that fucked my life up! I don't believe you was fuckin' with this nigga!" Kevin said with his teeth clenched and his hands balled up into fists.

"What? Dante is the cop who arrested you?" Kelly asked. She was hoping he was wrong. Maybe Dante *looked* like the same cop, but it couldn't be.

"Hell yeah, that's that muthafucka, I'll never forget that muthafucka's face."

Kelly's mind was reeling. She didn't know how to feel or what to think. With a lost expression on her face, and without saying a word, she zipped up her jeans, fixed her shirt, put on her bubble jacket, adjusted her headset, walked past her brother, and left her apartment.


Dante was sitting in his living room with a glass of Jack Daniel's in his hand. He had been drinking most of the day. Nightfall was upon them and he was still drinking. Dante thought back to the night that Kelly tore his heart out. He replayed the story of her brother and his arrest. Dante remembered that night very well, but he wouldn't dare make matters worse by telling Kelly that he had that same scenario go down and that he might very well be the punk-ass police officer that she was talking about. Kelly's account of the story brought back memories for him, memories that he had been trying to forget for the past five years.

His partner had come by to check on him. It was the second day that he had called out of work and she was concerned. Dante looked like shit. His partner could tell he was suffering. Dante sat wishing that he had never responded to the call that day on Broadway. He wished he had never met Kelly. If he had never met her he wouldn't be hurting so badly. Dante would have given anything to have Kelly back in his life. Why he loved her so, he had no earthly idea, but he couldn't deny the strong feelings he had for her. It was almost as if he felt responsible for her.

"Have you tried calling her?" Officer Brown asked.

Officer Deborah Brown had been Dante's partner for the past five years. They were rookies when she started out with him and they worked well together. The other officers at the precinct always messed with Dante and Deborah about their relationship. Most of the other officers thought for sure that they were more than just partners on the job. Rumors that they were sleeping together flooded the locker room on a regular basis. They both learned to ignore it. They had a great friendship and they didn't care what anyone said.

"She won't answer," Dante said, as he poured another glass of Jack.

"You're just going to have to give her some time."

"Her crazy-ass brother is probably in her ear telling her all kinds of bullshit about me."

"She knows who you really are, Dante. She'll come around."

Dante didn't know when that would be. He knew that Kelly was being placed in a very tough predicament. To have to choose between her brother and her lover was going to be beyond difficult. It just wasn't fair. But Dante had been a police officer in the city's toughest streets, so he was very well aware of the fact that life was anything but fair.

"All I wanted to do was make her life better."

"Dante, that's something she has to want for herself."

"She does want it. I know damn well she does."

He took another swig of his drink and slammed his glass down on his glass coffee table, shattering the glass of liquor on impact. He was willing to do whatever it took to make her life better, no matter what it took and if that meant not seeing her anymore, then regrettably that's what it had to be. But he owed it to the both of them to try to reach her just one more time.

Dante got up and grabbed his .45 and his overcoat.

"Dante, don't—"

"I'm going over there, Deb, I need to see her. I need to talk to her, I—I need to kiss her, Deb."

Deborah knew Dante and she knew that he had had way too much to drink. There was no way she was going to let him drive like that, especially to Colonial Heights. They would eat his ass alive.

"Dante, you're in no condition to go over there right now. Trust me, it's not a good idea. Sleep it off and try it again tomorrow, okay, sweetie?"

Dante wasn't trying to hear what Deborah was saying. He respected her as a partner and he appreciated her as a friend, but Kelly was the love of his life and all was fair in love and war as far as he was concerned.

"No, I'm going over there right now and ain't nobody stoppin' me."

Kelly had had a long night and she was glad that it was finally over. Although she was tired, she was determined to take a shower. Unwillingly, she cleaned the soiled tub and the entire bathroom. Kelly gathered her toiletries and her bathrobe and retreated to her freshly disinfected bathroom. Relief came to her weary body as the hot water ran over her velvety skin. She was still trying to put her thoughts and feelings in perspective about Dante's role in her brother's downfall in relation to how she felt about him. She was extremely torn between the two men in her life.

"Kev," Leek yelled over the headset.

"Yeah," he answered. Kevin never slept. He was obsessed with his newfound fortune and felt one minute of sleep could leave his business in a compromising position.

"Yo, we got a situation," Leek yelled. But before he could say what the situation was there was a pounding on Kelly's apartment door.

"Ay, who the fuck is banging on my fuckin' door?" Kevin yelled as he grabbed up his K9 and went straight to the door, unlocked and opened it. Kevin gasped. He was suddenly staring in the face of the man who had sent him off to prison. The man who made tears stream down his mother's eyes in the courtroom as they sentenced her baby to five years in the state penitentiary. The man who ruined his life and now was trying to ruin his sister's life by stealing her away from the only brother she ever had. He wanted to use his K9 to split open Dante's skull.

When Dante's eyes fell upon Kevin it had confirmed everything that he had been ruminating on. And it all made sense now: The reason Kelly had been acting so erratic and not returning his calls. Kelly's brother was the case that Dante could never forget. The case he used to have nightmares about as a rookie. Dante felt that Kelly had to be fighting an incredible battle within her own self. All he wanted to do was to see her, to talk to her, to hold her. But in more ways than one, Kevin was in his way.

"Is Kelly here?"

"Muthafucka, even if she was here, what makes you think I would tell your bitch-ass?"

"Look, I didn't come here to start any trouble."

"Oh no, then what the fuck did you come here for? Huh? How the hell did you even get in here?" Kevin asked. He was going to be checkin' Leek and Rich for their inadequacy.

"I need to see Kelly," Dante said.

"Oh, you need to see her, huh? Nah, nigga what you need to see is my K9 up in yo' mutha-fuckin' face."

"Don't forget, Kevin, I'm still a police officer, and whether I'm in uniform or out of uniform, you're threatening an officer of the law."

"Man, muthafuck you all day. You put me away, nigga, I didn't even get to spend my mama's last days with her."

"I apologize for that, man, but I didn't come here to relive the past."

"Oh yeah, what the fuck you come here for then? You damn sure ain't come here thinkin' you was gon' see my sister, 'cause you ain't seein' her."

Kevin was outside of his sister's apartment door, raising pure Cain in the hallway. A few of the other tenants, including Dora, opened their doors to see what was going on.

"Y'all get back in ya' muthafuckin' cribs, man, ain't nobody fuckin' talking to none a' y'all," Kevin told them, waving his gun.

"You know something, yo' ass is drunk. I bet you you ain't tell a muthafuckin' soul you was comin' over here, so if I popped yo' muthafuckin' ass right now, who would even know?"

"You would know."

"I wouldn't give a fuck."

"Kelly would know."

"She wouldn't give a fuck either," Kevin told him.

"Well, I would," Deborah said with her 9 mm pointed at Kevin as she stepped into hallway. She had been in the staircase the whole time. "Now, where is she?"

Dante was tired of listening to Kevin's empty threats. He knew how much Kevin hated him. He knew that if Kevin really wanted to shoot him then he would have shot him. Now he just needed to persuade him to allow him to talk to Kelly.

"You know I would think you would be happy about your sister dating an upstanding citizen instead of a thug, like yourself," Dante said sarcastically.

Kevin swung at Dante and Dante grabbed Kevin's fist and held it inside of his own. Deborah stood still holding her 9 mm on Kevin. She silently wished that Dante would stop talking. That was hardly the statement that was going to make Kevin change his mind. But she shortly realized that even intoxicated, Dante was still in police mode and what he was doing was trying to cause a commotion so that if Kelly was inside she would be forced to come out to see what was going on.

His plan was successful. Kelly had come out of the shower and heard all of the noise coming from her hallway. She threw on some shorts and a T-shirt and grabbed her .380 and went to join her brother in battle. She was stopped in her tracks when she saw who her brother's opponent was.

"Dante, yo, what are you doing here?" Kelly asked him in amazement.

"Kelly, I need to see you, baby," he told her.

"Of all of the pigs, it had to be this swine-ass stinkin'-ass nigga," Kevin said, looking like a hungry pit bull that was ready to have Dante as his next meal.

"Dante, why did you come all the way to the projects this late at night?" Kelly asked.

"Why the hell do you think, Kelly? I love you, baby. I don't care who knows it. I need you."

Dante's expression was a dispirited one, but Kelly was there, she was in front of him and he could physically see her; that alone made him feel better. The look on Kelly's face was a distant one. She had gone back to her life in Colonial Heights. She was now looking out for her brother's drug operation. And even though she played with thoughts of going to the Police Academy and being back in Dante's arms, her brother made sure that she understood, cop-lover or not, she was never to turn her back on her flesh and blood.

"I would give anything to see you smile," Dante said as he looked at Kelly with such desire.

Kelly couldn't smile. Instead, she wanted to break down and cry. She wanted him to go home. The sight of him reminded her of what she was leaving behind.

"Don't let your brother turn your world upside down."

"Fuck that, Dante, don't blame him, because it's you who turned my world upside down. It was you who had my brother locked up and it was you who testified against him and it was you who had my mother crying her heart out in court when they took him away. And I hate you for that shit, Dante, I swear to God I do! How can I ever trust you?"

"I was doing my job, Kelly."

"So, doing your job gives you the right to deceive someone you claim to love? I don't know if I want to join the force if it means deceiving and lying to the people I love."

*Join the force? Did I just hear her say she doesn't know if she wants to join the force?* Kevin and Dante thought at the exact same time.

"You played a major part in my brother's arrest and incarceration, and we can't forget about your part in Buddah's arrest and incarceration. Who's next, Dante, me?" Kelly asked angrily.

Dante understood Kelly's anger. He could see that she really did need some time to get her thoughts together. And as much as it killed him, he was going to have to let her be who she thought she was until she believed in herself to be who she was truly meant to be.

Kelly went back into her apartment and into her bedroom. She laid on her bed and cried. Seeing Dante was too much for her. It didn't matter to her now what he had done in the past. She missed him so much that her heart was literally aching. She could tell he had been drinking; she could smell it on his breath. Kelly knew that he was hurting just as much if not more than she was.

"I guess you know what time it is, huh, dawg?" Kevin asked Dante. He was glad that his sister made the right choice.

"Yeah, dawg, I know exactly what time it is, and you better know too," Dante told him, as he and Deborah left the way they came, through the staircase door.

# Chapter 12

*Choices*

"I just wanna hold you in my arms, can I do that?" Dante asked.

"Yes, please, baby, please hold me." Kelly needed to feel his strength around her. She needed his power to seep into her soul so that she could embody the strength and power that she was going to need to tell her brother that she was going to quit the drug game and become a police officer.

The day Dante left Kelly's apartment he had taken her heart with him and she hadn't been the same. A piece of her was missing and as soon as she had a free day she drove out to Dante's house and used the key that she had never returned. The very moment she saw him she felt whole and she knew that there would be no turning back. The moment he saw her he knew that his prayers had been answered and that he served an awesome God.

They held each other tightly as they lay naked in his bed. Dante was so thankful for Kelly having the guts to do what her heart was calling her to do. He knew what she was made out of. He had always known. Dante released Kelly from his grip and looked into her eyes. He had missed her so. He allowed his lips to feel the tenderness of her silky skin as he ran them across her neck. He rested his head and placed it on her shoulder and looked up at her.

"I love you, Kelly Morgan."

"I love you too, Dante Evans."

"I've been waiting for you," he told her, seductively.

Dante engulfed her in his arms and kissed her deeply. He slid his caramel body on top of her. His dick got hard instantly. Kelly smiled. She liked the way his dick responded to her presence. She parted her legs so that he could slide on in. Dante slid his hand down and played with her clit before he entered her.

"Oh, yes, I missed you, baby," she told him. She was getting wetter and wetter by each stroke of his finger.

He dipped his finger inside of her wet pussy and slid it in and out a couple of times.

"Stop teasing me. Give me my dick," she told him.

Dante did as his lady asked. Placing his hot dick in Kelly was like placing his arm in the sleeve of a shirt that had just come out of the dryer. He loved the warm sensation. *Damn, her pussy is nice and wet, wet, warm, and wonderful,* he thought. His body moved up and down and his dick moved in and out of her love. Kelly hadn't been with anyone else sexually. She didn't want to be. It would have been futile. Dante was the best. And she was in complete ecstasy.

"Yes, oh yes, give me my dick," she panted.

Dante rammed his dick up in her. He wanted to make sure that she was getting all of the dick that she needed. He ran his hands from her head to her neck to her arms to her waist as he grabbed her ass and skillfully made love to her.

"Aah, ahh, I love you, Dante. I love you baby," she said as her body jerked uncontrollably.

Dante sped up his strokes and dug his finger in her asshole and enjoyed the sensation as she came all over his dick. His cum came in waves like that of an ocean at high tide. He then guided himself to glory as his dick exploded with liquid and flooded her pussy even more.

"Oh my God, Kelly," Dante said.

She giggled. She felt the same way. Their lovemaking was soul-stirring. They lay together in each other's arms, smiling. Neither one of them had ever felt so good. Kelly wished the feeling could last forever, but she knew she had to get back to Colonial. Even though it was her day off, Kevin was bugging more than ever since Dante had showed up at the apartment. He was convinced that if Dante could get past Leek and Rich any other cop could too.

"I gotta get ready to go," Kelly told him regretfully.

"Aw, come on, Kelly, you just got here," he pleaded.

"I know, baby, but you've seen how crazy Kevin is. Ever since he saw you, he's been even crazier. I have to keep things cool around there."

"Kelly you'd better convince your brother to cool out around there, period. You know they've been watching all that shit. They're just letting him dig his own grave by waiting to get him on something big. He's too visible. He's not operating in a smart manner at all."

Kelly knew that Dante was right. She appreciated the fact that he had tipped her off about them watching her brother, although she already knew, it was nice to know that he was on her side.

"Dante, this whole thing with my brother is a big headache. I've been telling him to stop pumping in Colonial. He won't listen to me," she said. "I'm ready to get on a fuckin' plane and just be out."

"Running away isn't going to solve anything. The only place you need to be running is on the track when you start training in two weeks at the academy."

"You know, I'm really excited about that," Kelly told him, smiling. She was extremely excited. She just didn't know how she was going to get her baby brother to digest the information.

"You promise to come back as soon as you can?" he asked her.

"I promise," she said, as she kissed him and left his bed.


Kelly had made it back to the hood. It was almost eight in the evening. She saw the usual people doing the usual things. A couple of niggas were getting their hair braided by some hood chicks on the bench in front of the building. Leek was in front of the building with his headset in place, playing dice with a couple of the neighborhood heads.

"Leek," Kelly called.

Leek stopped what he was doing and came over to check Kelly.

"What's good, Kelly? You enjoying your day off?"

"I guess, if that's what you call it. Nigga, you out here playin' games and you supposed to be lookin' out."

"I got this shit, Kelly. You ain't the only one who can cover the front."

"Man, Leek, fuck the front, our front, back and sides need to be covered out this muthafucka. Where's my brother at?"

"Where is he always at?"

Kelly knew the answer to her question. She went up to her apartment, but before she went to her door, she went to Dora's apartment and rang her bell. It took a while for her to come to the door, but she finally did.

"What the hell do you want?" Dora asked her.

Kelly pushed passed her and went into her apartment. She couldn't take the chance of her brother hearing or seeing what she was about to do.

"Here," she told Dora, handing her an envelope.

Dora looked in the envelope and saw more money than she had ever seen in her life. Her immediate thought was the amount of crack she could buy. She was getting ready to shit all on herself thinking of how high she was going to be able to get.

"Now look here, bitch, I'm puttin' this shit in your crackhead-ass hands. There's five thousand dollars in there and I'm telling Buddah that I gave it to you. If for some reason you don't get this shit to his lawyer for him to get a bond, that's your ass. You'd better smoke your ass into an overdose if I have to come see you for my fuckin' money, Dora, so do the right thing and go get your dick out of jail."

Kelly looked both ways before she left Dora's apartment to go back into her own. She wanted to make sure no one saw her, especially Kevin. If he knew that she was helping to get Buddah out of jail he would surely lose it. She knew she was taking a huge chance putting the money in Dora's hands, but Kelly knew deep down that Dora loved Buddah and she was going to take that money—at least most of it—straight to the lawyer to try to get him a bond.

Walking toward the back of her apartment, she heard sounds coming from Kevin's room. The moans and groans were more than Kelly wanted to hear. He was in her crib fucking some chick and she didn't even fuck niggas in her own crib. That was it! He was disrespecting her space and she was tired of it. The operation had to come to an end and Kevin had to take his ass elsewhere and live and be the grown man that he was.

Listening a little more closely, Kelly realized she recognized the female's voice. She was trying to make out what they were saying, but they sounded like Waka Flaka to her so she couldn't understand a word of what they were saying with the door closed. Kevin's bedroom door flew open and Kelly confirmed her suspicion of who the trick bitch was that her brother had just bagged.

"You know, you's a trifling bitch," Kelly told Laquisha. "You gon' tell Buddah some snake-ass shit about me being a snitch, and then you come in my muthafuckin' crib and fuck my brother wit' ya' ho ass? Kevin you betta not give this trick-ass ho no fuckin' money. Get the fuck out my crib, bitch."

Kelly charged at Laquisha. Laquisha wasn't fully dressed, but that didn't matter when a bitch was coming at your head. Kelly's fist landed in Laquisha's face. She reached for Kelly's signature ponytail and pulled it, trying to get a face hit of her own. Kevin wasn't having it. He grabbed Laquisha by the waist to get her off of his sister.

"Fuck that bitch, let her go," Kelly said, wanting to get some more of her.

"Kelly," Kevin yelled.

"What?" she yelled back.

"Stop, we got too much to lose," he told her.

"Then why you got this thieving-ass bitch up in my crib if we got so much to lose? You fuckin' up. Out of all the bitches you could fuck, why her? This bitch got five kids working on ten and what, you want to be on Maury seeing if you one of her fuckin' baby daddies? This bitch is a baby-maker. I hope you had a rubber on."

Kelly didn't want to say too much in front of Laquisha. She just wanted the bitch out of her crib. She knew that Laquisha didn't mean her any good and she didn't want her around any longer. Laquisha had managed to get all of her clothes back on. She didn't care what Kelly was saying about her; she had just fucked the nigga that was getting all the paper in the hood and that was a notch in her hood belt.

"Get her the fuck out of here, Kevin," Kelly told him as she straightened herself out.

"Ay, yo, I'll holla at you," Kevin told Laquisha as he walked her to the door.

Kevin quickly came back into his room where his sister was still standing.

"You know I just don't know about you, yo. On one hand you're one of the smartest brothers I know, then on the other hand you're the dumbest muthafucka I know," Kelly said.

"A nigga just wanted some pussy, man," he admitted.

"Pussy has been a lot of niggas' downfall. And I bet when they think about it, the pussy wasn't even worth it," Kelly said. "Why that bitch? You already know she ain't shit. Why the fuck you ain't go to a hotel? It ain't like you don't have the money. She's a snake bitch. You talkin' about me and Dante—"

"You and who? Oh, so you been fuckin' wit' that stickin'-ass pig again, that's why you been actin' all strange lately. So now what, Kelly, you gonna choose that pig over your own brother?"

"You know what, Kevin, he's a pig and you're a dog, what's the difference, is one better than the other?"

"Kelly, I'm your blood."

"Kevin, you're getting ready to land your ass right back in jail and you don't even see it. Fuck who I'm sleeping with."

"What the fuck are you talking about?"

"Dante said the police have been watching everything and that they're just waiting for the right time to bust this shit open. I told you before that we needed to calm Colonial down. It's just too fuckin' hot."

Kevin took in the information that his sister had given him. He wasn't trying to go back to jail. Maybe it was time that he shut it down and move everything out to Brooklyn where nobody was on the radar.

"So this muthafucka is gonna try to take me down again?"

"Kevin, Dante is not on a mission to fuck wit' you. He just told me what he knew to tip us off. And he didn't have to do that."

"Man, fuck that nigga. I'll kill that nigga!"

"Kill him for what, for trying to keep you out of jail?"

Kevin looked at his sister as she broke it down to him. He had to admit she wasn't the same woman he had left behind before he went in to do his bid. The Kelly he left behind was an eager chick, a ride-or-die chick, who went hard in the streets for whatever her heart desired. She didn't think about tomorrow, she was satisfied with ballin' out for the day and then *if* tomorrow came she would figure out how to do it all over again. The Kelly he was looking at now was still a ride-or-die chick, but he could tell that she cared very much about her future, and his.

"So what the fuck, we just gon' shut it down, just like that?" Kevin asked.

Kelly's look said it all. Hell yeah, they were going to shut it down, just like that.

After arguing with her brother, she went into her bedroom and called Dante back.

"Hey, it's me," she said, flustered.

"Hey baby is everything okay?" Dante asked. He was really concerned about her.

"Yeah, I'm good, but there's been a change in plans, I've got some things that I have to handle before I come back out there, so don't wait up."

"Kelly, I know you, you're about to go and get yourself into something crazy."

"You want me to be a cop, right?"

She knew that would shut him up.

"Of course I do, baby, you know that, but I want you to want it too."

"I do want it. I want it very badly, but I have to bring this life to an end if I want my new life to begin."

Dante couldn't argue with that and he didn't.

"Do what you have to, Kelly. But if I don't see you or hear from you within a week, I'll be coming to Colonial to look for you. You have a class to start."

Kelly couldn't argue with him and she didn't. He had given her a week. She hoped that was enough time. She knew that he would do just what he said and she didn't want Dante back in Colonial.

"I know I didn't just hear you tell this mutha-fucka that you want to be a pig?" Kevin asked in dismay.

"Yes, I want to be a police officer, Kevin, a devil, a pig, all of the above. It's what I want."

"This nigga got you all fucked up. He must have really put it on yo' ass," Kevin said, laughing on the outside, but on the inside there was nothing funny. He was losing his money-making turf and his sister.

"Kevin, I'm just not fuckin' with this shit anymore. It's not worth the risk. The money was good while it lasted. We can do some things with it to legalize this shit and keep it moving. It's time for you to decide what you wanna to do with your life, besides grind, because that's only going to land you back behind bars eventually, and you know it," Kelly told her brother.

In his heart of hearts, Kevin knew that his sister was right, but he didn't know of any profession that would lace his pockets with the type of money he was making. He was a felon. He couldn't run get a job, like she could so his choices were a little different but he was going to make it a point of trying to figure something out. Secretly, he admired his sister for having the balls to want something more out of life than what the hood had to offer her. In the meantime, he had to figure out the best way to ease up out of Colonial.

Three days had gone by. Kelly had called Dante to let him know that she was wrapping things up in Colonial and that her brother didn't give her as much of a fight as she thought he would.

Dante was glad to hear that. He saw something in Kevin's eyes the night they stood face-to-face. He didn't quite know what it was then, but now he could see that Kevin had matured in his time away. The Kevin he accosted five years before wouldn't have hesitated to pull the trigger when he saw Dante at his door.

"I'm going downstairs to finalize some shit with the boys," Kevin told Kelly.

"A'ight, don't be fuckin' around with them too long, Kevin. You got shit you need to pack up too."

Kelly began packing up her clothes. She had no idea how she was going to get all of her shoes out of there. Dante had asked her to move in with him and she readily accepted. Kelly was in a majestic mood. She was ready to start training at the Police Academy. Living with Dante would only give her more insight on the life of a police officer and she welcomed the opportunity, not to mention she would be up close and personal with the man who possessed the best dick and head she had ever had. It just didn't get any better than that.

Kevin had made arrangements to go back to Brooklyn and live with Rayvon until he got his own place. He was still fresh on the scene from prison and since he had been held up in Colonial the whole time, he wasn't sure of where he really wanted to live, so until he made a solid decision: he and Rayvon would be roommates. Rayvon wasn't trying to quit grinding quite yet and Kevin wasn't either, but he was old enough to make his own decisions. Kelly told him he would have to live with the choices he made.

Leek was out in the front of the building. He was still on post. They had two more days and then Colonial Heights would be a wrap. The loyal fiends had been prepared and told where they could find some good diesel. Kevin wasn't stupid; he knew that even though his time may have been up in Colonial that there was still going to be drug sales made and since he had invested so much into the neighborhood, he felt that it was only right that he get a cut of the profits. Leek would be the man to keep it pumping along with a few new fearless recruits.

"Everything good out here?" Kevin asked him.

"Yeah, I mean, I seen a couple'a ducks, but I ain't give 'em no love."

"Yeah, yo, they comin' on strong. Shit, we may need to wrap this shit up tonight."

"Word?" Those were words Leek never expected to hear from his boss.

"Ay yo, Kev," Buddah called.

Kevin saw Buddah coming his way. He wasn't expecting to see him. He thought he was still locked up. It had been a long time since Kevin had physically seen Buddah. When Kevin came out of jail Buddah had just gone to jail.

"Yo, Buddah, what it do." Kevin put his hand out to give Buddah dap and was met with a gunshot to the chest. "Blou!"

Buddah held the gun to Kevin's head and pulled the trigger again. "Blou!"

Kevin lay still in a pool of blood in front of the building. Leek couldn't believe what was happening. He didn't know what to do. Leek didn't have a gun on him because of all of the extra attention they had been getting from the police. He used his headset to tell Rich and Kelly. He looked at Kevin and saw that there was no need to call 911. He was dead.

"Yo, they just shot Kev," he yelled into the mouthpiece.

Kelly didn't have her headset on, but it was near her and she thought she had just heard Leek say that they had shot Kev. *Please God, please, please, no, please.* Kelly put her headset on and heard Rich and Leek crying. She knew that it was true. She grabbed her gun and ran out of her apartment. Kelly didn't wait for the elevator. She ran down the stairs with her mind racing in a thousand different directions. Visions of her mother flashed through her head, followed by visions of her brother when he was a baby, then a little boy, then them together as teenagers. Kelly hit the lobby of her building and ran outside. She saw a crowd standing around and she went dead into it. She was halted in her tracks by the horrid sight of what was left of her brother. Kelly fell to her knees and threw herself onto Kevin's body. She began crying, yelling and screaming.

"Who did this? Who could do something like this?" she cried. Kelly sat on the ground with her brother's dreads in one hand and a gun in the other. Her brother's head was split in two and the bullet that had penetrated his chest tore straight through his flesh.

"Buddah did that shit," Laquisha screamed. She had heard the shots and ran down to see Buddah running off.

Buddah was on his way out of the projects when he was stopped by a police patrol car. Instead of facing the music like a man he turned the gun on himself and pulled the trigger like the bitch that he was. Buddah used Kelly to get him out of jail so that he could put an end to the man who stole his shine. In Buddah's eyes Colonial Heights belonged to Buddah and only Buddah. Well, now Colonial Heights belonged to whoever wanted to carry the torch.

The knot in Kelly's stomach was the size of a basketball. She couldn't breathe. She thought that she was going to die right then and there along with her brother. Her mother was gone and now her brother was gone, leaving her all alone in this world. Why would Buddah do this to her after she helped him get out? It was if she had killed her own brother. Kelly couldn't understand how people could be so devious, but she was ready to retaliate. *That bitch, Dora, I'ma kill that bitch,* she thought.

"Yo, Buddah just shot hisself," Laquisha screamed as ran back from seeing where he had gone.

Kelly kissed her brother on the cheek and slid his body off of her. She stood up, wiped her bloody hands on her jeans, and disappeared back into the building. There were cops coming her way and she had something she needed to take care of first. Kelly was glad to hear that Buddah had killed himself. That was one less person she had to kill. She took the stairs up and made it to her floor. Kelly walked toward Dora's apartment door with pure rage and hatred in her heart. Killing Dora was her only outlet. The amount of guilt she felt for giving Dora the money to bail out her brother's killer was overwhelming.

"Open the door, bitch," Kelly cried.

Dora's door didn't open and she didn't answer.

"I said open your fuckin' door, bitch," Kelly screamed, while punching and kicking the door.

"Kelly!" Dante called.

Immanently he knew that she needed him. So when Dante heard the call over the radio he immediately responded. When he arrived and saw all of what was going on outside of Colonial Heights he recognized Laquisha and questioned her. She admitted to him that Buddah had shot Kevin and that Kelly had gone back inside and that she had a gun.

"Come on, baby, it's not worth it," he told her, attempting with all his might to persuade her to stop her quest for death.

"Fuck that, Dante, my baby brother is gone," she shrieked.

"I know, baby, but he wouldn't want you to end your life too. Not like this."

Kelly cried as she continued to bang on Dora's door. She was taking her anger and frustration out on the metal door and it was taking quite a beating from her small, but strong hand.

"Give me the gun, Kelly."

"No!"

Dante came closer to her. He knew the condition she was in and he didn't want to push her. The locks on Dora's door began to unlock. Dante was hoping that the tenant did not give Kelly what she thought she wanted, which was the access to kill.

Dora kept her chain on her door and spoke through the door. She had watched the whole incident from her window.

"Kelly, baby, please, I'm sorry. I didn't mean for anything to happen to your brother. If I'da known that Buddah was gon' do him like that I swear I would'na got him out. I would'a smoked your money up," Dora said, crying sorrowfully.

All Kelly could do stand there and cry. Her heart had become so heavy. She knew that she couldn't blame Dora for Buddah's actions, and that Dora had only done what she had told her she'd better do, but Dora was the only one besides herself that was still alive that she could blame.

"Come on, baby, give me the gun," Dante said with his hand extended.

Kelly slowly handed Dante her .380.

"That's my girl, you made the right choice," he told her as he took the .380 into his possession.

All of a sudden a flood of police officers came rushing up and out of both staircases.

"Freeze," one of the police officers yelled.

Dante was in plainclothes. He turned around to show the officers his badge. Dante's sudden move made one of the rookies react prematurely as he shot his gun and it went off. All you could hear was screaming and yelling. Officers were yelling at the rookie officer for acting too soon. Dante was yelling at his fellow officers for not recognizing him for who he was and putting innocent lives in danger. And Dora was yelling at the police officers, accusing them of trying to kill her. With all of the confusion and drama surrounding her, Kelly slipped into her apartment to grieve.

# Chapter 13

## *New Beginnings*

Kelly was at the gun range. She had just shot 120 out of 120, which was unheard of for a police cadet. Dante stood by smiling. He was proud of his protégé, but little did he know, it was her late brother, Kevin, who trained her to be the expert shooter that she was. It had been six months and training was over with Kelly about to graduate at the top of her class. The last six months had been the most challenging and invigorating months of her life. She took criminal justice classes that really opened her eyes to the magnitude of the broad spectrum that law enforcement actually covered. The defensive driving training was an adventure. Kelly got a lot of satisfaction out of whippin' their vehicles around the driving course. She also learned how to perform CPR in order to save lives.

Besides Dante being there for her, she had made a lot of good friends in the Police Academy. Having good people in her life made the transition from the streets to the law a lot easier. It also helped her deal with the loss of Kevin. There were over a thousand people at her brother's funeral. Kelly was shocked to see so many people there, since he had been locked up for so long. She was glad, however, that so many people had come out to show her brother the love and respect that he deserved.

"You did real good out there today, baby," Dante told her as they drove home.

"Thank you. I'm havin' a lot of fun. I didn't know it would be like this," Kelly said, sincerely.

"I knew you would make a great police officer. I told you," Dante said, beaming from ear to ear.

"Yeah, baby, you did," she said, smiling back.

"You ready for tomorrow?" he asked her. Her graduation ceremony was taking place in the morning.

"Most definitely," she said with supreme confidence.

The graduation ceremony was an event that Kelly would never forget. Due to her graduating with honors, she was asked to deliver a speech for the ceremony. Kelly had never delivered anything except packages of drugs and money, but she dug deep and was told by her inner voice

to instead give a poem in honor of the memory of
her mother and her brother.

> *My mouth says I love you everyday*
> *But the scale will never tell you what my*
> *love truly weighs*
> *I was the reason for the burden on your*
> *shoulders*
> *As the burden got heavier, we grew stron-*
> *ger, as we got older*
> *As cold as this life is, thoughts of you*
> *should bring me to tears*
> *But now it's my turn to get my hands*
> *dirty—to protect and to serve*
> *To give you the daughter and the sister*
> *that you both deserve*
> *Hopefully making up for all of the years*
> *in which I didn't have the nerve*
> *I know I'm not perfect—none of us are—*
> *in any way*
> *But you were the perfect mother and*
> *brother for me—and I'll love you everyday.*

Kelly admired herself in the full-length mirror
inside of their bedroom closet. She looked fly in
her police uniform as she slicked her fiery red
ponytail back and adjusted her belt. This was her
first day on the force and she was excited and a

little nervous. Dante had already left to start his day. She didn't want them to arrive together. It was bad enough they were working in the same precinct. Kelly didn't want any favoritism shown to her because of Dante. He had insisted that Kelly work out of his precinct. If something happened to her and he wasn't able to get to her, he would never forgive himself.

The parking lot was almost full, but Kelly managed to find a spot and pulled her Lexus into it. She walked into the precinct as a New York City police officer for the very first time and it felt great. Kelly saw a man in uniform sitting at a desk. Being new to the job, she wasn't sure of what she should do first, so she asked. She found herself in a roomful of police officers. She scanned the room, but she didn't see Dante anywhere. The police sergeant began the roll call. Kelly spoke up when she heard her name called. After hearing several cases that were a point of interest to their unit, she was paired off with another officer, Officer Rouse. He was to be her partner. Kelly took a good look at the tall and lanky blond-haired, blue-eyed white male she was going to be spending her shift time with. She never really fucked with white people like that before. *This is going to be interesting,* she thought.

"Hey, there, Morgan, how are you feeling?" he asked her, then smiled with his thin lips shut.

"I feel good," she said in an upbeat manner.

"Good, that's a good thing. Well, let's hit it," he said.

They walked outside into the brisk winter air. Officer Rouse walked toward their squad car. Kelly followed him. Dante saw Kelly and pulled his Charger up alongside of their squad car.

"Hey there, rookie," he called to her, grinning hard.

"Hey," Kelly said, both happy and relieved to see him.

"You take care of her, Rouse," Dante told his fellow officer.

"Oh, I've got her, Evans," he assured Dante.

"Unit 7210 . . ." the radio dispatcher called.

Kelly heard the dispatcher on the radio and it was on. She knew this was it. Rouse looked at her as he answered the call.

"This is unit 7210."

"Unit 7210, we have a shoplifting incident at Payless Shoes on Broadway. Suspect is a black female approximately five-five and a hundred and fifty pounds. She has long black hair, not believed to be her own. I believe store security has her in their custody, but she's giving them hell."

"Unit 7210, copy, we're on the way."

"Roger that, unit 7210."

"Well, this is it, kiddo. This is what you signed up for. You ready?" Rouse asked her.

"As ready as I'll ever be," Kelly said. She looked over at Dante and winked as their squad car screeched away from the curb.

There was a crowd of people standing in front of the Payless shoe store on Broadway. As Kelly and her partner exited the vehicle they were met with boos and other snide remarks. Kelly now knew what it felt like to be on the other side. As she came into the store she could see the back of the female suspect and she was giving the security staff an earful of not-so-nice words. She immediately recognized the voice and she couldn't believe that this was going to be her first arrest.

"Fuck that, I ain't steal shit. Y'all better mutha-fuckin' let me go. Shit, I gotta get home to my kids."

"Tell it to the police," the security officer told her.

The female turned around ready to give the police the same drama she had just given the store's staff and security, but when she saw who was there to take her in, her mouth fell wide open, and so did Kelly's.

"Oh my God, you a fuckin' cop?" Laquisha asked

"Oh my God, you're pregnant again?" Kelly asked.

Kelly looked at Laquisha's swollen stomach. No wonder she was out there stealing again; she was about to spit out another baby that she didn't have the resources or the money to take care of.

"You know this lady?" Rouse asked.

"Uh, well, yeah, I know her, but I'm probably gonna know a lot of the people I arrest."

"Arrest?" Laquisha exclaimed. "Bitch, you gonna arrest me? I'm carrying your brother's fuckin' baby and that's how you' gon' do me, bitch?"

Officer Rouse grabbed Laquisha by her arm and swung her around to cuff her. All Kelly could do was play back what Laquisha had just said. *Could it really be Kevin's baby?* she thought.

"Morgan!" Rouse called, snapping her out of her daze. "Read her her rights."

Kelly looked into Laquisha's sad eyes and read her her rights. There was no way that she could do anything to help her. Not right then and especially not right there. Kelly did her job and arrested her. They led her out of the store for the crowd to see and put her in the squad car. Rouse drove back to the station so that Laquisha could be booked.

"When are you due?" Kelly asked, curiously.

At first Laquisha wasn't going to answer her, but she knew that Kelly was her only chance of getting out of the mess she had gotten herself into, so she went ahead and answered.

"In another two months," she said with an attitude.

Kelly thought about it. Laquisha was a ho, but she did sleep with Kevin right before he died, which would have been seven months ago.


The next two months were like a roller coaster for Kelly. She had begged Dante to pull some strings to see to it that Laquisha didn't have to stay in jail. Kelly wasn't sure if Laquisha was carrying Kevin's baby or not, but if she was, she knew that she had to help her. Dante told her that he wasn't going to be able to help all of her hood friends get out of trouble, but he did understand that this arrested development was indeed unique. Kelly was also trying to find out how she could prove the paternity of Laquisha's baby with her brother no longer living. She went on the Internet and got her answers.

The moods of the individuals in the hospital waiting room were mixed. Laquisha's older children were all upset. Another baby meant another baby for them to have to watch while their mother was free to run the streets. Her younger children were happy. They couldn't wait for their new playmate to arrive so that they could take him home and play with their new toy. Kelly's nerves were on edge for several reasons. She was there with a patch of her dead brother's hair to provide in order to determine the paternity of Laquisha's baby and although she had just finished her shift, she had to go back to the station to complete a host of paperwork: She had just shot her first suspect.

"You all have a new baby brother," the nurse announced, as she came through the doors.

Laquisha's children all yelled and cheered with happiness, even the ones who had just been upset. They all ran past the nurse to join their mother and to see their new baby brother. Kelly walked over to the nurse to see what it was she was going to have to do to have Laquisha's baby tested. The nurse gave her the instructions that she needed. While on her way, she passed by Laquisha's room; Kelly stepped back and peeped in.

"Come on in," Laquisha said, weakly.

"I—I don't want to disturb y'all."

"Bitch, come and see your nephew," Laquisha said, softly but proudly.

Kelly didn't know how Laquisha could be so sure that it was Kevin's baby, but she had his dread in her hand and she was going to find out the real deal. As Kelly approached and took a good look at the brand-new baby wrapped up in a blue blanket, her eyes began to tear, the dread fell out of her hand, and Kelly fell to her knees. *Oh my God, Thank you, thank you, thank you. I don't believe it,* she prayed.

"Can I hold him, please?" Kelly asked, getting up from her knees.

Laquisha handed her the baby. Kelly cried tears of joy as she stared at the spitting image of her baby brother when he was born, reddish-brown hair, light brown eyes, and all. Her brother's memory was going to live on after all and she still had a piece of him within the tiny life she held in her loving arms. And even though Laquisha was the baby's mother, she couldn't be happier to have him come into this world. She was going to be closely involved in his upbringing and she planned to be the very best auntie that she could be.

Kelly's cell phone rang. It was Dante.

"Hey baby, guess what?" she said happily. "I got a nephew!"

"Really now, that's all right."

"Yep, I know right."

"What's his name?" Dante asked her.

"His name?" she asked, as she looked at Laqui-sha.

"His name is Kevin Corey Morgan Jr.," Laqui-sha yelled out loud, smiling from ear to ear.

"Did you hear that?" Kelly asked, with her face beaming with glee.

"Yes, I did and it sounds real good. Now you finish on up there, and get to the station. I heard you shot a suspect."

"Yeah, I did." Kelly had forgotten all about it.

"All right, well go on and handle that, and then come on home and handle me. You know police officers need love too," he told her.

"Yes, we do," she lovingly agreed.

# Greed

by

*Meisha Camm*

# Chapter 1

"Ladies and gentleman, the pilot has confirmed it's now safe to use your electronic devices. A friendly reminder: Please keep your seat belts on at all times. Should you need to use the bathroom, it's located in the rear. Shortly, we will be taking drink orders. For today, the menu will be herb-roasted chicken or filet mignon. The steak will be cooked to your preference," the flight attendant announced over the intercom.

"First class definitely has its perks," I mentioned to Greg, before lowering the volume on my iPod. I was listening to Prince's song "Insatiable." This had been our last connecting flight heading to Norfolk International Airport. With seven days, six nights, and a staff waiting on my everlasting becking call on the secluded island of Fuji, it left me wanting to gear up for yet another vacation. We were devout Virginia Beach natives; however, we enjoyed getting away.

"Yes, it's the only way to fly. I can stretch my arms, no screaming babies, and the person to my right isn't hovered over me," Greg added while catching up on e-mails.

"I agree," I said, nodding, before gently sliding his hand, passing my dress to my pussy. Soon after, Greg's finger was greeted to dripping wetness. I couldn't help but guide that finger into his mouth. None of the other passengers were paying us any mind. The brick red blanket given to me by the flight attendant came in handy.

"You want it?" he asked, grinning, and then continued to lick his fingers.

"Meet me in the bathroom in six minutes," I confirmed, not trying to make it obvious that I was craving dick.

Greg wasted no time closing the door. He unloosened his belt and slid his pants down to his ankles, revealing only boxers. I held on tight as he pinned me up against the wall. Just as he liked it, Greg's face ended up landing in between my breasts. With his clenched teeth, he pushed the left side of my V-neck dress over. Before easing his eight-inch dick into my throbbing pussy, Greg teased my nipple with his tongue. The left one was his ultimate favorite. Soon after, his dick found its way to my G-spot.

"Deeper," I demanded.

"Yes, Jackie," he agreed.

"Fuck me harder," I commanded. Even though he would never admit it, I knew Greg loved it when I talked dirty in his ear. His strikes of pleasure made both of us cum.

"I needed that," he insisted and let out a sigh of relief.

"Again," I urged.

"Nah, I'm done for now," he replied, shaking his head.

"Let's do it one more time," I insisted.

"Jackie, what if someone needs to use the bathroom?" he asked, attempting to pull up his khaki pants.

"They can wait. Besides, the second time around, you don't take long," I added before playing with his balls in my mouth.

I could have gone a third go-round but I had tired Greg out. After the fun came to a halt, I let him exit the bathroom first. Once I washed up and picked up my ripped G-string from off the floor, I made the way back to my seat. The G-string had cost around sixty dollars but it was well worth seeing him tear it off me. Not to mention, Greg was the one that actually paid for it.

"Thank you for the performance," I giggled, before blowing him a kiss and taking refuge in my blanket. I quickly fell asleep.

# Chapter 2

Since I was the age of thirteen and Greg was fifteen years old, our parents have been longtime friends living in Virginia Beach. At first, we hated each other. Then one day I desperately tried to hold back the tears about my current boyfriend cheating on me with a chick who had bigger boobs. To this day, I tend to wear my heart on my shoulder. I couldn't help it. We were at his parents' house for a pig roast. After he finished playing basketball with his friends and noticed how sad I was, we took a stroll through the neighborhood and ended up near the lake that glistened from the sun. With his keen listening, a delicate caress on the cheek, and confessing his true feelings about liking me, we'd been together ever since.

Through the years, we'd had our ups and downs. The college years didn't make it any easier. He attended Morehouse College while I went to Bennett College. He'd cheated on me with the result of the other woman, Sara, stabbing him in the neck, barely missing a vital nerve. Coming home drunk from the club in the wee hours of the morning, she caught him from behind. Greg was too embarrassed and wanted to drop the charges. I could have choked him after he told me that tidbit of information. I informed him if he did decide to drop the charges, it would be over for us. Scared of losing me, Greg made the right choice and let them stick on Sara. Besides, even if he dropped them, the state would have picked up the case. We live in the Commonwealth of Virginia. Violent acts of crime aren't taken too lightly and neither from me. No one messes with my family, or my beloved Greg.

I intended to destroy Sara. First, I sent an anonymous letter to her supervisor about her current charges. When working for Social Services, it doesn't look too hot when you've been charged with attempted murder. She made the mistake of not taking a plea bargain. At the trial, she was found guilty. Sara was handed the sentence of fourteen years with no chance of parole from the goodwill district attorney, Derrick Harkman. Plus, I rode his dick a few times to convince him to be harsh. Yeah, I'm far from a saint. To this day, Greg doesn't have any idea about how many indiscretions I've had. I'm too sneaky and plan things out to ever get caught.

Sara had shaken Greg up for a while. After a few years, he worked up the nerve to step out on me a couple more times that I know of.

Thinking back, I wondered why we made the choice to commit to each other at such a young age. We should have broken up, but, not having Greg in my life wasn't an option. Through the extraordinary and ugly times of our relationship, I jotted down my feelings in my beloved diary. When I was nine, Mom gave it to me. I've been writing ever since.

His father, Greg Bell Senior and my father, Harold Montague, joined forces to make a drug called Pozor. Daddy was the nerdy scientist who developed the drug. Mr. Bell had the financial means and the backing from the Food and Drug Administration to pass it. Their pharmaceutical company, Colstice Drug Company, was born. Soon after, Pozor flooded every drugstore and grocery store you could think of and even Wal-Mart and Target. Over a three-month period of taking the drug, people have lost countless pounds of weight. It even targets that hard-to-lose belly fat.

Greg and I are simply enjoying the fruits of our fathers' labor. Private schools, elite colleges, luxurious vacations, and getting anything we want are the only way of life we've ever known. *I don't want it now, but I want it right now* has been my motto for years.

After we both graduated college, Greg received a high executive position at Colstice and I am in the accounting department. In other words, we don't do nothing but send e-mails to ourselves, take long lunches, and have phone sex every chance we get. Doing completely nothing productive but actually showing up can become exhausting. Not to mention, getting it on in the copier room was so exciting. Most of all, the thrill was knowing we could get caught. We didn't care. Since the other employees valued their jobs, they wouldn't dare say anything, either.

"Wake up, princess," Greg urged, tapping me on the shoulder.

"We're home?" I asked, before yawning and stretching. All I wanted to do was take a hot shower, eat, and catch the latest episode of *The Real Housewives of Atlanta*.

"Yes. We're the last to get off the plane," he said, nodding, before pulling me up out of the cozy seat.

Among ninety other passengers, Greg and I were patiently waiting for our luggage. Since I was catching up on e-mails, checking Twitter, Facebook, and MySpace personal accounts, I didn't mind at first. I even checked voicemails from my envious associates. They were more like vultures always trying to mooch off me and my glory. I didn't care because I was, hands down, the woman that ran the Hampton Roads of Virginia. With the latest fashion, endless money, and all-access card to the VIP events, I was unstoppable. Being the life of the party is what I lived for. It's like an indescribable rush knowing all eyes from men and women are on me. Girls dreamed about belonging to my clique of girlfriends. The bad part about my life was that the only person I could trust was Greg. He always had my best interest at heart and vice versa. Most of all, Greg always made me feel secure in his arms.

Back in high school, Greg was the captain of the wrestling team. Eight years later, he still maintained a chiseled body with a touch of charm, easygoing personality, and dark eyes. The ironic part was that he didn't work out at all. Decent eating habits and heredity have been used to his advantage. Women continue to drool over him. It makes me wet knowing another woman desires Greg, but, can't have him. Despite his infidelity, he never got a baby in me. Every woman has her own personal standards on what she can take and what she can't take. Another woman's baby fathered by Greg is on the top of my list.

Through middle school, I admit to have being on the chubby side. In high school, I joined the basketball team and those creeping pounds melted off. The boys didn't start cat-calling until I did something with my mop head. I was somewhat of a tomboy. At age thirteen, I vowed to keep my hair looking presentable. Along with the help of a Dominican salon, my do is nothing but stunning. Long hair down to my back is an automatic turn-on. Size thirty-six breasts and a size seven isn't bad for me, pushing my late twenties. Once I grabbed hold of everyone's attention, I'd been craving it ever since.

Before I knew it, a whole thirty minutes had passed. The constant looking at watches, shrugs, and sighs from everyone around me was starting to get under my skin.

"We need our luggage," I interrupted the flight service clerk, who was on the phone and then took a bite out of a roast beef sandwich after walking over to the counter.

"Ma'am, I'm on the phone. I will be with you in one moment," she suggested with a smile.

"Lady, hurry the hell up, look around. While stuffing your plump face with today's lunch special and giggling to your man how much you miss him, we still need our luggage," I demanded.

"Who needs their luggage?" she asked after hanging up the phone.

"Can you see out of your eyes?" I inquired.

"Yeah," she nodded and rolled her eyes.

"Can you understand the English language and the words that are coming out of my mouth?" I questioned.

"Hmm, mmm," she nodded, again.

"All right, then, take another look again, lady, because these people behind me and myself need our luggage. We've been waiting for our luggage for quite a long time. Do something about it right now," I insisted.

"Ma'am, there's something wrong with one of the belts on which the luggage comes out. The workers are trying to fix it as we speak. If you'd like to go have a seat, as soon as they're done, I will let you and the rest of the passengers know any more updates," she explained.

"It would have been nice to know this tidbit of information forty-two minutes ago," I replied, looking at my watch.

"I apologize for the inconvenience," she suggested, trying her best to appease me.

"You will be sorry before the day is over. Get your manager down here right now. Do you have any idea who the hell I am?" I proclaimed.

"No, I don't," she responded, shaking her head.

"Of course, you wouldn't, because you're fat. This miracle diet pill will do wonders for you," I added before taking out a pamphlet to hand to her. I never wasted an attempt to do business with anyone. I was proud of my father's accomplishments.

Suddenly, the clerk jumped over the counter, attempting to try to punch me in the face with a bottle of water. Small crevices of bread crumbs that lingered on her face flew to the floor.

Greg came between us before I could reach for her weave. Within seconds, I reached into my purse and grabbed the Bath & Body Works perfume called coconut lime verbena and sprayed it into her eyes.

"Please, my eyes. It burns, it burns," she continued to scream. Security came running over to us and finally the belt started moving and luggage started to appear.

*It's about time,* I thought.

# Chapter 3

I gave the head supervisor of the Norfolk International Airport my business card. If that worker wasn't going to be fired for her conduct and rudeness, then I intended to sue. The last thing I was sure this company wanted was a lawsuit. He had five business days to comply with my offer.

"Where's my silver Jaguar?" I asked while searching through my purse for my cell phone.

"You scheduled it to be here, today, right?" Greg inquired, knowing I had a tendency to get my days mixed up.

"Yes, I'm sure of it," I replied while dialing my mom and then my father's cell number. All I got was voicemail.

"I'm going to call the limo service. Someone will be here in less than fifteen minutes," Greg assured me.

"All right," I replied after dialing my parents' home number. Mom was supposed to arrange to have my precious Jag dropped off.

"Finally," I uttered while seeing Fred, the limo driver, come closer to where we were standing.

"Jackie, relax, I'm sure there was a screw-up with the day," he suggested, looking at my worried face.

"I'm sure you're right," I agreed, before getting in the limo.

"Where to, Ms. Montague?" the limo driver inquired before we took off.

"My house, but first, I'm in the mood for Chick-fil-A. Make a quick stop at the one closest to my house," I directed.

"Yes," he obliged.

"May I take your order, please?" the drive-through attendant asked.

"Babe, you want anything?" I asked Greg.

"Yeah, I'll take a strawberry milkshake," he replied after reaching in his pocket and handing me a twenty-dollar bill.

"Fred, what about you?"

"I just ate. Thanks anyway," he answered.

"Hi, I need two milkshakes," I answered.

"What flavors?"

"I would like a strawberry and a peach milkshake with whipped cream on it."

"Anything else for you?"

"Yes, a twelve-piece nugget meal with lots of barbecue sauce. Instead of coleslaw, replace it with a fresh ice-cold carrots and raisin salad. That's it for our order," I said.

"Okay, your total is sixteen dollars and seventy-nine cents. Please drive to the next window."

"Thanks," I responded.

"Here are your shakes, order, and change," she announced after handing everything to me.

Before driving off, Fred knew the drill about me looking into the bag to make sure the food was right. There's nothing worse than getting home and you have the wrong order because a dumb-ass messed it up.

"This order is all wrong," I blurted out after looking into my bag and tasting both of the shakes. It took a while for the lady to come back to the window. Each moment, I was becoming more enraged.

"Ma'am, is there something wrong?" she asked, after realizing we were still lingering around.

"Yes, my fries are cold. I wanted carrot and raisin salad instead of coleslaw. These shakes are chocolate and vanilla," I proclaimed, after throwing everything except the nuggets back into the drive-through.

Her face was covered in milkshake, while pieces of carrots, raisins, and fries were stuck to her shirt.

"Jackie, what the hell is wrong with you? Don't start this shit again today," Greg ranted, shaking his head.

"Lick your right cheek. It will help you taste the difference of strawberry and peach versus chocolate and vanilla," I informed the drive-through cashier.

"Fred, drive on. Let's get the hell outta here before Jackie gets us all banned from Chick-fil-A permanently," Greg demanded.

"No, Fred, I'm not going anywhere 'til I get what I ordered," I proclaimed.

"You've done enough for today. I'm tired. Let's just go back to your place. I'll fix your favorite, shrimp with linguine," Greg encouraged.

"All right," I replied, sounding disappointed. I still had a taste for those fries and raisin salad.

# Chapter 4

"Fred, thanks for bringing my suitcases to the door," I acknowledged, after getting out of the limousine.

"Yeah, thank him for carrying eight suitcases, to be exact," Greg added, after handing him a fifty-dollar bill for his trouble.

"You know I particularly have a personal image to uphold. Not to mention, we're the couple everyone dreams about," I proclaimed.

"I don't give a damn about any of that," Greg responded.

"What!" I blurted out, after noticing there was a padlock on my front door.

"I'm sure there's a reasonable explanation as to why the lock is on the door. It's probably a mistake," Greg suggested, trying to calm me down.

"I need to know what's going on," I replied, after dialing all of the phone numbers I knew for my parents. All of them were going straight to voicemail.

"Let's go to your parents' house," he urged, handing Fred yet another fifty-dollar bill to lug all my stuff back into the limo. Greg didn't like seeing me upset. As we headed to my parents' house, I couldn't understand why I was not able to get into my house, especially when there was plenty of money to go around; probably feed the city of Norfolk for six months.

"Mom, Dad, what's going on? I can't get into my condo," I exclaimed, hearing my echoing voice after barging into the front door with Greg and Fred following behind my trail.

"Jackie, baby, you're home. I'm in here," Dad greeted me after I heard his voice in the study.

There was a swarm of movers taking their furniture out and loading it onto a truck. *My old room still better be intact,* I thought, while giving one of the workers an evil stare down. Mom was nowhere in sight.

"There's a lock on my door. I'm tired, hungry, and have had a long day, which seems to be getting worse. Why are our belongings being carried out?" I questioned.

"Mr. Montague, sir," Greg addressed Dad, shaking his hand.

"Hello, Greg. You two can have a seat. Since both of you have been gone, a lot has changed. Well, you see, Greg Senior and I have severed ties. Twenty years ago, this house and your condo came with the job. Now that I'm moving on, we are losing them."

"Mr. Bell and you couldn't have worked something out?" I asked.

"Greg's father wants to move the company in a new, innovative direction. That's all. We still are remaining friends. Jackie, it's business," Dad commented, shrugging his shoulders.

"Mr. Montague, I'm sorry to hear about this. I'm sure my father was sorry to lose you," Greg suggested.

"Thank you," Dad said, nodding.

"What are we going to do now?" I questioned. "Losing my home is one thing, losing the home I grew up in is a stab in the heart. There are countless memories here."

"We'll make it," Dad assured me with a smile.

"Jackie, you're in the best hands with your father. I'm going to step out and give you a call later," Greg expressed, before giving me a hug. I didn't hesitate to walk him to the door.

"He's hiding something," I said, hoping Greg would confirm my thoughts.

"Yeah, something isn't right. I'm going to go probe my father and call you in a couple of hours," he decided.

"All right," I agreed, before he walked out of the door and stepping back into the limousine. I waved good-bye to Greg. My head started to spin. I found Dad in the living room, sipping on a bottle of wine with my mother. He cherished his wine and that's probably where a lot of the family fortune went. The bottle in his hand cost around five thousand dollars.

"I was saving this bottle of wine for the day you got married," Dad wallowed. His whole mood took a 360-degree turn.

*Was it just an act for Greg not to see Dad sweat?*

# Chapter 5

Mom's eyes were bloodshot red. It looked as if she had been crying for days with fresh tears on top of dried-up ones. Seeing the look on her face made me want to do the same thing. Once we made eye contact, she and I hugged each other for a while. I was trying to find comfort in her, while she broke down even more in my arms.

"Dad, what really happened? I thought you owned half of the company?" I inquired.

"About five years ago, I did. Then Greg Senior gave me an offer I couldn't refuse. I thought my job would be around for the long haul. The day after you left for your trip, he called me into his office and simply said my services wouldn't be needed anymore. It would surprise me if he got three more scientists to put on the payroll for the price of one of me. Even more humiliating, security escorted me out of the building. My office was ransacked and what was left of it was placed into a cardboard box and shoved at me," Dad made clear.

"He fired you," I replied in a state of shock.

"Yes, pretty much. In the corporate world, loyalty and friendship don't mean a damn thing.

"What are we going to do for money?"

"The money has run out. All three of us have lavish taste and it cost money. The good life, as we have known it, is gone. Just as fast as I would make the money, we would spend it even faster."

"Can't you just go work for another company?"

"I'm fifty-four years old. No one wants to hire an old-timer. Besides, I'm too much of a liability. Now, I'm not saying I won't try. I'm made some calls to a few contacts. Greg Senior had pretty much blackballed me. It's hard being optimistic."

"For more than twenty years, we have lived in this house. To leave like this is terrible. I keep thinking I'm going to wake up from this endless nightmare," Mom sobbed in disbelief, rocking herself slowly back and forth on the couch.

"Where is all of our stuff going?" I questioned.

"For now, it's going to storage, 'til we figure what's next for us. Over the years, I wasted a lot of money, however, I did have enough sense to buy a moderate sized town house.

"What am I supposed to do for money? I can't live just off credit cards. Do something, Dad! What are people going to think?" I declared, freaking out about how neighbors had probably been peeping through their windows as our stuff was being carried away.

"Jackie, we just lost our home. I don't give a damn about what anybody thinks anymore. I suggest you follow my advice. Be grateful and stop acting like a spoiled twit. Keeping up with the Joneses has left us broke," Mom announced.

Mom smacked me across the face with the back of her right hand. It left me with a nagging sting. She hadn't laid a hand on me since I was ten years old.

"We need to stick together," Dad suggested, trying to diffuse the tension in the room.

"You can come to the town house. If I hear one complaint, your ass is out on the street," Mom commented.

"All right," I agreed with my hand still clutched to my face.

"One more thing," Mom declared.

"What now?" I asked.

"Cut up all of those credit cards. Our days of gold plastic are over," she announced.

# Chapter 6

Two weeks later, the walls felt as if they were closing in on me. Mom's constant nagging of me getting a job was hard to tune out. Dad and she were going on and scheduling countless interviews, but I couldn't get in the groove of actually working. Thank God I still had Greg's credit card to rely on. For old time's sake, I flocked to Nordstrom in my Jag to pick up a pair of True Religion and Cookie Johnson jeans, Gucci pumps, and a Louis Vuitton Speedy bag. At the nail salon, I had my toes and nails painted my favorite color, gray.

I made it a point to keep a low profile and go to the places at times where people wouldn't spot me. Most of my haters were blowing me up on Facebook, text messages, and MySpace, desperately trying to get the scoop about why the biggest house on the block had a *For Sale* sign on the front lawn. Even though Mom thinks I'm wasting my time and gas, I've been driving to our old house and parking in the driveway just to stare out what we once had. Mom has been drilling into my head that it's time we move on, but I'm not as strong as her, nor can I adapt so damn quickly to change. Today, I couldn't help but to cry thinking about how I scraped my knee while Dad taught me how to ride a bicycle, to coming down the stairs in an amazing gown for senior prom. As of yet, the house hasn't sold.

"Hey," I greeted Greg after he opened the door.

"Why the long face? I see you got plenty at the mall," he teased.

"I can't believe this is happening. My mind just keeps hoping Dad will get another job soon. Once it happens, things will finally go back to normal."

"Me either," he agreed, shaking his head.

"I can't get a word out of Dad about why he was let go," I admitted.

"My father isn't talking, either," he added, leading us to the backyard.

Greg had prepared fresh shrimp with linguine, salad and a berry tart, picnic-style. He loved to cook. Fall was approaching. It wasn't too hot or too cold. In his arms, we watched the sun set. After going back into the house, we had fun washing the dishes. Once the last dish was dried,

I couldn't wait to throw soap suds on him. Before I knew it, both of us were covered in them and his kitchen floor was dripping wet. I cornered Greg to the stainless steel refrigerator. I quickly grabbed two ice cubes out of the ice maker and scooped them into my mouth. Wasting no time, I pulled down his jeans and boxer shorts and took his dick into my mouth. The hot-and-cold sensation was irresistible to Greg.

"Damn, I'm going to cum," he whispered.

"No you're not," I begged to differ, before leading him onto the sturdy kitchen table. I motioned for him to lie down on top of it and I gently slid down on his dick, going slowly up and down so he could watch me.

Greg turned me over, put me on all fours and entered my soaking pussy.

"You're on my spot," I screamed.

"Yes," he replied.

Soon after, we came together.

While I was recouping on the table, Greg cleaned up the mess we made.

Then he lifted me from the table and carried me into the bathroom, placing me in the tub.

We took a warm bath together.

As he washed me, Greg gave me small kisses all over my body.

# Chapter 7

On Thursday, I was just there and the FOR SALE sign lay tightly dug in the front lawn. Now, today, on a rainy and gloomy Tuesday, the sign was gone. An older couple with a moving truck had the nerve to be putting *their* belongings in the house.

"Excuse me," I stated, after getting out of the car.

"Yes, young lady?" the man asked.

"What the hell are you doing?"

"My wife and I bought this house. We're retired from upstate New York. Once on a visit down here, we fell in love with the area," he explained.

"There's no need for your life history. I don't give a damn. This is my house and you need to leave right now," I ordered after cutting him off.

"The ink is dry on the papers we signed. This is our house. You need to leave right now!" the woman butted in once hearing my ranting.

"I'm not going anywhere. Put your crap back into the truck and go find another house. This is mine," I pointed out, and grabbed the box out of the man's arms and threw it back on the truck.

The woman took her cell phone out of her jean pocket and quickly called the Realtor. Once confirming the house was theirs legally, she called the police. I was escorted off the property.

"Ms. Montague, it's either jail, or you can go on with your day," the police officer offered, after pulling my registration.

"I'm leaving, for now. I'll be back. Next time, I'll be parked on the street and you can't do anything about it because that's considered city property. By the way, I was trying to warn you. Your souls won't be at peace. The house is haunted. When the clock strikes eleven, they will come for you," I screamed before pulling off, hoping my scare tactic was successful.

# Chapter 8

Long lines and few cashiers was becoming a trend at Target. I didn't care because I loved this store and could spend the entire day exploring in here with a small bag of popcorn in one hand and a strawberry smoothie in the other. An agenda to pick up only one item turns into me putting an extra twenty items in my shiny red shopping cart.

"Are you in a hurry?" I asked the woman behind me, who kept looking down at her watch and had a frustrated look on her face.

"Yes," she replied, nodding her head.

"Well, I'm not. You can go in front of me," I offered.

"You sure?" she inquired.

"Yes, I'm sure," I responded, smiling.

"Thanks."

"No problem."

"Listen, because of your generosity, I'm going to get to my doctor's appointment on time. If you're late, they charge an automatic thirty-dollar fee. Let me pay for that bottle of Sprite," she suggested, eyeing it in my cart.

"Sure, thank you," I said, nodding, before skimming through an *Essence* magazine. Before I knew it, she paid for her things and the Sprite.

"Here's your soda," she proclaimed. The next thing I knew she was pouring it all over my head.

"What the hell is wrong with you? You're crazy!" I spat at her.

"Boo-boo, the stickiness of Sprite isn't a good look for your hair."

"Who are you?" I demanded to know.

"I'm Michelle Perez. You should know me. I'm the one you threw two milkshakes and raisin salad on at Chick-fil-A. Karma is a bitch," she giggled, before calmly walking away.

I had embarrassed her in front of her coworkers. She humiliated me in front of complete strangers in my favorite neighborhood store. I couldn't decide which one was worse.

# Chapter 9

Waking up at eight in the morning was unheard of. Waking up and actually going somewhere to get my hands dirty was something I never before could imagine. I'm definitely not in the early-riser category. Dressed in an oversized white T-shirt and sweatpants, I was on my way over to the storage unit to help my parents sort it out. It was filled to the rim. Sure, there were items we would definitely keep. The others would be divided in two piles. The first pile would go to Goodwill for a hefty tax write-off, and the other would be used for an upcoming yard sale. Mom thought it could drum up cash.

Mom's Lexus was nowhere to be found. This was strange because I know she mentioned to me last night they would be here.

I slowly approached the storage unit with caution. My lips quivered and my knees went numb as I noticed a trail of blood as I entered in, looking down on the ground. On a pile of Persian rugs, my parents laid dead.

"Nine-one-one," the voice acknowledged me.

I cried out in disbelief and shock. The storage unit had been tossed.

"Are you there?" the female dispatcher asked.

"I'm at—" I paused, desperately trying to get the words to come out of my mouth. I fell to my knees.

"Ma'am, is anyone hurt?"

"Mom and Dad have been shot," I screamed.

"Is either one of them breathing?"

"No, I don't think so," I replied.

"Where are you?"

"Webster's Storage Facility off Holland Road. Please, hurry, right now," I pleaded.

"I'm dispatching police officers and the paramedics. They are on the way. I'm going to stay on the phone with you until they arrive," she explained.

Were Mom and Dad looking for something or was the killer?

# Chapter 10

Dad died instantly. Mom was pronounced dead at the hospital. I hoped at least one of them weren't leaving me here all alone and helpless. I wept to the floor. Who would kill my parents? Was it mistaken identity? The police officers asked me questions over and over again. A knot had formed in my stomach.

"Ms. Montague, is there anyone I can call for you?" a nurse asked.

"Greg, please. His number is in my cell phone," I replied, sobbing and pointing to my purse.

All the things I should have said and done for my parents came to mind. I didn't appreciate and cherish them like I should have. Now, they were gone. I loved Mom and Dad with all my heart. I hoped they knew that.

Words still couldn't come out of my mouth, so the police officers explained to Greg what had happened. From that day, he never left my side. Days that followed, I cried every night in Greg's arms.

The following week, the wake and funeral were scheduled. Dad's brother, Uncle Harold, made all the necessary arrangements. Greg's parents set a scholarship in my father's name. Each year, they vowed to give ten thousand dollars for a college-bound student. It meant a lot to me. I didn't want Mom or Dad to be latest news and then be forgotten.

At the funeral, so many people who I knew and didn't know were coming up to me giving their condolences. Even more, I felt even worse not knowing how much Mom volunteered and gave donations in the community. She probably tried to tell me but I was too concerned with the latest fashion trends and bleeding them for money. I knew Dad was an avid tennis player; however, I didn't bother to play a single game with him. All these years, I thought they were the lucky ones to have me in their lives. Now, it was too late and I finally realized how lucky I was to have parents like them.

Relentlessly, I hounded the Virginia Beach Police Department. Detective Snyder had been assigned to the murder case of my parents. The storage unit was checked for DNA and finger-prints. People in the area were questioned. No leads were developing.

Two weeks passed and I was ready to sort out their financial affairs. Twenty years ago, Dad granted Uncle Harold the executor of their estate. The town house was mine: free, clear and paid off. Mom's Lexus was recovered at a junkyard. Most of the parts were stripped. Dad's Denali was mine with no truck payment. After paying off debt and funeral expenses, I was left with a mere fifty thousand dollars and a painting by Jacob Lawrence depicting African Americans leaving the South to migrate to the North. This painting was valued at ninety thousand dollars.

I was faced with getting a job. Thankfully, I was not having to pay a mortgage or rent, but cable, water, and lights were not free. It wasn't hard to see I would have to drastically change my lifestyle. Fashion and the hottest trends didn't mean much to me these days. I would give anything to have my parents back. Still, I dreamed about buying back the house I grew up in.

# Chapter 11

"Go home," I suggested to Greg. For the last three weeks, he'd been staying with me. I overheard his friend mentioning to him about seeing a game at Buffalo Wild Wings.

"Are you sure? I can stay with you," he offered.

"Yes, I'm sure. I love you so much. I appreciate you being there for me."

"It's what I'm supposed to do. There's plenty of food in the refrigerator. Call me if you need me," he explained, before giving me a kiss and a hug.

"I will," I assured, before he walked out of the door.

Today was bright and sunny. I needed to run to the bank and catch up on errands. After I got back home, I decided to go online to start looking for a job. I didn't want to depend on Greg. Right now, my parents would be proud to see me strong and independent.

\*\*\*

While driving on Military Highway, I noticed a woman on the side of the road with her Honda Accord not starting.

"Do you need some help?" I inquired, pulling behind her car.

"Yes, I don't know what to do," she replied. It was none other than Michelle.

"I have a road assistance card. I can get your car towed to a mechanic and then maybe take you home," I volunteered.

"That would be a great help. I think it's my battery or alternator. I need it towed to Sears repair center. It's the one on Independence Boulevard," she explained.

"Yeah, I know where that one is. By the way, I'm Jackie," I replied, dialing road assistance on my cell phone.

Road assistance took about twenty minutes to come.

"Listen, Jackie, thank you so much for rescuing me. I've been meaning to get another battery, but I've been working so many hours," she explained after getting into my car.

"You're welcome," I responded.

"One more thing—I apologize for pouring soda on you. I was just angry—" she revealed.

"We're even," I acknowledged, after cutting her off.

We both started laughing.

"So where do you live?" I asked.

"I live in Pine Grove," she commented.

"I live there too, on Linden Street. What street do you live on?"

"I live on Waterbury Street."

"Small world," I suggested.

When we reached our neighborhood, I invited Michelle to eat lunch with me. Greg's pork chops, steamed carrots, and mashed potatoes would come in handy. I finally had worked up an appetite. Once we got to my house, Michelle and I talked for hours. Her family was originally from the Dominican Republic. She was born in New Jersey. At the age of five, her family migrated to Virginia. We had a lot of things in common. For example, she and I were both Scorpios and we went to the same hair salon. Not to mention, we both realized each of us had tempers.

After she left, I decided to clean up the house. I left my parents' room the same for now. I took comfort in knowing their clothes were still there. An eerie feeling came over me that someone else had been in the house. Paying close attention to detail, I noticed a few folders, books, and magazines were out of place. The only person who had a key to the house was Greg. He wouldn't come to my house without me knowing.

The following day, I called a locksmith to change the locks and had a security system installed for peace of mind. People in this neighborhood walked their dogs at night. Still, you could never be too sure. Since the economy went bottom, home invasions had been on the rise.

# Chapter 12

Since the death of my parents, two months had passed. Nights were harder than the days. The home movies of us together on VHS, I had turned onto a disk. Back at the storage unit, I rounded up any photos of my parents. I earned money by selling some of my most prized possessions on eBay. Not to mention, Greg had been secretly been putting money into my account. Whenever I did bring the subject up, he looked at me as if I was crazy.

Michelle and I had gotten closer. We went to the movies, got our hair done, and went to see a play together. I could tell her friendship was genuine and she just liked me for me and not what I could do for her. I discovered her hidden talent of baking, especially brownies. They were addictive. My favorite ones were the marshmallow brownies. Even better, I ate them with vanilla ice cream.

\*\*\*

"Detective Snyder speaking," he responded.

I dialed the number so much, it was memorized in my head. "Hey, this is Jackie Montague. Did you get the DNA results back yet?" I inquired, wanting to skip the *how are you* greeting.

"Ms. Montague, I received the results this morning. The only DNA found at the storage unit was yours and your parents," he explained.

"All right," I replied, letting out a sigh.

"We are still pursuing this case. You have my personal word that I won't give up on finding justice for you," he declared.

"Thank you, I appreciate it," I commented and threw the phone across the living room. Not realizing my strength, I broke the cordless phone. I was so angry someone killed my parents and was still out there walking the streets. Not ever knowing what truly happened was my worst fear.

# Chapter 13

There was a knock at the door.

"Hey," I acknowledged Michelle, who was in tears.

"Come in. What's wrong?" I asked.

"My house," she responded after coming into the house with more brownies in her hand.

"You're trying to make me fat," I pointed out, trying to get her to smile.

"When I'm upset, I bake something sweet. More often, the brownies are what first came to mind," she commented.

"Thank you. Sit down. What's going on with your house?" I asked after placing the brownies on the coffee table in the living room.

"Two years ago, I refinanced my house to pay off credit cards and other bills to an adjustable rate mortgage. Well, it has ballooned. Starting in four months, my payments will be eight hundred more a month. I can't afford that. I'm barely making it, now. I want to refinance to a fixed loan but my credit score is low. If I lose my house, my family, especially my parents, will be so disappointed in me. Out of five kids, I was the first to buy a house. I'm not trying to move back in with my parents," she sobbed.

"Let me talk to my Uncle Harold. He runs an investment firm. First, can you see if your mortgage company can give you some more time?" I questioned.

"It's worth a try. I'm going to go home, sulk, and eat my other batch of brownies. Working thirteen-hour days is killing me," she confessed.

Later on that night, I couldn't sleep because I was worried about Michelle's situation. How could I help her? I didn't want her to lose the house she worked so hard for. At 3:45 in the morning, it came to me. I put on a coat over my nightgown, ran over to her house, and banged on the door.

Her boyfriend, Miguel, answered. "Do you know what time it is?" he yawned after opening the door.

"Jackie, what's the problem?" she asked with her bathrobe clenched to her body. The cold air was seeping in the door.

"It's the brownies," I announced after coming into the house, heading toward the kitchen.

"What about the brownies?" she questioned.

"The brownies are going to help you and me," I added.

"How so?"

"Everyone loves those brownies you make. We're going to sell them and call them Gabby's brownies after your late grandmother. Besides, they're her recipes. Now, I will need a picture of her to be our logo," I explained.

"You really think it will work? Do you think my brownies are good enough to buy? I never thought about selling them," she expressed.

"Yes, people love comfort food and brownies are one of them. When is your next day off?"

"Ironically, I have this weekend off. They're cutting back on overtime," she confirmed.

"Meet me at my house at nine in the morning. In the meantime, whip up a batch of marshmallow, walnut, and double chocolate chip brownies," I ordered.

"Jackie, I don't have any money to play with," she revealed.

"Neither do I. Right now, all both of us have is hope. I need you to have some faith and put a whole lot of love in those brownies," I replied, before she handed me a picture of her grandmother.

# Chapter 14

The next day, I made a call to Uncle Harold about Michelle's house. He strongly suggested that she talk to her mortgage company, Horizon Bank, to lower her payments to something she could afford. Uncle Harold thought the mortgage company would work with her because she hadn't missed a single payment.

"I can't do it," she spat out after taking a seat at my kitchen table.

"You can't do what?" I asked.

"I can't call the mortgage company. They're going to turn me down. One of my other girlfriends was turned down. She and her husband, two kids, one dog, and a bird have to vacate the premises in thirty days," she explained.

"Your case may be different from theirs. If I were you, I would at least try to get the bank to work something out with you," I encouraged.

Before Michelle had come to my house, I had run to Wal-Mart to pick up various colors of

Saran wrap to decorate the brownies. Then, I went to Kinko's to make stickers of Michelle's grandmother sitting in a rocking chair to be placed on top of the brownies. Trying to come up with a slogan for them diverted Michelle's attention. Two hours had passed before we agreed on a slogan.

"Gabby's brownies, rich in history, rich in flavor," I proclaimed.

Even though Michelle was scared and discouraged, she called the bank to negotiate a deal. Luckily, the representative on the phone agreed to have her payment stay the same for the next three years. By then, her credit would be good enough to refinance into a fixed rate.

This business adventure of ours would take her mind off creeping bills and it would help me cope with the loss of my parents. Mom was right. It felt much better to give than to receive. It was a crazy feeling, but I still felt their presence in the town house.

One of Dad's old associates, Mark Emery, had been at the funeral. He was the CEO of Emery Marketing. He strongly urged me not to hesitate to call him if there was anything I needed. I took him up on the offer. Later that afternoon, he was able to squeeze Michelle and me in his busy schedule.

# Chapter 15

"Ladies, Mr. Emery can see you now," the receptionist stated, smiling.

"Thank you," we replied in unison. I gave her a brownie.

We were dressed in our power suits. Michelle was wearing a navy blue suit while I was wearing a black one.

"Jackie, how have you been?" he asked after we took our seats.

"I take it day by day. Still, I can't believe they're gone. The lead detective in the case still doesn't have any leads. Eventually, the killer or killers will be caught," I responded.

"Yeah, your parents died so tragically. Your father would have given his last dollar to help someone in need," he expressed.

"Yes," I said, nodding.

"What brings you two here today?"

"My friend, Michelle, and I have a brownie that we believe is worthy of selling."

"Well, the fact you strongly believe in your product is the first step to success. If you don't mind, may I try a sample?"

"Sure." I nodded and handed one of each three flavors from our baskets of goodies to him.

After taking a small bite of each, we were anticipating his feedback.

"Hmm, these brownies are delicious. The only thing I'm missing is a tall cold glass of milk," he laughed.

"Now that we have your attention. What's next for us?" Michelle asked.

"First, you need to get a food handler's license to ensure proper protocol in handling food," he revealed.

Michelle and I were jotting his words of wisdom down.

"Next, I would get a patent as soon as possible. The fees may run you to about two thousand dollars. Are you two going into this business together?"

"Yes," we both agreed.

"With that being said, I recommend you establish a LLC, which stands for limited liability company, which means your personal finances won't effect the business assets."

"How much will it cost?"

"Around seven hundred and fifty dollars," he estimated.

"All right," I replied, circling those figures he just said.

"I love how the brownies are packaged and the slogan is catchy. The picture of the grandmother adds an element of history to it. Once these things are done, come back to me and we'll brainstorm together about various kinds of marketing strategies."

"How much will your services be?" I questioned.

"Free of charge. If it wasn't for your father, I wouldn't be where I am today. I was the first marketing firm Greg Senior and your father used for Pozor. Life has been good for my family and me," he revealed.

"We're going to take care of things right away," I replied, committed to getting it done.

"Mr. Emery, thank you for your time," Michelle commented.

"You're welcome," he said, before we walked out of the office.

"Those brownies are tasty. Where can I get them?" the receptionist asked.

"Don't worry, we will be in the stores, soon," I proclaimed, smiling.

"I'm glad you like them," Michelle added. I couldn't help but notice how it boosted up her confidence.

# Chapter 16

"Mom, Dad," I called out. We were sitting in the backyard with our dog, a Bichon Frise named Muffin, eating hot dogs and hamburgers. Muffin desperately wanted a bite of my hamburger so I gave it to her. The first bite turned into five more bites. She was a big ball of fluff. The day was peaceful and serene. We continued to eat and talk.

"Jackie, we love you," they both continued to repeat.

"I love you too," I replied, giving each of them a hug and a kiss. Dad talked about his day at work, while Mom shared what we planted in the garden. The next thing I knew, someone came from behind and shot them.

"No, no," I screamed.

"Jackie, wake up, it's just a dream," Greg whispered in my ear. I woke up in a cold sweat.

"Where am I?" I inquired, trying to catch my breath.

"You're at my house. You just had a nightmare. Baby, do you remember what you dreamed about?" he asked in a subtle tone, caressing my hair.

"Mom, Dad, Muffin, and I were having a nice day. All of the sudden, I see them dead. I miss them so much," I cried out.

"Baby, I know you do. I miss them too. Do you want to watch some more home movies?"

"No, not right now," I replied, holding on to him. "Greg?"

"Yes?" he answered.

"Will I be able to move on from their deaths?"

"No," he replied.

"Why can't the police catch whoever did this? Not one single arrest has been made," I vented.

"I don't know. As long as we keep fire under the detective's ass, he'll have no choice but to work this case," he responded.

"Once the killer or killers are found, maybe I will gain closure to all of this. Right now, my heart is so heavy. Sometimes, I can't stop crying. I'm so sad," I revealed in tears.

"Ssssh, I'm here for you always, Jackie," he whispered slowly, rocking me back and forth. To help relieve tension, Greg laid me facedown on the bed. He started to play jazz music and began fumbling through his bathroom. I giggled after he tripped over my sneaker.

"Ouch," he blurted out. From the bathroom, he grabbed a bottle of lotion and mounted himself on my back and rubbed me down. Next, he went to my neck, arms, hands, thighs, and feet, working out all of the kinks.

"Make love to me," I whispered into his ear after turning over to face him. Since Mom and Dad died, I hadn't felt up to it.

"Are you sure?" he asked.

"Yes." I nodded and confirmed what I wanted by kissing him. I truly missed his tongue. Greg began licking on my left nipple in a circular motion through my sheer beige bra. It made me wet. He removed my matching panties. Greg's dick found its way inside my pussy. I lifted my legs and spread them out so I could experience each intoxicating thrust.

The next morning, Greg cooked me breakfast in bed. After brushing my teeth, I couldn't wait to dig into French toast with a dust of powdered sugar and raspberry sauce, apple-glazed bacon, scrambled eggs with cheese, and a tall glass of orange juice. Today, my spirits were better. While Greg was getting ready for work, I turned on the television to watch *Good Morning America* on the ABC station.

He *still* had his position at Colstice. I thought it would be a conflict of interest if I went back to work there. The company fires my father and I still work for them. I don't think so. Besides, Greg's father would only hire me back because he felt pity for me. I wasn't any use there.

"Thank you," I commented on the breakfast while I helped him fix his tie.

"You're welcome. Baby, it's nice to see you smiling," he replied.

"I feel good today," I added. My cell phone started ringing. I almost missed the call.

"Hello?" I answered.

"Can I speak to Jackie Montague?" the man's voice requested.

"This is she," I responded.

"This is Brinks Home Security System, can you please verify your security code?"

"It's heart," I mentioned.

"You must have left your sliding glass door unlocked. About fifteen minutes ago, someone tried to walk in your house. The police are on their way," the representative explained.

"So am I," I commented, hung up the phone, and quickly put my clothes back on.

"What's happening?" Greg asked, concerned.

"Someone tried to break in the house. The police are on the way. I'm headed to the house."

"I'm going with you," he replied.

# Chapter 17

"Nothing appears to be out of order or out of place," I commented to the police officer. Once Greg knew I was in good hands, I convinced him to go to work.

"Of course there isn't. The burglar only had a two-minute window before the police were dispatched."

"I don't understand why anyone would want to break in my house. I don't have anything," I added.

"Home burglaries are on the rise, especially during the day. I'm going to get my men to start driving through this neighborhood a little bit more. A crowd is beginning to brew outside. Call me if you have any questions," he pointed out.

"Thank you." I nodded and took his business card.

"Ms. Montague, there is one other thing," he replied.

"Yes?" I remarked.

"Please, make sure all your doors and windows are locked whether you're in the house or not," he urged.

"Will do." I nodded again.

# Chapter 18

Michelle and I wasted no time getting the food handler's license. Once we went back to Mr. Emery, we set up a Web site called gabbybrownies.com with our slogan, contact information, and endless pictures of the infamous brownies. The profits from this business venture would be split down the middle. I was the CFO, the chief financial officer. Let's face it, I was good at numbers. I definitely knew how to spend money, but making money would be a new challenge for me. When I was employed at Colstice, I would sit in on the sales meetings to hear other people come up with different marketing strategies for the weightloss pill. Their goal was to touch the young to the old who were overweight and they did. Besides getting it on in the copier room with Greg, I had to admit, I did learn a lot working at Colstice.

Michelle was going to be the baker and perfect these recipes.

"How much more is this going to cost? It's all ready been another month," she complained.

"Don't worry about money. For now, I have it covered. Listen, I believe in this. Do you?" I asked.

"Yes, I do. I just don't want this to flop. You'll lose your money and I'll lose my home," she confessed.

"Michelle, you have to be patient. We have to go through the steps of getting the proper documents, permits, and licenses. The last thing I want is for the city or the health department citing us, or handing us hefty fines because we didn't do what we were supposed to. The last thing on the list is to open a business account at BANFIRST," I explained, crossing it off on the notebook.

"All right, I apologize. I'm so nervous and want things to go right. All my life, I've had to struggle for everything. Plus, Jackie, I've never had a friend like you who truly cared about me and my well-being," she said.

"Girl, I feel the same way about you," I giggled.

"I need to be positive and do what I do best, make those brownies."

"I agree. The fact that we're actually doing this is an accomplishment in itself," I declared.

"You're right."

"Don't be so hard on yourself," I pointed out.

# Chapter 19

"How may I be of assistance to you ladies?" Ms. Pilom asked after coming up to us.

"Hello. We would like to open a business account," I answered.

"Well, come right into my office so we can get started," she agreed and we followed behind her.

"It's a good thing you came in. We're running a special on business checking," she mentioned.

"What kind of special?" Michelle inquired.

"Well, once we get the business account opened, you'll get a hundred dollars."

"Wow, that could help us stock up on supplies," Michelle expressed, smiling.

"Ladies, every little bit helps," Ms. Pilom pointed out.

"It sure does," I agreed.

"Especially, with this economy, five dollars goes a long way. Now, what kind of business is this?"

"It's a brownie business. The recipes came from my grandmother. Here are a few samples,"

Michelle responded, pulling ten out of her bag and handing them to her. She and I decided no matter who we meet, we wanted people to start buzzing about these brownies. Getting them to taste these scrumptious delights was easy. It was almost noon, which meant lunchtime, so I knew Ms. Pilom wouldn't turn us down.

"Thank you so much," she commented.

"Please give some to other coworkers. We would love to have feedback on the brownies," I added, giving her a few business cards with our contact information.

"These are good. Plus, I love walnuts," she replied after taking a bite out of it.

Michelle and I were all smiles.

"Getting back to business, how would like the checking account to be set up?" she questioned.

"We would like for the account to be set up as a LLC," I replied.

"Do you have the documents?"

"Yes." I nodded and handed her the necessary paperwork.

"All right, I will need to see your identification and we can get this set up."

"Great," I mentioned, handing her my driver's license while Michelle handed hers over as well.

"Will you be needing checks and business check cards?" she inquired.

"Let's start off with two hundred checks. Yes, those business check cards will come in handy," I expressed.

"They sure will. Not to mention, when making purchases you can earn rewards points. Those points will surely add up. How much will you ladies be starting the account with?"

"Five hundred dollars cash," I replied, taking the money out of my wallet.

"Okay, everything is set up. I need to sign these papers. I ordered your checks and you should receive the business check cards within five to seven days in the mail. Do you have anymore more questions for me?"

"No. I think that's all for the business account. Would this be a good time to share those brownies with your coworkers?" I asked.

"Only the ones I like will be getting a sample. I'll be right back with the deposit receipt," she laughed, walking out of the office.

"Thank you for everything," Michelle expressed to Ms. Pilom while she handed her the receipt.

"You're most certainly welcome. It was a pleasure meeting you ladies. Please come back and see me. Once the profits start rolling in, you may want to consider opening up a business savings account. We offer credit cards too."

"We don't need any credit cards. It got me in a lot of trouble," Michelle admitted, laughing.

"By the way, I gave each one on the teller team a brownie. They loved them and had the nerve to ask when you're bringing more back here."

"Don't worry, we'll be stopping by to make deposits and get change," I assured her.

"Tonight, when I get home, I'm going to call my sister. She's addicted to brownies. I want to order of box of walnut brownies for me and a box of double chocolate chip brownies for her. How much will that be?" Ms. Pilom asked, pulling out her wallet.

"It's fifteen dollars a box so your total will be thirty dollars," I answered.

"Okay, how many brownies come in a box?"

"Twelve," I answered.

"Would you prefer we drop them off here or have them delivered to your home?" Michelle asked, excited about our very first order.

"You can drop them off here, that's fine. I'll lock them in my desk drawer so no one will steal them," she convinced us with a huge grin on her face, handing Michelle the money.

"I'll drop them tomorrow afternoon," Michelle confirmed.

"In the meantime, I'm going to the store on my lunch break to get a bottle of whipped cream. Brownies taste even better with whipped cream on them."

Ms. Pilom agreed to take a picture with us. This was a huge moment for Michelle and me. It was our first sale. Ms. Pilom took an extra step and asked if anyone else wanted to order brownies. We got four more orders. Michelle and I had a lot of baking to do. It's a good thing she decided to use vacation time for two weeks to get the business started.

Michelle urged me to take a six-week baking class. I had tried to bake the brownies myself, but I continued to burn them. We didn't need to be wasting supplies. I had to admit if the phone rang or there was something on TV I wanted to watch, I became distracted.

# Chapter 20

To celebrate our sales, Greg and Miguel took us out to dinner at Ruth's Chris. We had double-dated before. However, this time was extra special. While the guys talked about sports, Michelle and I looked at our Web site. I had downloaded the pictures of Ms. Pilom, Michelle, and me on it. I had never seen Michelle so happy.

"I finally broke down and told my parents what we have been doing," she revealed.

"And what happened?"

"They were so happy and proud of me. When my grandmother died five years ago, Pop took it extremely hard. Now he's honored to know I'm keeping her memory alive," she expressed.

"That's wonderful," I commented.

Greg had been really supportive about my new business venture. He ordered fifty boxes to give away to his colleagues, friends, and family members.

"Yesterday, I went online and found a reasonably priced printing company in Norfolk. Flyers would come in handy. We could pass them out and leave them on people's car windows at the grocery store and shopping centers," she suggested.

"That's a great idea. Let me know how much it is and we'll send a check out," I agreed.

The restaurant was packed. Even with a reservation, we had to wait thirty minutes just to be seated. I was starving. Later in the day, Michelle and I opened up a membership at Sam's Club and didn't hesitate racking up on supplies for the brownies. Each one of us had spare bedroom so that's where we stored the supplies.

I dug into my medium-well-done steak and succulent lobster tail. This day was also special because I hadn't cried over the loss of my parents.

Later that night, Greg and I had sex on the kitchen bar. He was the only man that knew how to touch me. One of the things I loved about him was when his huge hands wrapped around my body.

# Chapter 21

I managed to get a booth in the middle of the food court of both Lynnhaven and McArthur malls. We could use the heavy traffic. Michelle and I had the proper permits. In return, the general manager was hoping we would open shop in one of the many empty storefronts. Right now, it wasn't an option. The commercial monthly rent was quite expensive.

"Do you think people will like the new flavor?" Michelle asked nervously. Her hands were shaking.

"Yeah, people cherish peanut butter. It's an American staple," I assured her. A week ago, she and I made the decision to add peanut butter for the fourth option.

"Hello, would you care for a sample?" I asked a woman with a stroller with a newborn and two toddlers clinging to her legs.

"Sure, I'll try one," she agreed.

"We have double chocolate chip, peanut butter, marshmallow, and walnut. Which one would you like to try?" I inquired, smiling.

"I'll try the marshmallow one," she confirmed.

"Here you go," I replied, handing it to her.

"Wow, this is really good. Are you in the grocery stores?" she asked.

"Not yet, but we're working on it," I responded before her son started running toward the carousel. I quickly ran after him and brought him back. She seemed to be at ease with all these little ones. It would stress me out.

"Thank you," she expressed, letting out a sigh.

"You're welcome," I answered.

"Would it be all right to give the kids a brownie?" Michelle inquired.

"It's okay. Give them the peanut butter. If I let them, those two would eat peanut butter by itself."

"All right," Michelle said.

"Well, right now, I'm on maternity leave. I work for a consultant firm that recommends new products to grocery chains. My name is Valerie. Do you have a card? I may know of a store that could be interested in your product."

"I sure do," I replied, handing her six cards on purpose. The clock struck 11:15. The mall only opened up an hour ago. A crowd was beginning to form around our table. I wasn't worried because we had plenty to go around.

Michelle was all smiles when more and more people were coming up to us. Also, she was happy, because last night, I fixed my first batch of brownies that weren't burnt.

# Chapter 22

"Excuse me, are you Jackie Montague?" a man's voice asked from behind. I was in Starbucks sprinkling sugar, nutmeg, and cinnamon in my pumpkin spice latte.

"Yes, I am," I answered after turning around with a cup of coffee in my hand. I accidentally dropped my car keys.

"Let me get those for you," he offered, kneeling down to pick them up. He was a man who appeared to be in his mid-fifties, bald, round belly, and huge waist. I had to admit he still had a boyish look in the face.

"Who are you?" I inquired.

"My name is Alex Lucas. I was a friend of your mother's. I've been away on business for the last nine months. I would have attended the funeral. I just received the news of her death along with your father. I wanted to give you my condolences," he explained.

"Yes, I appreciate it," I responded.

"Could you tell me what happened?"

"I don't remember Mom ever mentioning you," I said, changing the subject and noticing the tone of his voice. I wondered if he was just a friend to Mom.

"She always mentioned you. Your mother and I went to high school together. I loved your mother. This may be a bad time, however, you need to know the truth. We had a brief affair, but I still kept in contact with her."

"That's a damn lie," I spat back, throwing my hot cup of coffee on him.

"Your mother wouldn't leave your father because she loved him instead of me. Jackie, I need closure. Please tell me what happened to your mother," he pleaded.

"So you're the one who has been putting fresh gardenias on her grave."

"I see you've taken notice," he replied getting a stack of napkins to wipe himself with. Brown spots were saturated all through this suit. By now, people had started to stare at us.

"I go to the grave site at least three times a week. Stay the hell away from me. For all I know, you could have killed my mom and dad," I ranted and walked out of the door.

While driving back home, I couldn't but wonder if that was true. Last month, I attempted to rummage through the items in the storage unit. I stumbled upon a picture of Mom and him together where they appeared to be out at a park. Was Mom leading a double life? I figured Dad and her were happy. Growing up, I did notice he was spending countless hours at the laboratory. Mom would get grumpy if Dad didn't make it home for dinner. My mind started thinking to see if had missed any clues or signals of Mom having an affair. She was a very private person.

During their marriage, was it possible that Dad could have had an affair? I wanted to doubt it because his nose was always stuck in a book, his eyes were glued to a computer doing research, or he was on the golf course.

I began to feel even more guilty for not being there for Mom. We didn't really have an open relationship. All I ever did was continue to take and demand things from them. Tears started streaming down my face.

Despite my emotional state, it was a scheduled night to make brownies. Tonight, we had fifteen orders to fill.

"Hey," I greeted Michelle after she walked in the door.

"Sorry about being late. The fry guy didn't show up and I had to step in."

"When we make it big, do you think you'll quit Chick-fil-A?" I asked her.

"I'm not sure. It's a great company to work for. They truly care about their employees. Thanks for getting things started. If we work hard and stay on schedule, you can be back home watching your favorite show, *Criminal Minds*," she expressed, changing the subject.

This month, we made an agreement to take Ms. Pilom up on her offer and open up a business savings account and deposit two hundred dollars a month.

"Are you all right?" Michelle asked, noticing my sour mood.

"Well, it's my parents. This guy came up to me in Starbucks claiming that he went to high school with Mom and they had a brief affair," I revealed.

"How does it make you feel?"

"A big part of me thinks he's a liar. The other part wonders. My mother and I were never that close. I was more of a daddy's girl. Besides, if she was having an affair, she probably wouldn't have told me. I guess my frustration grows every day not knowing who killed them. I wonder why did they have to die at all and so viciously? Who could have hated and despised them so much as to shoot them in the back of the head, execution-style?"

"Have you talked to Detective Snyder lately?" she asked.

"No, he's been on vacation," I replied, shaking my head.

"Jackie, I don't know what to say. Marriages have their ups and downs. During my childhood, my parents were at each other's throats. Eventually, things calmed down," she explained.

"There's so many gray areas in this thing we call life. I wouldn't think my mother was capable of cheating. She was my mother, for God's sake. Mom wasn't supposed to be doing those kinds of things," I responded while cracking the eggs.

"Did the guy have any proof to show you?" she inquired while stirring the brownie mixture and popping three walnuts into her mouth.

"Of course he didn't, although I did find a picture of Mom and him together," I confirmed.

"By the way, I forgot to tell you the owner of the storage facility wants to break the contract. No one is renting units since my parents were found dead there. It's bad for business, he explained to me in a nice tone."

"What did you say to him?"

"I said, fuck you. I'm not breaking the contract. If even tries, I will sue him for so much that even his great-great-grandchildren not even born yet will have the burden of paying off his accumulated debt."

"Damn right. Some people have got a nerve to say the remarks that come out of their mouths," she commented.

"Did you eat yet?" I asked.

"No."

"Do you want to make it a pizza night?"

"Sure," she agreed nodding.

"Okay. What toppings do you want on your pizza?"

"Are you up for trying ham and pineapple? The sweetness of the fruit and the saltiness of the ham give the pizza a different flavor."

"I will try something different," I replied, dialing the number to reach Papa John's pizza.

"Mom has been telling the ladies at her church about the brownies. I've got six more orders for next week."

"That's great," I proclaimed.

"You think the grocery chains will come knocking soon?"

"I think so. We just need to stay focused and never give up on our dream.

"Five orders finished and eleven more to go," I mentioned.

Now we were taking orders online. Within three to five business days, we could ship our brownies just about anywhere.

# Chapter 23

"I need to see Detective Snyder," I requested at the police station front desk, refusing to take no for an answer.

"Let me see if he's in today. In the meantime, please have a seat," he instructed me.

"Ms. Montague," the detective greeted me.

"It's about time. May we talk in private?" I asked.

"Of course we can. Please, follow me into my office."

"Did you have a nice vacation?" I inquired.

"Yes, I sure did. I took my kids to Hershey Park in Pennsylvania. My wife and I are divorced. When she does let me have them, I take advantage of the time. It's unbelievable how much chocolate my munchkins can eat," he said after we sat down, looking at a picture of his children.

"You got cute kids," I pointed out.

"Thank you," he acknowledged, smiling.

"Snyder, you know why I'm here. Have there been any more leads?" I asked quickly, changing the subject.

"Unfortunately, there haven't been any more leads. Ms. Montague, I gave you my word. I'm not giving up on finding the killer," he expressed.

"Do you think the person who attempted to break in my house is related to my parents' death?" I questioned.

"It could be or it might have been a home invasion gone sour," he answered.

"I'm so frustrated. Rage is festering inside of me. This is hard. I'm sick of waiting," I admitted.

"Ms. Montague, I can't give you a deadline. You have to be patient. I interviewed most of his colleagues. Do you think your father might have known something?" he inquired.

"I don't know," I answered, shrugging my shoulders. "With your men patrolling my neighborhood, have they seen anything that could be possibly suspicious?"

"No, you would have been the first person on my list to call."

"Glad to see you still have all my phone numbers. Please call me if the slightest thing develops," I strongly urged.

"I definitely will," he agreed before I walked out of his office.

***

Receiving an e-mail delivery confirmation from Amazon.com cheered me up. Since Greg had been so good to me, I ordered a Jimi Hendrix CD for him. It wasn't cheap, being this particular one stopped being made by the manufacturer.

*Should I go to his job or should I wait for him to get home from work?* I thought, driving down Lynnhaven Parkway. I had plenty of paperwork to catch up on and plenty of invoices to be looked over before I paid.

Since it was in the direction I was heading to, I wanted to splurge a little on a manicure and pedicure. A year ago, splurging would have been six-hundred-dollar bedroom sheets from Nordstrom.

After I was done at the nail salon, I made a pit stop to the house where I found the CD waiting for me in a box. When you live in a neighborhood where items are left at the door, it made me feel I had pretty good neighbors.

# Chapter 24

Back at Colstice, many people gave me dirty looks, thankful my reign of an overpaid and nonworking employee was over. Some came up to me asking sincerely how I was doing and if the police case was leading to a possible suspect. I got asked that question the most. Every time, I had no choice but to tell that person, "no, there haven't been anyone arrested."

"Hey, you," I addressed Greg after knocking on the door and walking into his office.

"Baby, hi, I didn't expect you today," he expressed with sweat starting to come down his face. He looked nervous and kept looking at his watch.

"I wanted to surprise you," I explained, pulling out the Jimi Hendricks CD he had been looking for.

"You found it. I looked online for hours. Not to mention, I called so many music stores," he replied, surprised.

"I can find anything. It's the thrill of the hunt I love so much," I admitted, hugging him.

"Thank you," he laughed.

"You're welcome. What do you want for dinner?"

"Hmm, I'm in the mood for Chinese," he requested.

"Will it be your place or mine, tonight?" I inquired.

"Mine," he confirmed with a soft kiss on the cheek.

"See you then," I giggled and left his office.

# Chapter 25

I may not have known how to cook; but I perfected ordering take-out. Greg's General Tso's chicken with white rice and my chicken lo mein with fried rice had just arrived.

Today, I accomplished setting up PayPal and being able to take all major credit cards from our clients. Not to mention, I finished six orders.

After Greg closed the front door, he placed a medium-sized brown box at my feet.

"What is it?" I inquired.

"It's what I didn't want you to see when you came and saw me, today. Out of all days, you had to show at the office today, almost blowing my surprise for you," he laughed.

"I couldn't wait to give you the CD."

"I know. By the way, I listened to it for the rest of the afternoon. Open it," he ordered, getting back to the matter at hand. It was a white, fluffy doggy, just like the Bichon Frise I had before growing up.

"Aah, she's beautiful. What's her name?" I cooed.

"Jackie, you're the rightful owner, now. The decision will be made by you."

"I'm going to call you Bella," I replied to her.

"You like her?" he asked.

"I love her already. Thank you," I responded, smiling.

"Before you ask, she's up to date on all of her shots. I got a water bowl, bed, and food in the car. Bella is only four weeks old," he explained, handing me her necessary papers.

"The food is ready."

"I smelled it as soon as I walked through the door."

"How does it taste?" I asked Greg after placing his food onto a plate.

"It's hitting the spot. Did you notice her collar? I hope it fits your taste," he pointed out. The collar was my favorite color: gray. Hanging alongside of it was a two-carat princess-cut diamond ring.

"Jackie, I love you. I want us to have good, wonderful, bad, and ugly times together. I want to grow old with you and make babies. Will you marry me?" Greg asked after slowly removing the ring from Bella's collar.

"Yes," I proclaimed with a kiss. Greg went to the car and got Bella's things so she could get acquainted with her new home.

For the rest of the night, we ate, laughed, and talked. I couldn't decide if I wanted a huge wedding or not. Greg told me I had full rein on the wedding. The honeymoon, on other hand, would be left totally up to him. I considered it a fair deal and we shook hands on it.

I couldn't stop playing and holding Bella. She made me so happy. Greg even agreed to watch *Dancing with the Stars* with me. "This is your night," he whispered into my ear.

Later on that night, Greg and I went sleep with Bella in the middle of us on the bed.

# Chapter 26

"Hello?" I answered the phone.

"Hi, may I speak with Jackie Montague or Michelle Perez?"

"This is Jackie. How may I help you?" I asked.

"I don't know if you remember me. My name is Valerie Stevens. We met at the mall a few months back."

"Yes, I do remember." I nodded my head, crossing my fingers desperately, hoping she had good news for me.

"I'm back at work," she revealed.

"How are your children doing?"

"The baby is getting big. The toddlers are bad as ever," she laughed.

"So you're still thinking about our delicious brownies?"

"Yes, I ordered an assortment box for each of my clients. Well, Wal-Mart, Kmart, and Food Lion are interested," she explained.

"That's great," I replied, jumping up and down. Bella was looking at me with a funny look in her eye.

"The pricing may need to come down to fit each store clientele. Are you willing to do that?"

"Of course we are," I responded. Slow money and huge exposure is way better than no money.

"I will be sending you the invoices and contracts. Congratulations. I have high expectations for Gabby's brownies," she declared.

"Thank you so much," I proclaimed and hung up the phone. Then I started texting Michelle's phone. It was the quickest way to reach her. As I waited for her to call me back, I picked up Bella and we started pacing the floor together. I wished Michelle could have been here. If she didn't call back within the hour, I was going to her job, knowing she would be on her break soon. Finally, after forty-two excruciating minutes, my cell phone rang.

"Hey," I greeted her.

"Hi, I don't have long to talk. The kids from the high school have added orders from the normal lunch rush," she informed me.

"Are you there?" I asked. The phone was losing the signal.

"Yes, I'm here."

"Wal-Mart, Food Lion, and Kmart want our brownies into their stores," I announced, jumping up and down again. Bella had started barking due to my excitement.

"What?"

"I repeat, Wal-Mart, Food Lion, and Kmart want our product."

"Is this is a joke?"

"Hell no. We've made it big time. Valerie, the lady from the mall, called me."

"I remember her."

"She will be sending out invoices and contracts soon. Depending on their order quantity, we'll need bigger mixers. What time do you get off?"

"After I go to the bank and make the deposit. I want to be out of here by three o'clock."

"Okay, come to my house. We need to go shopping. The Bed Bath and Beyond is having a thirty percent off sale on Kitchen Aid mixers," I encouraged.

"As soon as I can break away, and may even leave earlier, I will be at your doorstep. I'm so excited. We finally made it," Michelle confirmed.

"Yes, we have arrived." I nodded and hung up the phone. My next stop would be Chipotle for a spicy chicken salad and a steak burrito for Greg. Then, I was heading over to his house.

# Chapter 27

On the way to Greg's house, I called Mr. Emery to inform him about the extraordinary news. He was proud of us and wanted to order yet another box of assortment brownies. I was more than happy to oblige him. I pulled into Greg's garage. The garage door led into the kitchen. I threw the food on top of the counter. I had to tell him the good news, first.

"Greg," I called out. He was nowhere to be found. I didn't even bother to notice if his car was parked outside. Sometimes, he parked in the garage and other times he parked on the street. I searched every room. Finally, I found him in the upstairs television room along with another woman sucking his dick on the couch. She was buck naked. Greg only had on a pair of boxer shorts, which was down to his damn knees.

"Greg, what the hell are you doing?" I cried out.

"Jackie, is that you?" He could barely speak, probably because he was about to cum in her mouth.

I put a damn stop to that happening. I grabbed the woman by the hair and spun her around. Then I punched her in the face.

She quickly tried to grab her clothes. The only thing I let her have was her bra and panties. Before I knew it, she sped off in her car.

I turned my attention back to Greg. "How could you do this to me? We're supposed to be getting married."

"Jackie, Jackie," he repeated in almost a sleepy-like state.

"We're over. The wedding is off. I thought your cheating ways were behind us. I guess not," I declared.

"Please, wait," he begged. I wasted no time smacking him plenty of times in the face and kicking his dick. Believe me, I didn't forget about his balls, either.

Greg hurled over the couch in pain.

I ran out of the house, barely able to breathe. This was one of the worst days in my life. If Greg wanted to be with other women, why did he ask for my hand in marriage? Cheating while married to me was a definite no-no. Now I knew why women killed their husbands because of infidelity.

Resentment and hostility would take the place of the love I had for him.

# Chapter 28

Four hours had passed before Michelle showed up at the door. In between that time, I cried and cried some more on my bed. I took a hot shower and cried in the bathroom as well. I had to get my emotions together. Dressing up in a cute top, jeans, and boots made me feel a little bit better. Besides, I didn't want Greg's ignorance to spoil the accomplishments of our brownies. I made it a point to discuss the events of the day at another time with Michelle.

Chills continued to go down my spine every time Greg entered my thoughts. Right now, all I could feel was numbness.

"Ready to go?" she asked me before hugging me. "I sure am equipped with my coupons. How many should we get?" she inquired.

"I was thinking two. Plus, we could pick up some new pans and swing by Sam's Club. I'm low on eggs."

Greed 525

"I'm slim on chocolate chips," she added.

"Okay," I agreed.

"Besides trying to contain your excitement, what else did you do for the day?" she inquired.

"I ran a few errands and took Bella to PetSmart for her very first class in dog obedience school."

"How did she do?" Michelle asked.

"Terrible for her first day," I explained, letting out a small laugh.

"She'll get better as times goes on. At least she's not pooping and peeing in the house."

"I'm grateful for that. I make it a point to walk her as much as I can. It's funny, because she has a tendency to poop in the same spot," I explained, laughing.

After dropping Michelle off and putting supplies away in the house, I didn't feel like sitting at home crying over Greg again. I wanted to take a drive, not knowing where I would end up. Before letting out a sigh of disbelief of today's revelation, I popped in a Mary J. Blige CD.

# Chapter 29

"Jackie, what a pleasant surprise. Please come in," Derrick welcomed me into his home. Since the last time I was here, he had done some major upgrades. The new hardwood floors were shiny as ever and the granite countertop was impeccable.

"You made it a point to let me know your door was always open," I replied, smiling.

"I could never cancel on you. Beautiful as ever," he replied, caressing my face.

"Thanks. So how's the life of the prominent district attorney?"

"Hectic. I'm up for reelection. Would you care for a glass of wine?"

"No thanks," I quickly responded.

"I have Sprite, tea, or water in the fridge. Do you want that?"

"I'm fine. Do you think you'll win?"

"Well, my opponent isn't well liked. Along with your vote and the other gracious people of Virginia Beach, I will continue my crusade in protecting our streets."

"Enough said. What cases are you working on?" I asked, walking over to the brown leather couch and motioning for Derrick to sit down. I stood over him and started rubbing his shoulders. He paused for a moment before finally answering.

"Damn, that feels good," he assured.

"Don't worry, I'll keep going. Now back to your major cases," I reminded him. One of the things I liked about Derrick was that he was an excellent storyteller.

"I'm working on a case where a guy lost his job. His house was in foreclosure. He killed his mother, wife, two daughters, one-year old son, and their family cat. He's trying to play the insanity card but I'm not buying it."

"What are you pushing for?"

"I'm rooting for the death penalty," he confirmed as I walked over to the couch and faced him. I took off my clothes, revealing a canary-yellow bra and G-string panty set. I turned around for him to get a glimpse of my body and take off the condom I had pinned in between the G-string and my butt. He removed it from me and tore off the paper with his teeth.

"Climb on," he urged after putting condom on. With my back facing him, I glided down his dick and starting riding him.

"You like?"

"Keep it coming," he insisted.

I turned around to face him and slid down on his dick again. Derrick held on tight to my breasts as I rode him with such force. He loved every second of it. Before I knew it, he came. I didn't break a sweat. He, on the other hand, was drenching wet.

"I gotta go," I informed while quickly putting my clothes back on.

"You're leaving so soon. It's too bad you're engaged."

"You knew?"

"Jackie, word gets around. Congratulations, he's a lucky man," he confirmed. I started crying and ran out of the house. Once thinking about Greg, I couldn't hold back the tears. All I wanted to do was go home, cuddle up with Bella, and go to bed.

# Chapter 30

Two weeks later, I barely ate anything. Chicken broth was the only thing I had an appetite for. When my emotions were in disarray so were my eating habits. All I did was make brownie orders and send them out to be mailed. If they were local, I delivered them. I still didn't tell Michelle about what had happened between Greg and me. I was too tired and too sad to bring it to her attention. Between Greg and Derrick calling me, my voicemail stayed full. When I would hear Greg's voice, I would delete the voicemail without even listening to it. Two nights ago, he stood at the door for hours trying to explain. I didn't want to hear that bullshit. Derrick was leaving voicemails ready for dinner and round two.

The orders from the chain stores kept Michelle and me up at night. We were strongly considering renting a commercial space.

Taking a break, I decided to write in my diary. When I opened it, a DVD disk with a cover was in my beloved diary. At first, I thought it was one of Greg's stunts trying to win me back, but it couldn't have been him because he didn't know the security code on the alarm system. I have a tendency to change it. Ever since the break-in, I get an overwhelming feeling someone is watching me.

I quickly popped the disk in the DVD player. It was Dad. He recorded this a week before he died.

"Jackie, listen to me very carefully. I hope you listened to me and didn't tell Greg that I truly was fired. The real reason his father fired me was because during my research an ingredient was added to the weight-loss drug Pozor. During my trial research, the mice were suffering severe liver damage and eventually died. I showed this information to Greg Sr. I urged him to pull the new ingredient out, which was an antidepressant. Not only did he want people to lose weight but he also wanted them to feel good emotionally. It was a disaster waiting to happen. He refused, wanting to have the goal of becoming the next billionaire. Greg Sr. could make people who did have liver damage go away with hush money. With every mouse I tested, each one died from severe liver damage," he explained.

As Dad talked, he said he stumbled upon a news broadcast with a woman claiming the drug caused her liver damage. He simply thought it was an isolated incident, but Greg Sr. was killing people for a profit.

"Jackie, if you lose this copy, there's another one in the safety deposit box. I put the set of keys in your black Baby Phat coat. My life is in danger. I'm planning to take this to the Food and Drug Administration. Greg Senior is trying to kill me for what I stumbled upon. If anything happens to me, go to the police, FBI, the Food and Drug Administration or anyone else who is willing to listen to you about this vital information. On my last day at the lab, that's what Greg was looking for. Jackie, your mom and I love you with all of our hearts. Be strong," he urged and blew me a kiss.

"Daddy," I cried out. How did I know Greg wasn't behind this as well? Did he ask me to marry him and treat me so nice to keep tabs on me? I thought while dialing Detective Snyder's phone number. It went to voicemail. I left a long message explaining the disk and that I was headed to the police station. Bella and I weren't safe here anymore. Before leaving the house, I e-mailed the disk to Detective Snyder.

# Chapter 31

Greg stood hovering over my door after I opened it.

"Jackie, we need to talk," he insisted.

"I can't talk right now. I need to go make deliveries," I urged, trying to stay calm with Bella in my arms.

"I can barely remember anything. Mom came over. A strange woman was in my house. Then, you came and kicked me in my dick. I would never jeopardize our relationship. Jackie, please talk to me," he pleaded, getting down on his knees, holding on tight to my waist. My strength was no match for his. He overpowered me. I quickly dialed 911.

"Nine-one-one,", the dispatcher spoke.

"I have an intruder in my house. Please come to nine-forty-four Linden Street," I replied, terrified of what Greg might do to me. With all of the commotion, Bella woke up from her nap, barking her head off.

"Ma'am, the police are on their way."

"Damn it, listen to me. I'm not going to hurt you," Greg demanded, smacking the phone out of my hand. "I don't know what happened."

"Liar, you killed my parents. I hate you. Greg, you were the only person who knew I was going to the storage unit that day," I screamed.

"I didn't kill your parents—"

"Jackie, he's telling the truth. My son didn't kill your parents," a woman's voice commented after walking in the door. She quickly closed the door. It was none other than Greg's mother, Sharon Bell.

"Mom, what are you doing here?" Greg asked.

"I'm here to add the last piece of the puzzle, my dear," she spoke in a subtle tone dressed in all black. Even the gloves she wore were black.

"What are you talking about?"

"I grew up in Diggs Park. To feed my mother's habit, she would give my little sister and me to men and let them have their way with us. We were poor and starved many nights. My mother didn't care anything about us or my brother. I made a vow to never ever go back to sugar water and ketchup sandwiches. Jackie, if your father would have revealed the truth to the police, my life of luxury would have end," she explained, taking a gun out of her purse and pointing it at Greg and me.

"People would have eventually found out. Thirty people have already died. Their families were given modest settlements. In return, they were instructed not to go to the media at all. Your father refused to follow the rules. If only he had decided to keep his mouth shut, none of this would have happened and your life wouldn't have been turned upside down. Don't worry, Jackie, your parents didn't feel a thing. I shot them from behind."

"Mom, how could you do that to her parents? Jackie's mother was considered to be your best friend," Greg asked.

"The only friends I've ever had were my sister, who died of a drug overdose, your father, and most importantly, money. Greg Senior doubted it, but I knew your father had recorded his findings about the liver damage. I ransacked the storage unit and tried to find it in this place; but Jackie, you got smart and got that security system. If I would have found that disk or any kind of paperwork and you didn't get that security system installed, you certainly would have been dead by now."

"Mom, put the gun down," Greg pleaded.

"Boy, do you want to die now or later?" she asked, pointing the gun at his temple. "Yes, my dear son. I did come over that day and drugged you with roofies. That woman was an associate of mine. I knew Jackie was coming over because you mentioned it to me. The plan was set in motion. Ever since you told your father and me about the marriage proposal, I had to do something drastic to break you two lovebirds up. I couldn't let you marry the woman whose parents I took the lives of," she giggled in a devilish tone.

Little did Mrs. Bell know, this was all being recorded on the 911 dispatcher's phone line.

"Let us go," I demanded, holding onto Bella tight. She was so scared.

"Jackie, you're scheduled to die tonight, including you too, son," she told us with vicious, cold eyes.

"Mom, you would kill your only son?" he questioned.

"I'll do whatever it takes to preserve my lifestyle," she confessed. Greg's heart looked to be crushed right before my eyes.

"Mrs. Bell, put the gun down," Detective Snyder demanded, coming into the town house. By this time, other police officers had surrounded the house. During her ranting, she failed to lock the door.

"I'm not going back to the projects. Jackie and her parents were trying to take my life away from me. I can't let that happen," she declared while pointing the gun at my chest.

Detective Snyder was left with no choice but to shoot her in the foot.

The gun fell out of her hand and Greg quickly grabbed it.

Mrs. Bell was arrested and taken into custody.

"Jackie, I got your message and the e-mail. I'm taking this information to the FBI. Because of sheer greed, people have died," he proclaimed.

# Chapter 32

It turned out Greg's father didn't know about his wife killing my parents. Until people started dying, he didn't realize the seriousness of it. It was way too late to get a conscience, now. Greg Junior was distraught over the way his mother treated him. Every family has secrets. He didn't know how deep theirs truly were.

His mother was sentenced to life without the chance of parole at my request. Death was too good for her. I wanted Sharon Bell to remember the life she had were only distorted memories that danced in her head. I wanted her to never forget what she did to my parents. This case got Derrick Harkman reelected for another term of district attorney for the city of Virginia Beach.

Ever since the trial ended, Greg and his father have been estranged. Right now, Greg doesn't want him in his life. As far as his mother, he completely disowned her.

He and I decided to get married at the justice of the peace. I assured him we could make our own family together and shower our kids with love.

After the FBI ripped the Colstice drug empire apart, lawyers' fees were paid and the victims who suffered liver damage were paid for pain and suffering. I sued the company for a billion dollars and won. Over the years, the drug company earned twelve billion dollars. Once everything got paid, Greg Senior had a mere hundred dollars left to his name.

Michelle and I took a step out on faith and pursued our brownie company on a full-time basis. We rented a commercial unit and business profits were at a hundred thousand dollars and counting.